# A PRETENDER'S MURDER

CHRISTOPHER HUANG

This is a work of fiction. Names, characters, organizations, places, events, and incidents are either products of the author's imagination or are used fictitiously.



Published by Inkshares, Inc., Oakland, California
www.inkshares.com

Cover design by Tim Barber
Edited by Adam Gomolin
Interior design by Kevin G. Summers

ISBN: 9781950301720
e-ISBN: 9781950301737

First edition

Printed in Canada

**Praise for Christopher Huang**

"Delightfully twisty and chilling all at once—murder mysteries are rarely this fun." **—Jonathan Whitelaw, *The Sun***

"Huang's impressive debut will delight fans of golden age detective fiction."
**—*Publishers Weekly* (starred review)**

"[A] puzzle worthy of Golden Age detective fiction."
**—*Library Journal* (starred review)**

"We hope [this] will be only the first of many Eric Peterkin adventures." **—*Booklist***

"Christopher Huang's debut novel, *A Gentleman's Murder*, is set in post-First World War England, but incorporates themes—race, the psychic toll of war—seldom acknowledged in classic mysteries of that era." **—Ian McGillis, *The Montreal Gazette***

"A mystery that recalls the best of Golden Age detective fiction."
**—Andy Lewis, *The Hollywood Reporter***

"Dorothy Sayers is alive and well and writing under the name of Christopher Huang."
**—Rhys Bowen, *New York Times*-bestselling author**

"A must read for fans of Anthony Horowitz, Charles Todd, and Anne Perry." **—Daryl Maxwell, Los Angeles Public Library**

"A locked room traditional mystery that does justice to its inspirations, even as it aids in the genre's continuing evolution."
**—CrimeReads**

*The pallor of girls' brows shall be their pall;*
*Their flowers the tenderness of patient minds,*
*And each slow dusk a drawing-down of blinds.*

—Wilfred Owen, "Anthem for Doomed Youth"

# CAST OF CHARACTERS

**Eric Peterkin**: As the newly installed club secretary, former lieutenant Eric Peterkin shoulders many new responsibilities—including, it appears, a murder investigation.

**Avery Ferrett**: Eric's best friend. An occultist who prefers coffee to conflict, he nevertheless rises to the occasion when circumstances demand it.

**Penny Peterkin**: Eric's sister is determined to be included in his latest adventure, but may not be prepared for the reality of murder.

**Ted Cully**: The elderly club porter. His years of devotion and dedication place him above suspicion . . . to most.

**Colonel Hadrian Russell**: As acting president of the Britannia Club, the Colonel is charming, expansive, and popular—the last person anyone could want to see dead.

**Lady Alice Russell**: The widow of the Colonel's eldest son, George, remains in full mourning even now, having never forgotten . . . or forgiven.

**Madam Eliot**: Miranda Eliot is the widow of the Colonel's second son, Andrew. How ruthless must she really be, to succeed as she has in a man's world?

**Flora Grace**: The beautiful Miss Flora Grace, widow of the Colonel's third son, David, makes no secret of her romantic dalliances. *Her* secrets are more dangerous than that.

**Lucy Russell**: The waif-like widow of the Colonel's youngest son, Patrick, Lucy is more daughter than daughter-in-law—innocence personified.

**Captain Gregory Ward**: Was it really tuberculosis that had Captain Ward sequestered in the Swiss Alps for the past five years, or was it something else?

**Thomas Harvey**: The handsome young club attendant was on duty on the night of the murder. He has an alibi, but that doesn't mean he was uninvolved.

**Inspector Benedict Crane**: A decade in Hong Kong has given this Scotland Yard detective a taste for all things Chinese . . . and frustrated his ambitions.

**Dr. Gérard Duplessis**: Why is this French specialist in shell shock really so interested in tracking down the murderer?

**Madame Davidova**: A self-proclaimed spirit medium, swathed in silks and silver. She tells far more than she knows.

# PART ONE

# LONDINIUM

AT 5:27 P.M. on Thursday the fifth of March, 1925, Eric Peterkin slid the envelope containing the latest manuscript he'd evaluated, with his recommendations, through the mail slot of the Looming Press offices near Aldgate, where the bowler-hatted financial hub of London bled into working-class Whitechapel. That was one obligation honourably discharged. March, he'd once been told, was the first month of the ancient Roman calendar: the promise of spring, new life, and the true turning of the years. Thoughts of slates wiped clean spurred him on as he walked down to Tower Hill and the Thames. There was London Bridge: How often had it fallen down and been built up again since the Romans first established the outpost of Londinium? Eric knew without having seen them that the surviving pieces of Londinium's fortified walls had been incorporated into the buildings of modern London and absorbed by the growing city. Bankers now walked where centurions once marched.

In the spring of 1925, London was not a far-flung outpost, but the heart of her own empire. The Great War had come and gone, crumbling half the empires of Europe to dust in its wake—but London still stood, and the British Empire with her, ready to face a new era. In the nightclubs of Soho, the bright and the young danced to jazz under the sparkle of electric lights. In the ever-expanding

Metro-land suburbs to the northwest, new families gathered in solemn gratitude for their hard-earned peace. Among the more transient populations of the docks, perhaps it was enough to spare a thought for loved ones far away and half-forgotten.

An hour's walk and the brisk March wind brought Eric to the grand portico of the Britannia Club on King Street, St. James, and now it was dark. The lights were on in the Golden Lion pub across the street, and especially bright around the St. James's Theatre farther down. This was the momentary lull between the bustle of day and the glamour of night, just as winter separated this year from the last. Drawing in a deep breath, Eric turned and pushed through the great oak entrance doors.

*31 December 1924*

"Lieutenant Peterkin, sir!" Ted Cully, the elderly club porter, smiled warmly from behind the reception desk, a sprig of holly prickling from his lapel. "Welcome back. Business all taken care of, I trust?"

"Oh, yes." Eric had missed Christmas Day itself, thanks to an obligation to a former sergeant, but the Britannia Club celebrated all twelve days of Christmas, of which New Year's Eve was only the seventh. Under wreaths of holly, the walnut panelling gleamed as though soaked in oil, and the polished brass fittings flared in the flicker of candlelight. This was the one time of the year when guests were allowed up the grand staircase to the club lounge, so the marbled hallways echoed with the unfamiliar joy of those normally left behind.

The one sombre note amid this Christmas gaiety was the Roster of the Fallen, a wall of brass plaques naming those associated with the club who'd fallen in battle—not just members, but their sons and brothers as well. First in this litany of sacrifice was Fitzwilliam Peterkin at the Battle of Waterloo, and Eric touched his brow in salute to his venerable ancestor. There had always been Peterkins at the Britannia.

The roster's placement here had occurred sometime during Eric's absence. Prior to that, its place was in the entry vestibule.

"Can't think why we didn't have it in here from the very beginning," Cully said. "Easier to pay your respects without the draught every time someone came through the front door, eh?"

"Perhaps our forebears saw it as a reminder of what they'd left behind. Cold winter battles, freezing the blood on foreign soil . . ."

"That may be, sir, but I can't say as there's any need for our boys to freeze twice."

"You've got a point there."

Then, though he knew he wouldn't find it, Eric scanned down to the bottom of the roster in search of another name: Albert Benson. Rather than be killed and lost on a foreign battlefield, Benson had been killed right here in the club, and the resulting upheaval had turned the Brittania's board of officers completely upside down.

"We've cleared out Bradshaw's office," Cully said, referring to the white-bearded former club secretary—that genial Father Christmas in tweeds who Got Things Done. "It's ready for you to move in—and the sooner the better, I say. Everyone else is gone."

"Gone? What do you mean, *gone*?"

"Just that. Gone. The remaining officers found themselves quite unpopular after that business with Mr. Benson, and it got worse while you were away. They decided to make themselves scarce." The porter's friendly geniality was marred by a note of contempt. He'd never approved of Benson, who'd served as a stretcher-bearer instead of fighting.

"Benson was a gentleman, Cully. He didn't run away . . . like some."

"As you say." Cully looked aside, obstinate in his views. "Well. Nobody could say a thing against you, of course, knowing what you did to put that sorry business to rest. And as you were already named to take Bradshaw's place, we've been waiting for you to do just that."

"But . . . alone?" Eric was half-tempted to run away himself.

"Colonel Hadrian Russell will be acting president until a new board of officers can be elected. He was president back in . . . 1910,

I think. Just before the War. Anyway, he'll know what's what. It was his idea to move the roster in here."

That was all very well, but it was the club secretary, not the club president, who actually got things done. Eric tugged his now-stifling scarf away from his neck, and his hand came away damp with melted snow.

*Snow drifted across the shoulders of a sergeant twice Lieutenant Peterkin's age. There was judgement in the eyes of the enlisted men before him. One or two had been in the trenches from the beginning of the War, while the young lieutenant could only measure his time there in hours. "Your men, Peterkin," came the distant voice of the company's officer commanding. "They live or die by your leadership. You know what you have to do."*

*Was this melted snow or a cold sweat?*

Wiping the moisture away on his trouser leg, Eric muttered, "In that case, I'd better have a word with Colonel Russell."

Some people invite confessions. Others perform to an audience. More rare are those who do neither, but shine like a flame amid the fluttering moths drawn to their presence. They hold court where others merely converse, as Colonel Russell was doing right now at one comfortable end of the lounge. He was not the one speaking, nor was he, exactly, the one being spoken to; yet somehow he commanded the centre. The men orbiting him—younger, without his gravitas—spoke only through his indulgence.

Eric knew Colonel Russell by sight and by reputation. He was a handsome, silver-haired gentleman with the heavy shoulders of a former rugby hero, though his watch chain now stretched over a comfortably solid belly. He'd married one of the Carrington-Clarkes—Johanna, as Eric recalled. She'd passed away some fifteen years ago, leaving him four strapping sons; then the War came along and, with the dust of fallen empires, swept those same four sons away in its Stygian wake.

A lesser man might have crumbled in the face of such loss, but not Colonel Hadrian Russell—and such fortitude was worth as much respect as the sacrifice itself.

It took Eric a moment to breach the wall of hangers-on. Once through, the noisy hubbub, unusual for what was normally a sanctum of peace and discretion, seemed to fade into irrelevance. The warmth from the fireplace reminded Eric that he'd just come in from the cold, and that he had only to raise a hand for an attendant to materialise out of the aether and provide him with a gin and tonic. To one side, the tall window overlooking King Street was a panel of inhospitable midwinter darkness, snow drifting through the black void between them and the lights of the Golden Lion pub opposite.

"Seven passengers and the pilot, all dead," one reedy voice held forth. "And on Christmas Eve, no less. Bad enough flying in wartime . . . Sure, our boys in the RFC were heroes—excuse me, it's the RAF now, isn't it? But I'd wager half their dead were down to just accident and misadventure—"

Eric never saw who the speaker was. Colonel Russell halted the ongoing diatribe with an upraised hand and rose from where he was seated—enthroned, rather—to meet Eric with a broad smile magnified by the fluctuant curves of his silver whiskers. "Peterkin! Introductions won't be necessary, I trust? Come, join us! I mean, this *is* your personal armchair, isn't it?"

The Colonel indicated the chair in which Eric usually sat to evaluate his manuscripts—his Usual Armchair—but Eric smiled and shook his head. "Hardly! I doubt the club quartermaster—if we had one—would take kindly to any appropriation of club property."

"Then we'd better take it up with the club secretary. Hang on, that's you now, isn't it? Gentlemen, let us raise a glass to Mr. Eric Peterkin, successor to old Jacob Bradshaw: may we always be in such good hands!"

"Hear, hear!" laughed the men around them, and Eric, surprised at being toasted in such a public fashion, could only murmur an awkward acknowledgement. For a moment, he thought he saw old

Bradshaw in the shadows, a genial smile dying under calculating eyes. Who was Eric Peterkin to usurp the old man's place?

"You'll do marvellously," the Colonel assured him, dispelling Bradshaw's ghost. "I knew your father—a fine fellow—and if even half of what I've heard about you is true, then I can say with some authority that he'd have been pleased and proud to call you his heir."

"One does one's best," Eric replied with a self-deprecating wave of his hand. The Colonel's reception was growing a bit too warm for comfort.

"I knew your mother, too. Not well, admittedly, but enough to know she was a lady."

Was the Colonel trying to imply something?

The late Magdalen Peterkin, beloved wife of Colonel Berkeley Peterkin, had been Chinese, and that heritage came out strongly in the features of her son. Few people really cared in the trenches, there being somewhat more pressing matters at hand; in peacetime, however . . .

But Colonel Russell was already checking his pocket watch. "Speaking of ladies, mine—plural—should be here any minute. Gentlemen, family calls and I must take my leave. Try not to burn the place down in my absence, eh? Peterkin, walk with me, if you will."

"Don't you forget all about us, now!" one of the other gentlemen called as they parted to let Eric and the Colonel through.

"Ugly as you are, I wish it were so easy!"

More laughter. Returning a wink, Colonel Russell put his arm around Eric's shoulders and shepherded him away.

"I've never actually met your mother," Colonel Russell said as they stopped on the landing of the grand staircase, under a massive painting of King Arthur and his Knights of the Round Table. "I hope you'll forgive the fib. But one or two of our friends upstairs needed some convincing, and we can't have dissent in the ranks if we mean to get anything done." He nodded up at the painting. "People do tend to forget, don't they?"

"About Palomides?" Eric's eyes went to the Saracen knight, the one dark face among the crowd of pale Europeans.

"Hah! No, I meant Arthur."

King Arthur, in the painting, was a handsome fellow of dignified bearing, with piercing blue eyes and a mane of golden blond hair. Every knight around him had been modelled after a founding member of the club—Pellinore, for instance, had been modelled after Fitzwilliam Peterkin—but King Arthur himself, as befitted such a mythic figure, had been drawn entirely from the artist's imagined concept of the ideal sovereign.

Standing in Arthur's shadow was another figure: Sir Kay, Arthur's foster brother and seneschal according to the legends. Where the other knights had their swords drawn, Kay's was sheathed, his gauntleted hands folded in reserve. He was the knight who stayed behind while the others went out questing for glory, who made sure Camelot remained standing and welcoming when they returned—much like the club secretary, come to think of it.

Colonel Russell, his focus still on King Arthur, let out a sardonic chuckle. "Such a fine Anglo-Saxon face! Even though the legends say he was primarily concerned with defending the Celtic Britons *from* the invading Saxons, back when *they* were the foreigners. And Arthur wasn't even a Briton himself. All those stories describing him as the secret love-child of Uther Pendragon by the Lady Ygraine, they're just myths. The real Arthur Pendragon was Italian—yes, a dark-haired, dark-eyed Roman centurion by the name of Lucius Artorius Castus, with an aquiline nose and a swarthy Mediterranean complexion. Hardly the average Englishman!"

"I've never given it much thought, I admit." Perhaps Kay was an allegory for the Britain that had adopted Artorius Castus as their own.

"The Arthur we know is a myth, Peterkin. He never died in the Battle of Camlann: he went on to become the Roman governor of Dalmatia and died there. But what does that matter, when a man's been dead for so many centuries? Myths are distillations of meaning. We put this myth on the wall because it reveals who we are. Rome traced their heritage to Troy by way of Aeneas, and we trace ours to Rome by way of old Artorius Castus. We are the heirs to the Roman Empire, Peterkin—that's what the myth means. The Romans built London Bridge, and we rebuilt it every time it fell, because *that* is our legacy: Rome in all her imperial glory, not some godforsaken tribe of woad-painted Celts."

Eric didn't have to imagine the polish and discretion of the Britannia Club as an offshoot of imperial Rome: the columns of the lobby were already classical in form and placement, and the architectural detailing taken directly from Roman antiquity. High above, a waxing half-moon sailed over the enormous skylight of this modern atrium—

For a moment, he remembered Albert Benson, sprawled across a mosaic floor, stabbed to death like Julius Caesar in the forum.

Shaking the bloody memory away, he told the Colonel, "You're not the first to imagine a kinship with ancient Rome, I'm sure."

"Nor the last."

"Perhaps."

Colonel Russell considered him for a moment more. Perhaps he'd expected a more enthusiastic response. "The trouble with this modern generation, Peterkin, is we're far too caught up in causes that make no difference. We leave behind the constants; we forget that we still walk in the ways set down by Rome, and a man without a history is a man without a self."

"Should auld acquaintance be forgot, eh? That's a line from the woad-painted Celts—who, let's not forget, also claim descent from Aeneas of Troy by his grandson Brutus and the Trojan refugees he brought with him."

"Hah! The supposed first king of Britain, more of a myth than even Arthur!" Colonel Russell's demeanour brightened once again, and he clapped Eric on the back. "You're a good man, Peterkin. I've every confidence that between the two of us, we'll soon have this ruddy club sorted to our satisfaction. That's a campaign we'll want to discuss, and soon; but not, perhaps, right away. You want to meet my ladies first."

# MY FAIR LADIES

COLONEL HADRIAN RUSSELL, before the War, had four sons: George, Andrew, David, and Patrick. Four sons named for patron saints of the British Isles; four sons martyred for those same isles; four sons gone with four daughters-in-law in their place. The Russell widows were a familiar sight at the Britannia, meeting here as they did for lunch every Friday.

Descending the grand staircase, Colonel Russell pointed out two boys standing before the Roster of the Fallen. The elder looked to be about fifteen; the younger, perhaps eleven or twelve. They were searching the immortalised names with pointing fingers, and Eric guessed them to be the Colonel's grandsons, home from school for the Christmas break and looking for their father and uncles among the other fallen members of the club.

"Matthew and Mark," the Colonel rumbled. "George, my eldest, had the good sense to cement his legacy before getting himself blown to pieces in Flanders. Pity he couldn't have left a Luke and a John to finish the Gospel quartet, but you can't have everything."

Eric chuckled as he was expected to, but he understood that such callous jokes usually hid a deeper pain.

The boys were joined a moment later by a tall, handsome matron of forty in a black dress and a matching wide-brimmed hat, nearly a decade behind the fashions but with an undeniable gravitas.

This was their mother: Lady Alice, third daughter of the Earl of Colford, widow of the late George Russell, and de facto matriarch of the Russell clan after her mother-in-law, the Colonel's wife, was laid to rest in Highgate Cemetery. But Eric remembered her as Sister Russell, a nurse at a casualty clearing station not far from the front.

*The nurse was tall, straight-backed, and grim, stalking between the beds like Nemesis on a mission. Temperatures were taken, medication dispensed, shots administered, all with a ruthless efficiency. The wounded survived for fear of incurring her wrath.*

*"Sister Russell is a lovely lady, usually," another nurse told Eric. "But her husband was killed last week in a failed offensive near Aveluy Wood, and we must make allowances for her if she won't make allowances for herself."*

It wasn't until he ran into her again, here at the Britannia two years after the end of the War, that Eric saw what that other nurse meant. Lady Alice was a lady in every sense of the word. Her smile was gracious, and her stride was swift and purposeful, its time precisely marked by an ebony cane that was more swagger stick than walking stick. She bore down on them like a grand galleon in full sail, and the crowds parted like sea foam before her.

The elder of the boys, Matthew, came with her; but Mark, the younger, suddenly broke away to run back to the vestibule.

"Aunt Lucy!"

The girl who met him at the entrance seemed not much older than the boy himself. She caught him as he barrelled into her, swung him around, and then the two were laughing and running across the staid marble floor to join the group gathering on the stairs. Light gleamed on the butterfly-shaped buckle on her cloche hat, and under the weight of her winter coat, the pleated skirt of her sailor dress flared like a memory of some long-forgotten, pre-War summer holiday by the sea.

Lucy Russell had been married to the Colonel's youngest son, Patrick, and it took Eric a moment to remember that she was, in fact, a woman his own age—not a girl ten years younger.

*A pale, dark-haired girl sat motionless in the Britannia Club dining room, staring into her untouched plate. She hadn't moved since Eric, back in London on leave, sat down at the next table; but her dining companion was Colonel Hadrian Russell, a popular figure at the Britannia, and Eric couldn't help but overhear their conversation.*

*"Lucy, my dear, won't you eat something, at least? I thought a change of scenery—"*

*"Patrick's birthday is next week," the pale girl—Lucy—said without moving. "He would have been twenty-one. It isn't fair."*

"Lucy, my dear," Lady Alice said with more indulgence than ire as she ruffled her son's hair. "You really mustn't encourage this little scamp, or he's never going to grow up."

"It'll be my resolution for the new year," Lucy replied with a wink at her nephews. Mark grinned back, while Matthew tried unsuccessfully to appear aloof and unamused. Then she turned to Colonel Russell and said, "Hadrian, you've gone and left your keys at home again. Honestly, you'll forget your own head one of these days."

Colonel Russell reddened slightly as he accepted the proffered keys, but covered over his discomfiture with a bark of laughter. "Word of advice, Peterkin: have at least one daughter, in-law or otherwise. She'll take better care of you than any son."

But the near-simultaneous arrivals of Mrs. George and Mrs. Patrick seemed to have ignited a low, electric buzz in the other gentlemen of the club. After all, Colonel Hadrian Russell had four daughters-in-law, and if two of them were here now . . .

*Click-click-click.*

Madam Eliot—Miranda, widow of Colonel Russell's second son, Andrew—was small and exquisite in a sharply tailored jacket of rich burgundy tweed, auburn hair expensively bobbed and finger-curled, movements quick and precise as her heels rattled out a rapid staccato rhythm, *click-click-click* like a ticker-tape machine, on the marble floor. Rubies glittered at her throat and ears, and a wristwatch flashed gold. Eric almost thought he heard her very bones click as she extended a hand to him on being introduced.

"Mr. Peterkin! How lovely to make your acquaintance. I've seen you about, of course—you do rather stand out—and of course I'd heard from Hadrian before that you're to take Mr. Bradshaw's place as club secretary. Will that be for good, or is it only in the interim? I know Hadrian's only *acting* president, of course, until elections can be held at the annual general meeting in April, but I'm given to understand that the role of club secretary is so much more involved that it seems a shame to show one man the ropes only to let him go after a few months."

Madam Eliot talked the same way she walked: like a machine gun, and Eric was very nearly forced to take cover. This woman, he thought, must have murdered a few thousand tongue twisters as a girl.

"You mustn't overwhelm the poor man, Miranda," Lady Alice said, then turned to Eric. "I must apologise for my sister-in-law. Not content with running her own business—"

"Don't be ridiculous. If Carrington-Clarke & Associates were indeed 'my own business,' it would be Eliot & Associates." She *was* signing contracts for the firm, though, hence the need for a name that wouldn't change with remarriage. "I get things done. That's all."

*"I will not have my husband denied his honours," the woman in the smart black jacket was saying to Bradshaw in the club vestibule. Eric, finally free now the War was over, passed them on his way through to the lobby, but paused on the threshold, curious.*

*"The roster lists men who fell in battle or from wounds sustained on the battlefield," Bradshaw replied. "Andrew Russell died in a Parisian hotel room."*

*"He was assassinated while on the trail of German spies, and if that's not giving his life for king and country, I don't know what is." Something passed from her hands to his. A cheque? "Just get it done."*

Eric's gaze stole over to the Roster of the Fallen. Bradshaw, like Madam Eliot, certainly got things done—and Eric had large shoes to fill.

As the Russell widows chattered among themselves, Eric sought out their husbands, the Russell brothers, on the roster. George

Russell, the eldest son, the loving father, the devoted spouse; Patrick Russell, not much more than a boy, his young bride widowed before she'd even turned twenty; heroic Andrew Russell, nearly left out over a technicality . . . But first among these and first to fall was David Russell, Colonel Russell's third son—poet, scholar, athlete—and it was for his widow that the gentlemen of the club now waited, behind raised newspapers and feigned conversations, with bated breath.

Flora Grace. She'd gone back to her maiden name after the War. Her story was quite well-known around the club: David Russell married her on the eve of his departure for Flanders, and when he was severely burned by mustard gas, she defied all advice to the contrary, bullied the necessary papers out of his father's War Office contacts, and braved travel in wartime to be at his side. They were going to ship him back to England for medical treatment, but he expired the night before—in her arms, according to some rumours, or the moment her back was turned, said others. Eric could only imagine Miss Flora Grace, the former Mrs. David Russell, returning home without her husband—shattered, silent, alone, the grey waters of the Channel churning restlessly around her . . .

There she was.

Miss Flora Grace stopped just inside the lobby, surveying the room over the circular rims of her sun spectacles. Her fur-lined winter coat slid off her shoulders into the hands of an attentive attendant, revealing a cream-coloured silk blouse and . . . trousers? It was a fashion choice that seemed, by the conservative metrics of the Britannia Club, calculated to obfuscate her femininity yet somehow managed the opposite. Dramatically reddened lips curved into a knowing smile as she fitted a cigarette into a cigarette holder, and another attendant scurried over to provide her with a light.

Was she beautiful? Yes. So were a great many other women. Flora Grace did not hold a monopoly on clear skin or golden blond bobs or emerald-green eyes rimmed with long, darkened lashes. It was confidence more than cosmetics that made the society beauty.

If Lady Alice was a majestic galleon, then Miss Grace was a racing yacht—sleek, elegant, arresting. And she knew it.

No one said a word as she sailed across the lobby floor to join the rest of the Russells at the foot of the grand staircase.

"I do hope I haven't kept you waiting," she drawled. "I had an afternoon guest who simply would not leave. Such a bore! I doubt I'll be seeing much more of him in the new year."

Colonel Russell ploughed quickly over this business of an afternoon guest. "Here's Mr. Peterkin, Flora. He'll be taking over Bradshaw's duties as club secretary from here on."

"Will you, now?" Miss Grace's gaze was open and frank, with a touch of amusement that Eric found himself eager to reciprocate. "And here I thought Jacob Bradshaw of the Britannia Club would be the one true constant in our rapidly changing world. Now, if you could only see your way to accepting Alice here as a member. Heaven knows she's seen more of Flanders than some soldiers I could mention."

"Flora!" Lady Alice barked in mild approbation, but Miss Grace only smirked and retreated behind the smoke of her cigarette.

"You mustn't mind Flora," Lucy told Eric. "She spends entirely too much time listening to the speakers in Hyde Park, and they give her the oddest ideas."

"If we're all here," said Madam Eliot, "we really ought to move on to dinner and stop blocking the stairs. Hadrian, if you would be so kind as to lead the way?"

"Of course, of course."

The gracious widow, the glittering professional, the glamorous vamp, the girlish ingénue, . . . and, of course, the magnanimous patriarch. Eric had to suppress a twinge of envy: his only family these days was his sister, Penny, who'd elected to see the new year in with her own horse-mad friends in the country; and Eric's other option, his best friend, Avery, preferred to eschew the thundering warhorses of the Britannia Club in favour of his own circle of queer Bohemians. For the briefest of moments, the classical walnut-and-brass opulence of the Britannia Club felt hollow—then he found Lady Alice's black-gloved hand on his arm, and the Colonel, beaming with familial pride, pressed him into the party: "Seems to me, sir, that you're as far from home now as our friend Artorius Castus."

*5 March 1925*

"Peterkin? I say, Peterkin!"

Eric stirred. The hand on his arm was too large for Lady Alice's, and lacked the rasp of black lace. The glare from the electric light dazzled him, like the flash of Madam Eliot's jewels; he fancied he could still smell the smoky warmth of Miss Grace's perfume, and in his ears were the fading echoes of Lucy Russell's laughter . . .

"Sleeping on the job, are we? Some secretary you turned out to be!"

The words were jocular rather than critical, and the man speaking was Colonel Hadrian Russell, acting president of the Britannia Club until the elections in April. Eric stretched, yawned, and tried to regain his bearings. Wallpaper, window, desk, untidy stacks of club correspondence, a telephone, cabinets filled with files and ledgers. New Year's Eve was long gone. The month was March, and this was the office Eric now occupied as club secretary.

Occupied! It had been two months, and Bradshaw's beloved porcelain tortoises were gone, but that sense of being an interloper in Bradshaw's domain remained. Eric's pictures—of himself with the cricket team, with his regiment, with his parents and sister in India—failed to cover the unfaded patches of wallpaper left by Bradshaw's. The only thing of Bradshaw's left, for reasons best known to Bradshaw himself, was a framed watercolour print from some children's book, of a tortoise wobbling along a country lane on a bicycle. It hung over the desk, and in its reptilian gaze, Eric could only ever read smug contempt.

"What time is it?" Eric asked, rubbing the crick out of his neck. The office window, normally a panoramic view of the adjacent service court's dirty brick walls, was a nearly solid black. When was the last time he'd enjoyed the comforts of his Usual Armchair, stretching his feet out towards a crackling fire? Winter was all but over, spring was in the air—and here was Eric Peterkin, shut away behind a desk. Eric sometimes wondered if his nomination for club secretary had, in fact, been malicious.

"Past ten o'clock," Colonel Russell replied. "And you've been busy, I see?"

Eric followed the Colonel's gaze to his blotter, and the images doodled on it: a house plan, a candlestick, a spanner, a coil of rope . . . He blushed. "Something out of the last manuscript I was reading. Fellow has a talent for description."

"Fascinating, but I've got other fish to fry."

"Oh?"

"I'm leaving tomorrow for my annual fishing trip to Scotland, and should be gone until the sixteenth. Just in time to miss the season for trout, but I'd much rather have salmon. These things are meticulously planned, don't you know! Just think, Peterkin: ten days on the banks of a loch or a burn, nothing but you, your rod, and the open skies . . . and maybe a flask of a good single malt. The ladies will continue with their Friday luncheons, of course."

The next one was tomorrow, wasn't it? Eric recalled again the memory of dining with the Colonel and his four daughters-in-law on New Year's Eve. He could practically still taste the roast goose.

"Oh!" Colonel Russell cut short his exaltation of the Scottish waterways. "You mustn't think I woke you up just to rub your nose in it. That's not it at all. Look, this showed up in my mail today, but it's really more your bailiwick, isn't it?"

The letter was from a Captain Gregory Ward, announcing his return to England and requesting reinstatement of the club membership he'd allowed to lapse three years ago. Standard club business.

"His father was old General William Ward," Colonel Russell said, "who died just before the War. I remember young Gregory marching into the War Office with his father's service revolver the day war was declared, demanding to be let in. Not quite how volunteering works, but he got through the War with flying colours, only to come down with consumption the year after and be shipped off to a sanatorium in the Swiss Alps. He'd trained with both Andrew and David, you know, and was especially friendly with Andrew. He was actually there when . . ."

"When?"

Colonel Russell laughed and brushed it off. "You'll give our friend Ward a hero's welcome when he shows up, won't you? I don't believe he's met the ladies—not even Miranda and Flora, for all he was so friendly with Andrew and David. You'll have to do the honours of introducing them all."

# ULYSSES

THE MAN AT the office door was tall and distinguished, with honey-brown hair gone white at the temples, a face lined with a history of laughter and sun, and a long, thin scar curving across his left cheek. His eyes, bright blue and merry, met Eric's with one quizzically raised eyebrow.

"Hullo," he said. "You're not Jacob Bradshaw, or is my memory that far gone?"

"Bradshaw's gone on to better things, I'm afraid. I'm Peterkin; Eric Peterkin. And you must be Captain Gregory Ward."

"Yes, I wrote about getting my membership reinstated."

Laugh lines deepened around Captain Ward's eyes as he slid into the proffered chair. Eric would have put his age at about fifty, though his paperwork put him at thirty-eight. Noting his interest in the cavalry sabre mounted over one cabinet, Eric said, "That was my great-uncle Charlie's. He was in the Crimea, and a bit of a rogue if half the stories are true. Do you fence? I'm always on the lookout for another sparring partner."

Ward tore his eyes from the sabre with a flicker of embarrassment and a laugh. "Oh, no. I wouldn't know one end of a sword from the other, I'm afraid. Besides, my health isn't what it used to be. Consumption is a nasty thing to have."

His health? Ward appeared to be brimming with health, his apparent age no more than skin-deep—hardly the image of a recently recovered consumptive. Eric wondered if, perhaps, the ailment in question was something else entirely.

"I swear," Ward went on, "I lost more years than I actually spent in that old sanatorium. Lovely view of the mountains, of course, and the freshest air outside of Eden; but by God it was dull. And all those doctors poking and prodding at you in the most indecent fashion . . . I wouldn't recommend it, Peterkin. Sometimes I listen to the words coming out of my mouth and wonder if my time there hasn't turned me Swiss German."

"The bar in the lounge does have some German schnapps in stock, if you want to complete the transformation."

"Better not. If I'm honest, Peterkin, the War's done something to my memory, and my time away hasn't helped. I barely remember this place at all."

*"Something to his memory," indeed.* Eric suspected now that what ailed Ward was not consumption at all, but something nobody at the Britannia liked to admit. That the poor fellow was even alluding to any issues with his memory was an act of courage.

Eric dove into the papers overflowing his desk and finally extracted the paperwork for Ward's reinstatement as a member in good standing. "We're happy to jog your memory as much as you like," he said. Then, noting Ward's hesitation over the space for his home address, he added, "If you've yet to get your lodgings sorted out, the guest rooms are available."

"Yes! That would be helpful. I seem to recall an excellent dining room, too."

"There's a new head chef since you left. I'd venture to say he's even better than the last."

"I also remember a piano?"

"In the lounge, upstairs. Along with a billiard room and a reading room if you get bored with guzzling German schnapps."

"No one gets bored on schnapps," Ward declared, handing back the completed forms.

"Maybe not." Eric put his signature on the last of this business, then stood and held out his hand. "But welcome back."

Ward took Eric's hand with a firm grip, his grin nearly melding into his scar. "It's good to be back."

"There's just one more thing."

"Oh?"

Eric pulled out a five-year-old ledger and opened it to the relevant page. "It seems you took out a box in the club vault before you left for Switzerland and never gave it up again."

"So I did." Ward dug a small steel key out of one pocket and held it up. "I'd forgotten all about it until I found this again while packing for my return. Does this mean I've technically been availing myself of club services all through the past five years, and therefore owe you my club dues for that time?"

"For something so petty? Not at all. But don't think I'm not going to hold this over you when it's convenient."

Ward laughed—a hearty, honest laugh that shook the dust from the shabby cabinets. "Very good! We'd better go take a look, then."

The vault and its anteroom were down a narrow staircase across from Eric's office and isolated from the rest of the basement. Eric hated that cold, windowless place. Its decorative mosaic floor spoke of a nobler intention subverted to a more pragmatic use, like a bombed-out church appropriated for the storage of Army rations; and of late, there also seemed to be an unpleasant smell clinging to it. The vault was where poor Albert Benson had met his untimely end, and Eric, perhaps fancifully, wondered if there might be a connection—Benson's ghost stalking the darkness, the odour of death in his footsteps, a grisly harbinger of guilt . . .

It took three tries to get the combination right. The vault door swung open, and a harsh glare flickered on to illuminate the steel boxes lining the far wall of the little white room within. Eric found himself looking for signs of blood, but the floor, of course, had been scrubbed clean countless times over. Benson really was gone.

"Here we go, Ward. I'm afraid I've yet to get used to . . . Ward?"

Ward seemed to have lost track of his surroundings. He was staring at a pile of old posters mounted on cardboard, all shoved into a corner and forgotten. *Once a German, always a German!* they proclaimed over illustrations of barbaric atrocities ascribed to the German forces. And if these imagined wrongs weren't enough, there was the grave of Edith Cavell pictured near the bottom.

Sister Cavell was a British nurse in Belgium when the War broke out, and was there any British soul not outraged at her execution by a German firing squad? Ward's good humour had drained from his face, leaving it grey and bitter.

Eric laid a gentle hand on Ward's shoulder and tried to turn him away. "We've had a visit from the British Empire Union, and as you can see, they've left their posters. We should have thrown these out right away."

Ward stirred and stretched out a finger to trace the words printed on either side of Sister Cavell's grave: *1914 to 1918* on one, *Never again!* on the other. This poster was not a relic of the War itself, but something composed well into the aftermath.

"The War ended seven years ago this November," he murmured. "I wonder how long we must continue to live in its shadow."

"I know." The Britannia was full of men still overshadowed by the War.

Ward's finger stopped on the image of the grave itself: a simple cross on a mound of dirt, the name *Edith Cavell* on the crosspiece. "I was there, you know. In Brussels."

"When she was killed?"

He nodded. "She was a remarkable woman. She knew the price she'd have to pay for smuggling all those soldiers out of Belgium to safety, and she paid it with better courage than most men could muster. Before she died, she told her priest, 'I must have no hatred or bitterness towards anyone.' So I wonder what she would have made of this."

"Best thing we can do for her now is to live well; and we've been through enough," Eric said, drawing Ward away from the posters and towards the light of the open vault. The point, Eric knew, was not that a British nurse had been executed ten years ago on charges of espionage, but that her memory was now being invoked to keep the War alive. And the damage was done: a sullen shadow had descended upon Ward, dispelling all his previous *joie de vivre.*

Ward's box came out of the bank with an echoing rasp, like a casket out of a crypt, and Eric set it on the lone wooden table in the middle of the vault. Ward, his brow still clouded, drew closer only as Eric opened up the box itself.

They were immediately assailed by a strong odour of gun oil. The only thing in the box was a revolver wrapped in oilcloth: a Webley, with the distinctively curved "bird's head" grip of an older model. Was it a Mark IV from the Boer War, or a Mark V from the beginning of the Great War? Eric twitched aside a flap of the oilcloth for a closer inspection—

"Hands off," Ward snapped, slapping his hand away.

Eric held his hands up, palms open, then laid them flat on the table. He knew better than to pick a fight with a soldier in such a mood. But he peered at the Webley where it lay in the box, nonetheless, angling his head to not block the light. Ward had no objection to that, at least.

Scratched into the Webley's grip was a small rectangle divided into triangular quarters by an inscribed X.

"Your mark, Ward?"

Ward pulled the oilcloth back over the gun. "It no longer matters."

"You'll want to get that thing cleaned and properly serviced. After five years locked away in here, untouched and without maintenance, it's bound to be very nearly choked with rust."

"I'd sooner sell it."

Eric understood. He'd sold off his Webley, too.

Ward dropped a thick envelope into the box, on top of the Webley, with a violent gesture that made Eric jump. The name of Ward's sanatorium was stamped into one corner, and the envelope itself looked as though it might contain a written manuscript—was

Gregory Ward an aspiring writer? Ward snapped the box shut again and pushed it back in Eric's direction, saying with a curtness bordering on rudeness, "I'll keep this box a while longer. Put it back."

It was normally the member himself who handled the boxes once they were in the vault. Properly speaking, Eric's place was out in the anteroom, both to afford Ward some privacy with his personal belongings and to open the vault door again should some accident send it slamming shut. But Eric complied, nonetheless. There'd be time enough to remind Ward of how this worked later, when he wasn't caught in the grip of some dark memory.

And this, of course, was the moment something behind the walls went off like an exploding shell, causing just enough of a tremor that the vault door swung shut before either man could scramble around the table to stop it. The electric light above, linked as it was to the vault door, blinked out, and the room was plunged into a pitch-black darkness.

*Darkness. Blind blackness, something acrid in the air, and unyielding earth all around. Lieutenant Peterkin's ears still rang from the shell that had all but obliterated their position, but he imagined he could hear the more fortunate soldiers of his company scrabbling through the rubble for survivors. He felt around, pushing away as much of the collapsed dugout as he could without bringing anything worse down on his head. His fingers found fabric . . . a sleeve. Not his own sleeve. This was one of his men. Private Dent.*

*Just, as it turned out later, not all of Private Dent . . .*

*Stiff upper lip, man. You're an officer, and an officer does not lose his head in front of his men. He sets an example of absolute, perfect sangfroid. Stiff upper lip . . .*

Eric swallowed the horror rising in his throat and forced himself into the present. Stiff upper lip! The last thing a shell-shock case like Ward needed was another panicked soldier trapped with him. But—

"Peterkin? Are you there?"

"Here."

Ward's voice was tight. Controlled. Too even to be anything but a brave front. Eric groped through the darkness towards it, finally encountering the fabric of Ward's jacket.

*Private Dent's sleeve.*

The smell of rot was overpowering. That had to be only his imagination, surely? Eric put his arm around Ward's shoulders, and felt Ward do the same for him. They were each keeping a stiff upper lip for the sake of the other man.

What was that? Footsteps?

"Hullo!" Eric called out. "Cully, is that you?"

"Lieutenant Peterkin, sir! I think we've had a burst pipe!"

Eric heard the combination wheel spin. A moment later, the door swung open, and the electric light flooded the room with a blinding glare. Thank God.

Ward, shrugging out of Eric's grip, launched himself out of the vault and was gone before anyone could stop him.

"Don't give me that," Madam Eliot said into the telephone mouthpiece, so crisply she might as well have snapped. "The Sandalford Estate can wait. This can't. Yes, I know it's Friday. Why do you think I'm asking you to rush?"

Light flashed on the jewelled face of her gold wristwatch as she set the telephone down again with a sharp click. It had been Cully's idea to approach the former Mrs. Andrew Russell for help, as she was here with the other Russell widows for their usual Friday lunch. After managing all the builders and trades employed by Carrington-Clarke & Associates, she had to know what must be done for a burst pipe, and all the right people to do it. And so she did. Once unleashed, the woman was a virago.

"There. That's the water mains shut off, and a crew arranged to clean up the mess. That should give us all some breathing room. But the real trouble is that your burst pipe is buried behind a solid concrete wall, and judging by the smell, you've probably had a leak back there all through the winter. We'll have to break down the wall before we can get anything done, and that means time and work and money. Assuming, of course, you want us for the job."

Eric's nerves were still on edge from the vault, seeking an enemy that his brain understood to not be there. All he could see, really, was Bradshaw's damned tortoise-on-a-bicycle print framed over the desk. "Of course," he said, keeping his posture upright and his expression neutral. "It should go without saying that Carrington-Clarke will be the company for us. We're in your debt—"

"Only until our invoices are paid, I assure you."

"I'll leave this in your capable hands, then."

"Splendid." Madam Eliot slid off the edge of the desk, where she'd been perched while ringing up all the necessary people, and her heels hit the floor with a sharp *ka-click*. "In the meantime, you'll have to shut down the kitchen as there'll be no running water. That means no lunch. The others will be disappointed, but Flora should know of a good alternative."

"I'd better go and offer them my apologies."

They walked out together but stopped at the entrance to the lobby, where golden sunlight poured straight down onto a gleaming marble floor from the skylight above. After the darkness of the subterranean bunker that was the vault and its anteroom, this sunlit world felt like an illusion; and there, washed in the sun, stood Captain Gregory Algernon Ward in earnest conversation with Lucy, widow of Colonel Russell's youngest. In her white-and-navy sailor dress . . . Yes, it was spring now, wasn't it? The world was in bloom, with bursts of colour overwriting the grey of winter, and the brisk March wind was infused with the scent of new growth. Ward, smiling, looked for once like his actual thirty-eight.

"They make a darling pair, don't they?" Leaning against a column with trousered legs elegantly crossed, Miss Flora Grace looked as though she might have descended from the cover of a fashion magazine. A blue-grey trail of smoke from her cigarette in its holder floated up into the shadows like incense. "They ran into each other ten minutes ago—him out of the dark, her in from the light—locked eyes and have yet to look away. I'd be more concerned if he hadn't looked so pathetic, or if I hadn't recognised his name when he introduced himself. He *is* the same Gregory Ward who trained with my David, I assume?"

"He is," Eric said, and marvelled. Half an hour ago, even before being trapped in the vault, Ward had been sunk into the darkest of moods. "And this is love at first sight?"

"There's no such thing. He's quite taken by her, I'll give you that much. But that's the work of a moment, and I've seen the effects come and go a hundred times before. Whether this momentary infatuation actually turns into love on both sides depends entirely on how well they impress each other going forward."

Eric found himself suddenly wondering how well he'd managed to impress the lovely Miss Grace so far.

"Well, she's young," said another voice: Lady Alice, her habitual black mourning blending into the shadows beyond that sunlit meeting of lovers. "Far too young to be settling into a life of keeping house for Hadrian. She's been in a dark hole since Patrick died, though she won't admit it, and she really could do with someone to get her out of the darkness."

Miss Grace, the bright to Lady Alice's black, drew on her cigarette and nodded in agreement.

March really was the most difficult month, Eric reflected as he firmly shut his office window on the grey skies and plummeting temperatures of what he hoped was the last gasp of winter. Thank God, Madam Eliot's workmen had resolved the worst of the pipe issue, and they could reopen the kitchen tomorrow. Had it really only been five days since it happened? Yes, and it would be another five days before Colonel Russell's return.

Emerging into the lobby, Eric heard whistling from the vestibule: an improvised series of joyful cadenzas dancing on the marble and tripping out into the lobby like exultant birdsong. Someone, at least, was enjoying himself—and Eric knew who.

"Hullo, Ward. You're coming back from your dinner later and later every day."

"Am I?" Ward ceased his whistling to check his watch. "I've had good company."

"Lucy Russell? Or Madam Eliot?"

Ward had made it a point to take Madam Eliot out to dinner once, but that was merely a courtesy to her as the widow of his old friend Andrew Russell. Every evening since had been spent in the company of the former Mrs. Patrick Russell instead, and the club gossips were taking bets on Colonel Russell's reaction to this rather intense courtship once he got back from his fishing excursion.

"Dear Lucy." Ward's smile grew unbearably sweet. "Do you know she's reading Guy de Maupassant in the original French? She says you can never truly appreciate a translation, and I'm inclined to agree."

"If you're out any later, you'll have to trouble the night attendant to let you in. But the club dining room should be reopened tomorrow, so there's that—unless you'd like to proceed from there to some nightclub or other."

"Lucy doesn't care for nightclubs. She's . . . old-fashioned. Unspoilt. A wonderful girl."

Ward wandered on, up the stairs and past the Knights on the landing. There was a boyish spring to his step, and one almost wondered how he could ever have been mistaken for an old man of fifty. Eric watched and waited until the whistling died into the distance before turning to let himself out. March was regressing into a sullen wintry chill, and London might see one last snowfall before spring truly set in; but Gregory Ward, warmed by the sun of Lucy Russell's growing affection, likely felt none of it.

# ILL OMENS

"I NEVER SEE you anymore. It used to be that you'd stop by the Arabica almost every other night, after you were done with whatever nefarious skulduggery you get up to in this club of yours. We'd have a cup of coffee, and I'd read your fortune in the cards—or try to, anyway—and then we'd go out and burn the city to the ground—"

"Burn the city to the ground!"

"A fellow can dream."

Avery Ferrett, fine-featured and fair with an aristocratic nose, perched his lanky frame on the balustrade of the Britannia's front portico and flicked the spent remains of his clove cigarette into the street. He was excluded from the Britannia Club by virtue of never having fought—not that his Bohemian pretensions would have fit in, anyway—and usually whiled away his hours instead at the Arabica, an obscure coffeehouse just off Soho Square.

"Club secretary," Eric said, "has been more work and responsibility than I initially expected, and Bradshaw left no notes whatsoever as to how he kept everything running. A lot of what I managed in January, I had to do over in February."

"And now it is the middle of March. The thirteenth, no less—Friday the thirteenth. You know I wouldn't set foot out of doors on Friday the thirteenth if I didn't think it important."

"Well, I doubt this Friday the thirteenth can bring anything worse than last Friday's burst pipe." Eric paused, then grinned and reached out to pull Avery off the balustrade. "This might interest you, in fact. Come on in. I'll even treat you to lunch afterwards, now the dining room's open again."

"Don't tempt fate," Avery muttered crossly, though he seemed perfectly eager to follow Eric inside. Perhaps it was the prospect of oysters Rockefeller.

Eric signed him in with Cully at the reception desk, then took him down to the vault. A rough hole had been broken into one wall of the anteroom, and what lay beyond was a bit more than the expected crawl space. "The vault wasn't part of the original building plan," Eric told his friend. "It was installed later, and separated from the rest of the basement with these concrete walls. In the process, they also sealed away this room between the vault and the kitchens. The workmen found something in it after draining out all the floodwater and muck; they showed it to me, of course, and I thought immediately of you."

"If you say it's a cask of Amontillado, I'm leaving."

"For the love of God, Montresor!" Eric laughed. "No, but you'll love this more."

A few bare bulbs had been strung on electrical cables leading into the hole to give the workmen some steady light to work by. Eric flipped the switch and climbed in, Avery following after a moment's hesitation. On one side, a tight little alcove opened into a larger cavern choked with a forest of pipes snaking across the walls in every direction. Tangled shadows leapt and danced with the swaying of the naked bulbs overhead. And at their feet, the floor had crumbled around the pipes after a century of dripping water and neglect, finally collapsing into a deeper cavity beneath the foundation.

Eric reached up and gingerly angled a light bulb by its insulated base to cast light down into the cavity. "What do you think?"

"Is that . . . is that a Roman mosaic?"

The vault and its anteroom had mosaic floors, relics of an original intent lost to the march of time, but the thing at the bottom of the hole was something else. Glazed chips of ceramic had been arranged into an intricate pattern of intertwining vines, subtle differences of colour used to simulate shading and shadow. Seen from a distance, one might think this a painting instead.

"London," Eric said, "when it was the Roman outpost of Londinium, didn't reach this far west. You can still find bits of the wall if you know where to look. Westminster and St. James, in those days, would have been open countryside outside of the fortified walls. This might have been part of a Roman patrician's country villa. There were a few of those here and there, once the local Celts got used to living alongside the Romans."

Remembering Colonel Russell's remarks on King Arthur, Eric couldn't help but wonder if the patrician in question might have been Lucius Artorius Castus himself. It would mean that the Britannia Club was, quite literally, sitting on top of Camelot. Imagine the Knights—Gawain, Percival, Lancelot, and the rest—as Roman centurions marching out to enforce the Pax Romana, and the stalwart members of the Britannia following in their footsteps . . .

The light bulb sprang free of Eric's grip, causing the dark edges of the hole below to surge like a black tide lapping against the mosaic vines. Shadows swirled madly across the walls and against the pipes, making the room appear to pulse like the inner workings of a living beast.

Avery stared down into the hole several seconds longer, momentarily mesmerised, then backed away. "I don't like this," he muttered. "I wouldn't be surprised if this was originally some sort of mausoleum, and that mosaic thing was part of a sarcophagus. You may have unleashed something akin to a mummy's curse, Eric, but Roman rather than Egyptian. There's a very good reason someone sealed this room away."

"Yes. The very good reason being that it's cheaper to build a plain wall than one with a door, and someone was shortsighted enough to think that if the plumbing worked perfectly well then, it should work perfectly well forever."

"I'll feel better once you've had someone come in and identify any vengeful spirits that might want appeasing."

Eric followed as Avery beat a hasty retreat back to the lobby, where they were arrested by a sharp, irritable bark:

"Peterkin! What's this I hear about an exploded pipe, a Roman mosaic, and you going over my head to authorise works done on the club building?"

Colonel Russell was back from his fishing trip—three days early and with sour discontent overriding his usual geniality. With him was Madam Eliot; she must have told him all the news. Behind them, Cully was still in the act of gathering up the correspondence that had been left for the Colonel in the care of the Britannia Club rather than sent directly to his house in Knightsbridge. Avery stopped at the front desk and turned, distracted by the demands being made on his friend.

"Colonel Russell!" Eric snapped unconsciously into a straight-backed military stance as he briefed the Colonel on the situation as succinctly as possible. "It really couldn't have waited for your return, sir. I've only authorised what was absolutely necessary."

Colonel Russell glared fiercely, then broke into a sudden grin. "At ease, soldier! I know it couldn't be helped. If I'm cross, it's more because a plague of poachers on the Scottish waterways forced me to cut my trip short. You'll forgive me the joke at your expense, I hope. In any case, I trust your judgement, and Miranda knows what she's doing."

Madam Eliot, smartly tailored and brightly jewelled, had been in and out of the Britannia so much over the past week that Eric was beginning to think of her more as a business liaison than as the former Mrs. Andrew Russell. This was her cue to cut in.

"Mr. Peterkin! This won't take more than five minutes. You do have time for me, don't you?" Without waiting for an answer, she slipped her arm into Eric's and drew him away. Eric could see the Colonel turning to get his mail while Avery, all thoughts of ancient Roman curses forgotten, looked on in growing amusement. She continued, "Hadrian's brought up a very interesting point, which is that if a proper entrance to that new pipe room is to be installed, it really shouldn't be from the vault anteroom. Technically, both the vault and its anteroom are what we call 'above-stairs' spaces—that is, they're used primarily by the membership—which could mean having your respectable gentlemen tripping over plumbers and the like whenever maintenance needs to be done. So what I'm proposing is that we punch a hole through another wall to create an access from the kitchens. Oh, not *directly* from the kitchens, of course: it'll be the passage from the kitchens to the back door, across from the big storage room. Far more suitable, I'd say."

"Yes," Eric said, rubbing his forehead. "That would be best." Madam Eliot's rapid-fire attack had him vaguely off-balance, with any romantic notion of being built on top of Camelot itself now blown away by the everyday business of simply making things work. How did Sir Kay manage Camelot's dull and pragmatic side?

"Splendid." Madam Eliot scribbled something in her notebook. "And I'm returning your copy of the back door key. No, it's not that the workmen won't still be wanting free access at all hours—it's that Hadrian has given me his. He says you sometimes use that door while he never does, so this will be much more convenient all around. Our next order of business would be to get an archaeologist in to authenticate that mosaic fragment; but I see Alice is here for our Friday lunch, which means Flora and Lucy cannot be far behind. Though if Lucy prefers the company of her new gentleman friend, perhaps it'll be just the three of us today."

Indeed, Lady Alice, majestic as ever in black silk, was just now advancing on the front desk to welcome her father-in-law home. "And Mr. Ferrett! Fancy meeting you here. How do you do?"

Lady Alice knew Avery? She was already introducing him to the Colonel.

Eric didn't have time to question the familiarity, as Captain Ward arrived right then with Lucy Russell on his arm. It was as the gossips had speculated: How would Colonel Russell react to finding that Lucy, more daughter than daughter-in-law and perhaps the most present memento of his late son Patrick, was being courted behind his back? Ward, no doubt, had been planning to approach the Colonel in private, but now . . .

Ward faltered on spotting the Colonel. He stooped to whisper something to Lucy, then took a deliberate step away from her. Meanwhile, the Colonel's shoulders were knotted with tension at Ward's approach, and his conversation with Avery and Lady Alice seemed quite forgotten.

There was a guardedness about the two men, like wolves circling each other.

Ward stopped and smiled, his scar flexing, though his eyes remained wary. He said, "Colonel Russell, sir. It's Captain Ward. You received my letter, of course?"

"I never forget a face," the Colonel said, his voice low. Then he let out a boom of laughter and pulled Ward into a warm embrace. "Ward, my boy! How utterly delightful to have you back . . . among the living, as it were. You could have knocked me over with a feather. I'd all but given you up for dead, after all these years!"

Ward's smile finally hit his eyes in an explosion of laugh lines. "You know I'm not so easily gotten rid of."

Eric let out a breath and relaxed. As Ward and the Russells drew away to await the last of their number—Miss Grace—to join them for lunch, Eric sidled over to Avery and said, "It's all your fault, you know."

"My fault? What am I supposed to have done now?"

"All that talk about ancient curses had me quite on edge—made me think Ward and the Colonel were about to leap at each other's throats. But it's only that they haven't seen each other in ages, hardly the stuff of curses. And what would a Roman curse even look like, pray tell?"

Avery's expression turned grave, now he'd been reminded. "Look for a small square of paper-thin lead with the exact nature of the curse engraved on it. That's how the Romans used to work their magic. And in the meantime . . . beware the Ides of March."

"We are none of us Julius Caesar, Avery."

Nonetheless, Avery repeated: "Beware the Ides of March."

Overhead, a cloud passed over the skylight, dropping the lobby into a sudden shadow. Avery shivered, looped his scarf once more across his chin, and hurried away.

*Beware the Ides of March.*

Eric was following a trail of paper-thin lead squares through a forest of vines. His regiment was leaving for France, and he had to join them before the fifteenth of the month or be left behind; but the faster he ran, the slower he seemed to go—

"Peterkin? I say, Peterkin!"

Eric blinked awake. Colonel Russell was leaning over him, his breath heavy with whisky; the electric light above was blinding, and his office window showed only darkness.

"Saw the light on," the Colonel grumbled. "Making a habit of this, are you?"

"Not at all."

"So you say. What's this, then?" Turning his head, Colonel Russell peered at the doodles across Eric's blotter. "Something new since the last time."

"Oh. The vines from the Roman mosaic, the cipher Ward used to mark his service revolver, and . . . all the daggers from the murder of Julius Caesar. Ides of March, you know."

"Fascinating."

This time, the Colonel really did seem fascinated by Eric's blotter, but that was probably because of the whisky. Eric hadn't known Colonel Russell to drink to excess before. He stood, stretched, and checked his watch. Nearly midnight. "Time we were gone, Colonel."

"No one is ever truly gone, Peterkin."

The Britannia Club at midnight was unearthly in its silence. In the vast, shadow-shrouded lobby, moonlight pooled around the eternal sentinel that was the Roster of the Fallen with its brass plaques gleaming on oaken shields. The shadows were suddenly thronged with ghosts, and Eric shivered. Was that old Fitzwilliam

Peterkin at his shoulder? *All earthly pleasure and pain will pass, my boy, but this is immortality.*

Colonel Russell must have felt it, too. He stopped to gaze up at the Roster, with its constant reminder of lost futures and the present that might have been.

*George, my eldest, had the good sense to cement his legacy . . . Pity he couldn't have left a Luke and a John to finish the Gospel quartet . . .*

"You'd think," the Colonel said, his tone suddenly harsh, "that with four sons, at least one would have made it out alive."

This was a different Colonel Russell from what Eric was used to: one with the armour of good humour stripped away, a father bereft of family. One had to be careful of touching that raw, open wound. "A war like that," Eric said, turning their focus outwards, "isn't likely to happen again, at least."

"The war to end all wars." The Colonel laughed bitterly. "You're not that naive, are you?"

"I read the news. Civil wars, uprisings, border disputes . . . I know they still happen. But we've learnt from our mistakes. Something on the same scale—"

"Who knows, and who cares."

The shadows drew closer. They were in the Colonel's eyes.

"Do you know," he continued, "why I had the Roster moved into the lobby? More room. More room for future plaques, future wars. And there will be war, Peterkin. It is inevitable. From the moment Cain struck down his brother Abel, war has defined human civilisation. How do you think we got our empire, eh? Diplomacy? Not one of our colonial diplomats and governors would be worth tuppence without the regiments of fighting men behind them, all armed to the teeth with superior firepower. Pick up a copy of *Punch* or study our patriotic art—hell, empty your pockets, look at our coinage—and you'll find our great nation personified as Britannia, a warrior queen in a helmet out of classical antiquity."

"There's also John Bull," Eric said. "Rather more fun at dinner parties than Madam Britannia, wouldn't you say?"

"John Bull! That fat, self-satisfied farmer . . . John Bull is a myth, as Arthur is a myth, but of a different stripe. John Bull is how we'd like to be seen: genial, prosperous, a little bit stupid but otherwise well-meaning. It pays to be underestimated, eh? But make no mistake: strip off our mask and you'll always find bloodthirsty Britannia underneath. No one sings 'Rule, John Bull.' Our founding members didn't call this the John Bull Club. And that—" He turned an accusatory glare up at the great painting on the landing. "*That* is not John Bull with his feet up, downing a pint at a country pub."

King Arthur and his Knights gazed back down in solemn silence.

"Perhaps if we were John Bull . . ." Colonel Russell's tone softened. "Perhaps, without the ideals of King Arthur, we wouldn't have been so eager for battlefield glory, eh?"

"Colonel Russell, I realise you're mourning your sons—"

"And what is there to mourn, I'd like to know? War is inevitable, and people die in wars. That's how it always was, always is, and always will be. There will always be a certain percentage of slain, and if a man must number among the doomed, there is nothing you or I could do to make a difference. Not when David was drowned in mustard gas, not when George's attack on the German line went wrong, not when Patrick got picked off by a sniper. Andrew's death in Paris, mere weeks before the Armistice, was just . . . emphasis. Fate and futility."

There it was: the bitterness only hinted at by his pretended callousness over his eldest son's death and legacy. Eric laid a hand on the Colonel's arm, and for a moment, it appeared as though another outburst was forthcoming; but the older man deflated and said:

"At least we name them, eh? The Cenotaph on Whitehall commemorates all the dead who never came home, grandly and simply, but we name them. We make it personal, see? But that changes nothing. Even victory and defeat are meaningless in the long run. So what is the point in mourning? You might as well protest the moon."

With a nod befitting a Roman emperor, Colonel Hadrian Russell proceeded, as steady as if he were sober, to the entrance vestibule. Shadows and ghosts closed over his broad back, and then he was gone.

# THE IDES OF MARCH

ERIC SNAPPED AWAKE to an insistent pounding on his door. A German raid! The chill of melting snow shot through his spine—he could smell mud and smoke and damp canvas—as he fell out of his surprisingly comfortable cot onto the surprisingly clean planking of his quarters. Where was his Webley? He'd sold it . . . Why?

The shadows resolved themselves into shapes far too fine for the front lines. The smoke faded. There was a tall window before him, with real glass; and beyond it, the roofline of London houses—

"Lieutenant Peterkin! Lieutenant Peterkin, sir!"

Oh, dear God. Eric took a moment to shake away the last vestiges of Flanders, then hurried to answer the door. Cully was the only person in the present day who called him by the rank he'd long ago left behind, but what on earth could Ted "Old Faithful" Cully be doing here, so far from the Britannia, and at this hour of the night?

Cully pushed his way into the flat as soon as Eric got the door open, shutting it behind him. He'd thrown on a thick winter coat over his pyjama shirt, and his feet had been thrust into unlaced boots without socks; but his posture was stiff and soldierly, his eyes bright and alert. His voice was strained: "Sir. There's been a murder."

A what?

Eric recalled Cully's clear panic in the face of Benson's murder last year. Was this the same man? But the image of Albert Benson lying dead on the vault floor quickly eclipsed all other concerns. Last year? No, it had only been a few months ago. Surely lightning couldn't strike twice, and so soon?

Eric ran to get some clothes on. "You don't mean at the club?" A desperate hope, but why else would Cully be here? Eric had spent the day at the Arabica instead—stocktaking be damned—and this was the result. A sickening sense of déjà vu tied knots in his stomach, and the image of Albert Benson bleeding out over a Georgian mosaic melted into one of Gregory Ward bleeding out over a Roman mosaic . . .

Cully said, "It's Colonel Russell, sir."

"What!" That was nearly as unbelievable. Eric remembered parting ways with Colonel Russell before the Roster of the Fallen, just twenty-four hours ago. What was it he'd said? *"If a man must number among the doomed . . ."* Eric shoved his shirttails into his trousers. "You've called the police, of course?"

"Yes, sir, right before I came to get you. They should be at the club by now."

"And you got here by taxi?"

"It's waiting outside."

"Come on, then!"

Eric abandoned his waistcoat buttons—he could do them up in the taxi—and hurried down the stairs. Cully had the presence of mind to grab him a tie before following him down to the Beardmore taxi growling in wait. Ashen flakes of snow drifted down to melt instantly on the vehicle's black bonnet before rising again as breaths of steam. In the single-sided front, the driver was so heavily muffled against this last gasp of winter that nothing human could be discerned about him. He said nothing as Eric and Cully bundled into the back, and screeched away from the kerb before the door was fully closed.

Fumbling with his collar studs, Eric said, "Tell me what happened. From the beginning."

"There was a loud bang. It . . . gave me a fright. Then there was another bang, and a crash like breaking glass. I told myself it had to be a motorcar backfiring, not a gunshot, but that didn't explain the crash. So my next thought was—burglars! I caught up a fireplace poker and went to have a look around. There was a light on in the lounge, and one of the windows there was broken. It occurred to me that there was surprisingly little glass on the floor, like the window had been broken outwards, if you catch my drift?"

Eric nodded. He'd seen that clue more than once in the manuscripts he'd had to evaluate. "You had a closer look?"

"Colonel Russell was on the pavement outside. He must have gone through the window. There was blood and glass everywhere."

There'd be no hiding this one. The scene was right there on their doorstep and would remain there for as long as Scotland Yard dictated—at least another twenty-four hours. How much traffic was there on King Street on a Sunday? London had withdrawn and barricaded itself behind brick and stone for now, turning the void between her fortress-like edifices into a deserted no-man's-land.

Snow blew past as they sped on, white flecks dashing against the windows of the taxi's passenger compartment to leave darted threads of water, like shallow cuts in the glass. Light from a passing streetlamp made the taxi driver's reflection stand out, ghostlike, in the windscreen. The muffler pulled up to his nose looked almost like a beard . . . Bradshaw's beard.

*You're not thinking it's indecent, are you? To be worrying about how this tragedy might scandalise polite London society, instead of giving the dead his due respect?*

Bradshaw?

*I pulled an orchestra's worth of strings to keep Benson's murder out of the papers. So lightning's struck twice, has it? Now it's your turn. Colonel Russell served his king and country with honour, sacrificing four sons on the altar of Empire. It would be indecent* not *to protect his memory and preserve unsullied the club he loved. Others may mourn:* you *must guard against scandal.*

Eric straightened up and turned to Cully. "You're certain he was murdered?"

"Man wants to jump, he opens the window first. And he chooses a higher floor."

That was the other concern: that this might, in fact, have been suicide. The bitter fatalism of the Colonel's last speech still echoed in Eric's mind, and he knew that Cully understood.

"Who else knows about this? The night attendant, I'm assuming . . . Who is it tonight?"

"That would be Thomas Harvey, sir. Bright young lad, very personable—maybe too personable for his own good. I was giving him hell when we both heard the bangs."

"Hell? What for?"

"He'd brought a woman into the club, sir. I caught him with his trousers down—quite literally. I gave him a moment to get himself in order and the woman out the door. If I'd known what was to happen . . . Well."

Eric made a face. There'd have to be disciplinary action taken, on top of this crisis. But that would have to wait. "There's no chance this woman's our killer, is there? I mean, if you were occupied with Harvey . . ."

"Sir? Never! A big, strong man like Colonel Russell—he'd never, not against a woman. Besides, I had Harvey send her away, and that was *before* the murder."

"By the back door, I'm assuming. I wonder if Harvey remembered to lock it after her."

A new lock had been installed on the back door just last month, so there wasn't any question of extra keys wandering around. Eric had one as club secretary; the club president's key was currently in Madam Eliot's possession; and the last was kept in the door, on the inside. But what were the odds of some dangerous maniac just happening to be in the service court at the right time to notice if Harvey forgot to turn that key behind him?

But he was getting ahead of himself. "All right. Who else was in the building?"

"Only Captain Ward, sir. No one else. He showed up as Harvey and me were looking out the window. I told them to keep watch over the Colonel—his body, I mean—while I called the police and came to get you." His story told, Cully sat back and seemed to deflate. This was the anxious, obsequious Cully that Eric knew—the faithful retainer who looked to his officers for direction.

Eric remembered that brief moment of tension in the meeting between Captain Ward and Colonel Russell, and how it had been dispelled by the Colonel's welcome. But thinking about it now, hadn't the Colonel's cheer been a trifle overstated? Did he, in fact, secretly see Lucy's romance with Ward as a betrayal of Patrick Russell's memory, and was that the reason for his fatalistic mood that Friday night? Had he come to blows with Ward over it?

*Beware the Ides of March.*

"What was Colonel Russell doing at the Britannia at this hour? Drinking again?" Eric wondered aloud as the taxi swerved around the corner from St. James's Street to King Street. He could see the scrum of police cars in front of the club, and the distinctive silhouettes of police helmets bobbing to and fro under the light of the streetlamps. A handful of gawkers had gathered across the street, outside the Golden Lion: last call might be eleven o'clock, but it evidently took a couple of hours for the pub's patrons to actually finish their drinks and go home. They'd carry the news to all of London before the ink was dry on the morning editions.

"Harvey says the Colonel let himself in at about half eleven, sir, but he doesn't know what for. It's not his place to question the members, especially the acting president."

The taxi pulled up a few paces from the club, and Cully drew a deep breath, steeling himself to face the lions. It occurred to Eric that, despite his apparent panic last time, Cully had still carried out his every order with aplomb and kept all the attendants in line. He'd risen to the occasion then; and this time, Eric was around to see it.

"Cully." Eric laid a hand on the old porter's arm before the man could get out of the cab. "Listen. I'm glad you came to get me. It was the right thing to do, but the police won't see it that way. They'll say you left to dispose of important evidence and they'll be especially difficult on that account. This won't be like the last time. All we can do is put a brave face on it."

For the first time that night, amusement flickered in Cully's eyes. "With all due respect, sir, I think I know bravery. Besides, haven't we got members at the Yard?"

"That won't matter. Whoever gets put in charge of this case, it won't be anyone with an interest in doing us any favours. All the better to keep things honest, see?"

"I reckon so, sir. And forewarned is forearmed, as they say."

Getting out of the cab, Cully squared his shoulders, smoothed down his hair, and shook off the last of his anxiety. Hadn't he once crawled across a mile of the Transvaal with a bullet in his knee? There was more steel to Ted Cully, Eric realised, than anyone gave him credit for.

Up ahead, the helmeted policemen stood in a crude circle before the club, their boots stamping away the fine layer of snow still visible in patches up and down the pavement. There was a military tension about them, an alertness that brought Eric back to days of watching and waiting for the enemy's next move. Who was the commanding officer here? A big man in a trench coat, fair hair gleaming in the light from the open front door. Cully approached one of the lesser soldiers, and other shadows detached themselves from the crowd to surround him. Judging by the barking tones of the policemen, Cully was getting his head properly bitten off for having left the scene; but he stood firm, seeming to draw strength from the adversity. Eric waited for him to turn and beckon before crossing the street to join them.

"You'll be the man in charge of this fine institution, then?" the grim-faced constable said, glaring balefully. "Inspector will want to talk to you. You and Mr. Cully both."

Eric noticed that the policemen had positioned themselves in such a way as to block Cully's escape, should the old man—with a bad knee—try to run. Beyond the shield of their starch-fronted bodies, Eric could see the crumpled form of Colonel Hadrian

Russell on the pavement, surrounded by blood and glass. Light from the streetlamps caught on his whiskers and on one glassy, staring eye, bringing into grotesque relief the snarl frozen across his face. Swirling snow turned to mud around him, and Eric recalled with some irony that Colonel Russell had spent the War in London as a senior recruitment officer rather than actually in the field—

*Beware the Ides of March, when the murder of Julius Caesar finally tipped the Roman Republic into becoming the Roman Empire.*

Hadrian Russell had been named for a Roman emperor. That meant nothing, surely? Or was there actually something to Avery's superstitious nonsense?

"Mr. Eric Peterkin, is it?"

The man whom Eric had identified as "the commanding officer" approached with a lithe, light-footed grace, like a big jungle cat. His blond beard was cut in a fashion more common in Chinese caricatures, and his brows went up with interest on seeing Eric. "I'm Inspector Benedict Crane," he began, and then a series of lilting syllables poured forth from his mouth. It took Eric a moment to recognise the Chinese dialect he'd heard only once before, in Limehouse.

"I'm sorry, Inspector. I don't understand."

The Inspector's mouth snapped shut, and his expression changed. Disapproval? Or disappointment? Abruptly no-nonsense and practical, he said, "I was saying that I'm just back in England after ten years in Hong Kong, and that I hope we'll get this unpleasant business sorted before too long. As club secretary, you'd be the one in charge, I understand?"

"I am."

Eric glanced again behind him, where someone was taking photographs of the body from every conceivable angle. Up at the doors of the club, Ward shivered in his dressing gown and slippers; beside him stood Thomas Harvey, a tall lad with dark curls tamed by club regulations and storm-grey eyes tamed by nothing ever, the shirtfront of his livery like a beacon of white against the dark. Both had their hands tucked under their arms for warmth.

And there, of course, was Ted Cully, responding to the badgering questions of a police sergeant as though nothing on earth could shake him.

"Sooner we get the body to the medical examiner, the better," Inspector Crane said, looking back at the scene. "Carter! We done?"

The photographer raised the thumbs-up, and Crane gestured to someone to bring a stretcher over. Colonel Russell was rolled onto his back, revealing the patch of blood and gore spreading out from the hole in his shirtfront—Eric had seen enough men shot to recognise what he saw. And what was that, clutched close to his chest? A revolver: the Colonel's fingers were frozen around its barrel, leaving the curved "bird's head" grip and trigger guard free.

"Well, well," said the Inspector, brushing the snow from his shoulders. "There's the true cause of death, I reckon—and the weapon, wrestled away from his killer. Much obliged, Colonel. All we'll be wanting now is a formal interview with everyone present."

*Snow drifted across the shoulders of a sergeant twice Lieutenant Peterkin's age. "All right, Peterkin. You know what you have to do."*

"Yes," said Eric, squaring his shoulders as Cully had done. "Of course. Let me show you to my office. That and everything we have is at your disposal."

# NOBLESSE OBLIGE

THE SNOW WAS gone by daybreak, when Inspector Crane left to call on Colonel Russell's house in Knightsbridge. Once he got some idea of the Colonel's final hours from Lucy or the servants, he'd presumably move on to Lady Alice in Marylebone to officially pay his respects to the family as a whole. Even so, it was well past noon before Eric was allowed to begin dealing with the broken window, the horrifying stains on the pavement, the disorder left by a horde of policemen turning everything upside down in their search for clues . . .

The broken glass was cleaned away in a minute; the fingerprint powder took more time and effort. Eric's interest, however, was drawn more to the things left by the murder itself. There was a half-empty bottle of gin on the table next to the chair where Colonel Russell had presumably been sitting, along with a bottle of tonic water, a saucer of sliced limes, and an unused glass. Another glass was found broken on the floor by the chair and taken away by the police as evidence. They'd also dug a bullet out of the wainscotting opposite the window.

The evidence told the story. Two glasses meant the Colonel had been expecting someone. There must have been an altercation of some sort. The other person drew a gun, fired, and missed—hence the bullet in the wainscotting. Colonel Russell charged his assailant and tried to wrestle the gun away. The two grappled by the window until the gun went off again, killing the Colonel and sending him through to the pavement outside.

The entire business seemed unreal: first, that there should be a second murder at the Britannia Club, let alone so soon after the first; and then that it should have happened to Colonel Hadrian Russell, of all people. The lord of the club lounge! Popularity personified! What enemies could such a man possibly have? Eric half expected to turn around and find the man booming with laughter over the day's newspapers, which of course were reporting some other colonel who'd been killed in some other club—

"Eric!"

Avery waved from across the street, having spotted Eric through the broken window. Eric waved back and went down to meet him in the portico.

"Eric, I heard the news. I'm so sorry."

"Nothing I haven't seen before." Eric shrugged with false bravado. "I hope you're not here to say you told me so."

"You know me better than that." Avery gave Eric's shoulder a friendly squeeze. "I was going to ask how you were keeping, but I think I can tell by looking. So go on and talk my ear off, if that helps. I won't even insist on sitting down to coffee at the Arabica."

Eric indicated the men scrubbing the blood from the pavement. "You see what I've been dealing with all day. It's as if I'm not permitted to think of the man's death until I've cleared away the mess it's left behind. Until you came along, I was thinking how much I wanted to hit something."

Avery smiled.

"What's so funny?" Eric asked.

"You want to investigate the murder. Like the last time."

"I do not!"

"And why not? What did Albert Benson have that Colonel Russell doesn't?"

That made Eric stop. He remembered the struggles and the people he'd upset. He hadn't thought much of Bradshaw's fury then, but now that he was in Bradshaw's position . . . "One shouldn't make a habit of this sort of thing. With the Colonel gone, I'm in charge with no one to pick up the slack. I haven't the freedom. Besides, Crane seems to know what he's doing."

A flash of colour, above the roofline opposite, caught his eye. Was someone flying a kite over St. James's Park? It didn't appear again, though Eric watched and waited . . .

"You should call on Lady Alice," Avery said. "I'm just back from offering my condolences, myself."

"I meant to ask, how did the two of you get acquainted?"

"We met at a séance. She's a regular client of Madame Davidova's."

Really? Lady Alice always struck Eric as far too down-to-earth for the vagaries of spiritualism. Then again, she'd remained in black mourning even seven years after her husband's death. Eric looked back to the pavement: the stain was mostly gone, though his imagination supplied the shape of Colonel Russell still outlined in gore. Above the roofline, the kite he'd glimpsed earlier failed to reappear.

"This *is* one of your duties as club secretary, isn't it?" Avery said, and Eric could almost imagine Bradshaw and Colonel Russell both telling him the same thing. "The family could do with a kind word from some representative of Colonel Hadrian Russell's beloved club."

"You're right. Of course you're right." Eric checked his watch. "Too late in the day now, I'm afraid, but tomorrow, as soon as it's polite, I will do my duty by the Russells."

Lady Alice, despite her aristocratic pedigree, ruled the Russell clan from the middle-class modesty of Marylebone, a stone's throw from Regent's Park. Her house was a tall and narrow slice out of a uniform block, faced in stately white limestone on the ground floor and a more unassuming honey-brown brick above, with a narrow wrought-iron balcony running across the first floor. But for a few window boxes and potted plants, the street was all hard surfaces and austerity, buttoned up in its respectability and giving nothing away.

In the heart of that urban desert, Lady Alice's drawing room was an oasis. It was large and spacious, and made even more so by having the furniture pushed close to the walls. Three tall windows overlooked a grassy back garden shaded by a venerable chestnut tree, from whose branches a wooden swing rocked in the wind. Were they still in the city? Lady Alice had foregone the country estates of her aristocratic forebears, and she was only the third daughter of an earl, married to an untitled commoner; but as she crossed the rose-patterned Axminster carpet to meet Eric with a hollow-eyed smile, she might have been an empress, and this the grandest of throne rooms.

"Mr. Peterkin," she said, with a nod to dismiss the maid who'd shown him in. "How good of you to come."

Eric had half expected the grim Nemesis of that long-ago casualty clearing station; but evidently the death of a father-in-law, unlike that of a beloved husband, was powerless against the mask of decorum she'd worn since childhood. He took her hands in his; up close and without her usual wide-brimmed black hat, he saw that her hair was, in fact, styled in a faux bob, the long tresses curled under and pinned at the nape of her neck—a conservative woman's compromise with modern fashion. "My condolences," he said. "If there is anything I or the Britannia Club can do for the family, you have only to ask."

"You are too kind. Thank you. Would you care for some tea?"

Seated at a table by one window was Lucy Russell, wearing a black dress tailored more to Lady Alice's matronly proportions than to her own girlish figure. She gave Eric a wan smile and turned her attention back to the chestnut tree outside—and Eric could hardly blame her. He'd spotted a couple of kites flying over Regent's Park on his way here: red and yellow, ducking and weaving freely through the air, their tails fluttering behind them. Not the same kites he'd spotted over St. James's Park, of course, but the effect was identical. Spacious as this drawing room was, they were still stuck indoors on a bright spring day. The freedom of the great outdoors remained untouchable beyond glass.

The other person at the table was a man of perhaps sixty, tall and narrow, with a pince-nez on a scarlet ribbon. Lady Alice introduced him as Dr. Gérard Duplessis, an alienist with a specialty in war neuroses. He leapt to his feet with the energy of one who lived exclusively on strong coffee, shook Eric's hand, offered a calling card, and protested that no one could call him a specialist. "I was a physician for most of my life and have turned to psychology only recently. I still have much to learn." His accent was no more than a slight Gallic lilt, with the softened consonants of cosmopolitan Paris.

"Much to learn! Most people call it research. You really are too modest." To Eric, Lady Alice added, "Dr. Duplessis is attached to the University of London and has published a number of extremely well-received articles on the treatment of war neuroses. He spent the last week at Craiglockhart studying their methods, and the week before that, he was at Seale-Hayne. I had him look in on some of George's more troubled men last year, and his help has been invaluable."

"We should arrange for a lecture at the Britannia Club," Eric told the alienist. "We do take a certain interest in the subject there."

A certain *guilty* interest, he almost said. The servicemen of the Britannia knew the worst of war, and for all its grandeur, its halls were still haunted by the spectres of unwanted memories.

"Do you think so? I suggested it to Colonel Russell once, but—" Duplessis stopped, embarrassed, and Lucy cut in without looking away from the window:

"Hadrian belonged to that class of officer, usually high up enough to see very little of the actual fighting, who thought that shell shock didn't happen to men of strong moral fibre."

"Lucy!" cried Lady Alice.

"Attitudes *are* changing," Eric said quickly to the alienist. "One lecture at a time. You'd be doing us a service."

Lady Alice said, "I think Hadrian would want something of the sort done in his memory. I have always found that in times of distress, the best thing to do is to keep as busy as possible. You won't have time to brood, and you will at least have something worthwhile by the end of it."

Eric remembered Sister Russell stalking the wards of that casualty clearing station so many years ago, and thought that Lady Alice must have had recourse to a great deal of busy work over the years to save herself from grief. At the very least, discussing plans for a potential lecture series meant not having to think of the void left by Colonel Hadrian Russell's absence.

The man himself was watching them, Eric realised, from a framed photograph across the room: Colonel Hadrian Russell in his younger days, before the War, with his late wife Johanna and all four sons, still no more than boys, gathered around them. Their smiles might have lit up the room better than any electric light, but it occurred to Eric that there wasn't a person there now alive, and he turned his gaze to the other framed photographs around it: weddings, family gatherings, portraits . . .

Centred over a glass-fronted cabinet full of toys was a larger family portrait. In it, Lady Alice sat with a four-year-old Matthew Russell clinging to one arm of her chair and Mark Russell, barely a year old, staring wide-eyed from her lap. George Russell stood proudly behind with one hand lovingly on her shoulder: he was very nearly a carbon copy of his father, but with a receding hairline and the leaner build of one who favoured tennis over rugby.

A bronze memorial plaque was mounted just below: the so-called Dead Man's Penny, issued to the next of kin of all those men and women who'd given their lives in the War. It showed Britannia, accompanied by a lion, honouring the inscribed name of the dead. *He died for freedom and honour*.

Eric could easily guess the reason for Lady Alice's patronage of Madame Davidova.

"Your sons will be home for the funeral, yes?" Duplessis asked. Evidently, the matter of planning a lecture series had finally been settled.

Lady Alice nodded. "They should be arriving at King's Cross right now, in fact. Matthew insists he's quite old enough to shepherd himself and his brother home from there, and he's quite right. He's at that age where he's more anxious than anything else to be reckoned a man, and wants nothing to do with his mother's fussing; but I've a year or two yet with Mark, at least." She paused, following Eric's gaze to the family picture. "It broke my heart to leave them with their nanny in Hadrian's care when I went to France with the nurses. People called me irresponsible for putting myself at risk when their father—well. But I could hardly let my husband go alone, could I? Not if I could add even the slimmest of slivers to his chances of coming home safe."

But George Russell hadn't come home safe, had he? He'd been killed in a famously disastrous assault on the German lines. No one could say if he'd been shot or blown up or run through with a bayonet, because no one had come back from it. Eric wondered if his wife felt cheated, that her best efforts had been for nothing.

"Any nanny or doting aunt," Lady Alice continued, "can provide a child with material care and even love, but a parent represents the root of who the child *is*. A parent must be a hero, teaching by example the difference between right and wrong. If I had died as well, my sons would know I'd done the right thing, and that's more valuable than you know."

As if on cue, Eric heard the bang of the front door flying open and a babble of voices from the front entrance. A bark of baritone laughter silenced the others, the door slammed shut again, and then came the clatter of running feet. There was just enough time for Eric to recognise the flash of apprehension in Lady Alice's expression as she got to her feet, and then it was pure joy as Mark Russell burst into the room with a cry of "Mother!"

He hadn't changed at all since Eric last saw him at New Year's.

Lady Alice met him in the middle of the Axminster and caught him up in a warm embrace. "Mark, darling! Did you have a safe trip?"

"We're here, aren't we?" his older brother, Matthew, drawled with feigned scorn. Eric didn't remember him being quite this prickly at New Year's. Perhaps it was grief.

A third figure appeared in the doorway, the owner of the baritone laugh: Gregory Ward. But the levity was fleeting, and his scar deepened with sympathy. "I happened to be at King's Cross when these two ruffians got off the train, so I thought I'd get them a taxi home before they caused any trouble."

Matthew rolled his eyes. "Trouble. Honestly."

Any sign of Lady Alice's apprehension on hearing Ward's laugh earlier was gone as she turned to him with a gracious smile. "Captain Ward, you really shouldn't have."

"Nonsense. It was my pleasure."

Eric glanced around at Lucy. He had an idea that it was she, not chance, who'd directed Ward to King's Cross at just the right time. She wasn't staring out the window anymore, and there was colour in her cheeks. She stood as Ward approached, greeting him with a shy smile, and Eric rose from the table to give the couple more privacy.

Lady Alice, meanwhile, was fully occupied with her sons.

"It's the perfect sort of day for a kite," Mark was telling her. "They're going up all over Regent's Park. Please, may we?"

"You've only just got home! Don't you want to rest?"

"I slept on the train."

"Besides," Matthew interjected, "you've got company."

Lady Alice sighed. "All right. But mind you're home in time for dinner!"

Mark cheered and ran back down the hallway and up the stairs to fetch his kite. Matthew, with a long-suffering sigh of resignation, followed at a more sombre pace.

Eric had half a mind to join them. "They're keeping their spirits up, at least."

"Hadrian," Lady Alice said, "believed in shutting children away with a nanny until they're old enough to discuss politics; he was at best a distant stranger to his grandsons. Meanwhile, Matthew once overheard him tell George that a son is a thing of his father's—meaning that George was an extension of Hadrian himself, but Matthew took it to mean that Hadrian saw his progeny as no better than nail trimmings. That killed any inclination on

Matthew's part to endear himself to his grandfather; and Mark, of course, takes direction from Matthew."

Duplessis, meanwhile, was struck by a sudden recognition: "Captain Gregory Ward! Yes, we met on the ferry from Calais, remember? I was very rude, I am afraid, and I must apologise. I hope all is forgiven."

"Nothing to forgive," Ward reassured him. "I wish I had a penny for every Tom, Dick, and Harry who remarked on the old war souvenir, but that's what you get when you stick your face into an exploding shell, eh?"

Lady Alice's brow darkened, and she pulled Eric aside. "Mr. Peterkin. You told me earlier that you and the Britannia would be entirely at the family's disposal in our time of grief. You meant it, I hope."

"Of course I did."

"On your word of honour?"

"Lady Alice, what is this about?"

"This is about Lucy. I don't know if you've noticed, Mr. Peterkin, but Lucy isn't like other women. More girl than woman, I should say. Since Patrick's death, she's lived with Hadrian as his daughter and he's taken care of her. Now that he's gone, and gone like this, we all agreed that we simply cannot have the poor dear living alone in that house. So she came to me, but I see that wasn't enough."

"Ward, you mean? I'm sure—"

"Lucy's father-in-law—who might as well have been her actual father these past seven years—is dead, and Captain Ward has the audacity to come in and flirt with her. That is so much the height of bad taste, it becomes a mark against his character. Simply put, he's taking advantage of an innocent young woman just when she's at her most vulnerable. Besides, look at him. Look at her. He's old enough to be her father."

"He's thirty-eight."

"Old enough he should be looking elsewhere!"

Meanwhile, Lucy seemed to blossom as she leaned her head towards Ward's. Duplessis finally took the hint and left the table, ostensibly to study the photographs on Lady Alice's wall.

"You know he's a suspect in Hadrian's murder," Lady Alice said.

Eric looked sharply back at her. He'd be lying if he said he wasn't aware of how it looked for Ward, but this was the first time he'd heard it stated so baldly.

"He was in the building when it happened," Lady Alice continued, "and the only one there who knew Hadrian well enough to have even the possibility of a motive. Of course, nobody's saying he absolutely must have done it, but until the matter is settled . . . at the very least, better safe than sorry, wouldn't you say?"

At the tea table, Lucy stifled a laugh, and Ward laid his hand over hers. As Lady Alice pointed out, Lucy was really more daughter than daughter-in-law to Colonel Russell. The baby of the family was always precious beyond its siblings, and that position had been young Patrick Russell's legacy to his widow. Was Colonel Russell really so sanguine about her moving on to another man?

And what would it do to Lucy Russell if the hand enfolding hers was red with her father-in-law's blood?

"It occurs to me," Eric said, "that my sister, Penny, has recently had her heart badly broken, and could use the company of another young woman her own age. She lives just outside Barchester—the old family home—and I wonder if Lucy would object to a little holiday in the West Country. She really would be doing us a great service."

# INQUEST

INSPECTOR CRANE FISHED something black and gelatinous out of his congee and popped it into his mouth with evident delight. "This inquest should be no more than a formality," he said. "We'll get a verdict of wilful murder, and then it'll be all hands on deck."

Crane had taken a flat in Limehouse, of all places, and this tea-shop was across the street from it. It was a dingy, unprepossessing place, even in the light of morning, and the air within was thick with oil and spices; but Crane evidently loved it. The proprietor, a retired Chinese seaman, had addressed him cheerfully by name and in Cantonese, and provided him with more fried dough for his congee than was standard.

"I'm sorry," Eric said, "about interrupting your breakfast—if only I'd gotten your message sooner. But I thought you had urgent questions for me about what happened?"

"If this were business, I'd have come to you at my convenience; and if I didn't want you calling at breakfast, I wouldn't have suggested it. No, this is purely social. They told me, you know, what happened the last time you had a murder at your club."

"It's not a regular occurrence, I assure you."

Crane responded by pushing the plate of fried dough across the scarred tabletop to Eric. This looked like a two-inch-wide baguette fried to a crisp, golden colour throughout and sliced into inch-thick croutons. Aware that the teashop proprietor was watching him, Eric skewered one with a fork and found it not bad at all. Then, at Crane's insistence, he reluctantly detailed the whole story of his involvement in the investigation of Benson's murder, from beginning to end.

Crane listened attentively as he ate his rice porridge, interjecting with a question or two. When Eric finished, he said, "Well, I can assure you we shan't be making the same mistakes again. There is a balance to these things, and you shouldn't have had to get as involved as you did. We all want the same thing, don't we? So there's no sense in working against each other."

"I have no intention of working on this at all, I assure you."

Chuckling, Crane finished his congee and poured out the last of the tea for the both of them: Chinese tea, a clear, dark amber in colour, in teacups without handles. He expertly snapped up a piece of fried dough with chopsticks and said, "If there's one thing I learned from my time in Hong Kong, it's that we must have the public on our side if we intend to actually get any police work done. Amateur sleuths may get in the way, but we still want eyes and ears in all the street corners; helpful citizens such as yourself, with insight we might lack; specialists in all sorts of relevant subjects, from physics to chemistry to psychology—"

"Psychology?"

"It pays to know how the criminal mind works, Peterkin. I owe half my past success to a doctor of psychology at the Hong Kong College of Medicine. If only he were here now! We'd have this murder solved in time for supper."

Eric sipped his tea thoughtfully. It wasn't bad, but he was far too used to milk and sugar. Meanwhile, Crane waved the proprietor over and began gabbling in Cantonese. Eric couldn't tell what was being said, except that it went from laughter on both sides to something more serious. Crane placed a reassuring hand on the proprietor's shoulder, and his tone turned earnest. A promise of help over some secret trouble? As a Scotland Yard detective, Crane's patronage alone was a deterrent to the criminal gangs known to prey on immigrant communities. Unsurprisingly, no bill came when they were done; but Eric noticed Crane slip his payment for the meal under his plate: no one could say that Detective Inspector Benedict Crane took unfair advantage of his position.

They emerged into the morning light and the bustle of a new day dawning on London's East End. Despite its reputation as a Chinese stronghold, Limehouse was home to seamen of many more nationalities, often with their English wives, due to its proximity to the docks. They were all around now, a tapestry of strange tongues woven through with one that Eric felt more guilt than he wanted to admit for not knowing. While Crane seemed entirely in his element, Eric felt entirely out of place.

Eric said, "Why did you come back, if you don't mind my asking?"

"Eh? That should be obvious. I'm an Englishman. England is my home."

"And why did you go?"

"Why does anyone go anywhere?" Crane shrugged and turned to look down the street. "It seemed like a decent way to make a name for myself, and see the world to boot."

Eric's late father had said much the same thing about his time in India, though Crane seemed a bit more reticent about the details. Retrieving Dr. Duplessis's calling card from his pocket, Eric held it out to the Inspector. "You mentioned psychology as a tool for police work. Well, if it's an alienist you want, here's someone who might be of interest. I just met him yesterday; he's a family friend of the Russells."

Crane grinned as he accepted the card and tucked it away. "Now, *this* is the sort of cooperation I like. Now, come along: we've got an inquest to get to."

Inquests across the British Isles were infrequent enough that they were usually held in informal spaces like assembly halls and alehouses. London could afford something a little more formal, however, and for all Eric knew, the chamber arranged for this morning might, in fact, have been built for that specific purpose. It was wood-panelled, with a tall window behind a raised desk for the coroner; after the dinginess of Crane's breakfast teashop, the air of judicial austerity felt especially rarefied.

Perhaps this bastion of civilisation, like so much else one took for granted, had its roots in Rome. Colonel Russell would know, even if Eric didn't. One thing Eric did know, however, was that Rome loved its circuses, and the reporters squashed together against the back wall, notebooks and pencils at the ready, looked far too eager to turn this tragedy into theatre—much to Eric's distaste.

Cully was already waiting in a separate seating area arranged for the witnesses. Spotting Eric, the old porter approached with an envelope in hand. "Sir! I know you're out of London right after this, and I was hoping to have a word. This came in for Colonel Russell, and I don't rightly know what to do with it. Should I send it back?"

The return address on the envelope identified the sender as a Jean-Andre Garnier of Boulogne-sur-Mer. Might it have anything to do with the murder? Crane, watching from over Eric's shoulder, said, "One way to find out."

"Of course."

Moving into a more discreet corner of the room, Eric tore the envelope open and peered inside. Old newspaper clippings, all of them in French. A covering letter, addressing Colonel Russell as a "dear cousin," said only that these clippings had been sent "as requested," with no indication as to why such a request had been made in the first place. Eric picked one out at random and endeavoured to translate:

## ENGLISH SOLDIER ASSASSINATED, ESPIONAGE SUSPECTED!

Police were summoned to the Hôtel Aubert near the Gare du Nord last night, following the report of gunshots. There, they found the body of an English officer, who was identified as Captain Andrew Russell—

"Andrew Russell!" Eric exclaimed. "That's Colonel Russell's second son—his widow is Madam Eliot, who's been helping us with the repairs in the club basement. I know this story. He was assassinated while chasing spies in Paris, close to the end of the War. The French police eventually caught up with the spies and arrested them all. I wonder why Colonel Russell wanted this."

"I should think it's obvious," Crane replied with a touch of disappointment. "It's proof of his valour. Colonel Russell likely wanted these for a scrapbook, or to frame up on his wall. What proud father wouldn't?"

"But why now, of all times?"

"Why *not* now? God forbid we embark on any personal projects when we're about to be unexpectedly murdered."

Crane turned away and went back to his seat. But . . . this was the last thing on Colonel Russell's mind before his death, was it not? Surely it had to be significant. Shuffling through the clippings again, Eric came upon another familiar name: a certain Captain Gregory Ward was cited as a witness, having accompanied Andrew Russell to the hotel where he was murdered. His testimony was key to tracking down the spies . . .

What if one or more of those spies had escaped?

But the arrival of the coroner—a sleek, weasel-like fellow who waited for nothing and no one—signalled the beginning of the inquest proceedings, and both Eric and Cully had to scramble back into their respective seats.

The medical examiner testified that the Colonel had been shot at close range before going through the window, which likely killed him before he hit the ground. Aside from the technical details, it was nothing the press wouldn't already know or guess.

Inspector Crane described the scene as he'd found it, including the gun clutched in the Colonel's death-grip: a Webley in poor condition, probably of better use as a cosh—but the coroner had no time for such digressions. Was this definitely the murder weapon? Inspector Crane responded with a single word: yes.

Lucy Russell, in one of Lady Alice's mourning dresses, looked more than ever like a wide-eyed little girl playing dress-up in her mother's clothes. Eric could hear the pencils scratching more furiously behind him as she came to give her evidence: there was nothing like a "helpless innocent" for public sympathy. She was asked to identify the deceased, which she did, and about his movements that Saturday before his death.

"Hadrian rose quite late, missing breakfast. I think he'd been drinking the night before. He left for the club at about ten o'clock. Captain Ward came by later to take me out for the afternoon, and when we got back after dinner, we found Hadrian home already. That would have been about eight o'clock, I think. Captain Ward went to talk to him in his study, and I don't know what was said, but it seemed to cheer Hadrian up considerably—I think he was pleased with how Captain Ward and I were getting on. Captain Ward left at half past eight, and Hadrian stayed in his study until just before eleven, when he told me that he had business at the club and wouldn't be back until very late. I made sure he had his keys, and then he left and I went to bed."

"Did he say what this club business was?"

"He did not."

Eric's hand went to the envelope in his pocket. Could this have had something to do with wartime espionage?

The coroner continued: "What can you say about his state of mind?"

"You mean, did it seem at all likely that he intended to kill himself? The idea is quite ridiculous. Besides, I told you: Hadrian was in a jolly mood that Saturday night. He practically skipped down the front steps on his way out."

It was a far cry from Eric's encounter with the Colonel twenty-four hours earlier. Perhaps all he'd wanted was a good night's sleep—or assurance that Captain Ward's intentions with regard to Lucy were honourable. Might Ward have been the one to have sparked Colonel

Russell's renewed interest in Andrew Russell's death? Or was Lucy merely exaggerating, to further repudiate any idea of suicide?

Cully repeated his tale of finding the body, and Harvey corroborated it. Neither man mentioned Harvey's indiscretion, or the woman he'd brought into the club.

The thought of suspicion falling on either man was, in Eric's opinion, nothing short of laughable; but the volume of pencil scratching behind him suggested that the press thought otherwise. Eric made a mental note to thank Cully for his foresight in making Harvey come in his livery: that alone should tell the world that all was right between the Britannia Club and young Thomas Harvey, and no guilt attached to him.

If the press ever realised that he was to be sacked before the day was out, they'd conclude that he had something to do with the murder, and it would be all over for the poor lad.

Then it was Ward's turn.

"I was awakened by the gunshots and the sound of breaking glass. It took me a moment to gather myself, and then I went downstairs to investigate. I found Mr. Cully and Mr. Harvey in the lounge by the broken window, and they pointed out the body of Colonel Russell on the pavement below. Mr. Cully went to alert the authorities, while I volunteered to stand guard over the body with Mr. Harvey."

"Colonel Russell was found clutching a gun, the murder weapon, to his chest. Did you recognise it, Captain Ward?"

Ward's gaze flickered in Eric's direction. "Yes. It was mine."

Whispers rippled through the audience, drowning out the excited scribbling of the press. Eric could almost see the adjective *dashing* being scratched out and replaced with *sinister* in the description of Ward's scar. The coroner said, "How can you be sure of this?"

"There is a mark I cut into the grip back during the War, to distinguish it from those of my fellow officers. After the War, I put it in the club vault and forgot about it until only recently. I wished to be rid of it—after all, it wasn't as if I was putting it to any use—and Colonel Russell offered to pass it on to someone he knew. I imagine he was in the club that night to meet with this mysterious buyer. He should have told me. After all, it's my gun, I was just upstairs, and had I been present at that meeting, he might still be alive today."

Across the room, Eric caught Lady Alice's eye. Her nose was wrinkled in disbelief at this explanation for how Ward's gun came to be on the scene, and she looked once again like the looming Nemesis he remembered from the casualty clearing station in the War. *You see, Mr. Peterkin, why it is imperative that we put some distance between Lucy and that man?*

Ward disappeared from the room as soon as he was dismissed, no doubt to avoid the inquisition of the press—Eric heard a camera flash go off as the door closed behind him. The coroner proceeded as if Ward hadn't just effectively pointed the finger of suspicion back at himself, and a verdict was swiftly returned, as Crane had predicted, of wilful murder.

# FAITH OF OUR FATHERS

WHEN COLONEL BERKELEY PETERKIN moved his family home to England from India, it was into a long, low-slung, half-timbered house on the outskirts of the cathedral town of Barchester. Its walls were covered with ivy and honeysuckle, and its roofline complicated by an excess of gables and dormers. Eric fondly remembered a childhood among its trees, playing at soldiers and practising every lesson he could glean from Baden-Powell's *Scouting for Boys*. It was his now, to do with as he pleased; but his life was in the lights and bustle of London, and it was his sister, Penny, who actually lived in this West Country Eden. Eric availed himself of his room here only as an occasional escape.

It was past nightfall when they arrived, but Lucy was nonetheless delighted by her first glimpse of the house. "Oh!" she cried. "It's like something out of a storybook!"

Penny had come to fetch them from the station in the family motorcar, a Vauxhall D-type originally intended as an Army staff car. Stopping on the gravel drive, she said, "I hope you like horses, because I'm busy most of the day helping a local breeder train them. If not, you'll have to work out your own entertainment."

Eric busied himself with the luggage while Penny showed Lucy into the house. Aside from a suitcase, Lucy had also brought a bicycle, and Eric was just carrying that in when Penny met him outside the door with folded arms and said, "Robbing the cradle, are we?"

"Nonsense. Lucy was married and widowed seven years ago, so she must be in her mid-twenties at least. And I'm afraid that in this case, I'm less the knight in shining armour and more the wicked uncle."

Penny raised a brow. She took after their father far more than Eric did, and might have passed for Anglo-Saxon given the right lighting; and while Eric might have inherited Berkeley Peterkin's heavy brows, Penny had his way of turning them into a full interrogation. Faced with this, Eric could only sigh and set the suitcase down. "What do you want to know, Penny?"

"Anything. Your telegram was remarkably uninformative. And while this is technically your house and you're free to host whom you like, *I'm* the one actually living here."

Eric peered into the house and, satisfied that Lucy was occupied with the contents of a bookcase, drew Penny aside to explain the shadow of suspicion hanging over Captain Ward, and Lady Alice's desire to keep her sister-in-law safe from his amorous attentions—at least until his name was absolutely cleared.

"Well," said Penny, "do you think he's guilty? And are we to hold her prisoner in the meantime?"

Eric hadn't spoken to his sister much since the breakdown of her last romance. Perhaps he should have: she was clearly still in a sour mood about it. "Lucy's our guest," he assured her. "She's free to leave whenever she wants. This is only until Colonel Russell's death is resolved."

"God knows how long that will take. I hope you're applying that brain of yours to solving this murder, Eric, or I'll see to it that we're playing host to this Captain Ward, too."

"No, you won't. We haven't got another guest room available."

"Then they'll simply have to share the bed."

"I know why I'm here, you know," said Lucy from the doorway behind them, watching with an expression of blithe innocence. She might as well have announced a fondness for chocolate. Neither Eric nor Penny had heard her approach.

Penny was incredulous. "You don't object?"

"What good would that do? Of course I understand that poor Gregory is a suspect. I don't believe it for an instant, but fighting you or Alice isn't going to help his case, is it? Besides, it would be simply horrid to spend even one night in Hadrian's house right now; and nobody said anything about writing letters."

"You are not to write letters," Eric declared.

Lucy's smile didn't falter. "If you insist," she said demurely, but Eric recognised false acquiescence when he saw it. There was nothing he could do, short of actual imprisonment, to stop her communicating with Ward, was there? If not letters, then telegrams; and if not telegrams, then telephone; and if not telephone, then . . . Eric glanced at Penny. He had a feeling his sister would happily ferry messages for Lucy by word of mouth if asked to.

"All right," he said, relenting. "You may write to him, and I'll deliver the letter myself. But you are not to tell him where you are."

"Hurrah! I knew you'd see sense." Beaming, Lucy held out an unsealed envelope. "You can read it, if you like. That won't be too different from censoring your men's letters home from the trenches, will it? But I promise you'll be bored out of your mind."

Eric tucked the envelope into his pocket without a word, beside Colonel Russell's newspaper clippings.

"There," said Lucy. "Now that everything is settled, I think I should like to freshen up." And with that, she disappeared back into the house.

"And *I* think," Penny murmured, "you may have underestimated our little ingénue."

Mrs. Berkeley Peterkin had been a convert, taking "Magdalen" as her Christian name shortly before her marriage. Who she was before then was a mystery: her gravestone in the grassy churchyard of St. Tobias's gave no indication of any other name, family, or identity. Only the phoenix carved into the stone suggested a heritage outside of the British Isles.

"I suppose it must have been difficult," Eric muttered, standing over his mother's grave in the golden light of dawn. "Considering how you valued loyalty, I don't believe you were the one to turn your back on your family. They must not have approved of Dad."

Funny to imagine anyone disapproving of the honourable and eminently respectable Colonel Berkeley Peterkin, but that was looking through the lens of conventional British society. Presumably, his now-mysterious Chinese in-laws saw him as "only some damned foreigner." Eric remembered asking more than once, only to be met with vague deflections and outright distractions. Neither were willing to talk, and the secret now lay between their graves, never to be unearthed.

Eric laid a hand on the gravestone. Colonel Russell's death had brought back to mind all he'd said at New Year's about heritage and legacy, and his words were only underscored by the discovery of the Roman mosaic under the club. Where had any of them come from, and what did that make them now? "And to top it all off, I've got this Scotland Yard detective looking at me like I'm some sort of Judas for knowing as little as I do."

Dim memories flitted by, of Mum hiring a tutor to iron out all traces of a Chinese accent from her speech; Mum at the shops, exchanging gossip so all of Barchester would know she sounded no different from them; Mum's singing voice, clear and modulated as a violin solo, as they went carolling at Christmas. Mum was stiff in her adherence to all things English, and she held her head high despite the venomous whispers behind her back: *Who does that Mrs. Peterkin think she is?* She knew the struggle of having to prove one was English enough.

Eric hadn't anticipated a need to also prove he was Chinese enough.

In the east, the rising sun glowed red through a bank of distant storm clouds, though the sky above was clear, and a brisk wind ruffled the ivy on the grey stone wall of the church. There was no winning, was there? The stained-glass window was only a tall, black lancet on this side, the shapes and figures more like cracks across its dull surface.

St. Tobias's church dated back to the 1300s and boasted a fine set of stained-glass windows depicting scenes from the Book of Tobit—windows so fine that the parish refused to forget the story despite it being relegated by the Reformation to the Biblical Apocrypha. This was the parish into whose life Magdalen Peterkin had thrown herself with the convert's alarming fervour. She was mildly scandalised to learn that the church had been dedicated not to some obscure saint of that name, but to the Biblical character—a man who could hardly be called a Christian saint, having lived and died well before the birth of Christ. Still, one must pay one's respects to those who have gone before. Eric remembered his mother lighting a candle for Tobias—*that* Tobias, son of Tobit—every year on the anniversary of their arrival in Barchester. She lit other candles, too, but Eric never found out for whom.

*What's the use of mourning?*

Better to do something about it, Eric supposed—and there flashed in his mind those newspaper reports of Andrew Russell's death, still in his pocket. Eric imagined a German spy, starved for vengeance, watching the club for an opportunity and seizing it when Harvey shoved his paramour out into the service court . . .

No. Inspector Crane was a perfectly competent detective, and there was no need this time to get involved. Feeling in his pocket for a matchbox, Eric turned to enter the church.

The church interior was dim after the brightness outside, and the windows were brilliant mosaics of colour against the shadows. Here was Tobias's father, Tobit, digging graves for the destitute dead; next was his distant cousin Sarah weeping for the seven men she'd married, one after the other, only to have them each murdered by the demon Asmodeus on their wedding night; then, Tobias setting out with the angel Raphael to ask for Sarah's hand in marriage—

A stifled sob caught Eric's attention. Lucy was standing before the bank of votive candles under Sarah's window. Last night's excitement had left her, and Eric saw once more the grief-stricken girl he remembered from the aftermath of Patrick Russell's death.

Beside her, Penny looked up at Eric's approach. "Lucy insisted I bring her here, before even thinking of breakfast."

"I'm sorry," said Lucy. "It all just came crashing down on me again when I woke up. I'm being stupid, I know."

"You're not being stupid," Penny assured her, and Eric concurred.

Lucy drew a deep breath to compose herself, approached the candles, and set about lighting one. "Yesterday was the Feast of Saint Patrick. I always visit a church on the Feast of Saint Patrick, for my own Patrick. I didn't yesterday—it was so busy—and I felt just awful when I realised. It was as though I were forgetting Patrick."

Had Colonel Russell felt the same way about her attachment to Ward? Eric pushed the thought away. He wanted to think of alternatives to Ward, not of his potential motives.

"We'd been married only half a year," Lucy continued. "I remember . . . It was as if the world was going on without me, and all I could do was stand and watch. It was months before I even realised what day it was, or that I was still living in Hadrian's house with Flora and Miranda looking after me."

Penny sat Lucy down in a pew and tried to comfort her. "It's never easy, losing someone you love. I understand, as would anyone with sense."

"I'd forgotten." Lucy dabbed at her eyes with a handkerchief. "I'd grown so used to the way things are now, and what's my one loss, really? Others have lost more."

In the window above, Sarah raised her hands to heaven in desperation and grief. Seven skulls for the seven husbands she'd lost were ranged at her feet.

*Colonel Russell gazed up at four brass plaques for four lost sons.*

"People put on a brave face," Eric said. "That doesn't actually change anything. Not for them and certainly not for you."

"That's true." Lucy sat in silence for another minute. "Patrick was the baby of the family. George was already in the Army when the War broke out, while Andrew and David volunteered immediately; but Patrick didn't enlist until 1916. That was when we met. There was a dance to send off all the newly trained and commissioned officers, and Grandfather—he was still alive then—encouraged me to go and have a bit of fun. I remember, Patrick looked so handsome in his uniform . . . he told me he actually felt terribly silly meeting people in it, and I think that was when I fell in love. I don't think he really thought of me in that way, though; not until he came home on leave some months later and we met again. He looked as though he'd aged five years in the meantime, but I remember how his eyes lit up when he saw me, like a starving man discovering a feast. We ran away to Gretna Green to be married, not because anyone actually objected, but because there wasn't time to call the banns or obtain a special licence before his leave would be over. That was a great adventure. He was like an eager young boy again, and honestly, sometimes I'd wonder which of us was the elder."

She looked up suddenly and said, "Eric, do you ever wish you were back in the nursery?"

Startled, Eric could only stammer, "What? No, of course not." It took him a moment to notice she'd used his Christian name despite their lack of familiarity, as though he were a child—in much the same way the world called her by *her* Christian name.

Lucy stood and put her handkerchief away. "Patrick told me, just before he left again for France, that if this was what it meant to be a man, he'd much rather just be a boy again. That was the last thing he ever said to me. Six months later, he was dead."

The sun had cleared the roofs of Barchester now, and the windows over the sanctuary flared with a startling brilliance. Lucy looked up at the stained-glass depiction of Sarah's grief, and the dead young men who might each have lived happily with her otherwise. "What a horrible thing to memorialise," she murmured. "The poor girl."

Then she walked away.

The church doors opened on a world fully ablaze with the sun of a new day. The light caught on Lucy's girlish form as she crossed the threshold, gleaming on the butterfly buckle in her hat and drawing a halo around her head. Stumbling forth from the darkness of the club vault, Gregory Ward's first glimpse of her must have been something like this: child and woman and angel all rolled into one, not so much *young* as *ageless*.

"Eric." Penny halted him with a fierce expression. "Eric, please tell me you were listening to that poor girl's story."

"Of course I was listening."

"So what are you going to do about it?"

"What on earth do you imagine I could do about any of that?"

"You could find out who killed Colonel Hadrian Russell."

Hadn't he just been wrestling with that very question? In the shadows of the church, darker now he'd been half-blinded by the light, Eric imagined Colonel Russell watching him expectantly. He sighed. "Penny, that's a job for the police. The last time was a unique situation that's never going to happen again, and I've got enough trouble now just trying to pick up where Bradshaw left off, never mind the repairs in the basement. Colonel Russell doesn't need me to give him justice: the man they've got in charge knows what he's doing. In fact, it looks like he's already done it."

The newspapers were out in the window of the post office across the street, and the blaring headline, ARRESTS MADE IN CLUBLAND MURDER, were just visible from the church steps. Drawing closer, however, Eric's elation deflated, leaving a cold disbelief.

*Club attendant Thomas Harvey and longtime club porter Ted Cully were arrested this morning—*

Eric reread it twice to make sure his eyes weren't playing tricks on him, then let out an oath that might have got him excommunicated had he still been within the confines of the church. Heads at Scotland Yard were going to roll.

# PART TWO

# DAMNED IF YOU DO

THE DISTANT STORM CLOUDS Eric had noted at dawn were over London, pelting the red-and-white-striped turrets of Scotland Yard with rain when he pulled up in the family Vauxhall. Eric didn't care. He'd made just one stop on his way here, at the Britannia to drop off Lucy's letter for Ward and question the attendants as to what the hell happened.

*"They said they'd arrested Harvey for the murder, sir, which made Mr. Cully an accessory—"*

Storming into Inspector Crane's office, Eric was surprised to find Dr. Duplessis sitting there with a cup of tea. Neither Harvey nor Cully were anywhere in sight.

"Arrested?" Inspector Crane chuckled. "The papers exaggerate. This was just a friendly invitation to come and answer a few more questions."

"Most friendly invitations," Eric spat, "don't come with a pair of burly constables ready to drag you in by force should you refuse. Where are they now?"

"I've left them alone to stew. So, no, you can't see them. Though you're welcome to sit down and have some tea, if you wish, and tell me why you think I'm making a mistake."

Inspector Crane, only lately returned from Hong Kong, had yet to fully move in, and this office was not much more than a dull grey box. On one wall hung a horizontal scroll crawling with calligraphy that Eric could not understand, and on the desk was an elaborately carved rosewood paperweight. Everything else was still in boxes. Outside, the downpour continued unabated. Curling his fingers into the back of one rickety chair, Eric said, "Cully vouches for Harvey. He's the most trustworthy man I know. On what grounds would you even doubt his word?"

"Trustworthy isn't the same as truthful, is it? If I were in a bind, I might trust my best friend to lie for me. It's a question of loyalty. And Mr. Cully is more loyal to the Britannia Club than to the intangible concepts of law and order."

"Then he'd be demanding justice for Colonel Russell."

"Colonel Russell is dead. Thomas Harvey is not."

"Thomas Harvey is an upstanding young man, and you've got nothing on him."

"Upstanding? Is that why you gave him the sack immediately after the inquest?"

"That was nothing to do with the murder."

"Oh, yes. A woman, wasn't it? I got that much out of them once they understood the trouble they were in. A woman whom no one has seen, and whom neither man can name. I'm inclined to think she's an invention of Mr. Cully's, to save one of his men from the noose while setting him up for the lesser punishment of a good, old-fashioned sacking. Did you also know that Mr. Harvey had a flaming row with Colonel Russell earlier in the day?"

"I never heard of any such thing—and as club secretary, I'm the one who does the hiring and firing." Then again, he'd spent that all-important Saturday away from the Britannia. "A flaming row, indeed! If every argument I ever had were a prelude to murder, I'd be Jack the Ripper or dead a thousand times over."

"Mr. Peterkin." Inspector Crane's eyes narrowed as he stood and leaned forwards, hands braced wide on his desk. "Let's not pretend that the respective positions of Colonel Russell and Thomas Harvey in that club of yours don't matter, shall we? Attendants do not intrude on members, and members do not notice attendants. If an attendant raises his voice with a member, even if that member were acting president and therefore had cause for more direct interaction, it must be significant. Or can you offer me something better?"

"The clippings Colonel Russell sent for, concerning the death of his son Andrew in Paris. I have them right here—"

"I did wire Paris for the official report, as it happens. The case was solved and resolved seven years ago, and anyone who could want vengeance has been executed. Try again."

Eric hesitated. There was Ward.

Ward, whistling happily to himself as he returned from an afternoon's outing with Lucy Russell. Ward, bitterly wondering when the world would move on from the tragedy of the War. Eric remembered the reassurance of Ward's arm around his shoulders as they waited in the darkness of the vault for Cully to find them. He also remembered the tension around the first meeting between Ward and the Colonel. Was Colonel Russell really as pleased with Ward's attachment to his dead son's widow as Lucy believed? Could Eric hand a fellow officer over to the police in exchange for Thomas Harvey?

Could he leave one of his men to hang?

Eric glanced at Duplessis, who'd remained silent throughout the interview, and said, "Perhaps it was some maniac who got in off the street."

The alienist stirred. "People are always suggesting the homicidal maniac. They think it is that easy. But even the most deeply alienated individual would not break into a random London club solely to push through the window a man that he could not expect to find there. It is too much effort for too uncertain a goal. If this were the work of such an individual, I think it more likely that his goal was entry to the club itself, not murder. Look instead for inexplicable break-ins at other nearby clubs, or watch for another break-in at your own."

"Dr. Duplessis," the Inspector told Eric, "has been very helpful in our consideration of the very possibility you suggested, and I must thank you for giving me his card. As to what he just said, I can tell you that there has not been a spate of break-ins around St. James, and we found both your front and back doors locked. So, we're looking for someone with the keys and the freedom to come and go as he pleases, and the only such person we know of . . . is you."

That wasn't true.

*Friday afternoon. Madam Eliot. "I'm returning your copy of the back door key. No, it's not that the workmen won't still be wanting free access at all hours—it's that Hadrian has given me his."*

Madam Eliot?

It was easy enough to imagine Madam Eliot picking up a gun and firing, whether by accident or design. It was harder to picture her, diminutive as she was, throwing the much larger Colonel Russell through a window. But . . . Eric imagined the Colonel charging at Madam Eliot after the first shot, and the gun going off again just as his hands closed over it, while Madam Eliot twisted away. His own momentum would then propel him through the window . . .

Outside, the rain had stopped. Clouds parted around patches of blue, and sunlight glowed through the droplets of rain speckling the Inspector's window to separate the uniform grey of the room into light and shadow. Someone rapped softly on the door, and a constable peeked in. "Sir," he said, "there's a lady to see you—"

Flora Grace's voice cut through the air like a winter draught. "I'll take it from here, thank you."

She flowed past the constable, finding her way unerringly to the patch of sunlight cast from the window onto the floor. The shoulders of her trench coat were damp, and she slid it off now to reveal a white silk shirt over wide-legged fawn trousers. "I understand you've got a friend of mine in custody," she said as she tossed the coat to the staring constable and pushed him out the door. "I must protest. Tom Harvey has nothing to do with this dreadful business—as Mr. Cully's evidence should have made abundantly clear."

Trying to regain his balance, the Inspector began, "Miss Grace—"

"You think he and Mr. Cully made up some woman just for the sake of complicating their alibi, don't you? It's in all the papers."

"Do you know something more about it, then?"

Miss Grace let out a derisive laugh, and her reply was clarity itself:

"Do I really have to spell it out? *I* was that woman."

Inspector Crane, unexpectedly, received Miss Grace's admission with something like smug satisfaction. This, Eric realised, must have been his objective all along. Flaming row or no flaming row, Harvey's alibi had now been neatly corroborated by all involved—and where did that leave them?

Miss Grace on the scene. Harvey was supposed to have let her out of the building before the murder, but Eric could easily imagine the flustered young man showing her to the door but neglecting in his haste to make sure she actually left. She could have done it, but with what motive? And there was Ward, without an alibi. Were there alternatives? Colonel Russell's newspaper clippings rustled in Eric's pocket . . .

Duplessis departed as soon as he and Eric were ushered out of the office—he did not seem happy to have been roped in by the police today. Eric would have dearly loved to hear what Miss Grace was telling the Inspector now, but he could hardly listen at the keyhole with all these policemen running around. Instead, he sat and waited for his men to be released.

Harvey emerged first, looking rumpled and red in the face. Eric wanted to ask about the row Harvey supposedly had with Colonel Russell—was it something to do with Miss Grace? Had the Colonel found out?—but Harvey cut him off. "I've returned my livery, I've got my references, and you're no longer my boss."

Turning his back, Harvey drew himself up into the proud, soldierly posture Cully had probably beaten into him long ago, and walked away.

Cully came marching out next, his head held high. "I'm not your god-damned grandfather," he snapped, slapping away the hand of an attentive policeman. The fire disappeared as soon as he saw Eric. "Sir! You shouldn't have inconvenienced yourself."

"Nonsense. They didn't treat you too badly, I hope?"

"They barely asked me anything, to be honest; and you did warn me. Shame about that bloke from the Golden Lion seeing Miss Grace come out of the service court. We really were hoping to keep her out of it entirely."

There was "being a gentleman" and there was "being an idiot," and Eric was about to chide Cully for the latter when something struck him. "What do you mean, *someone saw her*? I was told no one ever saw any woman there at all."

"Yes, that's what Inspector Crane told everyone when he came for me, but he made it clear once we were alone that it wasn't the truth. Perhaps he was lying to keep her out of it, too?" But Cully seemed doubtful, and rightly so: Why draw attention to something that need never be an issue?

"If Crane knew about Miss Grace, why didn't he just call her in?"

"I don't reckon he knew it was her. Seems the bloke from the Golden Lion didn't see her face, just a woman's shadow in the streetlight."

So, this second interview had, in fact, been framed as an "arrest" in hopes of encouraging the woman to come out and name herself, in case Cully and Harvey refused to give her up under questioning. Eric almost had to admire the Inspector's guile . . . But if Crane had settled on Harvey rather than Ward as the one entertaining a woman that night, it could only mean that he suspected Ward of the murder itself.

"Should we be heading back to the club, sir?" Cully asked.

"You go on ahead. Miss Grace will want someone to see her home—and I want a few words with her."

# THE BAREFOOT KNIGHT

THE CENOTAPH ROSE, stark and white, just around the corner from Scotland Yard: a tall stone block, subtly tiered and bereft of any statuary to distract from its dignity. They were in the aftermath of the storm now, with blue skies deepening towards evening and pavements glistening with mirror-like puddles. The dust of the city, tamped down by the rain, had yet to rise again, leaving the air as cool and fresh as it ever got in busy, bustling, traffic-choked London.

"'No mockeries now for them; no prayers nor bells,'" Miss Grace quoted. "Nothing seems sufficient, does it?"

She'd been amenable to Eric's company but declined a ride in the Vauxhall: solely, Eric guessed, so she could stop by the Cenotaph to pay her respects. The former Mrs. David Russell had had to leave her husband's body behind in Flanders, he recalled, when she returned from his deathbed. He was buried there, one of the thousands for whom this representation of an empty tomb had been built.

"I've heard," Eric replied, "someone express a similar sentiment. 'What's the use of mourning? One might as well protest the moon.'"

"That's not the same thing at all." But rather than elaborate, she gazed another minute up at the Cenotaph, then turned again to Eric. "You don't approve of me, do you, Mr. Peterkin?"

"I thought it was brave of you to come forward."

"Even if it took me the whole day to do so? While I don't mind people talking, I do mind what the police might do. Alice is the reverse. She encouraged me to speak up when I went to her with this dilemma; but she was also the one who first suggested I go back to my maiden name, to put some distance between the Russells and my oh-so-scandalous behaviour."

King Edward III, retrieving the fallen garter of the Countess of Salisbury, might have addressed onlookers with the same scorn: *Honi soit qui mal y pense*—shame on him who thinks this evil.

Eric said, "I thought that was your choice."

"It had to be, in the end. If I'd wanted to remain Mrs. David Russell, nothing Alice could do or say would make me choose otherwise. But it fit with David's dying wish that I move on."

Newly washed by the rain, the Cenotaph flared a blinding white in a sudden shaft of strong sunlight. The noise of pedestrians and motorcars seemed to fade into silence, so Eric only heard Miss Grace's words. The earlier touch of amusement was gone now, leaving something soft and bitter as early snow.

"David volunteered as soon as war was declared, as did Andrew. They were so excited to go . . . all those stories about courage and honour and battlefield glory. They even worried that the War would be over before their training was done. I was equally caught up in the excitement. What girl doesn't love a man in uniform? It tells the world that he is brave and dutiful and in robust health, and she's lucky to have him. I settled into Hadrian's house while David trained, and we were married by special licence before he left for France. None of us questioned it. We knew, intellectually, that people die in wars, but we also knew with absolute certainty that David was going to come home a hero. Death was a thing that happened to other people. Not us. Not the Russells. Not David."

She was still mourning him, Eric realised. Like Lady Alice in her perpetual black and Lucy with her Saint Patrick's Day rituals, the former Mrs. David Russell had never forgotten the man she married. All her alleged lovers, including Harvey—had she simply been desperately trying to fill the void left by her husband?

"My strong, handsome David. I was with him when he died. I was lucky that way: none of the others can say that. Lucky! Do you know what mustard gas does to a man?"

There were men at the Britannia who wore their collars unfashionably high to hide their scars; or who relied on prosthetic masks; or whose shallow, uneasy breaths betrayed lungs forever ruined by gas. "Yes," Eric said, swallowing. "I know."

"Miranda tried to visit Andrew in France near the end of the War. She'd gone once or twice before to meet with Uncle Joss's French suppliers, but this time, even with Hadrian's paperwork greasing the way, she was turned back at Le Havre. I almost wish the same had happened to me. Almost." Miss Grace stared up at the Cenotaph until the light faded around it. "Well, David didn't want me to be faithful to his memory. It was the last thing he said to me. The ward was in the chapel of a French convent, and I remember the nuns and nurses hurrying around us, amid the groans of the other patients. I remember kneeling beside David's bed, and I knew it hurt him to move, but he reached out to put his hand on mine. He said I wasn't to mourn any longer than I needed for myself. To hell with all these artificial conventions about full mourning and half-mourning and all the rest of it, he said. He made me promise to do only what felt right for me, and afterwards to live my life and be happy without him. Memorials, he said, should be made of stone, not of human lives."

Miss Grace turned away and set off up Whitehall at a clip Eric associated more with the briskly businesslike Madam Eliot. Catching up, he said, "Your husband had quite the unique perspective."

"David was never satisfied with mere tradition as a justification. He questioned the world and he made me think. That's what I loved about him."

"You must find the hoary, tradition-bound Britannia Club dreadfully boring."

"I'm always surprised that you lot aren't angrier at the world in general and the Empire in particular. You were marched off by the hundreds of thousands to die in the most awful conditions, and for what? What was the War meant to do for anybody?"

A few pedestrians glanced their way but did not stop. They were passing the War Office now, where the decisions to march anyone anywhere were ultimately made. Its ornate facade, all columns and pediments and domes, was a far cry from anything Eric ever encountered in the trenches. He lowered his voice in hopes that Miss Grace would lower hers as well. "Should we have looked the other way while Germany trampled over Belgium and France?"

But there was an echo of Colonel Russell's last words to Eric: *"Even victory and defeat are meaningless in the long run . . . Perhaps, without the ideals of King Arthur . . ."*

"We did our duty," Eric said at last. "You can't fault us for that. If it weren't for duty, nothing would ever get done."

"That doesn't make the loss any easier to bear. First David, then George, then Patrick . . . We thought Andrew, at least, would return to us alive. And then, practically on the eve of the Armistice, after Alice had come home for good and we were all just waiting for him to complete the family picture, as it were, he was killed, too." She shook her head. "Hadrian took it well, I thought. Philosophically. But it's always the old men who survive these things, isn't it?"

## SPY RING UNCOVERED, SUSPECTS APPREHENDED!

Police conducted a raid yesterday afternoon on a printer's shop in Montmartre, after evidence found in the investigation of the murder of an English soldier, Captain Andrew Russell, suggested that the address was a home to German spies. For the past week, the police have had the shop under surveillance, confirming that the large postal traffic consisted of military intelligence being drawn in from various sources and then ferried out again to Germany via Spain and Switzerland . . .

Lounging on the wide sill of a Chicago window overlooking Bloomsbury from four floors up, Miss Grace browsed with languid ease through Colonel Russell's newspaper clippings, which Eric had produced for her inspection. Her flat was as avant-garde as she was: bright and modern, its furniture fluidly curved in lacquered wood. The paintings on the wall were of nothing but colour, their purpose distilled down to its purest form. She'd requested that Eric remove his shoes on entering, and Eric felt oddly vulnerable with his stockinged feet digging into the luxuriously plush carpet.

Her perfume was a warmth coiling around his body like a cat weaving about his ankles.

"The Garniers are distant cousins," Miss Grace said, tapping ash from her cigarette into an ashtray of moulded amber glass. "Distant enough that we might be strangers, though we must have been close enough thirty or forty years ago that Monsieur Garnier got to be Andrew's godfather. That's probably why he collected all these clippings."

*We*. Miss Grace might have dispensed with the Russell name, but she was still one of them. Considering the clippings, Eric said, "Sentiment? Or a claim to notoriety? Either way, I assume he wouldn't have sent them all over unless the Colonel insisted."

"I don't pretend to know what went on in Hadrian's head. He could be remarkably opaque. That perpetual mask of hail-fellow-well-met. Lucy calls it Hadrian's wall. Have you shown her these clippings? She sees and hears far more than people give her credit for."

"I was going to, but this business with Harvey's arrest got in the way. And there's one thing more that puzzles me: Andrew Russell was never attached to military intelligence, was he? It was never his job to go hunting spies. So how did this come about?"

Miss Grace blew another smoke ring and watched it dissipate. Her cigarette was spent, and she took another moment to crush it out in the ashtray. "I think," she said, "that may have been my fault."

"Your fault?"

"You know how my eldest brother-in-law, George, was killed leading an assault on the German line? Andrew practically worshipped George, and was convinced that something so meticulously planned could only have gone so terribly wrong if the Germans somehow knew it was coming. Which meant we had a spy in our midst."

"And you were the one who pointed him at Paris."

"Yes. Let me show you something."

Miss Grace slid off the windowsill and disappeared into her bedroom.

Outside, the sunset flared into shades of rose and peach, a wash of colours to match the abstract paintings on the opposite wall. Four floors down, the streetlamps glimmered into brightness one by one as the lamplighters ambled by. To the east was the venerable dome of the British Museum; to the west, the electric glow of Soho's nightclubs, beginning now to unshutter just as the rest of London shuttered for the night. Was it only this morning that he'd watched the sun rise over his parents' graves in a country churchyard?

"No one would listen to Andrew," Miss Grace said, startling Eric from his reverie. "He was only sore about losing his beloved elder brother, they said, and what could he do about it? Not much, not until we realised the truth behind these."

She'd returned from her bedroom with a pair of old letters, and a third that was crumpled and incomplete as though it had been rescued from the bin. They were written in a loose scrawl with a curious backwards flick in the extended tails of the lowercase *F*, addressed to *Flora, ma chère cousine*, and signed *Monique*.

"Monique Garnier first wrote to me early in the War, supposedly because we were cousins in similar situations: newly married to men who'd gone off to fight. David didn't know her, but he knew about the Garnier relations. Hadrian encouraged me to write back, and so I did. We wrote continuously through the War, a letter every month or so. Then, Andrew ran into his godfather, Jean-Andre Garnier, while visiting injured comrades at a French hospital, and he mentioned Monique. Monsieur Garnier, greatly puzzled, replied that no such woman existed. So who was I really writing to? Who was writing back?"

"A spy."

"Andrew wrote at once to warn me. I was mortified. What had I done? Had I let anything slip that might have put our men in danger? Was I responsible for what happened to George? To Patrick? To—to David?" She stopped, and her usual languid sensuality gave way to a blank-faced grief. "I didn't go back to my maiden name because Alice asked me to, or because David encouraged me. I did it because—how could I call myself a Russell, knowing all that?"

Eric reached out to comfort her and found himself wrapping her into an embrace. "You can't blame yourself," he said. "This was their doing, not yours. And you can't have been alone. For this to work as a means of gathering intelligence, there must have been a host of other women being duped as well. It's too inefficient otherwise."

"That's what Andrew said. He knew I was innocent. All he wanted was the address in Paris to which I'd been sending my letters, and he would use his upcoming leave to investigate. And you know what happened then."

*Andrew Russell gunned down in a Parisian hotel, the last Russell man of his generation, mere weeks before Armistice.*

Eric continued to hold her as the sunset outside faded into shades of indigo, and the newly lit lamps cast a yellow glow up into the night. The silk of her shirt was as warm and soft as the skin beneath it, and her perfume, that heady mix of leather and vanilla and smoke, was a cosy cocoon around them both.

Finally stepping back, he said, "It wasn't in vain, was it? In the course of investigating his murder, the French police caught up with the spies and arrested them all."

"The guillotine was too good for them." Miss Grace's tone was venomous as her grief crystallised into rage. "If Hadrian wanted suddenly to dig this old story up again, I can only assume that it's somehow relevant to the present. And if Hadrian was killed right on top of that, it should be obvious cause and effect. I don't know what Inspector Crane must be thinking, dismissing this out of hand. Then again, I trust the police about as far as I can spit."

"You won't mind if I add these letters to the clippings, then?"

"Take them. Make your inquiries. And if it turns out that one of these spies actually escaped justice all those years ago, you had better hope you find him before I do, because I would really prefer not to hang for that bastard's murder."

Eric folded Monique Garnier's letters into his pocket and bent to gather up the newspaper clippings from the windowsill. So, Andrew Russell's hunt for spies had been based on more than a vague suspicion. It began with the Russells being preyed upon, and who was to say it hadn't ended that way as well, seven years later? It was just as well that Crane had dismissed this avenue of inquiry: Miss Grace had been implicated enough already without these letters.

When Eric straightened up again, he was surprised to find Miss Grace standing barely an inch away, with a wildness in her eyes that might have shocked a barbarian queen.

"Miss Grace—"

Her lips burned on his cheek, and continued to burn after she'd stepped back, still watching him with the same wild expression.

"Consider it a lady's favour to her knight errant," she said, and Eric wasn't sure if she meant the letters or the kiss. But her perfume, warm and smoky, threatened to overwhelm his senses, and her words seemed to register in his head without actually being heard: "And call me Flora."

# THOMAS HARVEY

ERIC SLID INTO Avery's booth at the Arabica, wondering if the world could smell Flora's perfume clinging to his person. These evenings at the Arabica had their own scent, of sandalwood and patchouli, perhaps powerful enough to overcome all others. He wasted no time in presenting his friend with both the newspaper clippings and Monique Garnier's letters.

Avery was impressed. "Espionage! And the police won't consider it? That settles it, then: you're playing detective."

"I'm taking a passing interest in the inquiry."

"If you say so."

Avery hid a grin behind a sip of coffee, and the clove-scented smoke of that cosy little back booth suddenly felt a trifle warm—like Flora's perfume. The Arabica favoured pretensions of Arabia and India, with faux oil lamps over each table and soft, intricately patterned fabrics. It was a far cry from the modern austerity of Flora's flat, yet the effect was not much different.

Perhaps it was more the proximity to Flora than anything to do with the flat itself.

"Monique Garnier." Avery squinted at one of the letters. "I feel like I ought to know something about this. Well, I'm sure it'll come to me in time. Now, if both the club attendant and the porter have been cleared . . . What about Captain Ward, who doesn't have an alibi?"

"Ward doesn't have a motive."

"You don't sound too sure."

"Don't I?" Eric gave it some thought. "Lucy gave the impression, at the inquest, that Colonel Russell was happy with Ward courting her. But I remember how the Colonel looked at Ward when they met, and I can't help but wonder."

"It's not his business to keep his daughters-in-law wrapped up in cellophane. I mean, the lovely Miss Flora Grace gets up to worse, and there's not a peep out of him."

"He blew up on Harvey, though—I assume because of their affair. But why pick on Harvey at all, unless . . . Might he be taking out on Harvey what he couldn't say to Ward? I mean, Ward is a respected officer, while Harvey's a lowly attendant who can't fight back. As for why he cares about Lucy when he's never said anything before about Flora, Lucy's practically his daughter, while Flora's distanced herself from the Russell name. It's different."

Avery set his coffee down, brows raised. "Oh, it's 'Flora' now, is it? What happened to 'Miss Grace'?"

Eric shot his friend the coldest look he could manage in this overheated establishment and changed the subject.

The only record the Britannia Club had of Thomas Harvey's address was the Working Lads Institute in Whitechapel, part of a Methodist mission for the betterment of boys of uncertain future. Harvey had come to his employment at the Britannia Club through the auspices of that mission, and had been lodged in the Institute's hostelry at the time of his hiring. Of course, he'd since moved on to decent lodgings of his own, giving up his bed to another of the many Whitechapel lads in desperate need of hope, and Eric had to hope himself that the Institute possessed some notion of where these new lodgings were.

Located right next to the Whitechapel Underground station and across from the London Hospital, the Working Lads Institute was a tall building of red brick, with three columns of bay windows to draw light into its depths. The two doors on the ground floor were headed "lecture hall" and "gymnasium" respectively, neither of which was what Eric wanted. The former seemed more likely to lead to an administrative office, but, as he paused on the pavement before it, a young West Indian man emerged and turned towards the Underground. Seizing his chance, Eric stopped him.

"I say, I wonder if you could help me. Do you know a Thomas Harvey?"

"Oh, Tommy? Yeah, I know Tommy." Dark eyes swept over Eric, taking in the affluence suggested by his cleanly tailored suit. "You an old boy, too?"

"No, I'm afraid not."

"Never does to forget where you came from, sir." The young man grinned and jerked his thumb at the door behind him. "Tommy's up in the old reading room, if that's what you're asking. Just follow the clickety-clack of that typewriter of his."

The young man disappeared into the Underground before Eric could inquire any further, and Eric had little choice but to head inside.

Eric knew two things about the Working Lads Institute: first, that the inquests for Mary Ann Nichols and Annie Chapman, two of Jack the Ripper's victims, had been held here; and second, that it had served as something of a sanctuary for West Indian soldiers during the War. The administrative office, he discovered, had since been transferred elsewhere, and the building itself now functioned more as a hostel for young men of all races and creeds as they sought to better themselves.

The Institute reading room spanned the front of the first floor, much like the lounge at the Britannia, but without the bar. A desk had been pushed up close to one bay window; on it were a type-writer and several folded newspapers. Harvey stood waiting beside it, having evidently seen Eric's approach through the window.

"You're persistent," Harvey remarked. "So now I wonder what you want from me. I'm sure my livery was all in order, and I've been paid what I'm owed. Though I wouldn't say no to an extra bob or two."

"I spoke to Miss Grace yesterday."

"Yeah?"

"Among other things, she claimed to have made the first move, and you weren't to be blamed for what happened. Then again, I doubt you were forced into it on pain of death."

The colour rose in Harvey's cheeks. "Did you come here just to preach at me?"

"Sit down, Harvey."

Harvey folded his arms but remained standing. So be it. Eric hitched himself up on the opposite edge of the desk and looked him straight in the eye. He had an inkling that Harvey would not be too keen on cooperation, and, until he was, any questions pertaining to the night of the murder would have to be approached indirectly.

"You've been with us for a year and a half," Eric began, "and we don't cut ties with our men lightly. Even without Miss Grace's endorsement, we take an interest in your future."

"And I thought Bradshaw was the busybody," Harvey muttered. To Eric, he said, "Sure, an interest in my future. You know why I'm *here*, yeah?"

"Is there a reason you shouldn't be?"

"This isn't a club, Mr. Peterkin. I'm supposed to have moved on, given up my bed to the next poor beggar. Fact is, my old landlady's gone and tossed me out. She runs a respectable establishment, she says, while I'm a notorious murder suspect, practically Jack the Ripper. Hah. Good on Miss Grace for speaking up, but it's done me no good whatsoever."

Eric hid his discomfiture. "Did Colonel Russell find out about you and Miss Grace?"

"He got me just as I was going to rest up for the night shift. One of the other Russell ladies must have let it slip. That damned hypocrite wouldn't have known me from Adam otherwise."

"That's what you fought about, earlier in the day."

Harvey nodded. "When Florrie showed up at the back door wanting one last . . . kiss, I reckon it was mostly out of spite that I said yes. What difference would it have made, now? That the Colonel was up in the lounge right then only made it that much better." Harvey finally unfolded his arms and dropped into his chair. "And now, here we are."

Outside the bay window, open blue skies soared over the grime of Whitechapel Road. A trio of Jewish scholars wandered by in long black coats and curled sideburns, arguing some theological nuance; they seemed oblivious to a pair of Arab sailors laughing at something in a shop window, while a lorry trundled past bearing beer into the City. Rather than the fabled degeneracy of the Ripper era, Eric saw an echo of Crane's Limehouse digs: colour overlaid on a humble, hardworking respectability.

This was the truth of the Empire, more so than the starched-and-polished affluence of St. James, and the streets of Rome might have been the same. You couldn't expand your borders to encompass the world, without eventually finding the world within your borders.

"If Colonel Russell was expecting someone," Eric mused, "do you suppose he let them in himself? As acting president, he had the keys."

"He could have waited in the ground-floor meeting room, if that's what he wanted."

"Perhaps he wanted to help himself to the bar."

"Not bloody likely. That sort of thing makes no difference to a man who doesn't think twice about having some poor blighter run up and down the stairs fetching his brandy." Harvey frowned, thinking. "Mind you, that should have told me something was amiss that night."

"What?"

"Look. It's half eleven, and Colonel Russell comes in the front door. All right, he's got the keys. He locks the door behind him and goes straight up to the lounge. We've had words, so I'm thinking it's my bad luck to be on duty tonight, but the Colonel doesn't even notice I'm the same chap he tore into earlier. He asks if there's schnapps in stock. Doesn't *tell* me to fetch the schnapps, mind: *asks*. Not like him at all. I tell him what we all know, that yes, we've got a full bottle of schnapps, but no one's touched it since the War and especially since the British Empire Union came around telling everyone to say no to all things German. Colonel gives a nasty sort of laugh and says to fetch the Tanqueray instead. Along with two tumblers and a bottle of tonic, of course. Then he told me to stay away until he rang for me."

This joke about the schnapps sounded like gloating to Eric, and why would the Colonel bring it up at all? Was he meeting with an old German adversary? At the very least, it seemed like a grasping connection to the espionage case that had gotten Andrew Russell killed. And while the downstairs meeting room might have the advantage of convenience, the lounge had a wider view of King Street—much like the view of Whitechapel Road from this reading room.

Eric slid off the desk and took a seat close to Harvey, leaning forward. The room was empty, dust motes floating in the sunlight past scuffed bookshelves, and they were co-conspirators now. Eric lowered his voice. "You've told all this to the police?"

"I answered their questions."

Meaning he'd yet to completely lose the distrust of the police that he'd learnt in the East End gutter, and saw no need to be any more forthcoming than he absolutely had to be. Having been bullied into a police interview room and made to sweat it out probably didn't help.

Eric said, "All right. Let's think about that night. Really think about it, I mean. You've got a good head on your shoulders, and you're probably the most likely to know something that will point us in the right direction."

Harvey raised a brow. "What about . . . ?"

"Captain Ward? Of course. But let's try to eliminate all other possibilities first, get a lay of the land. Miss Grace came calling after you left the Colonel in the lounge. How long after?"

"I'd say about five minutes. Maybe ten. I was in the staff room all that time. I didn't see anyone or anything."

"The back door? Any chance someone was waiting to slip in behind her?"

"Could be. But I know I locked the door once I'd let her in. We were kissing, and I had to reach around her to turn the key. I remember because it was . . . inconvenient."

Eric coughed. "I imagine you were rather distracted at the time."

"Not *that* distracted." Harvey's smile widened into a grin before he remembered the circumstances and straightened his expression. "Florrie—Miss Grace, I mean—and me, we wound up in the storage room next to the staff room. I reckon we weren't quite as quiet as we thought, because all of a sudden, there's Mr. Cully screaming in my ear. Florrie's frantically trying to get her trousers back on, and Mr. Cully, at least, has the decency to look away. 'Send her off,' he tells me, 'then see me in my office and don't keep me waiting.' Don't have to tell me twice! I point her at the back door and rabbit off to Mr. Cully's office where he proceeds to give me what for—"

"Wait. You just 'pointed' Miss Grace at the back door? You didn't actually make sure she left, or lock the door behind her?" The key would still be in the lock, of course—that was standard practice. Flora would have no trouble getting out on her own. Locking the door again once she was outside, however, was a more difficult business.

"I nipped around to turn the key after Mr. Cully left to get you. Didn't want anyone asking uncomfortable questions that might lead to me having to tell them about Florrie."

"But this means that anyone could have walked right in after she'd gone. How long were you in Cully's office getting your head bitten off?"

Harvey looked crestfallen. "No more than two minutes. That couldn't have been enough time, surely?"

To slip inside, find the Colonel, and shoot him? Perhaps, if the killer had been following a plan; but no plan could reasonably depend on chance to open the club's back door.

"All right," said Eric. "Let's move on. You heard the gunshots, and the crash of breaking glass. And both you and Cully went to investigate?"

"We got out into the lobby and saw the light still on in the lounge upstairs. I tell Cully that's the Colonel, and we go to check on him. But first thing I see when we get there is he's gone, and the window's broken. We go in for a closer look, and there's Colonel Russell in a heap down on the pavement. There's people coming out of the Golden Lion, too, and they're shouting something, I don't remember what. Mr. Cully shouts back that he's calling the police. Then he turns to me, and he's all business, which is never a good sign. He says, here's what we have to say if we're to keep Florrie out of this mess. I'm more than happy to go along. That's when Captain Ward comes running in."

"How'd he look?"

"Like he's just fallen out of bed. He's got a dressing gown on, but I can see he's missed a button on his pyjama shirt. The scar on his face makes him look fierce, like he wants to eat us all alive, but he's properly horrified when he sees what's happened. Someone's got to mind the scene, he says. Make sure no one interferes with it. Mr. Cully tells me to go, and Captain Ward says he'll go with me. I don't mind saying I was glad of the company. I mean . . . well."

He shrugged, but Eric understood. Poor Harvey was too young to have seen the War, and this was his first encounter with violent death. It must have left quite an impression, standing there in the midnight chill with the fog slipping damp fingers down his collar and the Colonel's corpse bleeding all over the pavement not two feet away. Eric wondered how he himself had managed to stomach death in the trenches. Perhaps he'd grown used to it then, and was now, finally, beginning to forget.

Eric asked, "Was there anything else you remember about waiting there? Did Ward say anything to you, or did you happen to overhear anything from the people at the Golden Lion?"

"Captain Ward was muttering to himself; I couldn't quite make out what. He seemed quite upset and trying to hide it. Didn't help he was out there in his pyjamas and dressing gown—he was shivering himself to pieces. I didn't hear what the folks at the Golden Lion were saying. If I'd known one of them had seen Florrie leaving, I mightn't have lied about her not being there at all."

So what had they learnt from all this? That the back door was unlocked when Flora left the club building shortly before the murder, and it remained so until after Cully left to get Eric. Harvey would have no way of knowing if the door had been left unlocked by an escaping assassin or by his escaping paramour.

But the easiest escape would be up the stairs to a guest room, then back down again pretending to have only just heard the commotion. Ward had taken a bit longer to get to the scene, too—long enough for Cully to plan a case of petty perjury. Why was that?

As Eric pondered the question, Harvey sat back and fixed him with a knowing look and a smile. "You're not so bad after all, are you?"

"Eh? What do you mean?"

"I'll admit I missed Bradshaw. We all did. That man was an institution all on his own. But I don't see him ever sitting here without knowing he was doing me a favour and that I bloody well owed him. I reckon it's because he was so much older. He lived in a different world. But you and me, we know *this* world, don't we?"

The newspapers on the desk were each folded around the Help Wanted section of the classifieds. Harvey had been prominently named as a suspect in Colonel Russell's murder, and, if his landlady's reaction was any indication, his search for employment must be running into similar difficulties. Meanwhile, blue skies soared over the respectable walls of the London Hospital. Eric thought of Ward stumbling out from the darkened vault to find Lucy waiting in the sunlit lobby, and of light piercing the darkness of a collapsed dugout as soldiers worked to rescue those trapped within.

This was what the Working Lads Institute really offered, Eric realised: legitimacy, always preferable because it was easier than the uncertainty of chaos. A single public library probably did more good than a dozen policemen—and thanks to Crane's tactics, Harvey was back in the gutter where he'd started.

"You know," Eric said, "none of the other lads back at the club seem too keen on the night shift. It's been difficult."

"Rubbish. O'Mara's more awake at midnight than at midday, and—"

Eric held up a hand. "I'm saying, Harvey, that there's few people around at night to notice that the night attendant should have been sacked ages ago. We really could use the extra pair of hands, and you already know what needs doing."

Pride, of course, demanded a token show of resistance. "You don't owe me anything. You know that, right?"

"It's just the night shift for now, and the old staff quarters—" Eric stopped. No one had been up to those attic rooms in years, and they might not be habitable. "We can set aside one of the guest rooms, temporarily. All I ask is that you don't make the same mistake again."

"Never fear: Florrie and me are done, and she's probably all over some new bloke by now. All right, then. I'm not so proud I can't accept a hand up when I'm down." They shook hands, and Harvey, taking a step back, said, "I know what you're doing, by the way. Everyone knows it was you who sorted out Mr. Benson's murder, not the police, and you're doing the same again. And I wish you the best of luck. Anything to put one over Inspector Bloody Crane, right? That man's a bad egg if I ever saw one."

Eric wanted to protest, but Harvey was right. Just yesterday, he'd told Penny that he'd play detective when pigs took wing over a snow-covered hell; and now, here he was, doing exactly what he said he wouldn't do, all because one of his men had been pulled in by the police. Feigning disinterest, he said, "I reckon it's no more than what Bradshaw would do."

"Bother Bradshaw. I told you, didn't I? He's one of the old men. He wasn't one of us."

# THE RAZOR'S EDGE

IT WAS LUNCHTIME when Eric got back to the Britannia Club from Whitechapel, though a quick glance into the dining room showed it to be practically empty, its usual patrons having yet to forget that there'd been another murder on the premises. The same was likely true of the lounge upstairs. Cully, at least, was still behind the front desk. Eric approached him and said, "I've some news about Harvey, but first: Is Captain Ward anywhere about?"

"I believe he's lunching elsewhere—the traitor. He's taken it into his head to explore London through its eateries, a different place every meal. Shall I tell him, when he comes in, that you want him?"

Eric shook his head. "I was just curious. You knew him when he first joined, didn't you? Before he left for Switzerland."

"Well, enough to say hello, sir; not much more. I remember him mostly because he was friends with Andrew Russell, and they joined together in . . . 1917, I believe. Only time we really spoke was after the War, when he was demobbed. He asked after Mrs. Andrew—Madam Eliot as she calls herself now, being an important businesswoman—and I suggested he call on her himself. He replied that he didn't actually know the family outside of the Army, and he didn't intend to change that. He blamed himself for what happened to Andrew Russell, you see. I tried to tell him otherwise, but . . ." Cully shrugged. "He took a room and was gone the next morning."

"And then he came down with consumption, or so the story goes."

"That sanatorium made a new man of him, I think. All that fresh air and exercise! Mind you, he's lost weight, and the whole thing's gone and aged him something awful."

"The white at the temples is new, I take it."

"And the scar."

"The scar? Didn't he get that in the War? I heard him say it was from a shell."

Cully frowned, considering, and finally shook his head. "No, I'm quite sure he never had that scar before. I'd remember him better if he did."

"I see . . ."

Could Cully be mistaken? It was not that Eric wanted to point the finger at Ward. Far from it. But these tiny little questions kept cropping up wherever he looked, and, like it or not, turning a blind eye to the admittedly real possibility of Ward's guilt would be at least as negligent as dismissing Colonel Russell's newspaper clippings out of hand. Something had to be done, if only so Eric could tell himself that belief in Ward's innocence was more than mere wishful thinking.

"Cully, do keep an eye out for Captain Ward, will you? I'm about to indulge in some ungentlemanly behaviour, and I would much rather he didn't know about it."

Ward, as it turned out, had given up his vault box as soon as the police were done poking around the club, and its contents were long gone. The Webley was in police custody, of course, though the fat envelope from the sanatorium remained a mystery.

This was one fewer thing to worry about, at any rate.

Eric headed next for the second floor, where Ward had taken one of the larger rooms overlooking King Street. In addition to the usual spartan accommodations—a bed, an armchair, and a chest of drawers with a mirror on the wall above—this room came with a gas ring and a small teakettle, in case a gentleman didn't want to summon an attendant just for a cup of tea. Ward's occupation was evidenced by a dressing gown slung over the armchair and, among the toiletries laid out with military precision atop the chest of drawers, a razor case with an embossed eagle and insignia on its lid.

This was one of the Gillette safety razors, with disposable blades, that had been standard issue to the American troops. Eric knew one or two men who'd used safety razors before the War, but since then . . . Well, the societal effects of the War weren't always obvious or political. Before then, for instance, the watch on his own wrist would have been seen as either an affectation of the Boer War or jewellery better suited to a lady. And now, half the men of his acquaintance had either wristwatches or safety razors or both—petty fruits of a grim harvest.

Eric checked inside the razor case but found nothing unusual. He took care to replace it exactly where it was. He had no intention of rousing Ward's suspicions by leaving anything noticeably out of place.

The drawers of the chest were similarly tidy. There were three new shirts, blinding white and crisp, which Ward must have purchased only recently. The other clothing looked old and shabby. Presumably, Ward had little recourse to a tailor in the five years he'd spent at his sanatorium, and these older clothes were relics from before his stay there.

Guilt prickled on Eric's consciousness: Was it really his place to invade this man's privacy, considering what he'd lost? Four years to the War, and another five to the sanatorium. What must it be like to come back into the world after that? Everyone else would have moved on without you.

Carefully poking through the folded socks, Eric encountered cardboard . . . a small carton, labelled in German. It rattled as Eric picked it up, and he understood the label enough to know the contents before he looked. Bullets. Not the 11.6 mm cartridges that would have gone into a Webley revolver, but tiny 6.35 mm pellets more likely to get lost in a Webley's chambers than strike a target.

So, Ward was carrying another gun, probably a pocket pistol of some sort. His sanatorium had been in the German-speaking region of Switzerland, and presumably he'd purchased his ammunition there before beginning his journey home.

Eric replaced the carton between the socks, and his eye fell next on the battered suitcase tucked halfway behind the armchair. He hesitated. Surely he'd done enough?

But what was that on the suitcase's scuffed canvas side? A spot of ink? More dot than spot, really, and here was another one just an inch away, and another, and another . . . a whole pinprick constellation of ink, still sharp and clear, though the travel labels had long faded to illegibility. Spray from some accident with a bottle of ink? A star map? No, just stains from being used as a makeshift writing desk, and recently.

Well. If there was a line to be crossed, he'd done it already. Sitting down in the armchair, Eric laid the suitcase across his lap and opened it.

Notepaper, blotting paper, a bottle of ink, a tin stationery case containing two pencils and a fountain pen . . . but most interesting of all, an old journal, with Lucy's letter slipped inside its front cover. Eric set the letter aside and opened the journal.

*The alps are lovely, to be sure; but their beauty wears thin once one realises that there is very little here for an invalid to do. The doctors, of course, insist you do even less . . .*

Eric flipped to the final entry.

*Werner came by again this afternoon with the newspaper, and we played chess. We talk less and less of late, yet I would say we are closer than ever. In the long silences between us, I find it is enough that we understand. Nobody else in this peaceful slice of Eden does—they think the War was a thing that happened in the news—or else they speak no English.*

*I am reminded that I have yet to write a will. One would think, given my circumstances . . . but then, I have had no one since Mother's passing last year. Or so I thought. It occurs to me now that Werner has become like a brother to me . . . and if that is not proof that God loves irony, I do not know what is. I shall have to engage a solicitor and make my intentions known.*

*Though I would, of course, keep this a secret from Werner. Let us not forget that he tried to kill me when we first met!*

What?

Eric flipped back to the beginning of the journal, skimming through the entries for mention of this Werner.

*The caretaker who cleans my room is a cheery fellow by the name of Karl Werner. I am being sarcastic: he is as gloomy as rain on the moors . . .*

Further on, perhaps?

*Werner brought me the newspaper and read me the headlines, translating as he went. My German improves, but not enough, not yet. We read of the ceasefire in Ireland with some relief, but agreed: you'd think that the War to End All Wars would actually end a few wars . . .*

Had Eric missed the entry detailing this supposed attempt on Ward's life? He went back again, more carefully.

*The locals speak a dialect called Romansh, but Werner is more comfortable in German. I think he intimidates the doctors, being better educated than his position would suggest. Certainly he intimidates his supposed peers. I shall have to keep him close, if only because he can get me an extra helping of pudding at dinner . . .*

Was that a creak on the stairs? Eric snapped the suitcase shut over the journal and pushed it back into place. He peeked out the door. No, it wasn't Ward. It was another member, unsteady from a glass too many, stumbling into another room.

He'd been too lax, Eric decided. Complacent. Settling down into an armchair was assuredly not the right thing to do if one were concerned about getting caught. Nor could he afford to get distracted. Opening the suitcase a crack, he got out the blotting paper.

This was a common trick in the manuscripts Eric had read. Writing with pen and ink meant, of course, pressing a sheet of blotting paper over the document afterwards to soak up the excess ink, effectively printing fragments of the document onto the blotting paper. Turning to the chest of drawers, Eric held the blotting paper up to the mirror and tried to make sense of what he saw.

*Dear Lucy . . . course I didn . . . hat I tol . . . tween us. H . . . I loo . . . n Peterkin's membership fi . . . ddress in . . . if you think I shou . . . o, but . . .*

Eric nearly dropped the blotting paper. Ward had been investigating *him* just as he was now investigating Ward! And what did his membership file have to do with any of this? It contained a brief summary of his war record and his original application—

Oh.

At the time of his application, his address was the house in Barchester. Ward must have guessed that if Eric was playing courier for Lucy, then Eric might also be playing host. Not at his own London flat, of course, not without causing a scandal; but a house in the country with a sister to play chaperone? That was different.

The thought of membership files stirred something else in Eric's memory. He'd taken note of Ward's regiment while processing his reinstatement, of course; and now he thought about it, they'd never been posted anywhere near Brussels, had they? Yet Ward had spoken of Edith Cavell's execution as though he'd personally witnessed it.

Replacing the blotting paper, Eric checked the corridor again. All clear. He had to dig deeper. The two pencils in Ward's stationery case appeared to be well-used, but for what? Eric saw no pencilled notes among the notepaper . . .

And here was another trick he'd read about more than once. A pencil bore down on paper with significantly more force than a fountain pen, leaving an imprint on the next sheet. Taking one of the pencils, Eric began to gently shade the top sheet of notepaper; and in the manner of a stone rubbing, the words imprinted from the sheet before began to form, white and ghostly, like magic:

*Werner came by again this afternoon with the newspaper, and we played chess. We talk less and less of late, yet I would say we are closer than ever. In the long silences between us, I find it is enough that we understand. Nobody else in this peaceful slice of Eden does—they think the War was a thing that happened in the news—or else they speak no English.*

Eric stopped. This was a passage from Ward's journal.

Why was Ward copying passages from his own journal?

Could this be how Ward coped with the lingering effects of shell shock? He'd said once that the War had done something to his memory. Then again, there were the other little inconsistencies: whether or not he got his scar from the War, for instance, and whether he'd actually been in Brussels for Edith Cavell's execution. What about his connection to Andrew Russell's murder, seven years ago?

Eric pocketed the shaded notepaper and replaced everything else in the suitcase just as the stairs creaked again, louder than before. Scrambling for a plausible excuse in case it was Ward and he was caught, Eric darted to the door and peeked out.

It was Cully.

"Sir? Captain Ward is back. I told him you wanted to speak to him, and that he was to wait in your office while I came to get you."

Eric sighed in relief. "Good man, Cully. I don't know what I'd do without you."

"I'm afraid Cully misunderstood," Eric told Ward breezily as he settled down behind his desk. "It was someone else I wanted—one of the builders working on the pipe room downstairs. Colonel Russell's funeral is tomorrow, isn't it? I'll speak to Madam Eliot then. I do apologise for the inconvenience, but since you're here, won't you stop for a while? I'll have someone bring us a pot of tea, unless you'd prefer something stronger."

Ward looked cold and sullen. Ignoring the offer of tea, he drew a sealed envelope from his pocket and held it out. "I wanted to see you anyway. Would you be so good as to pass this on to Lucy Russell?"

This must contain the full letter, phrases from which Eric had only just read off Ward's blotting paper. Eric took the envelope, put it in his own pocket, and told himself that he was absolutely not going to steam it open later. He endeavoured to maintain a friendly tone, saying, "Of course. Though you could always give it to her in person. At the funeral, I mean."

"That would defeat the purpose of writing at all. I shan't be attending the funeral. I get the distinct impression that I shan't be welcome."

"That's a shame."

"Do you really think so little of me?"

It took a moment to realise that Ward meant Eric's part in separating him from Lucy, not Eric's search of his room. "I'm sorry. I promised Lady Alice to help the family in any way I could, and this was the 'help' she demanded."

"The hell you say. I ought to punch your bloody lights out. I've never been so insulted or humiliated in all my life."

"I'm sorry."

"I didn't kill Colonel Russell, Peterkin. I swear it on my honour." Ward dropped into a chair and rubbed both hands over his face, the initial anger and resentment fading into a tiredness that left him looking even older than his first impression. "Lucy and I have been seeing each other for only a week. Of course I can't expect her to rally to my side on the strength of *that*. Of course she'd want some distance between us. I know how it looks, and even if it didn't, she might want time alone to grieve. All the same . . . a week is nothing in the balance. She'll have forgotten all about me long before this has all blown over."

Poor Ward. His distress seemed genuine. And yet, there were the inconsistencies. Was that business with his rewritten journal entries a cause for pity or for suspicion? Eric said, "Isn't there anything you can do or say to clear your name?"

Ward shook his head.

"You must have seen something on your way down to the lounge that night? I mean, it sounds as though you took a while to get there."

Again, he shook his head. "I was having a bad dream. I didn't realise right away that the noise was real."

Eric tried a different tack: "Colonel Russell seemed to be looking into the circumstances surrounding his son Andrew's death, before he died himself. Do you know anything about that?"

"What?" Ward's brows shot up in surprise, then crashed together in consternation. "No. Yes. Let me think. We did talk quite a bit about that, but I thought it was simply because Andrew was someone Colonel Russell and I had in common. It's possible that meeting me was what got Colonel Russell thinking about Andrew's death, since I was there as a witness, but that's as much as I know about it."

"Do you think wartime espionage could be at the bottom of the Colonel's murder?"

A moment of silence, then Ward let out a single bark of laughter. "Impossible. The French police caught everyone involved in that spy ring. Trust me: I was there."

"Tell me what happened."

Ward sat back to think, evidently reassured by this line of questioning that Eric was not, in fact, endeavouring to see him hanged. "Andrew and I were on leave. We went to Paris because Andrew had got it into his head—rightly, it turned out—that someone there was probing his family for information. We checked into a hotel barely a minute from the Gare du Nord, and I left him to his own devices: we were in Paris, after all, and I had no intention of wasting a minute of it. I got back to the hotel just after dinner, and was talking to the concierge when we heard the gunshot. The concierge and I went up to investigate and found Andrew dead. We called the police, and

I told them what Andrew was up to. They followed up on the clues he'd already gathered, broke up the spy ring, and that was the end of it. I watched them conduct the raid on the spies' base of operations with my own eyes."

It was much as Eric had gathered from the newspaper clippings. "They never actually charged anyone with the murder, did they?"

"These men were already facing a firing squad for treason. There was no need to guillotine them as well."

"'Let there be no hatred or bitterness,'" Eric observed. "As Edith Cavell said."

"She was a great woman."

A great woman executed by the Germans for espionage . . . and a thought occurred to Eric. "Ward, you mentioned that you were there when she was killed, didn't you? In Brussels."

"That's right."

"But see here. I looked up your regiment—part of the paperwork—and it was never posted anywhere near Brussels."

Ward's scar flexed with sudden tension, then relaxed. "Oh! I meant I was in Brussels *where* she was killed. That was after the War, on my way to Switzerland—something of a pilgrimage. A final goodbye, if you will. There is a sort of coming-to-terms that only happens in the aftermath, after enough water has passed under the figurative bridge. If there's one thing you realise when you're told you have a life-threatening illness, it's that life is short. I was not about to spend what might be my last months on earth still weighed down by the War."

So, either Ward had misspoken, or Eric had misheard. That was all. As for the rest, they understood each other on the persistence of memory. There was a grim wisdom in what Ward had done. *I should go back to Flanders, too,* Eric thought, though his stomach lurched at the notion. *Say a final goodbye to that dreadful place, then watch some farmer run it over with a plough. Would it really be that simple?*

Ward, at least, seemed to have set aside his earlier unhappiness at being separated from Lucy. He smiled reassuringly as he rose to leave; and Eric, distracted, almost let him go.

"Wait. One more thing. A small thing. I'm sure you must get tired of people asking, but I was curious about your scar. You told Dr. Duplessis it was from an exploding shell?"

"That's right."

"Cully says he doesn't remember you having one after you were demobbed."

Ward froze. For a moment, his face took on a ghastly hue . . . and then he began to laugh.

"Oh dear. I'm afraid I've been found out. I began telling people this was from shrapnel, as a joke. One rarely encounters shelling at a Swiss sanatorium, after all! And then the joke took on a life of its own."

"You didn't get it shaving, though, did you?"

"Oh, didn't I?" Almost absently, Ward slid one long barrel cuff down and began to fiddle with the cuff holder attaching it to his sleeve. "I can tell you that I got it from a razor blade. I get all my scars from razor blades."

The holder came open, along with the stud, and the barrel cuff sprang free. Ward held his hand up in a fist, curled back to better expose the deep scar across his wrist.

Eric could only gape. It was half a year ago, and he was standing where Ward was now, learning from Bradshaw about the uncomfortable prevalence of suicide among the seemingly happy and well-adjusted soldiers home from the Great War—about the faltering of stiff upper lips, the lies told to preserve honour—

"I put up a bit of a fight when they wrestled the razor away from me," Ward said, though Eric had to strain to hear. "The doctors insisted I use a safety razor instead, after that—not that I intended to try again. When you've reached such depths of despair, and someone cares enough to save your life . . ."

Ward's voice broke.

"I'm sorry," Eric managed to choke out. "And I do understand."

"No. You think you understand. You don't. I cannot put into words what it is to wake up the morning after you've decided to never wake up again, and realise the mistake you almost made.

Second chances are beyond all riches, Peterkin." Ward paused to gather up his cuff, holder, and stud, then turned back to the door. "I was twenty-six when the War started. I hadn't married because I thought I had all the time in the world. Now, I'm nearly forty, with nothing and no one to show for the years since then except this: a second chance. And then, on top of Inspector Crane's inquisition, I have you. Don't think I don't know what you're up to. The whole club knows what happened the last time."

"Ward—"

Ward sighed and bowed his head. His tone melted into a sadness that cut deeper than any attack. "I want to live, Peterkin. *Lucy* wants to live—youth is too precious to waste on an old fool who doesn't appreciate her, and God knows if she'll get the same second chance when she's my age. Don't we both deserve that much?"

After everything he'd endured, of course he deserved some measure of peace. But he slipped out of the office before Eric could form the words, and the door closed behind him with a firm click of finality.

# OUR GLORIOUS DEAD

COLONEL HADRIAN JOHN RUSSELL was afforded a funeral with all the grand solemnity befitting the sacrifices made both by his sons and by the man himself, and he was interred amid the verdant foliage of Highgate Cemetery on the morning of Friday, the twentieth of March, 1925.

It had rained sometime in the wee hours, and the ground was muddy still. The smell of wet dirt and wood was in everyone's nostrils, a cold earthiness redolent of abundant new life creeping forth on hair-thin legs and glistening bellies. Perhaps it was only the novelty of fecund spring following barren winter, but the fronds now unfurling over the dead stone monuments seemed especially green, and the light filtering through them was a mottled green-gold, like verdigris on brass.

"'Look up, and swear by the green of the spring that you'll never forget,'" Flora quoted as she perched on one sturdy, stolid monument and drew on a cigarette through a cigarette holder. She was no less striking for having foregone her usual avant-garde trousers in favour of a sober black dress for the occasion, and might have been a bird of paradise intruding on the tame English landscape.

"You should get down and join the others," Eric told her. "Or they'll think you've abandoned them."

"In a moment."

The other widows were farther up the path, saying their long goodbyes to the crowd of mourners; Penny was with them, keeping close to Lucy. Such a turnout meant a multitude of reconnections among old chums, greatly slowing the exodus. Even Avery had made an appearance: he had barely known the Colonel, but he was friendly with Lady Alice through their shared spiritualist interests, and perhaps that was enough.

Matthew and Mark Russell, meanwhile, had wandered off to explore the interesting nooks and crannies of the cemetery. "I imagine they're re-creating the chariot race from *Ben-Hur* around the Circle of Lebanon," Flora said, gesturing towards the cedar crowning that ring of vaults. "That's what I used to do when I was a girl. That, or pretend I was Boadicea, warrior queen of the Britons, and each mausoleum another Roman villa to be sacked. My father, before he got his position at Oxford, brought me here at least once a week, and he let me play all over the place. To this day, I can't walk past a gravestone without wanting to climb it."

"What did your mother say to that?"

"Nothing. She was dead, only I didn't know it at the time. My father had some misguided notion of sparing me the grief, so all he said was that she was 'away,' and I was too young to question it. Years passed before I realised the real reason we came here so often, and by then, I was so used to not having a mother around that there was no true grief left to be felt." Her cigarette finished, Flora hopped down from her perch on the monument and dusted herself off. "It might have left something of a hole in my soul, but that's more something that I know in my head than feel in my heart, if you know what I mean. Life goes on, whether you like it or not—which may be what Sassoon meant about swearing to never forget."

Eric supposed there was something poetic about the wealth of greenery curling over the monuments of this dead necropolis—like poppies flooding the fields of the slain.

Up by the Colonel's grave, the last of the mourners were now drifting past the widows for a final goodbye. An elderly gentleman, stoop-shouldered and unsteady, was holding up the queue by wringing Lady Alice's hands with a grief more evident than hers. This was Jocelyn Carrington-Clarke, brother of the Colonel's late wife Johanna. The principal of Carrington-Clarke & Associates, he was such a faded ghost that it came as no surprise that he needed Madam Eliot to manage the day-to-day of his business.

Flora excused herself to join her sisters-in-law, and Avery wandered down to take her place.

"Popular bloke, your Colonel Russell," Avery remarked. "I haven't seen such a crowd since King Edward hopped the twig."

"He was the heart and soul of the Britannia," Eric replied with feeling.

Mr. Carrington-Clarke, leaning on Madam Eliot for support, stumbled past them. Once they'd gone, Avery said, "You never told me what you found out from that attendant of yours. Was he still willing to talk despite getting the sack?"

"What? Oh. Yes." Retreating behind a mausoleum, Eric briefed Avery on his findings over the past twenty-four hours, including his search of Ward's room. "It's left me with more questions than before, but I'm fairly certain now that Ward didn't do it. Nobody credits the idea of a random homicidal maniac, least of all Duplessis, who should know. So, where does that leave us? Andrew Russell's spies."

"Or Karl Werner." Avery seemed quite taken by the account of Ward's friendship with the sanatorium caretaker. "That does seem rather an odd friendship, don't you think? I wonder if there was more to it."

"Karl Werner might have been a former German soldier. When Ward wrote about 'understanding,' he clearly meant shared experiences in the War."

Avery frowned and looked away. "Yes. That must be it."

"You're right about it being an odd friendship, though. I mean, Ward did mention an attempt on his life. But he might not have meant it literally. From what little I saw, he tended to be quite flippant about things."

"Well, I think it's rather telling that Ward's final journal entry mentions an intention to leave everything to Werner. That sort of thing tends to change relationships."

That was a thought. Had Ward actually made a will? Avery had a friend at Somerset House who could look it up for them. Marriage to Lucy Russell would have nullified such a will—that could be a motive. What if Ward had been the target all along? Eric imagined this hypothetical Karl Werner watching the club building, slipping inside when he saw Flora leave, and running into Colonel Russell in his search for Ward . . .

Surely a man like Colonel Russell couldn't be the casualty of someone else's story?

"Mr. Peterkin! There you are. I've been meaning to speak to you about that Roman mosaic." Madam Eliot, standing right behind them, made them jump in surprise. Eric had somehow missed the clatter of heels that normally announced her arrival, and he'd nearly forgotten about the Roman mosaic they'd found under the floor of the excavated pipe room, too. Before he could come up with a plausible excuse, Madam Eliot rattled on:

"I've been speaking to a Dr. Linwood at the British Museum, and he seemed quite interested in authenticating the mosaic. You haven't found another expert, have you? Not that it would matter: I don't think these academic types begrudge each other the opportunity to study these historical artefacts, and a second opinion only means we shall be twice as sure."

Eric glanced over to Avery for help, but Avery murmured vaguely that he wanted another word with Lady Alice. "Besides," he whispered, "you'll manage this faster and better without me in your way."

Curse or no curse, Avery had yet to lose his unease over the Roman mosaic.

"Dr. Linwood won't be available right away," Madam Eliot said as soon as Avery was gone. "He has some business up north, but he should be at our disposal in a week or so. I'll just make the necessary arrangements, shall I? And tell the crews to halt their work. No sense paying for a trickle when you can get things done in a torrent after the mosaic's been sorted."

"Of course." Eric glanced back again to the little black knot gathered farther up the path, which Avery had just joined. "Is this really something you want to discuss right now, though? I'd have thought that under the circumstances—"

"Hadrian's death, you mean? I'm known for a spectacular lack of feeling." Madam Eliot snapped open her purse and extracted a silver cigarette case. She lit a cigarette with a silver lighter, drew deeply, and expelled a plume of smoke. Eric had never seen her with a cigarette before. "Andrew hated to see me smoke," she remarked.

Madam Eliot's lips creased around the end of her cigarette as she sucked the smoke into her lungs. The business of managing things at Carrington-Clarke would take its toll on any man, Eric reflected, and the effect on Madam Eliot's nerves was plain to see; but Eric rather got the impression that she thrived on the constant pressure. It gave her no time for self-doubt.

Eric said, "You took over your husband's job when he went to war, didn't you?"

"As did thousands of other wives in my position. And it was a much-needed paycheque: the Russell men are hopeless when it comes to money. I know Hadrian lives—*lived*—closer to the bone than you'd expect."

"It can't have been easy."

"Putting it mildly! That first day, seeing the stack of obligations demanding my attention, I nearly cried. But as it turned out, most of my difficulties were nothing more than Andrew having left a snarling mess for me to clean up. Look." She pointed out one straight-backed and sombre mourner, just now walking away from the grave. "That's Bill Tyler, one of our building foremen. He won't say a word against Andrew now, because Andrew saved his life in the War—but I remember how he used to grumble at Andrew's less-than-satisfactory managerial skills. I did a far better job, but of course Andrew would have expected to take up the reins again afterwards as if nothing had happened. That's the natural order of things, isn't it? Andrew's death was almost a blessing."

A *what?* Eric stared at the urbane little woman surrounded by lush greenery and, beyond her, the stone monuments embedded in earth. "You don't mourn for him, then?"

"Of course I mourn for him. Don't be stupid." Madam Eliot cast down the remains of her cigarette and ground out the ember beneath her heel. "Andrew was my husband and I loved him. But let's not be blind to his particular shortcomings, shall we? He was a proud man. Pride demanded that he take a different path from his brother George, even though his strengths clearly lay in the military; and pride demanded that he be the principal breadwinner regardless of our respective abilities."

Funerals had a way of encouraging discussions of the departed, and Madam Eliot was opening up about her husband. Would she be so candid otherwise? This seemed like Eric's best chance of getting some answers about Andrew Russell's final objective. What were the others up to? Dr. Duplessis, looking both embarrassed and out of place in a long overcoat of green wool, had joined the other Russell widows; between him and Avery, it looked as though they might carry on for hours.

*Carpe diem.*

Eric lowered his voice to a conspiratorial whisper. "Listen. Just before he died, Colonel Russell asked your husband's godfather for all the news articles he'd collected about your husband's death in Paris. We all know Andrew Russell was assassinated by the same spies he was chasing, and that the French police, following the leads he left behind, managed to finish his work for him. But I wonder if one of them got away and came back seeking vengeance."

"Against Hadrian? You must be joking."

"The fact remains that Colonel Russell asked about one murder, and then got murdered himself."

Madam Eliot said nothing. She scrambled for another cigarette, though she appeared to have lost all sense of coordination in her hands. The cigarette case flashed in the sunlight and nearly tumbled to the ground. Next, the lighter. Snap. Snap. Eric drew out a matchbox to offer her a light, but she waved him away. Snap. Third time lucky, and she practically sucked the flame off the lighter in lighting her cigarette.

"Madam Eliot, you're the most likely to know what your husband was planning that night. Didn't he say anything to you about what he'd discovered or what he suspected?"

"Andrew would never dream of sharing anything so important with a mere woman." Madam Eliot's tone was bitter, but there was a faint stammer to her normally precision-cut diction. Her stark black-and-white was tinged with the verdant green-and-gold filtering down through the shifting shade of springtime overhead. "I don't know what Captain Ward told you, but he's mistaken if he thinks Andrew's death has any bearing on Hadrian's."

"I understand your reluctance to reopen old wounds, but—"

"My husband is dead, Mr. Peterkin," Madam Eliot snapped. "Let him stay dead."

"Madam Eliot, the French police found the spies connected to your husband's inquiries, but they never determined who actually shot him. Don't you want justice for him? If these spies were behind his death—"

"They were not."

Eric stared. How could she be so certain?

"They were not," she repeated, glancing around for potential eavesdroppers. "Andrew was shot with his own gun, and don't you think an assassin would have the good sense to bring his own tools for the job? Andrew shot himself. I knew—I always knew—that it was suicide."

Silence froze their little corner of Highgate, so completely that Eric wondered if he'd just gone deaf. And perhaps he had. He couldn't possibly have heard that right. "But the reports from Paris—"

"There is no possible world in which a confrontation with my Andrew would have ended with his gun in his assailant's hands. And I'm grateful, Mr. Peterkin: grateful that, somehow, nobody thought to ask that question, grateful that Captain Ward thought it was murder and managed to convince the police of the same, because it has at least saved the family a little bit of shame. We can say he was a hero cut down in the execution of his duty, and not that . . . that the War proved too much for him in the end. But I knew."

"But, surely," Eric said, shaking off the shock. "Surely, the French police would have matched the fatal bullet to Andrew Russell's personal sidearm. They told you this?"

Madam Eliot nodded. She was pulling her cigarette down to ashes with alarming speed. "So, please, Mr. Peterkin. Let it be. Suicides have no place on the Britannia's Roster of the Fallen, do they?"

No. They didn't. Not if anyone knew.

Eric knew Bradshaw to have covered up a host of suicides, and the old man's words echoed in his memory: *"I let them have their dignity. That's more important than the truth, sometimes . . . I dare you to look their widows and children in the eye and tell them I was wrong."*

Madam Eliot flung this second cigarette down after the first, her heel snapping over it almost before it hit the ground. "I can count on you to keep this quiet, I hope."

Eric nodded. There was a curiously large number of suicides among the ex-servicemen of the Great War. They'd brought the darkness of the trenches home with them, and Eric didn't need to ask why Andrew Russell, universally acknowledged as a jolly fine fellow, might want to put a gun to his head. Perhaps the crushing weight of that darkness finally outweighed his determination to root out the spies he held responsible for his brother George's death.

"There's one thing I don't understand, though."

"Mr. Peterkin. Leave it. I have nothing more to say."

"Why go to the trouble of booking leave—"

"I don't want to hear it!"

"Travelling to Paris and taking a hotel room—"

Madam Eliot held up a hand for silence. Rather than fill it with some form of explanation or speculation, she turned away and began her rapid-fire stride back towards the others. Eric had to run to catch up.

"Madam Eliot—"

*"No!"*

Eric sprang back, hands up with palms out. He hadn't even realised that he'd laid a hand on her arm—a mere touch, but she'd jumped as though he'd struck her. For a moment, the poised, polished businesswoman was gone, and in her place was a cringing, cornered animal. Her purse fell to the ground between them, bursting open to scatter its contents across the cemetery path and into the dense undergrowth bordering it—cigarette case, lighter, pencil, notebook . . . pistol? Yes, a sleek little pocket pistol, dull black and without Madam Eliot's usual glitter . . .

Farther on, where the other Russell widows were gathered with Avery, Penny, and Dr. Duplessis, the low buzz of conversation came to an abrupt halt. Madam Eliot was already on her knees, snatching up her purse and its spilt contents—including the little pocket pistol. "I'm such an idiot," she muttered, her cheeks flushing as red as the rubies she favoured. "No, I can manage. Leave me alone."

Avery jogged up just as Madam Eliot began plunging her hands into the damp foliage after her lighter. "I say, Eric, has something happened? Here, Madam Eliot, let me—"

"I'm fine!"

Madam Eliot got to her feet, snapped her purse shut, and shot Eric a fleeting sideways look of nervous apology. Then she skittered back into the safe embrace of her sisters-in-law. Lady Alice's expression, directed at Eric, might have frozen wide swathes of hell itself.

Eric himself was dumbstruck. Madam Eliot had done her best to hide it, but he knew the look she'd given him when she'd first sprung away. He'd seen it before, in the faces of former soldiers startled into the grip of an old wartime memory—the look of a blind, undying terror that continued to exact tribute long after having outlived its cause.

# OLD WOUNDS

"THE DISTINGUISHING FACTOR of war neuroses," Dr. Duplessis said, "is, in my opinion, not so much in their effect but in their cause. Madame Eliot need not have gone to war to have developed the same symptoms as someone who has, but such behaviours do not spring out of nothing. She must have suffered something in her past, something with at least as great an impact on her mind as the War on the average soldier."

But what could that something be? Had she been assaulted? She was a woman who worked in the admittedly rough world of construction, after all.

"That might be why she's got a gun in her purse," Eric said unhappily. The thought of violence befalling that tiny, delicate woman was like smashing a Fabergé egg.

Duplessis nodded sagely and drained his coffee.

It was early afternoon, after the funeral, and they were waiting in the Arabica coffeehouse for Avery to return from a visit to his friend at Somerset House. Eric wanted a professional's insight on Madam Eliot's unexpected behaviour, and Duplessis, muttering something about having to catch a train that afternoon, agreed to a spot of lunch—even if it was only the mediocre fare served at the Arabica. The alienist managed just half a sandwich, but pronounced the coffee "exceptional."

"Incidentally," Duplessis said, "I should demand an apology. You gave my card to Inspector Crane, and that promises to be a deeply exhausting relationship."

"I didn't realise it would be so bad."

Duplessis shrugged. "*C'est la vie*. He believes you intend to make your own inquiries. That is why you were pressing Madame Eliot for answers, yes?"

"He had two of my men arrested. Of course I had to get involved."

"But that matter has been settled, has it not?" Duplessis paused to signal for another cup of coffee, then gave Eric an appraising look. "I think this is something I have seen before: men, unable to answer the big questions of the War, project these questions onto smaller, more manageable mysteries. In the resolution of their fictions, they find a satisfaction that their realities could not give them, so you feel compelled—"

"Nonsense. I learned in the Army to always sort things out for my men before calling in a higher authority. That's all. It's the same thing again, now that I'm club secretary."

The bell over the Arabica's door tinkled. It was Avery, back already from his detour to Somerset House. A cup of coffee was handed to him over the counter without him having to ask for it, and he swept up to join Eric and Duplessis in their booth. "Hullo," he said. "Fancy finding you here. Usually it's the other way around."

"I thought you'd be another hour, at least," Eric remarked.

"You give the efficiency of His Majesty's bureaucracy too little credit. More to the point, I might have been longer had there been anything to find: Captain Gregory Ward never made a will. Or perhaps it was never registered. Is that allowed? One reads stories about lost wills and hidden legacies, which would all be quite silly if one could simply walk into the registry of wills and demand to see a copy of the latest thing."

Duplessis looked curiously from Avery to Eric and back. "Captain Ward's will? Why are you asking about his will? Will he not tell you himself?"

Eric said, "There's a German caretaker, presumably a former German soldier, named Karl Werner, to whom Ward may or may not have left everything. Let's just say that some minor skulduggery was involved in discovering this information, which I'd much rather Ward didn't know about, and leave it at that."

"A German soldier!"

"They met at a Swiss sanatorium," Avery added, "and became the best of friends. Remarkable, isn't it? Two enemy soldiers making peace over the shared horrors of the War."

Duplessis grunted. "I suppose empathy from the other side is better than no empathy at all."

"But I was thinking." Avery lit up a clove cigarette. "Andrew Russell was after German spies. And now, here's this German caretaker, Karl Werner. They must be connected."

"Of course," said Eric. "Because all Germans are the same German."

Duplessis looked lost again, and Eric had no qualms about showing him Colonel Russell's newspaper clippings.

## PRINT SHOP SPIES EXECUTED!

The four men arrested as the Print Shop Spies, so-called for having run their operation through a Montmartre printer's shop, were executed by firing squad this morning. This concludes the saga begun when one of their number assassinated English officer Captain Andrew Russell, who had been seeking to bring them to justice . . .

Or not, if Madam Eliot was right. Aloud, Eric said, "Crane got the official police report from Paris, and he doesn't care to pursue it any further. But I wonder if we might learn more from a face-to-face conversation. There's always some mess that doesn't make it into the neat and tidy final package."

Like Monique Garnier's letters. They were chatty, banal, and deceptively innocuous in their fishing for intelligence. Flora had given them to Eric expecting discretion, so these he kept to himself.

Duplessis, meanwhile, considered the clippings with interest. "So. Andrew Russell was assassinated by German spies. Meanwhile, his widow exhibits symptoms of a neurosis rooted in fear and violence. I wonder if the two are connected."

"Oh!" Avery laughed. "They're not. Lady Alice told me all about it. You know how the Germans used zeppelins to drop bombs on London—or tried to—during the War? Madam Eliot's house was completely destroyed by one of those bombs. That's how she wound up living with Colonel Russell through the latter half of the War, though I understand she lives in Chorleywood now. Honestly, I'm surprised she isn't more of a nervous wreck: I know I'd be if someone dropped a bomb on me."

Eric shook off an unbidden memory of shells landing around him, a dugout collapsing in on his head, and the hours of darkness afterwards awaiting rescue. He understood exactly what Madam Eliot must have gone through. There was something profoundly depressing about the horrors of war reaching an innocent woman at home, far from the front lines, and to see the effects echoed now in someone who should have been safe.

And this was Andrew Russell's widow, he reminded himself. Madam Eliot believed her husband had committed suicide, even as the world believed he'd given his life to set things right. Either way, Eric felt honour-bound to set things right as well.

"But if we're talking about spies," Avery went on, "what about Ward? What if *he* was the spy? He was there when Andrew Russell was killed, and it would explain how he got so friendly with this German fellow. Perhaps they were working together, and Colonel Russell found out!"

"Avery," Eric said, "be serious. Ward?"

"I am wary of your Captain Ward," Duplessis said, frowning in thought. "There is something about him that feels wrong, though I cannot say what. I do not think he can be your spy, however. As a young Army captain, he would have been far too busy with his duties on the battlefield to worry about deceiving multiple unsuspecting women. At least, that is how it was in the French army: I saw enough as a medical officer to know. Perhaps it was different for you."

Avery hesitated, darting a glance at Eric.

Duplessis's brows went up a notch. "Do you not know, Monsieur Ferrett?"

"I spent the War in Argentina—my health, you know—"

Was that disapproval in Duplessis's expression? Avery hurried on:

"Well, that's beside the point. You're quite right, of course, now I think about it. I mean, as an officer, he'd have all the information he'd want already, wouldn't he? No need to go wheedling it out of anyone back home. But couldn't he have killed Andrew Russell, still? If he's friendly with one German soldier now, who's to say he wasn't friendly with the Germans as a whole back then?"

Eric rubbed his head in exasperation. "Avery, I think you've crossed the line from mere speculation to unadulterated fiction."

"Then we'll simply have to go find out the truth for ourselves, won't we?"

It might be worth actually visiting Paris for a word with the Sûreté about Andrew Russell's death. The alternative was a trunk call, which might end up costing more when coupled with navigating the bureaucracy of a foreign police force.

Duplessis checked his watch and stood up. "Messieurs, it has been a pleasure, but I have my own business in Paris tomorrow. I would have left this morning if not for the funeral; as it is, I must catch the eight o'clock from Victoria—"

"Bother the train," Eric said, coming to a decision. "I've got the family motorcar. If you don't mind waiting a few minutes for me to throw some clothes into a suitcase, I'll drive you down to Dover and we can catch the ferry together."

Eric packed with the swift precision of a soldier preparing to move out and was ready in ten minutes. He found Duplessis waiting outside his flat at the north end of Bloomsbury, and then it was across the river to pick up Avery from his flat in Lambeth. Avery, however, was barely halfway through his packing.

"Honestly, Eric. We're not in a race, and an earlier crossing won't get the overnight train into Paris any sooner than scheduled."

So Eric was shooed out of the flat and made to wait in the car. He had to admit that Avery was right. The French police archives would still be there whether they got there tomorrow or a week later. It was only Duplessis who had to be in Paris by tomorrow for whatever reason, and he was reading a medical journal without a care in the world.

A distant whistle tore at Eric's nerves. Avery's flat was uncomfortably close to the railway tracks—possibly the reason he spent his every waking hour at the Arabica—and Eric could see the trains rumbling in and out of Waterloo Station. Perhaps one was bound for the ports of Southampton . . . Eric remembered gathering with hundreds of other soldiers at Waterloo Station eight years ago to go to war in a foreign land: the impatience he felt now was an echo of the anxiety he'd felt then. Waterloo Station at that time had been under construction, a twenty-year-long project to bring order to the most chaotic, godforsaken snarl of railway tracks in the Empire. Now, eight years later, the scaffolding was gone; the platforms and tracks were in order; the main entrance was marked by the Victory Arch to commemorate the rail workers who'd given their lives in the War.

The War was supposed to be over. That's what memorials like the Victory Arch meant. Order had been restored to the world just as it had been brought to the platforms of Waterloo. Yet here they were, still cleaning up the detritus of four years in Flanders.

*Darkness. Rubble from a collapsed ceiling closed in on all sides. Groping blindly, Lieutenant Peterkin's fingers finally encountered fabric: not the familiar khaki wool of a soldier's uniform, but a lady's jacket, sharply tailored from rich burgundy tweed—*

"Eric! Away with the fairies, are we?" Laughing, Avery tossed his suitcase into the back seat and leapt in after it. "I thought you were in a hurry."

"And whose fault is that?" Eric started the Vauxhall and drew away from the kerb. They rounded the corner, and there was Waterloo Station itself, with the Victory Arch flanked by the Roman personifications of war and peace. The twin goddesses gazed down—one grim, one gracious—on the beginning and end of a thousand journeys . . .

"Eric, why have we stopped?"

"No reason."

Eric stamped down on the acceleration pedal, and the Vauxhall leapt away again, this time with a lurch that nearly cost Duplessis his place in his reading; and then they were off—to Paris, and the reopening of old wounds.

# THE SLEEPING BEAST

ERIC HAD BEEN to France just once since the War: last summer, to see the Olympic Games in Paris. Both Penny and Avery had been with him then, and the journey was marked with a great deal of laughter and high spirits. He remembered some good-natured ribbing when another Eric, Scottish runner Eric Liddell, refused to run the 100 m because the heats were scheduled for a Sunday; and he remembered the cheers and back-thumping when Mr. Liddell went on to set a world record for the 400 m instead.

Mr. Liddell was born in China, where he was returning this year as a missionary—unless he'd already gone. Presumably, he spoke the language like a native. Inspector Crane was bound to have a few choice words for Eric about *that*.

In any case, the festive air surrounding the Olympic Games meant that Eric's prior experiences on French soil barely registered in his conscious mind. But that was then. This time, he was on a mission, with all the tension it entailed. He could think of nothing but the shadows of the War rising again in defiance of electric-bright modernity.

The train left Calais at half past eight, threading its way southwards along the coast to Boulogne-sur-Mer and Étaples before veering inland. It was dark by then, and the French countryside was a sea of dark shapes washing past, in which one might imagine any menace. While Avery and Duplessis slept, Eric remained wakeful until Amiens—a three-hour stop amid deserted platforms in the haunting silence of the wee hours.

This was where the end of the War began, Eric recalled: the Battle of Amiens, an eight-mile advance after years of stalemate and a thorough breakdown of German morale. Eric knew the story of how Australian troops captured and commandeered the locomotive on which the Germans had mounted the infamous Amiens gun. The original station was badly damaged by shelling, so this vast, echoing cavern of empty platforms had likely never seen the War; but Eric still imagined the Amiens gun rolling in, crowned by a squad of hooting Australians . . .

A conductor ambled by, yawning and apparently heedless of the station's hidden scars. Was it the same throughout the city? Brooding over the stillness, watching for he knew not what, Eric finally drifted off into a troubled sleep.

Duplessis had his own flat in Paris, but promised to call on them at their hotel that evening; in the meantime, inquiries at the Sûreté led Eric and Avery to an Inspector Alain Michaud: a small, comfortable-looking old man with a pink face and white hair. Watching him fuss over his five-year-old granddaughter, one would never have guessed that he'd spent the better part of his life up to his elbows in some of the most gruesome murders behind the Parisian veil of *joie de vivre*. He was retired now, but he was happy to sit down to coffee and pastries under the chestnut trees of an open-air bistro, and discuss the murder of Andrew Russell:

"But yes, of course I remember. It was a feather in my cap—a triumphant close to my career. But I don't mind saying, since you are asking about it, that in my eyes and in spite of what the newspapers say, it was a failure."

Eric raised an incredulous brow. "A failure, Monsieur Michaud?"

"We never actually identified Monsieur Russell's murderer, no? Oh, the public believes, when they think about it, that it was one of the four men we executed as spies; but who can say which? As a group, they would all be morally responsible, but is that the same thing?"

"You didn't follow up on your own afterwards?"

"Monsieur, in the first place, a police detective has no time to chase after cases that no longer concern him; and in the second place . . . I am retired, and such things concern me even less. We must put away the things of yesterday when a new day dawns, must we not?" The former inspector raised his cup to the distant Eiffel Tower, spearing up from the Champs de Mars through newly green trees into a cloudless blue sky. "You know, of course, that la Tour Eiffel served as a radio communications relay during the War? Now she, too, is retired, and serves as a thing of beauty. My son-in-law works for Citroën, and he tells me there are rumours of a plan to cover the tower with thousands of electric lights spelling out the company's name. Is it not poetic? Citroën began by making weapons to hasten death in the War. Now they ease our lives with motorcars, and tomorrow, if such a plan passes, they become the brightest light in the new world of modern France."

Indeed. Paris was a phoenix rising from the ashes of war, with bright lights in the street and music from a hundred nightclubs to dispel the darkness of yesterday. Monsieur Michaud's granddaughter had been named Edith, after Edith Cavell—it was not only the British who honoured her memory—but she was born in the light of this post-war world, and would never know what the older generation, her namesake especially, had endured.

Eric cleared his throat. "Returning to the subject of Andrew Russell—"

"Aha, so you wish to reawaken the sleeping beast. It was a long time ago, in another life. I do not know if I remember the details. Although . . ." Blue eyes darted to a nearby confectioner's and twinkled with mischief. "A box of marrons glacés might do wonders for my memory."

"Are you asking for a bribe?"

"I am no longer with the police—"

"Say no more!" Avery was out of his seat before Eric could stop him and back a minute later with the requisite bribe, which he placed in the middle of the bistro table.

Michaud chuckled and opened the box, revealing an array of candied chestnuts whose glazed surfaces glowed like amber in the sun. He popped one into his mouth, advised little Edith that she could have just one, and gestured for Eric and Avery to help themselves. "In truth, I'd have told you everything regardless; but what is life without a marron glacé, eh?"

Avery grinned in agreement. "Don't look so scandalised, Eric: I'd have gone for these even if Monsieur Michaud here hadn't asked for them. What is it that Penny keeps telling you? 'Live a little. Stop and listen to some jazz.'"

Sitting back with a satisfied smile, Michaud sipped his coffee, advised his granddaughter that she could have "just one more," and began in earnest:

"We received the alert in the evening, I should say about eight o'clock, and we were on the scene within fifteen minutes. The concierge of the hotel is a worthy lady by the name of Jeanne Aubert. She is still there, I believe. According to her, she had been in conversation with another guest, a friend of the dead man named Gregory Ward, when they both heard a gunshot upstairs. They went to investigate and found Monsieur Russell dead in his room. Monsieur Ward stayed to guard the body while Madame Aubert went to fetch us."

Poor Ward! Waiting beside the Colonel's body must have awakened quite an unpleasant memory for him. Did the retired French inspector know of this sequel to his old murder inquiry?

"Mrs. Andrew Russell," Eric said, "is convinced that her husband shot himself."

"The poor woman! He was shot in the head, just above the right brow, which may have looked like suicide at first glance, but no firearm was found in the room; and later on, it was determined from the lack of powder burns that he was shot from a distance, so it was as clear a case of murder as you like. Perhaps she misunderstood when we suggested that the assassin escaped with her husband's weapon."

"That's possible."

Monsieur Michaud shrugged and returned to his story. "Monsieur Ward told us that Monsieur Russell was sacrificing his leave to pursue a ring of spies operating out of Paris. There was an address written in the notebook of Monsieur Russell, a printer in Montmartre. We spent some time watching it and closely examining the post coming in and out. Within a week, we were rewarded: military secrets, written in code and destined for Germany! We knew, too, how many men would come and go from that place, and we were able to capture nearly all of them together at once."

"Nearly?"

"As far as the public knows, four men were apprehended, and those same four men were later executed. In fact, we caught six men. Two of them died in custody." The little man absently rubbed the knuckles of his right hand and helped himself to a marron glacé. "We learned from interrogation that there was a seventh accomplice: a Karl von Werner—"

Avery was quick to pounce on the name. "Werner?"

"Von Werner. There is a difference."

Eric put a restraining hand on his friend's shoulder and said, "What else could you learn about this person?"

"This was their actual contact with the German military. Three of our captured spies had never actually met him in person; of the other three, two died in custody—as I mentioned—before they could tell us anything; and the last . . . Messieurs, there comes a point in any interrogation when all the truth is extracted, leaving only the lies your suspect thinks you want to hear. We reached that point with this one. One moment, Karl von Werner was an aristocrat of middle age; another moment, he was a young officer eager to prove himself. For myself, I believe that 'Karl von Werner' was an assumed name, and the actual person was a woman."

"A woman! Why?"

"Where Monsieur Russell was shot, we found a footprint in the blood. A woman's footprint—too small, certainly, to belong to any of the men involved; and with the brand of a shoemaker that distinguished it from any of the women at the hotel. Ergo, it belonged to an outsider, perhaps one of the spies Monsieur Russell had come to find. And as all the spies we caught were men, I concluded that the one we missed—the so-called Karl von Werner—must be the woman. It is clever, no? A woman may hide her face behind a veil, while a man may not; and a woman caught in the wrong hotel room is no threat at all." Michaud chewed thoughtfully on another marron glacé, then added, "I always wondered if Monsieur Ward recognised that mark. He seemed surprised when it was pointed out to him, and from that moment on and throughout our interview afterwards, I had the sense that there was something more he wished to tell me. But intuition is not evidence, and in any case, the spy ring was dismantled without any further assistance."

"Perhaps," Avery mused, "it's an English shoemaker's brand, one he knew."

"If you wish, I can ask my friends to send you a picture of that footprint. We keep records of everything."

"Please do." Eric gave the address of his hotel and grinned at Michaud's surprise. "Yes, the same hotel where it all happened—I even managed to get the same room."

The hotel was on the Rue La Fayette, across from the Église Saint-Vincent-de-Paul and a stone's throw from the Gare du Nord where the train from Calais had deposited Eric and his companions at half past seven that morning. It was small, family-owned, and family-run, and while the intervening years might have eradicated all physical clues, the general layout and disposition of the rooms hadn't changed. The room that had been Andrew Russell's was on the first floor, a large room with high ceilings and elaborate plaster moulding, shabby but spotlessly clean. Here was an old-fashioned double bed, its tightly pulled sheets faintly tinged with an indigo wash to counter the yellowing of age and use. On either side were matching bedside tables, painted white. Porcelain lamps, threadbare carpet, a pair of high-backed armchairs in a corner . . .

"He was lying over there," said Madame Jeanne Aubert, flowing around Eric and Avery to indicate a spot near the foot of the bed. "On his back, this terrible look of fury on his face. Monsieur, I believe that if he had not been killed, there would have been a different man killed here that night."

Madame Aubert was a youthful-looking forty, slim and graceful as a swan, with the slight frown of one trying to navigate the world without the aid of the spectacles in her pocket. She'd graduated from concierge to manager since the War, but seemed quite happy to relive this one exciting night of her earlier life. She moved a lamp from the bedside table to the floor and turned the table itself onto its side. "This is a new lamp, of course: the original one was broken. There must have been a fight, and the killer fell against the table when he was struck."

Or, if Inspector Michaud's suspicions were correct, when *she* was struck. But a single overturned bedside table and a broken lamp might just as easily be indicative of a man drunk on cognac stumbling over unfamiliar furniture.

"We worried," Madame Aubert remarked, "that the scandal would put us out of business. But the notoriety brought us tourists eager to see things for themselves; and after that, the world moved on and all was forgotten."

"We should have a séance," Avery said. "To contact the spirit of Andrew Russell. I'll bet he could tell us a great deal more than anyone else could."

Madame Aubert looked disapproving, but only murmured that they must not disturb the other guests.

Eric, meanwhile, was peering out the tall window. The balcony outside was a shallow thing, more decorative than useful, and littered with ground-out cigarette butts. It ran across the whole of the street facade, past the similarly tall windows of the neighbouring rooms, whose doors were left unlocked for the convenience of the cleaning staff unless occupied. A hotel guest lounged at the far end with a cigarette—hardly an unusual sight, apparently. Across the street, the Église Saint-Vincent-de-Paul offered no witnesses but the saints ranged across its parapet. Escaping this way should be easy.

But how did the killer get in? Madame Aubert was happy to explain.

"Monsieur Russell and Monsieur Ward arrived together at about two o'clock. Business being slow that week, I was able to give them each their own room at a fair price. They went their separate ways for the afternoon. Monsieur Russell returned first, with a bottle of cognac. He seemed pensive, and I remember he went into the salon rather than up to his room. But then it was time for my dinner. The family *appartement* is a little away from the front desk, but that is why we have a bell, no? I heard it ring while I was away, and I came to answer it, but I found no one waiting. It was only later that I came to realise that it must have been the killer, but it is not the first time that a guest rang the bell and changed his mind. I had no cause to be suspicious."

"Of course," said Eric. "No one intending murder would announce himself like that. You were right to have no suspicions."

"But naturally! I waited to see if the person calling had simply wandered around a corner, but no one came, so I went back to my dinner. Five minutes later, I was back behind the desk, and another five minutes after that, Monsieur Ward returned. I told him his friend was waiting for him in the salon, but he looked and said there was no one there. He was more interested in what I had to say about the sights around Paris, in any case—all the places a soldier on leave might want to visit. We were talking when we heard the gunshot. Monsieur Ward went immediately to investigate. I hesitated to follow. Next minute, he was shouting for the spare key, so I took that and went up to open the door for him—and you know what we found then."

Andrew Russell, dead in the middle of the room; upset furniture; and a cold draught coming in through a gap where the window wasn't quite closed. How had it all come about? Eric imagined Andrew Russell coming in the door to find an assassin waiting for him—no, why wait to have an altercation, when one could simply shoot on sight? Come to that, why kill him here, when one could just as easily push him into the path of an oncoming bus, or accost him in an anonymous dark alley? Perhaps the killing hadn't been planned. Perhaps the so-called assassin had only come to steal whatever evidence Andrew Russell may have found, and was surprised in the middle of his—or her—search . . .

Eric's thoughts were interrupted by a knock on the door: the new concierge, seeking Madame Aubert's help. "They are fighting in the salon—a loud American and the doctor friend of these two gentlemen—and I do not know what to do!"

# THE IRON HARVEST

"LIKE HELL YOU'VE never played before! You're a hustler, that's what you are—a shark. And where I'm from, we shoot the sharks."

"Monsieur, I assure you—"

But the American was already on his feet, pulling a terrified Dr. Duplessis up with both fists curled into his shirtfront. Eric, hurrying into the hotel salon, caught only the tail end of the conversation—if it could be called a conversation—but the scene told him all he needed to know. He was on them in an instant, hands interposed to pry them apart.

"See here," he said, "put the man down. He's half your size and twice your age—hardly a sporting fight."

The American, red-faced, snarled down at Eric. "You weren't just taken for a ride by this slinking, lying shark, so what do you know? Go see to the laundry!"

"There is no need to be rude," Eric said, ice in his tone. "Duplessis?"

"Monsieur l'Americain was showing me—"

But Eric's familiarity with Duplessis seemed to have only added fuel to the American's ire. He let out a roar of fury, threw Duplessis back down, and swung around to face Eric.

What was that smell? Mud and blood and cordite, the acrid stench of expended gunpowder . . . Eric caught the American's hand as it flashed out for a shove and thrust it wide, gripping the wrist hard enough to leave bruises. The American was thrown off-balance, and while he could have recovered and tried something worse, something in Eric's demeanour gave him pause.

"If you cannot be a gentleman," Eric said with a dangerous calm, "I suggest you leave."

They stood there motionless for one long, anxious moment, their gazes burning between them. The American faltered, then finally deflated as Eric released his wrist with a gesture of contempt. He cast one last venomous look at Duplessis and slunk out of the room.

Duplessis was staring wordlessly at Eric.

"What?" Eric wanted to shake his head clear of what felt like battlefield smoke, but settled instead for righting the seat overturned by the American's outburst and gathering up the scattered playing cards—fussy, civilised movements to obfuscate the decidedly uncivilised beast now leering from the darkest corner of his soul. He saw, once again, the faded velvet upholstery and the organic art nouveau curves so popular at the turn of the century. Night had fallen while he was interviewing Madame Aubert. Through the window, he could see the slender square towers of the Église Saint-Vincent-de-Paul; turn left, and the Rue La Fayette would take him straight into the 9th Arrondissement, to the Théâtre National de l'Opéra and, for all he knew, the phantom said to lurk in the catacombs beneath—also named Eric, according to the Gaston Leroux novel.

*This* Eric had his own phantoms to worry about.

Back at the door, Madame Aubert stood with her niece, alarm fading from their faces as they saw the situation resolved. Reassured that there was no need to call either the police or, God forbid, the *gendarmerie*, the pair withdrew to the lobby, brushing past Avery in the doorway. Avery, nose twitching on high alert, looked from Eric to Duplessis and back.

"Is it safe?"

"Oui. It is safe."

It was plain from Duplessis's inflection on the word *safe* that he considered Avery a coward, and Eric held out little hope that his friend hadn't noticed.

"Well, what set this off, then?" Eric said gruffly, turning to drop the needle of a nearby gramophone onto a record. Louis Armstrong's brassy jazz trumpet filled the room.

"Monsieur l'Americain was teaching me a game called poker," Duplessis said, sitting down primly. Eric and Avery sat down with him. "I found it quite fascinating. It has much to do with creating false impressions, with intimidation, and with the careful husbanding of resources. It is a shame, but my teacher was not at all a good liar. I could see through him every time, which is how I came to win so much. It convinced him I was cheating."

"You're just better at reading faces than most," said Avery.

If Avery was hoping to win Duplessis over with flattery, it failed. Duplessis merely shrugged at the compliment and said to Eric, "My sincerest apologies. I hope your inquiries this afternoon were fruitful?"

"Fruitful enough."

"There was another spy," Avery burst out. "A Karl von Werner, though the Inspector thinks it was really a woman. But we know better. That's Karl Werner! It has to be! It's the same name!"

"And I am the phantom of the Opéra, when I'm not running races for Olympic gold." Truth be told, Eric's curiosity had been piqued by the name as well. He was simply in no mood to acknowledge it.

"Come on, Eric. We absolutely must continue to Switzerland now. Besides, what about Ward's will? Ten to one, he made it with a Swiss lawyer, and that's why I didn't find anything at Somerset House."

"If Karl Werner really is the villain of the piece," Eric snapped, "he'll be in London, not Switzerland. We might as well go home: there's nothing else for us here, anyway."

"Bite your tongue!" Avery laughed. "We're in Paris, Eric! You'd be mad not to make the most of a night in la Ville Lumière."

Eric's lip curled in response, but he said nothing. He *felt* mad.

The record ended, and Avery got up to put another one on. "You can sit here feeling sorry for yourself, if you like, but it's Saturday night, the Folies Bergère is practically next door, and if we can't get in, there are a dozen other cabarets to choose from. We've done what we came to do, and now we've got the time, we don't want all this to pass us by."

Bright lights on brass instruments, and trombone slides punching into the air. Paris by night was an electric jewel, hard facets flashing to defeat the dark. There was dancing to be done, and interesting new cocktails to be sampled. At Duplessis's suggestion, they sought out a nightclub called Le Grand Duc on the Rue Pigalle. The manager, Duplessis said, was a black American named Eugene Bullard, who'd been heavily decorated for his wartime exploits as a pilot in the French *aéronautique militaire*. The hero was otherwise occupied that evening, however, and Eric had to satisfy himself with cheap brandy from the bar, while Avery took lessons in the Charleston from a woman with a laugh that swept the room much as the music ground on his bones.

Eric didn't recall Paris having such a souring effect on his mood last year when he came to see the Olympics; nor earlier in the day when he was occupied with gathering information. It was only in the moments of stillness—like the station at Amiens—that one let one's guard down, and the beast within stirred from its slumber.

Lady Alice's words echoed in his head: *"In times of distress, the best thing to do is to keep as busy as possible."*

The brandy, cheap as it was, burned his throat, while jazz music did the same with his ears. Eric made a pretence of searching his pockets, then offered to buy his neighbour a drink in exchange for a cigarette. He never carried the things, not being much in the habit, but every so often, one wanted the ritual of lighting and smoking—more so than the taste itself . . .

Outside, the stars were overcome by the lights of the city, and the sky was tinted orange around its edges. It would be worse if Citroën really did follow through with that plan Inspector Michaud had described, of covering the Eiffel Tower in electric lights. Or was this conquest of the night a thing to celebrate? The blare of the jazz music was muffled by the closed doors, at least, but so, too, was the laughter and chatter of the nightclub's patrons.

*If you can't be a gentleman, then you should leave.*

"Monsieur Peterkin." Duplessis had emerged from the nightclub as well; but not, apparently, for a smoke. "Monsieur Peterkin, you are not disappointed about having missed Monsieur Bullard, are you?"

The last thing he wanted right now, Eric realised with surprise, was to exchange war stories with a decorated flying ace. He shrugged and mumbled a polite denial. "I have a lot on my mind. That's all."

"Perhaps." Duplessis considered Eric for a long moment. "If you'll pardon my saying . . . You are, ordinarily, a civilised gentleman—an honourable, magnanimous John Bull—yes?"

*John Bull is how we'd like the world to see us . . . But make no mistake—*

"I'd like to think so," Eric replied.

"Earlier, you showed a different face."

*—strip off our mask and you'll always find bloodthirsty Britannia underneath.*

Eric scowled down at his cigarette as it burned. "It was the War."

"Humanity has a capacity and a desire for violence, however much our civilised superego tries to distance us from it. You control rather than suppress. That mastery of the violent id suggests to me that it is natural—not a case of mental alienation at all."

"Mastery!" This supposed control was tenuous at best. Eric scoffed and repeated, "It was the War."

"It was your training as a soldier. You think it was the War because you have, until now, only called upon it in the context of its horrors."

Why did everything always have to come back to the damned War? That thing which had defined his entrance into adulthood . . . What was it Lucy had said of her husband? *"If this was what it meant to be a man, he'd much rather just be a boy again."*

"I noticed," Duplessis continued, "that as we left Calais, you changed your seat so you could look out the left side of the train. The right side, westwards, was the better view, with the coast and the last light of the sun; but you had eyes only for the darkness of the opposite direction, as if you thought you might find something out there."

Eric dropped the burnt-out cigarette, ground it out under his heel, and tried not to think of Madam Eliot doing the same at her father-in-law's funeral. "Is that a crime? Paris is inland. Obviously I was only anxious to arrive at our destination."

"You were facing backwards, not forwards. Northeast, in other words, and in that direction . . . that would be Flanders."

Eric's breath caught in his throat. He remembered the dark shapes flying past, the formless fields and the distant tree line against the night sky, and stars unobscured by the lights of Paris. *I swear I know that horizon, but not like this.*

"All right. I couldn't sleep, and of course it's always interesting to see how time has changed a place you once knew all too well. At Amiens—" Eric grimaced. It was a mistake to have admitted any interest in the old trenches. "It's not important."

"It is more than an interest, I think." Rather than speculate on Eric's curiosity, Duplessis chose to address it: "They are rebuilding the villages, just as they are rebuilding Amiens. The muddy battlefields are returning to nature, even if some places must remain untouched for years to come because of the mines, the gas pollution, the unexploded ordnance . . . Every year, men clean a little more away, in what we call the *récolte de fer*—the iron harvest—and the grass grows a little taller . . ."

"And ordinary life goes on."

There might be children laughing and playing over the trench, now filled in and covered with sod, where Eric had watched his men die. Eric remembered Flora's story of playing in Highgate Cemetery as a child, and the image that had come to mind then of poppies flooding the fields of the slain . . .

Duplessis nodded. "It is the nature of life and the world to move on. Every man who has been in the War has his own 'iron harvest' to bring himself back into the world. You do not want to be so lost in the past that you lose your present."

*Memorials should be made of stone, not of human lives.*

The nightclub door swung open to emit a pair of very drunk patrons, and for a moment, jazz music drowned out the world. Eric caught the door before it closed and gruffly said to Duplessis, "Time we were back to the dancing, then. That's what you want, isn't it? To live in what's right under my nose?"

"You are stronger than you realise, Monsieur Peterkin, and have less to fear than you think. You have only to ask yourself who you are."

Eric turned and flung himself back into the sea of music, laughter, and light.

Morning brought sunlight stronger than the electric bulb and, as it was a Sunday, flocks of respectable French Catholics to the doors of the Église Saint-Vincent-de-Paul. Eric rose early despite falling into bed late, and stumbled down to the salon with last night's excesses throbbing dully in the side of his head. Through the window, he watched the churchgoers troop into the embrace of God, as they'd done every Sunday since Christianity first established itself in the then Roman province of Gaul.

The world didn't change, as Colonel Russell once said. Or did it? Gaul became France, Camelot disappeared into legend, Londinium became the heart of another empire . . . Political entities might come and go, but ordinary life carried on regardless.

Eric settled into an armchair and looked around the salon. From here, he had a good view of the hotel entrance and the stairs up to the guest rooms, but not of the front desk. He rubbed at his aching head. Why was he here again? Because Colonel Russell was dead immediately after having requested information on Andrew Russell's death. Andrew Russell had been murdered by spies—his widow's belief in his suicide notwithstanding—and the investigating policeman believed that one of those spies, a woman going by the masculine name of Karl von Werner, was still at large.

Had Colonel Russell been killed by this escaped spy, for daring to dig up ancient history? It seemed no less far-fetched than the idea of Gregory Ward being the murderer.

Emerging into the lobby, Eric found the front desk unmanned. The concierge must be at her breakfast, and that reminded Eric of Madame Aubert's claim of having been at dinner when someone rang the bell. How long did it take to answer a summons? With an eye on his watch, Eric hit the bell. Exactly thirty-seven seconds later, the young concierge emerged from the door behind the desk, brushing croissant crumbs from her skirt. "Oui, monsieur? May I help you?"

"I was wondering if anything came in for me last night."

Thirty-seven seconds. Even the most impatient of guests would wait at least that long, and to disappear without a trace meant leaving the lobby without waiting at all. Eric had been certain until now that this was something completely unrelated, but what if he was wrong?

What would a spy seeking something in Andrew Russell's room have done? They'd have checked the register, which was right there on the desk, and taken the spare key—

No. The spare key was still there that night for Madame Aubert to open Andrew Russell's door, so the spy must have picked the lock instead. But why not steal the key, if the desk was momentarily unmanned and the key rack undefended? Why ring the bell?

And how was it that it took all of Madame Aubert's conversation with Ward before any violence occurred? Andrew Russell must have already gone upstairs while she was at her dinner, or she'd have mentioned seeing him afterwards. Had he been in the toilet all that time, thus not encountering the spy in his room until right that minute?

Besides, whether the intention was to kill Andrew Russell or to search his room, how did the spy even know where to find him? Andrew Russell had only just started asking his questions that same afternoon. The story made less sense the more he looked at it, but somewhere in this tangle must lie the solution to Colonel Hadrian Russell's murder seven years later.

"Monsieur?"

"Oh! Excuse me. I've a bit of a headache, that's all."

"This was delivered by hand late last night, but you were in no condition to receive it."

So, Inspector Michaud had come through after all! Eric accepted the envelope and tore it open immediately. A photograph slid out—a photograph of a photograph, in fact, which did little for its clarity, but the footprint was easy enough to make out nonetheless.

Eric frowned.

Michaud had mentioned a shoemaker's brand on the sole, but Eric didn't think this symbol edged in black blood was anything of the sort. A rectangle, quartered by diagonals . . . This was the same mark from Gregory Ward's service revolver.

# PART THREE

# THAT NEVER WAS

WHAT COULD THAT mark mean? It had to be a way of identifying secret members of the spy network. Why else would it be on the assassin's shoe? But then, why would it be on Ward's service revolver? Unless—

"I'll tell you what it means," Avery said. "I'm surprised you haven't thought of it yourself already, Eric. It means that Captain Gregory Ward was in league with the Germans. Ten to one, he was supposed to keep an eye on Andrew Russell and guide him into a trap, and then to keep the hotel concierge occupied while the assassin did the job. You said yourself that he didn't look like a recovering consumptive. Clearly, that so-called sanatorium is a hideout where traitors like him could stay out of sight and out of mind until it's safe to come back into decent society. Andrew Russell was killed by a Karl von Werner, and Ward's closest friend in the past five years was a Karl Werner. Obviously, they're the same person—probably Ward's contact in German intelligence. Colonel Russell found out, so Ward killed him. Mystery solved!"

"But why?" Duplessis argued. He'd come ostensibly to return his winnings of the night before to the American gambler, as a gesture of good faith, but seemed more interested now in discussing

Eric's inquiries. "Why go through the trouble of teasing information out of Mademoiselle Grace if Captain Ward could just tell the Germans himself?"

"Besides," Eric added, "Inspector Michaud thinks 'Karl von Werner' was a woman. A man like Andrew Russell wouldn't think to fear a woman he caught entering his room."

"You are making connections where none exist," Dr. Duplessis said, picking up the photograph of the incriminating footprint. "Designs cut into the soles of shoes have a way of wearing away. What you see here may be only a part of a more elaborate whole."

Eric took the photograph back and studied it closely. He didn't see any fading lines to indicate the wearing away of a larger design. They were back to the question of the same mark being on Ward's service revolver, linking him to the spies. And as Avery had already pointed out, it wasn't the only suspicious point, was it? "We'll have to go to Switzerland. We need to find out more about Ward—and about Karl Werner."

"Eric! If that sanatorium really is a nest of spies—"

"The War has been over for seven years, and they're on neutral ground. Unless they're also traitors to the Swiss, no one cares. Though, in my opinion, we're more likely to discover that the sanatorium is really a hospital for shell shock." Eric thought of Ward copying and recopying his own journal entries, and the scar on his face echoing the scars on his wrists. Whatever his sins—

"Tuberculosis runs its course in two years," Duplessis said. "Monsieur Ward was at that sanatorium for five."

Eric and Avery turned to him in surprise.

"So I am coming with you. It is questions such as this that I may ask of the sanatorium doctors—I speak their language, oui?" Duplessis's expression hardened into a savage determination. "Besides, all I have heard since the funeral is that German espionage lies at the bottom of Colonel Russell's murder. Have they not done enough? I lost my son to the War, Monsieur Peterkin, and if nothing else, I owe it to *him*."

Truth be told, Eric was reluctant to continue to Switzerland. He wasn't sure why, unless it was a fear of confirming Gregory Ward's guilt. There was something gratifying about the man's blossoming romance with Lucy Russell, which Eric was loath to destroy, and he couldn't forget having his nose rubbed into Ward's tragic past the last time.

The sooner this was over with, the better. Unfortunately, the next train into Switzerland—a sleeper—wasn't until 8:30 p.m., which left Eric with nothing to do for the rest of the day but read and evaluate the manuscript that was his current work assignment—or try to, at least, while Duplessis and Avery attended to their own business.

> Harry checked the chambers of his revolver but found them empty. His highly sensitive ears detected the movements of the assassin at the end of the warehouse, getting closer. A normal man might have despaired, but the former Captain Harry Thompson was made of sterner stuff; besides, after Flanders, was this really a thing to fear? Harry waited until the assassin's footsteps drew within three yards of his hiding place, then hurled the useless revolver into the darkness. He was gratified to hear the assassin turn in alarm, and that was all he needed to launch an attack of his own.

"After Flanders, was this really a thing to fear?" Eric circled the line in pencil. Of course, there were men who drew strength from their experience in the trenches; but Eric hated to romanticise it. All it did was put him in more of a temper about the upcoming journey to neutral Switzerland.

By the time their train finally steamed out of the Gare de l'Est, Eric was in a morbid state of mind. He slept, if that was the right word, and woke again in the predawn darkness to an awareness of having drawn, obliquely, ever closer to where the trenches once were. They were stopped at Delle, which was on the Swiss border and still on the French side of the trenches; but they'd actually cross the border at Basel, and that would be on what was once the German side.

Eric sat up in his berth. Outside was darkness, faintly fading into light in the east, as dawn prepared to break over this far end of the trenches. Could he see any lingering sign of the War? Did he want to? The soft stirring of early risers reminded him of the barracks, of men rising at dawn for another day of anxiously awaiting death. It occurred to him that while the men of the Britannia might have been damaged by the War, none were so badly off that they couldn't still navigate society with ease. But if he was right about Ward's sanatorium treating shell shock rather than consumption . . . Eric shuddered.

This was it.

This was the source of his earlier reluctance, this gnawing anxiety over coming face-to-face with another pointed reminder of the War—

And then, without him having spotted so much as a muddy scar in the landscape, they were in the Swiss city of Basel, with the morning sun shining on spotless white walls and painted shutters, coloured roof tiles laid down in geometric patterns, flowers budding in window boxes . . . The air seemed cleaner, crisper, purer for having never known chlorine or mustard or phosgene. The War might have never happened.

Another train took them from Basel to Zurich, and yet another from Zurich to Chur, past the still waters of fathomless silver lakes reflecting jagged ridges of white rock striped with green forest. Eric spent the time forcing himself to listen as Duplessis described to him the treatments he'd seen at Seale-Hayne and Craiglockhart: "As for what to expect here, should this place turn out to be a similar hospital, I cannot tell you. Some places are more progressive than others, and some are less. During the War, for instance . . ."

"Yes?"

"It does not matter what the treatments were then. Look on the mountains: they would lend themselves well to the gentler methods of peaceful rehabilitation. You may hope for that."

A third train from Chur brought them to a lonely country station at sunset: Ward's sanatorium and its attached village were another hour's walk up the mountain.

"You must be joking," Avery grumbled.

"You are welcome to turn back, if you like," Duplessis shot back.

Reddening, Avery flexed his grip on his suitcase and straightened up. "I was only commenting on the inconvenience. Let's get on with it, shall we?"

Duplessis's barbs never quite crossed the line into rudeness, but there was a coldness in his attitude towards Avery that left the other man increasingly out of sorts. Eric waited until the alienist, as the most fluent of them in German, went to make arrangements for the final leg of their journey, then approached his friend.

"I'm quite all right," Avery said, his tone uncharacteristically brusque. "I know he doesn't like me, and hasn't since I mentioned spending the War in Argentina. Don't worry. It's nothing I haven't seen a hundred times before."

Though Duplessis's attitude was no doubt worsened by having lost a son to the War.

Snapping open his lighter, Avery pulled flame into a fresh clove cigarette and blew out scented smoke through clenched teeth. All indulgence in marrons glacés aside, it seemed that Avery was struggling with his own inner beast, much like Eric himself.

The village was a trim and well-kept collection of Alpine cottages spread out along the side of a mountain, with more churches and chapels than seemed reasonable for its population, and goat statues everywhere. It had, apparently, served for centuries as a stop on one of many pilgrimage routes to Santiago de Compostela in Spain: even before the creation of the sanatorium, its prosperity was derived from the accommodation of visitors.

The sanatorium itself loomed over the comparatively ancient village like a pretender to a baronial seat: an austere, whitewashed edifice festooned with wide wooden verandahs. Approaching in the early morning after a night at the local *gasthaus*, Eric was bemused to find those verandahs filled with consumptive patients in lounge chairs.

Not everything, he supposed with an inward laugh at himself, had to be about the War.

"That doesn't mean the doctors aren't all German spies," Avery muttered.

"If they are," Eric countered, feeling lighter than he had since leaving England, "then they're all retired, and we have nothing to fear; and if they're not retired, they'd be in the capitals of Europe rather than here in the middle of nowhere."

"Well, I don't like how everyone's staring at us."

It was true, every head on every verandah was turned in their direction; but the sanatorium director, meeting them outside the front door, was quick to dismiss the issue. "You are the most excitement they have seen in weeks. We do not like to excite our patients."

His name was Dr. Leonhard Keller, and he was a tall, aristocratic-looking gentleman with an excessively firm handshake. His English was fluent, if heavily accented; and he sported a clean, straight scar across one cheek, similar to Ward's. A relic of the War? But mention of the War elicited only a disdainful shrug. "That was nothing to do with us here in Switzerland."

He welcomed them into his office, a place of sun-drenched white walls and herringbone parquet, furnished in lacquered wood of utilitarian design. The one departure from this sleek modernity was the head of an enormous mountain goat stuffed and mounted on the wall, with horns the size of bull elephant tusks curving halfway across the room. An orderly brought them coffee and a platter of cold cuts and cheese, while Dr. Keller set a gramophone to play a Mozart concerto. Eric was reminded of Lady Alice welcoming him into her drawing room.

"I am afraid you will have to be satisfied with speaking only to me," Dr. Keller said as he took a throne-like seat under the mounted goat's head. "Karl Werner gave us his notice over a month ago and has not been back since. I do not know where he is now. May I ask, what is your interest in him?"

"His name came up in an inquiry we're conducting in England," said Eric. "Yes, we're sure it's the same man—the reference was quite specific. If he's not around, we'd be grateful for any information at all."

"What is there to say? He came looking for work, and we had work for him. Do you know what it is to run a tuberculosis facility? Not everyone wants the risk of catching the disease. Well. He said he was from Berlin, and that he no longer had any family. He worked hard and he kept to himself. I had no complaints. Is that all you wanted to know?"

"Surely, you must know more. What was he like?"

Dr. Keller's lips compressed briefly with impatience. "He was fond of his schnapps, and he tried for a while to become a drunkard. He did not have the temperament for it, however, and for that, I suppose we can be grateful. I take care of my workers, Mr. Peterkin, but it is not my business to be their friend."

"Why did he leave?"

"He did not say."

"You must have some suspicion."

"He was friendly with one of the patients. That patient died—as tuberculosis patients sometimes do. I suppose he was greatly affected by the loss, as I myself suffered the loss of a bottle of schnapps soon after the funeral. But he handed in his notice before I could confront him about the schnapps, and then he was gone."

"We know he was friendly with a patient by the name of Gregory Ward. Do you remember him?"

"You are yourself a friend of Mr. Ward?"

Eric nodded, and Avery followed suit. Duplessis seemed to have barely registered the question, being occupied with studying the academic credentials framed on the wall around the mounted goat's head.

Dr. Keller's impatience relaxed into amusement. "Mr. Ward! Such an irrepressible sense of humour. He kept things lively for all of us—perhaps too lively. I had to speak to him more than once about the rest both he and his fellow patients required. Did you know him well?"

"He was a member of my club before he came here; but I first met him only three weeks ago, when he came to have his membership reinstated."

Dr. Keller sat up in surprise, and then his brows came down in a fierce scowl. "You are lying to me. What is this about?"

"What? Of course I'm telling the truth. Why would you—"

"Mr. Ward died here two months ago. *He* was the friend I told you about, whose death affected Herr Werner so deeply. Now, I ask you again: What is this about?"

# JOB

"THERE MUST BE some mistake," Eric said. "You deal with a great many patients at a time. You must be thinking of someone else."

But Dr. Keller was adamant. "I know my patients. Mr. Ward is dead. His grave is in the local churchyard, if you care to see for yourself—with an epitaph in English, no less."

"But see here," Avery said. "If he's really dead, then who's the chap back in London? He's about so tall, with brownish-blond hair going white around the temples, looks to be about fifty, though he's supposed to be—what was it, Eric? Thirty-five? And he's got this scar, right here, just like yours, Doctor—"

Dr. Keller stood up. "You are describing Karl Werner."

A cloud passed before the sun, and for a moment, the stark brightness of the office was suffused in muted greys, and a chill that had nothing to do with the mountains ran up Eric's spine. This explained so much. The hint of a German accent? It was natural, not something picked up from his time in Switzerland. Edith Cavell's execution? Eric hadn't misheard, nor had "Ward" misspoken. Karl Werner had been present, possibly even as part of the firing squad. And the passages copied from the real Ward's journal? Not a memory aid, but practice at mimicking Ward's handwriting.

And . . . Oh God, Lucy! If this was all true, then the poor girl was being deceived in the worst way possible.

Eric cleared his throat. "They were similar in appearance, weren't they?"

Dr. Keller had to pause to consider the question. "Superficially, perhaps—much as Mr. Ferrett and I are similar in appearance, having the same height and colouring. Herr Werner looked a decade older, though he was, in fact, a year younger; and of course, there was the scar. We were not in the habit of mistaking one for the other."

Given a five-year absence and the known ravages of a wasting disease, even a superficial resemblance might be sufficient to fool a few people. Ward's closest friend in the Army was Andrew Russell, and Andrew Russell was dead. None of the Russell widows, not even Madam Eliot, had ever actually met him. But Colonel Russell had. Surely *he'd* have seen through the masquerade? Or was their acquaintance less than the Colonel made it out to be?

Perhaps the Colonel *had* seen the truth. Perhaps that was why he had to be killed.

Dr. Keller stood up. "I am sorry that you have come all the way out here only to learn that you have been duped. But there is nothing I can do."

"No," said Eric, shaking away the last vestiges of his shock. He wanted to rush back to London immediately. He wanted to wire his sister with a warning. But first—"There *is* something you can do. We need to know everything about both Gregory Ward and Karl Werner. There is, you see, the matter of a murder."

The room that the real Gregory Ward occupied as a patient had already been given over to another patient, and there was nothing of him left there. Dr. Keller showed them instead to the attic, where Ward's meagre belongings had been neatly stored away in the same steamer trunk with which he'd arrived.

The sanatorium director was quite forthcoming, now he'd been made aware of the stakes. Perhaps he felt responsible for both the late Gregory Ward and the errant Karl Werner, much as an officer feels responsible for the men in his charge. He said, "Mr. Ward was with us for five years, with minimal improvement. Most patients finish their treatment in two years, one way or another. I believe that what ailed him was not tuberculosis, but *cancer of the lung*. Regardless, he came to believe he would die here, and against *that*, no amount of mountain air can prevail."

"A misdiagnosis," Duplessis murmured. "Of course."

Eric, meanwhile, made a quick search of Ward's trunk. Clothes, all old but well-made; a spectacle case; a set of watercolour paints and brushes. The paintings themselves were tucked into a narrow space behind the trunk. Avery picked one at random and held it up to the dormer window's light. He turned it around in a futile effort to determine which way was up, and finally said, "He wasn't much good, was he?"

"It was something to do," Dr. Keller replied. "We could not allow him the excitement of daily practice. He was supposed to be resting, after all."

Eric closed the trunk and pushed it back in place. It reminded him of searching Werner's room at the Britannia, which made him wonder: Why go to the Britannia Club at all? Colonel Russell couldn't be the only member to have known the real Gregory Ward.

"Much of Mr. Ward's belongings disappeared with Herr Werner when he left," Dr. Keller said. "They were friends, as you know, and Mr. Ward made it clear that whatever he owned, the other as good as owned; he intended to make a will saying so, but he died before a lawyer could be summoned. Herr Werner didn't care about the mere goods and chattel. He snapped at me once, when I referred to his friend as dead. Gregory Ward lived on, he said: he knew that better than anyone."

Duplessis frowned. "A curious friendship. Monsieur Werner was a German soldier, I think? Monsieur Ward mentioned it in his journal. A few years earlier, and they might have killed each other on the battlefield."

"Herr Werner owed the other man his life."

Eric recalled Werner, as Ward, showing him the scars on his wrists. He'd spoken of "someone" caring enough to save his life. Did he mean Ward? Regardless, the pieces were falling into place: Colonel Russell knew "Ward" for an imposter, sought to confirm his suspicions, and was killed for it. Did it follow that this Karl Werner was the same Karl von Werner named by the apprehended members of the Parisian spy ring? But what about the woman's footprint? And why risk exposure at the Britannia Club?

Dr. Keller looked around the dusty attic room, then beckoned them back out to the corridor. "We have yet to assign a new member of staff to Herr Werner's room. That is what you wish to see next, yes?"

It was. Dr. Keller accordingly took them to a room as austere as a monk's cell, and crowded once all four men were inside. Beside the narrow iron-framed cot, a chest of drawers held a few books on top and looked barely adequate to contain even what little Eric had packed for this jaunt into the continent. The only respite was a dormer window just high enough to look out of, with a view of the village basking in the Alpine sun. It reminded Eric of the sky over Whitechapel, as seen from the wide bay windows of the Working Lads Institute. He'd thought of hope, then: of impoverished youngsters reaching for a now-attainable future . . .

*Second chances are beyond all riches.*

"Werner has scars from a failed suicide attempt," he said. "Was that what you meant about him owing Ward his life?"

Dr. Keller nodded. "He was unhappy, and he could find no solace in schnapps. The arrival of Mr. Ward worsened his misery: he confided in me that he recognised Mr. Ward from the War, though the other man seemed unaware of any previous meeting. After a month of this, Herr Werner took a razor to his wrists and settled into a bathtub to die."

"There was no struggle to wrestle the razor away from him, I take it?"

"No. Mr. Ward found him and called for help, all the while trying to stop the bleeding himself with a tourniquet improvised from the belt of his dressing gown. Herr Werner was too weak to resist by then, and he became a patient in his own right for a while afterwards. He had a small pistol, which I think he would have used if he possessed the bullets for it; I took that away and did not return it until he left. I also took away his straight razor and suggested he grow out his beard. But Mr. Ward visited—against my orders—and provided him with a safety razor he'd got from an American comrade in the War. From that moment, the two were inseparable."

Ward would have felt responsible for Werner. Eric understood that impulse all too well.

Avery, meanwhile, had picked up one of the books from the chest of drawers. "This one's in English. Edgar Allan Poe, bookmarked at 'Ligeia.'" He flipped back to the front and examined the bookplate. "Eric, look: Karl Josef von Werner. I told you they were the same person."

"That's still not proof, Avery." All the same, Eric had to wonder. Had Colonel Russell recognised Werner not simply as an imposter, but as a former German spy? And was that the reason for his sudden interest in Andrew Russell's death?

Avery turned to Dr. Keller. "Forgive me if I'm wrong, but doesn't the 'von' prefix mean some sort of aristocratic background? You've been calling him just plain 'Werner' instead of 'von Werner' all this time."

Dr. Keller glanced into the book as Avery held it out, and his mouth twitched. "Unless his family came from a place called Werner. But I will say that we all suspected he was highborn. He spoke in a very precise *Hochdeutsch*, for one thing, and the accent grew stronger rather than weaker when he drank."

Why was such a man sweeping the floors for an isolated Alpine sanatorium?

Eric looked out the window at the wide, open vista beyond. The little white buildings of the village blazed in the sun like blocks of salt and sand; from one chapel wall, a towering mural of St. Christopher ushered missionaries on to foreign fields. "Werner's scar. He lied that it was from his suicide attempt. But if he really did come from the upper classes, and if he had the education to match . . . It's a mensur scar, isn't it? Something they do at a lot of German and Austrian universities: duellists inflict these scars on each other, and having one is supposed to be a sign of courage and masculine worth—"

He looked around at Dr. Keller, whose own scar stood witness to the practice. But Dr. Keller's expression had turned cold: he seemed to have retreated back into the aloofness with which he'd greeted them earlier. He said, "Herr Werner claimed it was from a bayonet, but nobody believed it."

The silver chime of a church bell echoed through the crystal air. Eric checked his watch and grimaced. "We'd better go. If we don't catch the three o'clock from Chur, we'll be delayed another twenty-four hours—and that's assuming the trains are all on time and running perfectly."

Dr. Keller gave a start and shook off whatever it was that had offended him. "I have a motorcar. Allow me to take you to Chur myself."

They needed proof of Gregory Ward's death, like a death certificate or a signed statement by a reputable witness. While Dr. Keller set about obtaining these, Eric hurried down to the local post office. He shot off a wire to Penny, warning her of the imposter Ward. Forewarned was forearmed, and Penny would have insisted she could take care of herself; but Eric couldn't be satisfied with that. After some consideration, he wired Cully an instruction to send Harvey. Hopefully, Werner—he'd have to start thinking of "Ward" as "Werner"—wouldn't be standing at Cully's shoulder when the telegram arrived.

And then, there was the police—but Duplessis stopped him. "Not yet. I think Dr. Keller has more to tell, and I have a theory about what is happening. After you have heard it all, then you may do as you please."

Eric hesitated. Duplessis had no love for the Germans, but he was also an alienist. If he thought that special care should be taken in approaching a German threat . . . Eric stepped away from the postmaster and indicated that his business there was done.

To Duplessis, he remarked, "I thought you'd have more to say to your fellow doctor. Shoptalk, if nothing else."

"I observe. That is all." They left the post office and turned their steps towards the *gasthaus* where Dr. Keller was to meet them with his motorcar. "I observe, for instance, that a significant number of the menial staff at the sanatorium are young men: many with scars or signs of old injuries, at least two with nervous tics, and all speaking German instead of the local Romansh. Which may not mean anything—German *is* the official language of the region, after all—but it occurs to me that the sanatorium shares much with what I saw at Seale-Hayne: a peaceful environment, close to nature, with simple work in which an old soldier may lose his troubles."

Eric looked sharply around and nearly tripped over himself. All his earlier anxiety, relieved on seeing that the sanatorium really was set up to treat tuberculosis, seemed to kick him in the gut. "Shell shock?"

"Who knows? Monsieur Keller may be telling the truth when he says that the locals do not care to expose themselves to disease, but I wonder if that is the whole truth."

A few more steps brought them to the *gasthaus*. Dr. Keller's motorcar was already waiting there with their suitcases piled into the back, but the doctor himself was outside the church across the road, speaking to Avery: "Yes, Switzerland was precisely the same for me, which is why I never go back—"

He stopped short at Eric's approach and beckoned them all into the churchyard, to a peaceful grave facing the morning sun. "I thought you might want to pay your respects before we left."

*Gregory Algernon Ward*
*1887 – 1925*
*On, Ward, to glory.*

"Seems he died with his humour intact," Avery remarked. "I suppose there's no question of foul play?"

"None," Dr. Keller replied firmly. "I was there to the end."

Duplessis, looking solemn, stepped forward and laid a hand on the sun-warmed gravestone. Eric followed suit. Neither man said anything, but Eric thought: *I'm sorry, Ward. Werner was your friend, and I'm sure you never imagined it would come to this. But for what it's worth, I'm sorry.*

# ANASTASIA

"HAVE YOU HEARD of Madame Anna Tchaikovsky?" Duplessis asked, once they were on the road to Chur.

Avery, reading the Poe anthology he'd borrowed from Karl Werner's room, glanced back from the front passenger seat. "Tchaikovsky, the Russian composer? You mean his wife?"

"You are thinking of *Antonina* Tchaikovsky. And while she is an interesting case in her own right, it is the other who is of relevance."

It was not quite noon, and the sun was blazing from a cloudless blue sky onto a river rushing along beside them, swollen with the spring thaw. By Eric's estimate, they should be in Chur before one; and while it wouldn't get them into England any earlier, the extra time should be sufficient proof against the vagaries of train travel. In the meantime, what did this Madame Anna Tchaikovsky have to do with anything?

Duplessis shifted into a corner of the back seat so he could address everyone else in the motorcar. "Five years ago in Berlin, a young woman attempted suicide by jumping from a bridge into the *Landwehrkanal*. She was rescued and sent to an asylum, where she demonstrated no memory of who she was. Another patient identified her as the Grand Duchess Tatiana of Russia, which brought in a parade of Russian émigrés, some of them very close to the former imperial family, to determine the truth of this claim. When it was concluded that this woman was not the Grand Duchess Tatiana, she pointed out that she'd never actually made that claim herself. No, she was the Grand Duchess *Anastasia*, and that has been her story since. She goes by Anna Tchaikovsky now, a convenient alias, and she lives on the good will of her supporters."

"I take it," Eric said, "that you don't believe her claims. You think Anna Tchaikovsky is, like Karl Werner, carrying on an elaborate ruse."

"I think that Anna Tchaikovsky is and always has been an ordinary German peasant. But I do not think she is lying, per se. It is my humble opinion that she really and truly believes herself to be the Grand Duchess Anastasia."

Dr. Keller glanced back from his driver's seat, his interest piqued. "You mean Herr Werner now believes himself to be Mr. Ward? He gave no sign of it when we last spoke."

"I met him on the ferry from Calais, and he presented himself then as an English gentleman by the name of Gregory Ward. If his intention was merely to commit fraud, would it not be better to remain hidden until he arrived in London? And once there, would it not be better to limit the deception to a meeting with a bank manager, transfer all of Gregory Ward's assets to his own account, then disappear?"

Eric frowned. "Or he could save himself the bank transfer by settling down somewhere else as Ward, far from anyone who'd recognise him. You're right, and I've been asking myself that very question all day. Why go to the Britannia Club and risk being exposed?"

"Because he is walking in the footsteps of his friend, in the places his friend would frequent. In his mind, there is no fraud to be exposed. It is not that he wishes to pass as his deceased friend, but that he believes himself to *be* that deceased friend. He is not simply *living as* Monsieur Ward. He *is* Monsieur Ward."

The theory sounded preposterous, and yet . . . Eric remembered the faces of soldiers suffering from shell shock in the War, and he'd heard stories of men who'd come home seemingly sane, only to fall apart later at some innocuous trigger. And what about the rumours of men who lost hours, if not days, during which they had no idea what they'd been doing? Duplessis was the expert in this mysterious field, and he was right: a sane man would have conducted his deception differently.

"But how?" Dr. Keller asked. "How could this come to be?"

*The War*, Eric thought; but Duplessis said, "You know the state of the German economy in the years following the War, of course?"

Everyone nodded, even Avery. Just two years ago, one could light a fire with a bundle of German Papiermarks and it would still be cheaper than tearing up old newspapers for tinder. It had taken the abolition of the Papiermark in favour of the new Rentenmark to stop prices from doubling every two days. By then, many once-prosperous Germans had been rendered destitute and desperate for work of any sort, anywhere, solely to survive.

"We do not know the specifics," Duplessis said, "but circumstances suggest that Madame Tchaikovsky and Monsieur Werner have this in common: they were both ruined by the collapsing German economy after the War. Why else would a seemingly highborn, well-educated German—with a mensur scar, speaking *Hochdeutsch*—be sweeping the floors of a Swiss sanatorium?"

What must it have been like, Eric wondered, to return from the War and find one's home spiralling into ruin? What would he himself have done if he'd found Penny dead, the house in Barchester gone, and the British pound worth nothing? He imagined Karl von Werner turning his gaze westwards, to France and to England, with a heart screaming for vengeance . . .

Dr. Keller seemed excited by the idea. "I always thought that when Herr Werner spoke of having no family, he meant a recent loss. That left a void, but his mind survived. Mr. Ward came to fill that void, and then Mr. Ward died. This time, his mind broke. He seemed sane enough when he left us, but now I wonder. If anything, he was *too* sane, as though Mr. Ward's death had never happened, and he had no cause to grieve."

"These delusions do not spring fully formed into being, not even into the void left by such loss. Consider Madame Tchaikovsky.

When she first arrives at the asylum, she is a blank slate, completely broken by tragedy. It is another patient who connects her with a grand duchess, and now she is confronted with a history of plenty and privilege, something so different from her present ruin that she leaps for it, embraces it . . . It is a comfort. She tells herself that, perhaps, she really is a grand duchess, and perhaps that world of privilege really is hers by right. Perhaps the claim frightens her, so she settles on Anastasia, the youngest and thus the least of the daughters of the Tsar. And then, her mind still weak from shock and tragedy, she convinces herself that this is the truth. She really is the Grand Duchess Anastasia. The mechanism by which she copes with her situation becomes a reality that she cannot put down—an *idée fixe*. It becomes, in a word, *her*."

Dr. Keller looked grim. "I think I understand. Herr Werner never truly recovered from whatever misery it was that drove him to attempt suicide. It was only his friendship with Mr. Ward that held him together, but once his friend was gone . . ."

"It is likely that Monsieur Werner has repressed feelings of envy for his friend. Like Madame Tchaikovsky, perhaps he begins by imagining what his life might be like if he really were this more prosperous version of himself instead. This is compounded by a desire for his friend to not have died. He begins to tell himself that Gregory Ward has not died, because *he* is Gregory Ward. The mechanism of coping, the delusion that Ward lives, that he is Ward, simply becomes *him*. Monsieur Ferrett, where did you say was the bookmark in that book?"

"What? At 'Ligeia.' Why?"

"Do you know the story?"

"I think so. This man marries a spiritually powerful woman named Ligeia, who dies. Much later, he remarries, only to have his second wife die almost immediately after. He's sitting up alone at night for the second wife's wake—better him than me—when the body comes back to life. But when the funeral shroud comes off, it's Ligeia, the first wife, underneath."

"Oui. One dead woman resurrects herself in the flesh of another. I have no doubt that this tale played a part in Monsieur Werner's delusion."

Eric cleared his throat. "So he goes to England to claim his rightful place. Right. And Colonel Russell?"

"A man in Monsieur Werner's condition might react with violence if confronted and pressed on the matter."

Perhaps the first shot from Ward's revolver had been fired by Colonel Russell and aimed at Werner; and in the ensuing struggle, Werner managed to turn the revolver on the Colonel. Eric said, "Or Werner knows exactly who he is. He stole Ward's identity and killed Colonel Russell to keep it."

But again: Why risk exposure at the Britannia Club?

Avery said, "Have you considered that Ward might have wanted it this way? He wasn't able to get a will written in time, so on his deathbed, he told Werner to take his place instead."

Duplessis scoffed and rolled on as though Avery hadn't spoken. "You understand why I hesitate to set the police on Monsieur Ward-Werner. They are not gentle with the alienated, the police. They will confront him with force and do immeasurable damage in the process. If I am wrong, we lose nothing in staying our hand another twenty-four hours and dealing with him ourselves; but if I am right . . . If I am right, M. Werner is on the brink of sacrificing his own memories in favour of these other false memories plucked from the life of his dead friend. And that is a great tragedy." His voice trembled with emotion. "A man who loses his history, he loses everything."

Duplessis's theory still seemed outlandish to Eric's mind, but he couldn't dismiss it so easily. No one had ever heard of shell shock a decade ago, and now the halls of the Britannia were steeped in its malevolence. Was this another manifestation of it? Was Werner that unstable?

Did it really follow that he must have killed Colonel Russell?

Arriving in Chur with an hour's breathing space before the next train to Zurich, Eric spotted a gun shop near the train station; and recalling the carton of ammunition he'd found among Ward's—Werner's—socks, he went in to make a few inquiries.

The gunsmith was an otherwise nondescript gentleman with owl-like eyes magnified behind thick spectacles. He was unfamiliar with either a "Karl Werner" or a "Gregory Ward," but he did remember an Englishman with what he'd at first assumed was a mensur scar; yes, about so tall, with just that colour of hair, of perhaps forty-five or fifty years. This Englishman's German was passable, if somewhat broken, and he wanted bullets for a Bayard 1908 pocket pistol.

So, this early on his journey to England, Werner was already presenting himself as English, even adopting Ward's faulty command of German. Giving a false name was easy; hobbling one's ability to communicate was more of a challenge. Would Werner have done that if he were not in the grip of a delusion, as Duplessis believed? Or was he simply that thorough in his deception? They wouldn't really know until they got back to London and spoke to him again.

Returning to the station, Eric found Avery and Dr. Keller with their collected suitcases, deep in conversation once again. They fell silent at his approach, and Avery elbowed the doctor, hissing, "Go on. Tell him."

What was this about?

Dr. Keller cleared his throat awkwardly. "The Karl Werner I knew is not a killer."

"His idea of Gregory Ward might be," Eric replied.

"Some things are bred too deeply to be swept away by a mere delusion. For Herr Werner, it is his nobility." With evident reluctance, Dr. Keller touched his scar. "I will tell you this if you tell no one else. This scar of mine? I . . . I made it myself, with a razor. I had neither the money nor the pedigree when I was a student at Heidelberg to enter the sort of club where such things could be earned honestly. Herr Werner found out. He did not sneer at me, or laugh. He told me instead that . . . that my nobility went deeper than mere scars, because of my work at the sanatorium. That was the sort of man he was. That was the sort of thing he valued. I cannot believe that he would forget it even if he believed himself to be someone else. Karl von Werner, at his very core, is not a murderer."

Beet red from embarrassment, Dr. Keller snapped a sharp bow, muttered a significantly less-sharp "*auf Wiedersehen*," and hurried away. Eric watched him go, then turned to Avery with brows raised in question.

"Well," said Avery, "that was hardly the sort of thing he'd tell an old warhorse like yourself, or a jingoistic Frenchman like Duplessis, was it?"

"When I found you at the church earlier—"

"We'd been talking about missing the War, me in Argentina and him here in Switzerland. I thought he was perfectly justified, being actually Swiss by birth; but after all his time at Heidelberg, he said he felt like a fraud."

Eric could fill in the blanks from there. Keller had scarred himself in an effort to pass as the sort of gentleman Werner actually was. It must have turned his world upside down when Werner appeared at his door begging for work.

"That explains his particular interest in Werner," Eric mused. "And what of Duplessis himself? Rather curious how determined he is to see that Karl Werner gets the help he needs, now he's got it in his head that Werner might be another neurotic case. Professional interest? I got the impression when he decided to join us that he was eager to take the fight to a German enemy—for the son he'd lost to the War."

"That's one way of putting it."

"What do you mean?"

"The afternoon before we left Paris, while you were stalking about like a caged tiger, he visited his son—the same son he'd 'lost' in the War—in the psychiatric ward of the Saint-Maurice Hospital. Amnesia, I think."

*Duplessis, laying his hand solemnly on Ward's gravestone. And later: "A man who loses his history . . . he loses everything . . ."*

It was nearing time to board their train. Picking up his suitcase, Eric said, "Poor fellow! No wonder he turned to psychology after the War, and no wonder he feels as he does about the Germans—"

Avery's response was a muffled curse as the Poe anthology he'd obtained from Werner's room clattered to the station floor and was accidentally kicked several feet away. Eric picked it up as his friend struggled to disentangle himself from his overlong scarf.

"Honestly, Avery. If this is how you treat your possessions—"

Something fell out of the book, and Eric stopped short on seeing what it was: a torn envelope tucked between the pages as a bookmark, addressed to a Monique Garnier in Paris.

# DELUSION OR DECEPTION?

MONIQUE GARNIER. SHE didn't exist. She'd been invented by German spies to wheedle information out of Flora Grace—Mrs. David Russell as she was then. There was no way Werner could have got his hands on this envelope addressed to her without a connection to her gang of spies—no doubt, as the same Karl von Werner named by Inspector Michaud.

Eric barely noticed the whole process of boarding their train. As soon as he was in his seat, he seized both envelope and book for a closer examination. Nothing in the envelope, of course: only Flora's elegant penmanship and her misplaced trust. As for the book, he dug out Monique Garnier's letters to compare against the bookplate. Karl Josef von Werner. It wasn't a large enough sample for certainty, but the handwriting *looked* identical. There was that curious backwards flick on the tail of the lowercase *F* . . . Was that standard German penmanship?

No. There was a dedication pencilled onto the title page: *Für meinen Bruder—fröhliche Weihnachten*. "For my brother—happy Christmas." It betrayed none of the same idiosyncrasies despite this unnamed sibling having presumably learnt penmanship from the same copybooks.

"You were right," Eric told Avery. "It's the same Karl von Werner. He's the one who actually wrote all those letters to Flora. This ties everything together: Colonel Russell, Ward, Paris. Everything."

Avery, to his credit, refrained from saying *I told you so*. "I'd have thought that a trained spy would get rid of anything that could implicate him. All the letters from Miss Grace as well as the envelopes they came in."

Eric shook his head. "Implications work both ways, and an informant, especially an unwitting one, has more to lose than a spy. You hold on to everything in case you can use it to extract more information later, and that's true no matter which side of a war you're on."

"Are you saying the War Office engages in blackmail?"

"There is a reason I didn't follow my father's footsteps into military intelligence."

Outside, the sun blazed on snowcapped peaks and fathomless lakes of still, glassy water. Inside, Eric sat back and tried to organise his thoughts. Karl Werner was a spy trying to extract intelligence from Colonel Russell's daughter-in-law. Andrew Russell discovered the ruse, investigated, and was killed. His friend, Gregory Ward, gave evidence that ultimately led to the downfall of Werner's spy ring. Werner went on to lose everything after the War, winding up as a caretaker at a Swiss sanatorium . . .

What a bitter coincidence it must have been, for Ward to wind up at that same sanatorium, and then for it to be Ward who saved him from suicide! Who'd have guessed? Ward linked Werner back to Colonel Russell, who knew Ward well enough to spot an impersonation, and . . .

Was it delusion or deception?

Eric picked up the book again and studied the pencilled dedication. *Für meinen Bruder*. Werner no longer had any family, according to Dr. Keller. Would he have left behind this memento of a lost sibling if he were even partially himself?

Whatever the case, Scotland Yard would be merciless. If—no, *when*—it came out that "Ward" was not only a German imposter, but a former German intelligence officer whose primary job it was to deceive innocent Englishwomen into betraying their brothers, husbands, and sons, it might not even matter what he was accused of. There were isolated police cells where anything might happen. There were other prisoners who, whatever their sins, still sang "God Save the King" with patriotic gusto. And if he did survive to see trial, there would be jurors who laid annual wreaths of poppies on memorials over empty graves.

The question of whether he'd actually murdered Colonel Russell would be lost in the confusion, just as the question of who killed Andrew Russell was lost when the French police rounded up the spies he was chasing. And what if Karl Werner was innocent? Could they hand him over to the police, knowing he'd be condemned regardless?

*Private Dent sat shivering in the cramped confines of the dugout. "Shell shock," his officer commanding sneered. "Good men get over it soon enough, and Dent had over a week between his last so-called spell and his desertion yesterday. You're free to talk to him if you like, Peterkin, not that it'll make any difference. If the court-martial doesn't end with a firing squad at dawn, I'll eat my hat."*

*Of course, the shelling fifteen minutes later rendered a court-martial quite unnecessary . . .*

Arresting Werner might be no different from court-martialling Private Dent, but did they have a choice? If it was delusion, Werner would have to be apprehended as a potential threat to those around him. If it was deception, he'd have to be apprehended as a thief.

On the other hand, there was one more thing they were in danger of forgetting in the excitement of these revelations: the symbol on the real Ward's service revolver and on the bloody footprint at the scene of Andrew Russell's murder. Where did that fit in?

Avery and Duplessis spent the journey from Chur to Basel reading their respective literature, and slept from Basel to Paris. Eric did not.

The twelve noon from Paris was a fast train with a dedicated ferry connection, promising an arrival at Victoria by half past seven. Eric, however, still had his Vauxhall stashed away in Dover, and he practically leapt from the ferry the moment it docked to run for the rented garage. Five minutes later, they were racing the train for London, with both Avery and Duplessis united for once in urging Eric towards caution.

They didn't drop to a more sensible speed until they saw the clockfaces of Big Ben shining before them like yellow moons in the otherwise moonless night. Crossing Westminster Bridge, Eric abruptly turned onto the Embankment and pulled up to the kerb. He stared ahead to the turrets of Scotland Yard and said, "We should inform the police."

"You do not sound convinced," Duplessis observed.

Eric shook his head. What little sleep he'd got last night had been haunted by dreams of Private Dent's aborted court-martial, and the vacant stares of a dozen shell-shocked soldiers. Rationally, however . . . "Dr. Keller mentioned a pocket pistol—a Bayard 1908—and I happen to know not only that Werner still carries it, but that he's now got the ammunition for it. It might be better to go in with police reinforcements, in case he gets violent."

"Then we must be careful to give him no cause to draw his gun. Let me speak to him and assess the situation, and we can call the police with our findings afterwards."

"How long would that take? Suppose I just drop you off at the club and come back for the police? That would give you about half an hour, I think, before the police got there—"

"That won't work," said Avery. "Duplessis and I can't just walk into the Britannia and demand to speak to Captain Ward. We're not his friends, and we're not members. You're the only one who can do that. And do you really think Inspector Crane is going to listen if Eric Peterkin tells him to be careful of a potential neurotic case? You need Duplessis here for that."

Eric ground his teeth. He did not like the idea of confronting an armed man without some form of backup or insurance.

Perhaps if he could get his hands on a firearm. He'd sold off his Webley from the War after having been inexplicably denied a firearm certificate—required by law since 1920, and supposedly trivial for any *Englishman* to obtain. He did have friends who'd kept their sidearms. Forrester, now: that man collected the damned things, but visiting him would require too much of a detour. Alternatively, perhaps Madam Eliot would be looking in on the basement repairs, and he could borrow the pocket pistol out of her purse. Then again, deluded or not, Werner was in the position of having nothing to lose. Such a man *might* shoot an unarmed adversary, but certainly *would* shoot an armed one.

"We'll ask him to dine with us," Eric decided, glancing back at the illuminated dials of Big Ben. Hopefully, Werner wouldn't have left to find his dinner already. "Duplessis, you can talk to him over food and try to determine how far gone he is, or if he's gone at all. With enough people around, he might hesitate to draw his gun; and I'll have a few attendants nearby, ready to wrestle it away if he does. You'll have until the end of the meal to make your assessment—"

"Impossible!"

"I'm sorry. You can probe further afterwards, but only if we convince the police first that this is a case of mental alienation. We can't do that without some initial assessment. Meanwhile, there is no way that the attendants I enlist to ensure your safety will remain completely blasé once they know the truth. If we don't get Werner either behind bars or in a padded cell by the end of the night, there will be blood."

"Ward! Heading out to dinner? Cully mentioned you've been exploring the culinary landscape of London. What you've got against our own dining room here, I do not know."

Werner stopped in the Britannia Club lobby as Eric approached him. His face broke into an easy, guileless grin. "One does like a bit of variety," he said.

Eric couldn't tell if there existed anything more behind the imposter's words. He was keenly aware of the clink of silverware coming from the dining room, and the rich aroma of roast venison set his stomach yearning. Cully was behind the front desk; gentlemen wandered by, pausing to glance up at the Roster of the Fallen before continuing up the stairs. Someone on the gallery above let out a burst of discreetly stifled laughter, and the Knights of the Round Table gazed down from their painting on the grand staircase landing as they'd done for close to a hundred years. It was probably Eric's own imagination, but he thought Kay, in the shadow behind Arthur, looked a little smug.

The Britannia Club had gone back to a complacent normalcy in his absence. It was as though Colonel Russell had never been murdered, and the resulting upheaval had never happened. But here was Karl Werner, nevertheless, calling himself Gregory Ward—delusion or deception? Eric had to find out.

"You know Dr. Duplessis and my old friend Avery, of course? We were about to get something to eat, and Duplessis was telling me about his research into treatment for shell shock. Not a lot of difference between that and the treatment for consumption, I was saying, but you'd know far more about that, wouldn't you?"

"I was rather curious about your experiences," Duplessis said. "We did not speak of it the last time, as I recall."

"Well—" Werner began, but Eric wasn't about to risk him excusing himself.

"Tell you what. Why don't you dine in tonight and talk it over? I'm sure you've forgotten the miracle of our salmon mousse by now, and need to be reminded. I've got some business with Cully, so if you could order me the—let's see—lamb chops. Yes. And the salmon mousse to start, of course. We'll worry about the pudding later."

Eric hurried off before Werner could protest. From the corner of his eye, he saw Avery and Duplessis walk into the dining room with a somewhat befuddled Werner between them. They'd been lucky to arrive just in time to catch Werner before he left, and there was something to be said for trapping Werner with the task of ordering on his behalf. However, it left Eric with no time to make the proposed arrangements with the attendants beforehand. He'd have to do that now, taking him away from the action, and he could only hope that his co-conspirators would be adept at improvising over any unforeseen developments.

Cully, at his post behind the reception desk, hailed Eric as he approached. "I've left Monday's stocktaking on your desk—"

Eric shushed him. "We'll talk in your office. Come on."

Stepping around the reception desk, Eric ushered Cully through to the little cubby sandwiched between the cloak room and the office corridor. Glancing back out to the lobby, Eric satisfied himself that Werner was not making a run for it, then shut the door and whispered, "Did you get my wire?"

Cully nodded, suddenly anxious. "I sent Harvey to your sister, like you asked. What was that all about?"

Eric had refrained from telling Cully about Werner's impersonation of Ward in his communication. In the first place, the full story would be too many words for a telegram; and in the second, Cully was not so smooth an actor as to maintain a know-nothing facade through twenty-four hours of dealing with Werner. He told Cully now, as quickly as he could, and watched Cully's eyes grow wider.

"Sir! Does that mean he killed Colonel Russell?"

It did seem to follow, but only because the obvious motive—to avoid exposure—seemed so overwhelming. All the same, Eric couldn't help but doubt. "That's a question for later, Cully. Right now, I need a couple of attendants to keep an eye on Ward—Werner, I mean. They'll have to be quick on their feet and inconspicuous. Our man's got a gun, and I want someone ready to pounce before he has a chance to draw it. At the same time, I don't want him to notice he's being watched."

Cully nodded. "You want Harris and O'Mara. I've known those two to pop up out of nowhere to catch things before anyone even noticed they'd been knocked over."

Harris was the attendant at the back door when Eric left the Vauxhall in the service court earlier. Eric had instructed him to bring their suitcases to his office, and he knew the man would now be cooling his heels in the staff room. Indeed, there he was; along with another attendant, a burly fellow named Parrish, whom Cully dispatched to fetch O'Mara before Eric could decide it would be better, in the interest of time, to settle for him instead. Well, three heads would be better than two, or so one hoped.

Parrish returned with O'Mara in a thankfully short time. Harris, Parrish, and O'Mara . . . They were a keen-looking trio—two blades and a bludgeon—alert and interested by this prospect of something unusual.

*Your men, Peterkin. You know what you have to do.*

There was a subtle reassurance in slipping back into the boots of Lieutenant Peterkin, and Eric understood, clearer than ever, how Cully could panic in one moment and calmly carry out his orders in the next—why Madam Eliot found comfort in the demands of her career. It was easier to focus on *what* had to be done than to dwell on *why*.

Once briefed, the three attendants slipped out the door and down the back stairs to the kitchen. They'd approach the dining room that way and become the party's most attentive servers. Cully went with them, to tell the waiters what was happening. That left Lieutenant Peterkin alone in the staff room, deflating back down into his civvies. He drew in a deep breath and let it out in a long sigh. There was a relief in seeing a mission set on its course. All he needed now was to join the unwitting party and pretend that nothing was amiss.

Eric adjusted his collar, crossed the back stair landing to the office corridor—and froze.

The light was on in his office.

It hadn't been when he passed this way just ten minutes earlier to gather his men for the mission. Who could be in there? Eric stole cautiously forwards and looked inside.

Werner was standing among the suitcases, and in his hand was the book Avery had brought with him from the sanatorium—Werner's own book, the Edgar Allan Poe anthology, with his name written in the bookplate. Harris must have left it on the desk when he brought the suitcases in.

Eric swore inwardly. The best-laid plans, indeed. Deception or delusion? If the former, then the jig was up: Werner knew they were onto him. If the latter . . . Did he recognise the book? Did he know what it represented?

Perhaps he could be trapped here if Eric closed and locked the door—but then there was the window. In that moment of hesitation, Werner turned and their eyes met.

"Hullo, Peterkin." Werner's tone seemed pleasant enough. "You were taking rather a while, and I thought I'd come look for you. Instead, I found this. The others didn't say anything about having just come back from a holiday."

Eric stepped into the office and closed the door behind him. He wished he still had his old Webley, and never mind any justification as to the likelihood of Werner shooting at an armed adversary versus an unarmed one: he'd still feel safer with something to even the field between them.

"Duplessis had his research," Eric said, trying to hide his readiness to jump on Werner if necessary. "And Avery had a sudden craving for marrons glacés. He's got a box of them in his suitcase, and I'm sure he won't mind if I got it out for the table."

"Is that so?" Werner's eyes flickered down to the open book in his hand. "Whose book is this, then? It's not your name on the bookplate."

"I got it secondhand. Why?"

"I knew a Karl von Werner once. He's dead now."

Werner snapped the book shut and laid it down on the desk. He had to be contained, regardless of any questions as to delusion and deception. All Eric had to do was keep him busy. Cully and the attendants must be wondering by now about Werner's absence from the dining room. Perhaps they were hoping that Eric himself had met him in the lobby and was shepherding him back. It might take another minute to realise that that was not going to happen.

"We should be returning to the others," Werner said. His lips retained the shape of his easy, guileless smile. His eyes were hard.

"We should," Eric replied, without moving from the door. If Werner were to attempt an escape through the window, would Eric be able to cross the room and stop him in the time it would take to break the glass?

Werner's fingers twitched upwards, towards his breast pocket.

Eric tensed.

A sudden rap on the door made them both jump. "Eric!" It was Avery, speaking in an urgent hiss. "Eric, Werner's wandered off and I can't find him—"

Werner's hand sprang inside his jacket, and Eric leapt to stop him, only to be sent flying into a file cabinet as, with a roar, Werner flung him off. For a minute, Eric saw stars. Something lanced into the floor—Great-Uncle Charlie's cavalry sabre—nearly skewering him. He heard the telltale racking of a pistol slide as the door flung open and Avery charged in. Werner made to throw Avery off as well, but Avery had managed to get a better grip on Werner than Eric had, and the two went down in a tangle of flailing limbs.

Eric staggered to his feet. A shot rang out, narrowly missing him, and he dropped to the floor again. Tiny as it was, Werner's Bayard didn't thunder like a normal pistol, but its report rang in Eric's ears nonetheless. He could smell the acrid stench of expended gunpowder—the mud and blood of Flanders—and somewhere in the gunshot's echo, he heard shattering glass.

Across the room, Werner was struggling to extricate himself from Avery, who, despite not knowing the first thing about fighting, was at least quite good at clinging on. Eric began to get up, and the Bayard went off again. This time, Eric smelled blood—real blood, not the all-too-real memory of Flanders.

Werner was on his feet, horror and regret in his face and the Bayard still smoking in his hand; but Avery was crumpled against the office wall with dark red blooming across his waistcoat front and seeping out between clutching fingers . . .

The next moment, Werner was gone.

Eric scrambled across the office floor to his friend's side and slung off his jacket to press it over the bullet wound, hoping to slow the bleeding. He was vaguely aware of the black trouser legs of liveried attendants crowding into the doorway, frozen in shock. Somehow, he'd expected muddy boots and khakis.

"Don't just stand there," Eric barked. "There's the telephone. You! Call the police! And you! Get a medic—Duplessis will be in the dining room—get him here, now, and all the clean napkins you can find! The rest of you, search the club. You're after Captain Gregory Ward. Start at the back door and work your way in. Now go!"

The black trouser legs rattled off on their respective missions, and Eric turned back to Avery. His face was whiter than Eric had ever seen it before.

"I'm dying, aren't I? I don't want to die."

"You're not dying. Not yet. I've seen this sort of thing often enough to know."

In truth, Eric had seen far too many men die from gunshot wounds to the abdomen, but his words had the desired effect: Avery bit his lip in an effort to calm himself, and said, "It's been rather fantastic, hasn't it? Spies and amnesiacs and murder . . . Who would ever imagine this sort of thing actually happened in real life?"

"People would be amazed at the things that actually happen in real life."

Avery, however, was unresponsive. Not dead, thank goodness, but fainted dead away.

*"Come on, man," Lieutenant Peterkin barked, then stifled a cough. "You're not stopping now, are you? Private Dent's still in there."*

"Monsieur Peterkin! Monsieur Ferrett! I thought we had a plan!"

Eric gave way to Duplessis, who began barking orders to . . . someone. Eric was in the queer, emotionally deadened state that often came over him after a skirmish, when the guns fell silent and nothing in the world felt quite real. There were men swarming around him, and he couldn't tell if they were policemen, club attendants, or gawking bystanders. He could almost hear the more vocal members of the club sneering that nothing like this would ever have happened on Bradshaw's watch, and perhaps they'd be right. Bradshaw would have known how to handle Werner. Hell, he'd probably have known the real Gregory Ward well enough to spot the impostor right away, and none of this would have happened. Colonel Russell, that expansive and benevolent lord of the club lounge, would still be alive.

The thing that had shattered from the Bayard's first shot was the glass front of that damned tortoise-on-a-bicycle print Bradshaw had left behind. The bullet had torn a hole right through the tortoise's head. And with that thing destroyed, Eric thought grimly, Bradshaw was well and truly gone.

# WAR COUNCIL

ERIC'S FIRST INSTINCT was to leap into the ambulance when it came to rush Avery across the river to St. Thomas' Hospital; but as was firmly pointed out, his presence could do nothing for his friend. Duplessis went instead, leaving Eric to explain everything to Inspector Crane.

"I'd have thought," Crane remarked, "that you were used to the sight of wounded men, after the War."

"This isn't the War, is it? Even if it were, Avery never signed up to be shot at."

Eric and his men, even the conscripts . . . they all knew what they were getting into when they put their boots down in Flanders. Avery had more in common with the simple farm folk who'd woken up one day to find themselves in the middle of a battlefield—the innocent victims of someone else's violence.

Well, Avery's fate was all up to the doctors now. Meanwhile, Werner was gone—presumably down the back stairs and out the back door. He certainly hadn't run out through the lobby, and the vault anteroom across from Eric's office was a dead end.

"I'm calling back to the Yard for more men to search the area," Crane said. "In the meantime, Peterkin, you're going to give me the full story of what happened."

Eric had to tell the story no less than three times. Once for Inspector Crane, once more for his superior at Scotland Yard, and a third time in an emergency meeting with Crane, the superintendent, and all the policemen who could be mustered together on such short notice. The torn envelope, Monique Garnier's letters, and the newspaper clippings had to be handed over, with Crane pretending to have never seen the last before. Duplessis, his cuffs crusted rusty brown with Avery's blood, arrived to repeat his own theory regarding Werner's mental state, reinforced by whatever assessment he'd managed in the few minutes of conversation he'd had in the dining room, and its parallels with the case of Anna Tchaikovsky.

"Monsieur Werner believes himself to be Captain Gregory Ward, and reacted with violence because he was faced with a challenge to his delusion. Monsieur Peterkin, did he ever admit to you who he really was?"

Eric, occupied with worry for Avery, took a moment to realise what was being asked of him. "We didn't speak long enough for that, but he did say that 'Karl Werner' was dead."

"That would be how he'd see it. But I think also that the delusion is not complete. There is a part of him that remains Karl Werner, and that is why he recognised this old book of his as a challenge. He can still be saved, if we can only get him safely into our care."

Outside, Big Ben had just chimed midnight, and the streets were quiet with the unearthly, empty silence of the limbo between worlds. Inside, the single electric light above cast a yellow glare over the crowd of uniformed policemen crammed into Inspector Crane's office. Duplessis had been careful to avoid levelling any sort of accusation against Werner, but Eric knew what the gathered policemen were thinking: that Werner, whether it was his delusion or deception that had been challenged, must have killed Colonel Russell in a reaction similar to what had happened with Avery. They were here to capture a dangerous fugitive, and none of them cared what Duplessis wanted after that.

Crane himself was blazing with energy—moments like this must be the part of police work that he loved the best—and that energy commanded the attention of the war council . . .

War council. There was no other term for it. They were crowded into a cramped dugout in the dead of night, going over the plans for the upcoming offensive, their voices hushed as though the silence might carry their words to the enemy across no-man's-land. Eric had been here more than once, the chill of the cold night air creeping through the warmth of packed bodies around him. There'd been grievously wounded comrades each time, too, like Avery now; but one had to soldier on regardless, or there might be more.

One policeman raised a hand. "That's all very well, sir, but what's that mean for us?"

"It means," Duplessis told him sternly, "that, in this matter, you should not be asking yourselves what Karl Werner would do, but what *Gregory Ward* would do."

A low, interested murmur rippled through the crowd as pencils scratched furiously in notebooks. This was no longer simply a routine hunt for a fugitive criminal, and Eric suddenly understood Crane's eagerness to embrace Duplessis's theories: ambition. Werner's delusion made this a new game, with new rules, and victory here would distinguish the Hong Kong detective from his London-bred peers.

Inspector Crane clapped his hands, taking charge once more of the discussion. "All right, men. This makes our job much simpler. We know nothing about Karl Werner beyond what Mr. Peterkin and Dr. Duplessis have discovered from the sanatorium in Switzerland. Higgins, I want you to wire that sanatorium and tell them to send us whatever additional information they can. No sense in leaving that stone unturned. The rest of you, think about where an ordinary English officer who's down on his luck might wind up."

"St. Martin-in-the-Fields," said one policeman. "Over on Trafalgar Square. Any soldier of the War without a place to rest his head is welcome to bunk down in the church vaults. That's where I'd go if I were Mr. Ward."

"Good! You and Jones, go there now. And if our man isn't there, wake the vicar and tell him what's what. Peterkin, you have Captain Ward's personal details on file, don't you? His old address, his regiment . . ."

"If you like. Though you'd get better details from the War Office."

Inspector Crane nodded curtly and turned back to the assembled policemen. "We'll want everything Werner might have learnt from Ward in their time together at the sanatorium. Here's the journal from his room at the Britannia Club. Higgins, once you're done wiring Switzerland, I want you to go through this journal and take notes. Where did Ward go to school, and where did he grow up? If Werner really does believe himself to be Captain Ward, he'll want to go to the places that ought to be familiar to him."

Duplessis nodded with enthusiasm. "Yes, but yes! The search for such familiar points will be exactly what drove him to the Britannia Club in the first place!"

"And if," Eric said dourly, "he's not deluded at all, and this is all a ruse?"

"In the first place," the Inspector said, "anything is possible when it comes to madmen, and I've seen some things that would never be credited as plausible in a book."

Was Werner a madman? Eric called to mind, for the millionth time, every interaction he'd had with the man, searching for such evidence. But Eric wasn't an expert, was he? No, that was Duplessis, whom Crane had been consulting from the beginning. Perhaps the Inspector was simply prejudiced in favour of the psychological. "And in the second?"

Crane smirked. "In the second . . . Does it matter? Without the delusion theory, we have only a handful of measures that we'd have taken regardless of the case. With the delusion theory, we have those same measures, *plus* something more. You see? The best of all possible worlds."

Eric chose not to argue. "All right, then. Regardless of whether he's Werner or Ward, there's one person he'll want to see. Lucy

Russell—the former Mrs. Patrick Russell. She's currently staying with my sister at the old family house in Barchester. The plan had been to put some distance between her and Ward, but I have reason to think that Ward—Werner, I mean—has found out where she is."

Something flashed in Crane's eyes. He almost smiled, then turned to the superintendent with only the hastiest shred of deference due to a superior. "Sir, have we a house we can put this Mrs. Russell in? A house we can watch, in a place we know?" Almost before the superintendent could finish growling an affirmative, Crane swept on. "I will fetch and question her myself—with Mr. Peterkin, of course. She's bound to know something about our man that we shan't find in any war record. Archer, arrange a bodyguard detail. And Watts, I want you at Paddington, watching the trains bound for Barchester and the surrounding area."

"Don't forget the other Mrs. Russells," the superintendent rumbled. He was a large, lugubrious walrus of a man, with the expected moustache but not, thank goodness, the tusks—though it was a near thing. "Remind me who they are again?"

"The widows of Colonel Russell's four sons: George, Andrew, David, and Patrick—"

"England, Scotland, Wales, and Ireland. Understood. Mrs. Patrick's the one staying with Mr. Peterkin's sister."

Crane ticked the remaining Russell widows off on his fingers. "Mrs. George—Lady Alice—is the head of their little coven. Next is Mrs. Andrew, who goes by Madam Eliot for business reasons. Lady Alice has been married into the family the longest, while Madam Eliot's late husband was actually a good friend of Captain Ward. If he had any dealings with the family outside of the Army, one or the other of those two would know about it. Last, Mrs. David—Miss Flora Grace. You'll remember she was seen leaving the Britannia Club the night of Colonel Russell's murder, supposedly after an assignation with one of the attendants, and now there's this business with her letters. Wouldn't hurt to put some pressure on her, see if she comes up with any new surprises."

Avery. Lady Alice was friendly with Avery. She'd have to be told. And Madam Eliot—

Thoughts of Madam Eliot brought Eric back to that moment after Colonel Russell's funeral, when she'd gone so suddenly from polished businesswoman to frightened animal. He remembered the terrified look on her face, and her insistence that Andrew Russell's death had been a suicide and therefore could have nothing to do with the Colonel's murder.

Eric shook the image away and looked through the crowd for Duplessis. Crane was focussed now on assigning jobs to his men, with input from the superintendent and many minor discussions on what exactly he needed done. Eric and Duplessis had said everything required of them, which gave Eric leave to think of Avery again. Elbowing his way through to where Duplessis stood with his green overcoat slung over one elbow, ruefully inspecting his ruined cuffs and sleeves, Eric beckoned him out into the empty corridor where they could speak more freely.

"Avery," Eric said, wasting no time. "He's all right?"

"I told you when I came in. He was in surgery when I left him."

"Yes, yes, but surely you know more than that. You're a doctor. You must have your own opinion on his chances. I saw men shot in the stomach, in the War, and I remember only one surviving. Is there hope?"

"Monsieur Ferrett was shot with a pocket pistol, which has not the power of a rifle or even an ordinary-sized handgun. The bullet was small. It went through a folded-up silk handkerchief in his waistcoat pocket—Monsieur Ferrett has surprisingly expensive tastes—which helped to reduce the harm. And we are not also battling the filth of the trenches for him. We have the best of modern medical science at our disposal, and the surgery was going well. So yes, I would say there is plenty of hope."

Eric had to take comfort from that. "I should go see him. Crane won't mind if I take five minutes before we head off to Barchester, surely."

"Monsieur Ferrett will have been pumped full of morphine, for the pain. He will not be conscious, and they will not let you see him—not until this evening at least."

Eric made an inarticulate sound of frustration and kicked at the wall. Hope was well and good, but certainty would have been better.

Duplessis gave up fussing over his ruined cuffs and peered at Eric. "You think highly of Monsieur Ferrett, and you value his friendship. Curious. I cannot think of two men more dissimilar than you and him. You? You are like Monsieur Bullard. You remember the American manager of that nightclub, Le Grand Duc? You came to our aid though you had no need. Monsieur Ferrett, meanwhile . . . he stayed in Argentina 'for his health.'"

"He also jumped on top of a man wielding a gun. Was that the act of a coward?"

"Perhaps not."

"You were in the War, too, weren't you? A medical officer, you said. You saw all the grief and suffering we went through. You know, perhaps even better than I do, how it still haunts us. Can you blame Avery for saying no? I can't."

There was a long silence, broken only by the ongoing murmurs from behind the half-open office door, as Duplessis bowed his head. When he looked up again, his eyes were sad. He said, softly, "You did not have to contend with German troops advancing over your land."

And that was true, too.

"Forgive me," Duplessis said. "I admit I may have judged your friend more harshly than he deserved. But you see how I might be a little prejudiced when it comes to matters pertaining to the War and the defence of France against Germany. My son—"

He broke off.

Eric extended a hand and placed it on the other man's shoulder. "Avery mentioned that your son was warded at the Saint-Maurice Hospital?"

Duplessis's shoulder went rigid under Eric's hand, and the alienist pulled away. "That is no business of yours," he snapped, then swung his overcoat across his shoulders and scurried off down the corridor.

Poor fellow! But he was entitled to his grief, Eric supposed.

The office door slammed open, pulling Eric back to the present, and Inspector Crane came striding out. Behind him, the lesser policemen streamed off in a heavy tramp of boots to their assigned tasks, while the superintendent glowered despondently.

"Peterkin!" Crane said. "There you are. Don't run off on me now, not while there's work to be done. Where's Dr. Duplessis gone? To his own bed, I'm guessing, not that I blame him. It's late. We're all grateful for his help, of course, but you and I can take it from here."

"You'd better," said the superintendent. "We've had minimal progress in the two weeks since Colonel Russell's murder, and let's not forget that it's this fine gentleman who's been out doing your job for you, eh?"

"Sir!"

The superintendent made a low, rumbling sound in the back of his throat and turned to Eric. "Give my regards to Cully, and tell him that recent events make me even more reluctant to get my membership reinstated." Shooting one last baleful glare at Inspector Crane, he added, "Doesn't mean I don't take a particular interest. Russell's boy Andrew saved my boy's life in the War, and I want that debt repaid, understand?"

And then he lumbered away.

# IN A STRANGE LAND

"CLUBS," INSPECTOR CRANE said gloomily. "We had clubs in Hong Kong. Exclusive ones, too. Prestigious. But not like here. All along Piccadilly, up Pall Mall and down St. James, is there a building that isn't a club? In Hong Kong, if you said 'the Club,' everyone knew what you meant. Here, it's like a minefield. Back away from one and you'll blow yourself up on another."

Eric didn't answer. He could do nothing about Avery, and there was Penny to worry about. He would never forgive himself if the same thing happened to her. Harvey should be with her now, but was he enough? Crane had enlisted a burly young constable to take notes and play bodyguard on the way back, and the fellow was now snoring in the back seat of the Vauxhall. The sooner they got to Barchester, the better. Even if the moonless night rendered the roads dark and difficult; even if, at this rate, they'd arrive before dawn and have to rouse both Penny and Lucy out of bed—and Harvey, too, most likely. Eric would have set out even sooner if everyone else hadn't insisted he change into something that wasn't covered in blood.

Crane, still brooding over his own troubles, went on: "Well, it hardly matters if the superintendent's a former member of your club or not. He's got a vested interest in the successful resolution of this case, and if I don't give that to him . . . I've got a lot at stake here,

Peterkin. The whole of the Yard is watching me, wondering if the new boy from the colonies is going to fall flat on his face. I took a bit of a demotion when I came home, you know, with the understanding that it was only until I got my bearings—hah! Until I proved myself, more like. I'm jockeying for a promotion like everybody else, and I'm up against men who've been friendly with the brass for years. One of them's a bloody Victoria Cross, Peterkin. Can you imagine going up against that? 'What did you do in the War, Crane?' 'Nothing, sir, I was too busy drinking tea and playing mah-jongg.' God Almighty. I wish I'd stayed in England for the War."

"You wish nothing of the sort. Be thankful you got out of it with your honour intact. No one can say you ran away." *As they did with Avery.*

"Oh, can't they, now?" Crane grunted dismissively. "Well, if I don't get that promotion, I might as well hop on the next boat to Hong Kong and never speak English again. Do you really speak no Chinese at all? Not Cantonese, or Mandarin, or any of the other dialects?"

The sudden change in subject caught Eric off guard. He hazarded a glance at Crane and thought sourly to himself, *Does the average Englishman normally do business in something that isn't an unholy union of Saxon German and Norman French?* Aloud, he affected a disinterested tone and said, "I know the Mandarin word for 'umbrella.' That's the extent of my Chinese."

"Bloody useful if you were caught in a rainstorm in Limehouse. I'm sorry I brought it up. You may know a thing or two about not fitting in, perhaps, but you wouldn't be secretary of a prestigious gentlemen's club if that were ever a real issue for you. This is the world you've always known, after all."

Eric bit down the instinctive protest that much of his childhood had been in India, not England. He was in no mood to discuss the existential angst of an expatriate Englishman returned to an England he no longer recognised, but he had to wonder: Had his father adjusted to his return better than the Inspector, or had Eric simply been, as a child, blind to the troubles of grown-ups? What had Berkeley Peterkin's repatriation meant to his Chinese wife?

Inspector Crane went back to his brooding. He meant England when he spoke of "home," of course, but Eric had an inkling that his heart had never actually left Hong Kong.

"Mrs. Russell—"

"Call me Lucy. What is this about? I know you wouldn't be here, and at this hour, unless something's happened, so what is it? Is it Gregory?"

"Lucy," said the Inspector, mouth wrapping around the name as though he'd never pronounced it before. "As I said. We just have a few questions for you."

They were seated around the heavy, ancient table of the Peterkin house kitchen. The patterned ceramic wall tiles around them were a relic of a kinder age . . . and Lucy Russell in her drop-waisted sailor dress, sitting on her hands with a kettle on the hob behind her, might have stepped out of that same rose-tinted memory of domestic bliss—quite at odds with what Eric considered a desperate situation.

It was still dark out. Harvey stood by the window, arms folded and expression surly. Eric and the Inspector had arrived to find him sitting up with a book, a pot of strong coffee, and a big stick. He knew from Eric's telegram to Penny that "Gregory Ward" was a dangerous imposter, and was annoyed at knowing nothing more than that. So was Penny. The two had agreed to keep Lucy in the dark, on the grounds that they didn't yet have even half the story, which seemed to please Inspector Crane. The Inspector, Eric knew, wanted to break the news himself.

"For the record," the Inspector asked Lucy, "how long have you known Captain Ward?"

"About three weeks. It feels like more."

The police constable scribbled the Inspector's question and Lucy's answer into his notebook, the scratching of pencil on paper filling the silent night.

"Can you tell us about that first meeting?"

Lucy described arriving at the Britannia for her usual Friday luncheon with her sisters-in-law. Eric remembered, too, seeing her in the lobby, showered in sunlight. He knew the effect it must have had on Werner. From Lucy's point of view, Werner—or Ward, as she still thought of him—had come stumbling out of the darker office corridor looking like a kicked puppy. "The poor dear seemed positively spooked, but I knew better than to pry. He just needed to feel safe, first. He'd tell me what was bothering him if it was still important later."

"Safe? That's an interesting choice of words. Did you think he'd been threatened?"

"It's only human nature, isn't it? I'm sure there's a cleverer way of putting it. I mean that it's usually much better to let people choose things for themselves, in their own time."

Like the old fable, Eric thought—about the sun removing a traveller's cloak not by forcibly tearing it away, but by patiently warming the traveller until he took it off himself. Crane was lucky: in much the same way, Lucy was willing to patiently answer his questions, knowing he'd tell her what she wanted to know in due course.

"And did he eventually tell you what was bothering him?"

"He mentioned being accidentally locked in the club vault?" Lucy's eyes darted to Eric for confirmation. "He didn't elaborate."

"So you felt sorry for him."

"You could say that."

Her expression and tone did not change, but Eric suspected she actually meant, *No, but it's not worth arguing the point.*

Crane continued: "What else did you make of him, at that moment? I want all your first impressions."

"Well . . . He seemed nice. The scar was a little frightening, at first, but a lot of men came out of the War with something of the sort, and one gets used to it. He told me it was from an exploding shell, and he laughed when I said it was jolly brave of him. Scars like his were proof that someone was worth knowing, he said. That was a joke, of course: he wasn't half so stuck up as it makes him sound."

Crane gave Eric a meaningful look. Did Werner still know who he was, after all? Or was the significance of a mensur scar so great as to transcend identity?

"Your sisters-in-law. What did they think?"

"Alice liked him well enough at first. She said I couldn't spend all my life keeping house for Hadrian and that I should think about getting married again. She changed her mind after Hadrian died, though. She was very upset with me when I got him to bring my nephews Matthew and Mark home from King's Cross—I just thought they'd want help with their school trunks, and he was coming to call on Alice anyway."

Crane nodded and moved on. "What about Miss Grace and Madam Eliot?"

"Flora hadn't much patience with any idea of 'having' to get married again, but she did agree that I should get out of the house more. She knew about Gregory from her husband, long ago, and that was enough for her. It was only Miranda who wasn't too keen on poor Gregory from the beginning. I don't know why. Gregory was friends with Andrew, so might it have been something Andrew told her? She did say something very odd to me afterwards. She said that if I were unhappy about anything, I mustn't be afraid to tell her. Or Alice. They'd help me out no matter what, and there was no sense trying to be 'brave' about some things."

Interesting. Did Madam Eliot suspect Werner from the beginning? But if she did, surely she'd have said something to someone—probably Lady Alice.

Inspector Crane said, "Tell me about your meeting with him on the Friday before the murder."

Lucy's brow furrowed as she cast her mind back. "That was the day Hadrian got back from Scotland, wasn't it? Gregory joined us all for lunch. It was quite last minute: he actually wanted to have a drink with Hadrian and talk about old times, but Hadrian had other business to take care of. After lunch, we went for a walk through Hyde Park, and I remember that Gregory was happier than I'd ever seen him before. Excited, rather . . . nearly bouncing on his heels."

"Did he say why?"

Lucy shook her head. "I assumed it must be from meeting Hadrian again. They were old friends, I think, and Gregory admitted he hadn't many of those left."

"Did they meet again?"

"You know they did. I said so at the inquest."

"Your story was that on Saturday the fourteenth of March, Colonel Russell left for his club at ten o'clock. Our focus then was on the Colonel's movements. Now we'd like to know about Captain Ward's. You said he came to take you out for the afternoon. What time was that?"

"Two o'clock. He'd spent the morning looking for suitable lodgings, and he had quite a few stories to tell me about the flats he'd seen. We wandered around Hyde Park, dined out at the Grenadier, and got home at about eight. Hadrian was back by then."

"You said at the inquest that Captain Ward and Colonel Russell spent the next half hour sequestered in the latter's study. You have no idea what about?"

"I don't make it a habit to listen at doors, Inspector."

"You said that Colonel Russell emerged in a good mood. What about Captain Ward?"

Lucy bit her lip. "He . . . he looked quite glum. He barely even said goodbye to me." She watched the constable scribble this down in his notebook and added, "I hope you don't think they had some sort of a row, and that Gregory killed Hadrian because of it. I'd have heard something. And anyway, Gregory would never do something so awful."

Had Colonel Russell actually confronted Werner about his identity then, and not four hours later at the club? Surely the reaction would have been immediate, as with Avery's shooting. But Eric also remembered the one time he'd seen Werner as "glum" as Lucy described: in the vault, after studying the posters left by the British

Empire Union. The emotion had eroded his facade then, and the man who'd offered Eric his support while they were trapped in the vault had been Werner as himself, not Werner being Ward.

Crane said, "He never spoke to you about what upset him?"

"No. The next time I saw him was on Monday, after the murder. We were all too devastated to think, and no one wanted to discuss *that*."

Eric remembered that day at Lady Alice's—Lucy stifling a laugh as Werner, fully immersed in his role as Ward, laid his hand on hers. They hadn't seemed particularly devastated, but people handled grief differently, didn't they? For all he knew, that veneer of good humour might have been the only thing keeping Lucy from dissolving into hysterics.

Crane continued with a few more questions about Lucy's previous interactions with Werner, while Eric wondered: What exactly was Lucy thinking and feeling now? Anxiety was expected, given the situation; but aside from her initial burst of apprehension, Lucy seemed quite unperturbed . . . politely attentive, rather, like a schoolgirl at her lessons.

"Gregory didn't like talking about the War," she told Crane. "I don't know that anybody does, really. I think he had a brother who died of the Spanish flu. His father was a general in the Boer War, but he died just before the Great War. I think Gregory actually volunteered out of some idea of family pride—he said he took his father's revolver as his personal sidearm. His mother went with him to Switzerland and died there. He mentioned that one of them was a suicide, but didn't say which, and I didn't ask. I mean, that's not the sort of thing you discuss with a girl you only just met and whom you're trying to impress, is it?"

How much of that was Ward's actual family history, and how much was Werner filling in the blanks with details from his own life? He could only know what Ward had told him, after all. Duplessis had laid the blame for Werner's delusions—and those of Anna Tchaikovsky—on the economic ruin of Germany in the years following the War; for Eric, these dire circumstances amounted to a few scattered headlines lost amid many others. The only Germans one met outside of Germany were those still affluent enough to travel, and no one spared a thought for the rest. But it was telling that Duplessis, despite his prejudice, should have changed his tune so completely after learning of Werner's situation. There were some things one couldn't wish on one's worst enemy.

Colonel Russell *had* said something about Ward going off to war with his late father's service revolver. But the suicidal parent, Eric guessed, was likely to have been Werner's rather than Ward's. And the brother who'd died of the Spanish flu?

*Für meinen Bruder . . .*

Did any of this change if Werner were fully himself all along, a dangerous spy preying on innocents? Eric thought back to the man who'd just shot his friend. His expression had been one of horrified dismay—because, as Dr. Keller had asserted, he was not a killer at heart? Or because his plot had failed?

"Of course, he didn't intend on staying at the Britannia Club forever," Lucy continued. "I told you he was looking for a flat the day Hadrian died, and he'd been doing that for a while. He was looking for work, too. I suggested he speak to Uncle Joss—"

"Uncle Joss?"

"Jocelyn Carrington-Clarke, Hadrian's brother-in-law. He owns Carrington-Clarke & Associates, the company that Miranda works for. They build houses, though I think there's more to it than that. You'll have to ask Miranda about it."

"Do you know if Captain Ward did, in fact, apply to Carrington-Clarke for work?"

Lucy shook her head. "He was in no hurry, and Hadrian's murder happened before he could do anything. As far as I know, I mean. Miranda is practically Uncle Joss's right hand, and she said she never heard from him. But Gregory did say he was looking at flats and houses around Willesden Green, where Uncle Joss's office is located."

Something bumped into Eric's shoulder. Penny had prepared tea for everyone while they talked, and here was his cup. As he reached out for it, she caught his hand and peered at his fingers. Avery's blood was still crusted under his nails, Eric realised, and Penny's gaze when she met his eyes was a fierce demand for answers.

Meanwhile, Lucy's mask of placid attentiveness was beginning to crack. All things come to those who wait, perhaps; but there were limits. "Inspector, what are all these questions about? If you want to know what Gregory's been up to, couldn't you ask him yourself?"

"I would," said Inspector Crane, snapping his notebook shut. He seemed satisfied with the results of the interview, and was now watching Lucy intently. "The trouble is, he's been dead for the past two months."

For a moment, the scene seemed to freeze: the cheerfully coloured ceramic tiles gleaming in the yellow electric light, the bright copper kettle with steam drifting from its spout—and Lucy Russell caught like a bird in mid-flight. "I knew it!" she cried, half rising from her chair in horror. Then she dropped down again in consternation. "What do you mean, the past two months?"

"You knew it, Mrs. Russell?"

"I meant that I knew something must have happened, or you wouldn't be here. *What do you mean, the past two months?*"

"Captain Gregory Algernon Ward died in Switzerland two months ago. The man you met at the Britannia Club was someone else."

"That's impossible. Eric, tell him it's impossible."

"I'm afraid—"

"Don't you men know anything?" Lucy shouted, then clamped her mouth shut. The schoolgirl mask had shattered, and her fists were clenched tightly on her knees as she struggled for self-control. She took a deep breath, then said in a dangerously measured tone, "Who was he, then, if he wasn't Gregory—if he wasn't the real Captain Ward?"

"A German officer," Eric replied in the Inspector's stead, "called Karl Josef von Werner."

Eric heard a muttered oath from Harvey: the younger man unfolded his arms and came to join them at the table, his eyes burning with interest. Inspector Crane glanced at him and quickly smoothed away a frown; then, turning to Lucy, he said, "According to Dr. Duplessis, Mr. Werner really believes himself to be Gregory Ward. As such—"

"Well, I believe you're all perfectly stupid. And this is stupid. I won't have it."

Pushing herself away from the table with a violence that sent her chair crashing onto the floor, Lucy ran from the kitchen. They could hear her feet on the stairs, and then the slam of her bedroom door.

Penny started after her, then stopped and rounded on Eric and the Inspector. "You've got a lot of explaining to do, the both of you. And that? That was just cruel."

The Inspector, unfazed, said, "But necessary."

"Necessary!"

"Do you imagine she'd have answered my questions if I started by telling her what this was about? You saw what happened."

Penny glanced upwards, in the direction of Lucy's room. "I'd better go to her. I don't know what I can say to her that would be any help at this moment, but I know I must at least try. There aren't any further bombshells you want to drop on us, are there? The reason my brother's got blood under his nails, for instance?"

Eric looked down at his hands again. "Avery's been shot."

"What!"

"He's at St. Thomas'. They haven't let me see him yet—"

"Mr. Harvey," Inspector Crane said, "Mrs. Russell is in distress and I think you should see that she's all right. Give her a shoulder to cry on, if need be."

"What?" Harvey glanced at Penny, perplexed; then his brows came down in a scowl. "If you want me out of the room, you could have just said so."

He stomped out of the kitchen. A moment later, they heard the stairs creak again.

Once Harvey was gone, Inspector Crane turned to Penny. "Miss Peterkin, once Mrs. Russell has quite calmed down, have her pack her things. You'll want to pack a suitcase of your own. Karl Werner is a dangerous man, and there's a chance he knows exactly where you are. Scotland Yard has therefore arranged for you to be moved to a house in Harrow—"

"Harrow! We might as well move into the heart of London!"

"It's close enough for us at the Yard to keep an eye out without drawing too much attention, and far enough that there's little chance of an accidental discovery. And with no known connection to you, your brother, or the Russells."

"And I suppose, since you made Harvey leave the room before telling me, that *he's* not to be a part of this?"

Inspector Crane shook his head.

"You don't have to like it," Eric said. "Just don't be a bore about not liking it."

Penny ran both hands through her hair. "I don't believe this. Ward an imposter. Avery shot. I'll have to tell Mr. Stanhope that I shan't be helping with his horses for the foreseeable future—he's going to be furious."

She didn't wait for their response, but hurried out of the kitchen after Lucy and Harvey.

# NO HATRED OR BITTERNESS

WITH TWO WOMEN to watch and three men to watch them—four if you included Harvey—not to mention two hastily packed suitcases and a bicycle, it seemed better to leave the Vauxhall in Barchester and make the return journey by train. A pair of police motorcars, too black and anonymous to be mistaken for anything else, met them at Paddington, where Eric bade farewell to Harvey with a cheque for three pounds.

"A week's pay for two days of just waiting around," Harvey remarked as he tucked the money away. "I could get used to this."

Once Harvey had disappeared into the train station crowd, Penny addressed Inspector Crane: "Is there any objection to simply giving me the address of this house where we're supposed to sit and wait for danger to show up, so I can join you later?"

"It's Mrs. Russell who needs protecting. You're free to do as you please."

"Good." Penny shoved her suitcase into the Inspector's hands and turned to Eric. "I'm coming with you."

"What? What about Lucy?"

"All she wants is a sleeping draught and time alone." And Penny herself was too angry to accept a passive role. "I suppose there's no question of visiting Avery yet?"

"Not until this evening, I'm told."

Penny made a face. “Well, someone’s got to keep you out of trouble in the meantime. Besides, my life’s just been turned upside down, and if you think I’m going to be left behind while someone else deals with it, you’re as mad as our friend Werner.”

St. Martin-in-the-Fields, at the northeast corner of Trafalgar Square, had been suggested as a likely place for someone claiming to be Captain Gregory Ward to end up. There was no reason why Werner shouldn’t have learnt of it in the week he’d spent at the Britannia; and even if he wasn’t under any delusions of identity, it might still be safer to play the British soldier than admit the truth. Watching the church’s front portico from the monument to Edith Cavell a little farther up, Eric remembered the bitterness with which Werner had quoted the martyred nurse’s final words, added to her monument just last year: *I must have no hatred or bitterness towards anyone*.

“No hatred or bitterness! Hah!” The ragged tramp spat, then muttered an unrepentant apology to Penny. Eric could smell the alcohol on him, overlaying the musk of too many days unwashed. “I was conscripted in January of 1916. Two years in hell, and then I come home to . . . Well, there’s no one who’ll take me on, and the Army won’t take me back. And you’re telling me, ‘No hatred, Johnny! And no bitterness, neither!’ While German Jerry sets up shop right in front of me, fat and happy as you like! Sister Cavell’s a saint, but me? I’m only human, aren’t I?”

The tramp stopped as a well-dressed group entered the church with music sheets in hand: choristers showing up for practice, Eric guessed. Overhead, the early afternoon sun floated over Nelson’s Column and flooded Trafalgar Square with light; but a chill in the wind made the tramp shiver. He pulled his coat closer around him and chuckled darkly before continuing. “To answer your question: no. I’ve been watching ever since the coppers told us who Captain Gregory Bloody Ward really is, and I’ve seen neither hide nor hair of him. Wish we’d known! We’d have given the blighter what for, and maybe more.”

Eric said, "You've met him, then?"

The tramp grumbled to himself, then said, "Aye. I found him wandering around Charing Cross and brought him here when he asked about a good place for a soldier down on his luck to bunk down. Didn't think he'd turn out a soldier for the other side—"

"Wait. He stayed here, then? When was this?"

"Two weeks ago, maybe? Three? He stayed a week, then disappeared—to some swanky club on Pall Mall, so I've been told."

King Street was close enough to Pall Mall that Eric saw no need to correct the man. In any case, he was too taken aback by this news, that Werner came here *before* appearing at the Britannia.

"What was he like?" Penny asked.

"Kept to himself. We all do. Nobody likes questions asked, so nobody asks questions, and it's nobody's business what any of us gets up to in the day. But I remember he was living out of a nice-looking suitcase, which made me think he was new to the life. A rucksack's more handy, see? Maybe that should have been our first clue."

The tramp had little else to add. Eric gave him a shilling and left him to continue his vigil.

Once they were some distance away, however, he stopped and said to Penny, "I should have realised. Duplessis spent the two weeks before the murder visiting Craiglockhart and Seale-Hayne, but Werner only came to the Britannia one week before. If they met on the ferry from Calais, that leaves one week unaccounted for—the week he spent hiding out at St. Martin's. I wonder why."

"Perhaps he wanted to get a lay of the land? He wouldn't know London no matter who he thought he was—perhaps he told himself he'd lost his memory to shell shock."

"Perhaps. But he could still explore at his leisure—call it 'refreshing his memory'—after settling down at the Britannia." Eric frowned, thinking. He'd seen enough men snap to know that it was never so sudden as others pretended; that, and Duplessis's description of Anna Tchaikovsky, made it seem believable that even if Werner were in the grip of a delusion, he might have arrived in London still in some small part aware of himself. But then, this extra week at St. Martin's sounded like *reconnaissance*, and while Eric wanted to believe in Duplessis's theory, he'd never been fully convinced. If German intelligence officer Karl von Werner was enough himself for such a calculated move, what would he do now?

Eric turned to Penny. "Crane thinks that adopting Duplessis's theory gives the police more avenues of inquiry, on top of the ones they'd already pursue regardless—and I think he's a little in love with the idea of the alienated criminal, anyway. He never really stopped to think about what else they could do, assuming Werner was fully himself. So let's think about it. What would Karl Werner do, and where would he go for help?"

St. George's Lutheran Church was in the northwest corner of Whitechapel, near Aldgate and the city's financial hub—a stone's throw from the Looming Press offices, as it so happened. The plain brown bricks of its facade seemed particularly humble after the white stone elegance of St. Martin's, and the neoclassical bell tower just beyond the point of its gable was a defiant flourish. The neighbouring buildings pressed in close on either side. East of here were the sugar refineries, bakeries, and other industries—fading away now—to which German immigrants had devoted themselves over the past century. Eric had often heard it called "the German church," and while the German community didn't advertise itself much in these post-war days, St. George's must surely be its centre.

Eric and Penny arrived in time to see a wedding party pour from its doors: a small and modest one, and though much of the passing conversation was in English, Eric could catch the odd snatch of German passed about among the older guests. It took him a moment more to identify the pastor, who'd changed out of his vestments to join the party—but both pastor and party were spirited away in waiting taxis before Eric could approach either.

"Can I help you, sir?"

Only one man remained out of the departing crowd: a stout, florid, genial-looking man of middle age. He needed only the Union

Jack waistcoat to become John Bull, brought to life from a *Punch* cartoon, and his English was perfect—too perfect. It reminded Eric of his own mother and her efforts with an elocution tutor.

"If you're looking for the pastor," the man continued, "you've just missed him. I'm Miller—John Miller. One of the wardens."

Eric introduced himself and Penny. "There's a man we're looking for. We were wondering if he might have found his way here, to St. George's."

"It has been a while since I've noticed any new faces among the congregation. Why do you think you'd find him *here*, of all places?"

"His name is Karl Josef von Werner. He was a German intelligence officer in the War."

Did Mr. Miller's smile falter?

"He might seek out St. George's for the familiarity," Eric hastened to add. "I don't mean to imply anything more than that."

"He might try to present himself as someone else," Penny said.

Mr. Miller's tone was dry and almost mocking. "As a Charles Joseph Warner, you mean?"

"No," said Eric. "As a Captain Gregory Algernon Ward."

"Ward . . . I've seen that name before. In the news. A murder in St. James, wasn't it? There was a Captain Ward who gave evidence at the inquest and admitted to ownership of the murder weapon."

"That's the fellow. I have a deeper interest in the case than the papers. And no, I'm not a journalist."

"No, you are a typical Englishman with typical English interests." The geniality had disappeared entirely from Mr. Miller's demeanour now. He looked Eric and Penny up and down, and seemed to come to a decision that was very much against his preference. "I suppose it's in the church's best interests to cooperate. Come inside. We can sit down, which is better than lingering in the doorway."

Mr. Miller led them into a long and narrow nave, with wide galleries above and box pews crowding the floor. White-washed plaster trimmed with unpainted wood—a Protestant austerity overlaid with garlands of angel-white camellias from the wedding earlier. The door slammed shut behind them, making Eric and Penny jump; but Mr. Miller proceeded, oblivious, to indicate the coat of arms mounted above the pulpit: "Those are the royal arms of King George III. Whatever our origins, we have always been loyal to the Crown. From the day the first brick was laid, in fact. I imagine that is something you must understand very well."

Had it been a mistake to walk so willingly into the den of one who might be sheltering a dangerous fugitive? Surreptitiously searching the shadows, Eric replied, "Your loyalty must be unimpeachable and constantly proven."

"Just so."

"If Karl Werner were to come here, you would inform Scotland Yard immediately."

"Our numbers are smaller now, after the War. It would be easy to know if someone was harbouring a dangerous fugitive, or if someone knew more about it than they ought."

"You mean, those still loyal to Germany went home to fight, leaving those—"

"No." Mr. Miller's demeanour grew stony. He took a step closer, and the whisper of an accent crept into his voice. "Sit down. I had hoped that you, of all people, would understand. We have something in common, *ja*?"

Was Karl Werner, in spite of Mr. Miller's insistence, lurking in the shadows behind the camellia wreaths? When Eric, rather than sit down, shifted to come between him and Penny, Mr. Miller took a step back and a deep breath. The accent faded again, and he sounded instead like an Oxford don:

"I meant internment and deportation. I spent most of the War locked up at Alexandra Palace with a few thousand men of fighting age, whose only mistake was in retaining their German name. 'Hans Mueller' became 'John Miller' the moment I got out, though it was too late to do me any good. Our own pastor, bless him, did his best for us until he was shipped back to Germany in 1917. It took him three years to find his way back, and why would he come back at all, I ask you, after England had all but turned its back on him—on us? You know what it is to love and not be loved back. Don't you?"

Eric would have bristled, but the shadows of the galleries seemed all at once to deepen around them, the camellias floating like ghosts in the darkness. Eric remembered his mother in the church choir, her voice raised with pride in the knowledge that she sounded as English as her Anglo-Saxon neighbours, and perhaps even more so. He knew that when they stepped outside again, the mid-afternoon sun would be a shock, too bright after the muted half-light of this meeting between races—a different sort of no-man's-land.

For a moment, he saw the legions of Rome withdrawing from the British Isles, their villas and forts becoming the foundation for a new empire after their divorce from the old . . .

Penny stirred and stepped forward around Eric. "I apologise," she told Mr. Miller. "There's nothing here to discover, and I'm afraid we've only wasted your time."

If a ghost lurked in the shadows, it wasn't Karl Werner.

The genial smile returned to Mr. Miller's John Bull countenance. He waved off Penny's apology and walked them back the way they came. At the door, however, Eric turned to him again and said, "It must have been a difficult decision, and I respect that; but I wonder, do you ever regret it? Choosing England, I mean." *Over the land of your roots.*

"Do you?"

"That was never my decision to make. I grew up knowing nothing else."

No, that had been his mother's choice. A Victoria sponge for an afternoon tea, cricket on Saturdays, and a Sunday roast. Eric knew nothing of what she'd left behind. On the other side, there was Inspector Crane back from a decade in Hong Kong, hanging up a Chinese scroll on the wall of his Scotland Yard office . . .

*You can never go back. Not really.*

No more than Karl Werner could ever go back to the Germany he'd left behind, before the War.

# PATIENT MINDS

IT WAS PENNY who reminded Eric that he owed the remaining Russell widows the moral support of a visit. It had been nearly a full week since Colonel Russell's funeral, and in all the madness over Karl Werner, it was easy to forget that these women had more at stake than he did himself. So, when inquiries at the German Gymnasium in St. Pancras proved even more of a dead end than St. George's Church, they made their way back to Marylebone to call on Lady Alice as the primary representative of the Russells.

The street was exactly as before: quiet and guarded in its respectability, doors and windows shut tight against prying eyes. Overhead, gathering clouds dulled white limestone to shades of grey and honey-brown brick to mud. Lady Alice's maid answered the door with her habitual taciturn efficiency and ushered both Eric and Penny into the softer, more gracious world of the spacious drawing room with its view onto the verdant back garden.

They could hear Madam Eliot's voice raised in high dudgeon before they got there.

"Don't you think I hunted down every single workman we had on the Britannia Club job to see if they heard anything, as soon as the police were done with me? God only knows what the neighbours must think, seeing the police waiting outside your office for you in the morning. Uncle Joss would throw a fit, and that would really be the end of him—"

Eric and Penny were shown into the room just as Flora Grace interrupted her sister-in-law: "Miranda, do focus. What did you hear from your workmen?"

The police must have spoken to them about Karl Werner by now, and in the face of this crisis, the younger Russell widows had all flocked to Lady Alice. She stood between them now like the Rock of Gibraltar, steadfast and steady in eternal black. Madam Eliot, despite her smartly tailored polish, seemed to tremble where she stood: Eric could see her hand shake as she raised a cigarette to her lips. Flora, meanwhile, lounged in a chaise longue, her apparent languor betrayed by the nervous, rhythmic kicking of one elegantly trousered leg.

Flora! A sudden recollection of the warmth of her skin and the scent of her perfume—that night when she'd given him those letters—nearly bowled him over. It had been a week since they'd last spoken, and Eric suddenly found himself bitterly regretting that week, almost as much as he regretted having to tell Inspector Crane about her part in this mess. She was only an unwitting pawn, after all—of the German spy who'd come back, knowingly or not, to wreak havoc on her life.

Meanwhile, Lady Alice's two boys played chess in a far corner: Mark seemed totally absorbed in the game, but Matthew was clearly listening to his mother and aunts with undisguised concern, quite at odds with any prior pretence of aloofness.

Before Eric could say anything, and before the maid could announce him and Penny, all three widows descended on them like an unkindness of ravens.

"Mr. Peterkin!" This was Lady Alice, her practised grace gaining dominance. "And Miss Peterkin. How good of you both to come. We're in quite a state here, I'm afraid—dashing around in circles like chickens with our heads cut off. All we know is that Captain Ward is a dangerous imposter, that he's quite probably mad, and that the police are chasing him all over London, if not the whole of Great Britain. You must know more, I'm sure."

"The policeman who saw me," Flora said, "let slip that you were in this to your neck."

Eric did his best to summarise his adventures in Switzerland, the revelation of Werner's identity, and Duplessis's theory that Werner might actually believe himself to be Gregory Ward. "Until we can prove otherwise, it seems safest to not challenge him."

Flora said nothing, but her half-lidded gaze echoed Eric's doubts.

"Poor Lucy," said Lady Alice. "She's safe, at least?"

"Under police protection," Penny told her. "We've been uprooted and relocated. Not that I'm allowed to say where, for our safety. Well. *Her* safety, rather. As you can see, I'm still permitted to roam as I please, provided I'm careful about being followed when I go back."

There was another moment of silence as the ladies digested the information, and then Madam Eliot burst out: "So that's the story, then? This . . . Karl Werner, you said his name was? He decides he's Captain Ward and comes to England to take over his dead friend's life. I suppose Hadrian must have realised the truth, and called him onto the carpet, and then . . . Well, there's no 'going mad' if you're already mad, but it seems plain that the imposter reacted badly and killed him. One hears about homicidal maniacs but I never thought—"

Lady Alice laid a calming hand on Madam Eliot's shoulder and fixed a shrewd eye on Eric. "There's more, isn't there? He's not just a former German officer?"

Eric glanced at the others, then at the boys in the far corner. He didn't want to betray any confidences. "Among Werner's possessions, we found a torn envelope addressed to a certain individual connected to a case of espionage. It's almost certain that he was an intelligence officer tasked with getting information out of British civilians."

It took Flora a moment. "'A certain individual'! You mean Monique Garnier—"

“Boys!” Lady Alice barked suddenly, arresting Flora with an upheld hand. “Scoot!”

“But, Mum!” Mark whined. Matthew, however, silenced him with a whisper. The look he fixed on Eric as he carried the chessboard from the room was half scrutiny and half plea.

Lady Alice waited until they were quite gone before telling Eric, “Miranda and I know all about it, of course; Lucy, too. But I’d rather my boys didn’t.”

Flora said, “I take it the police know all about it, too, now?”

Eric nodded.

Flora’s lips tightened in displeasure. “That explains the persistence of their questioning. I expect Crane intends to spring this on me later, when he thinks he’s got something more damning, and see how I panic. But if Karl Werner was one of the spies Andrew was after, does that mean . . . ?”

“It’s possible.” Eric turned to Madam Eliot, who seemed to have frozen in place with her mouth half-open. “You told me of certain concerns you had about your husband’s death. I want to assure you that you can rest easy. His gun was missing, and there was clear evidence of an assassin—”

Madam Eliot jerked back with a violence that nearly sent her toppling onto the carpet. “That’s enough. What happened to Andrew is ancient history and can have nothing to do with anything happening now.”

“But Miranda, my dear,” Flora drawled. “If Karl Werner also killed Andrew—”

“You can speculate all you like. I, for one, have work to do.”

Madam Eliot snapped up her cigarette case from the table and slung it into her purse, then marched out of the room, her heels rattling like machine-gun fire. Penny made to go after her but was stopped by Lady Alice: “Let her be. She’ll sort things out on her own time.”

A moment later, they heard the front door slam.

Meanwhile, Eric couldn’t help but recall Avery’s speculation that Ward himself—the real Ward—might have been involved with

Werner's spy ring. It would explain their easy friendship later. Then again, it was Ward who'd pointed the French police at the spies . . .

Avery's theory was based on the same mark being on both the assassin's footprint and Ward's Webley. But suppose that gun actually belonged to the assassin?

Eric imagined the assassin escaping with Andrew Russell's gun by mistake, leaving their own weapon behind. And then, Ward coming through with Madame Aubert the concierge and leaping to the same conclusion as Madam Eliot, that Andrew Russell had committed suicide. Madame Aubert left to get the police, and Ward seized the opportunity to remove what he thought was his friend's gun, to better make the case for this being murder, and point the police at the spies Andrew had told him about. It was the most he could do without Madame Aubert noticing. He'd know it really was murder once the police arrived and found the bloody footprint, but it would be too late by then to present the revolver as evidence. So Ward returned to England with the assassin's gun and, not wanting to simply toss it into the Thames in case it became important, hid it away in the club vault.

"Well," said Flora, "I think it's a damned shame. There's a man I'd like to see boiled in oil, but he can't be sorry for what he can't remember, can he? I hope Dr. Duplessis is wrong. How on earth did he come up with such an idea, I'd like to know?"

Eric tore his mind away from Andrew Russell's murder, and repeated Duplessis's reasoning: Werner's fall from grace, his attempted suicide, the loss of his last friend, and the parallels with the case of Anna Tchaikovsky.

Lady Alice murmured, "I had no idea."

Flora, less impressed, scowled and got up to leave. "I almost feel sorry for him. Almost. None of this tragedy is an excuse or justification for what he's done. None of this is justice."

Eric's instinct was to offer to walk Flora home, but Penny had no intention of leaving just yet, and Lady Alice deserved to hear about

Avery's situation, being acquainted with him through their shared spiritualist interests. Of course, the plan had always been to continue to Saint Thomas' Hospital after this; now, Lady Alice insisted on joining them. Late as it was, the thickening cloud cover made it seem later still, and Eric hoped that enough time had passed that Avery could receive visitors.

Once in the back seat of the taxi, Lady Alice fell silent and said nothing until they reached the Houses of Parliament, and Westminster Bridge came into sight.

"You must forgive Flora. She feels rather strongly about things—oftentimes, things you wouldn't expect a girl like her to care tuppence about. Her heart's in the right place, whatever else she might do."

Penny said, "I thought she was perfectly right. Are you inclined to forgive Karl Werner, then?"

"'Forgive' is a strong word. Let us just say that I understand the man's position. I know something about what it is to come down in the world." It took Lady Alice a moment to realise the implications of what she'd said. Blushing furiously, she hastened to add, "Not that I ever looked down on George! That's not what I meant at all. George was a better gentleman than most who claim that title, and I won't have anyone thinking otherwise."

"What did you mean, then?"

"I meant Daddy. Oh dear, that's not quite right, either."

The taxi brought them right to the main entrance of Saint Thomas' Hospital, a venerable collection of ward pavilions turned towards the river for maximum light and fresh air. It had been requisitioned by the Army for the Fifth London General Hospital during the War, with huts erected on the grounds when the numbers of incoming wounded outstripped the available beds. The huts were gone now, but one could easily imagine the men in the Hospital Blues, sitting up in this sunny and well-ventilated place with the basket-weaving and embroidery they'd been encouraged to take up as hobbies while they rested and recovered from injuries very much like Avery's. Penny, Eric knew, still owned the needlework picture she'd picked up from an exhibition the hospital once held of those old warriors' handiwork.

Lady Alice climbed the front steps and stopped there, seemingly lost in thought as Eric paid their driver and sent him on his way.

"Daddy put on a brave face," she said when Penny nudged her from her reverie, "but I knew for years how bad things really were for us. With no son or distant cousin to inherit the title, Daddy knew the earldom would die with him. His investments went bad one by one, and the estate was so dreadfully mismanaged there was no saving it without a sudden influx of money. What could I or my sisters do? Daughters marry *out*, don't they? They and their fortunes belong to their husbands, not the other way around. George could be a duke or a dustman, and it would make no difference to the family coffers. Once my sisters and I were all safely married to decent, reliable husbands, Daddy quietly sold what remained of the estate to pay off his debts, ignored the whispers and pitying looks, and retired to Singapore, where a pound sterling means a little more than it does here. That's what I meant about coming down in the world. It wasn't Daddy's fault—he did the best he could—and it certainly wasn't George's."

Penny reached out to her, saying, "The world isn't what it was in our grandparents' time."

"No, and Daddy's story is rather common now, from what I hear. In a way, I'm glad. With nothing more to lose, I was free to marry for love rather than money or status—or not at all, if that was my choice."

"You were happy with George Russell. That's better than any number of jewelled tiaras."

It occurred to Eric that Lady Alice wasn't simply in full mourning: she was in *outdated* full mourning, as though time had stopped for her the day her husband died. What was it Flora had said? *Memorials should be made of stone, not of human lives.*

But Lady Alice saw nothing pathetic about her situation. "Of the four of us, I think I was the luckiest. George and I had seven lovely years before the War began, enough to learn that the thing which draws a couple together before marriage is only the promise of love, not love itself. Love comes later, from sharing in each other's blood, sweat, and tears. Flora and Lucy never got that far in their marriages, so what can they really know of it? They each enjoyed a fairy-tale romance and each now mourns a fairy-tale prince. *I* mourn a man of flesh and blood."

In that moment, atop the front steps of Saint Thomas' Hospital, Lady Alice was more a monument than ever: a basalt Madonna with eyes haunted by a thousand generations—

"Lady Alice! My darling, I knew I would find you here!"

A woman, swathed in floating silks and dripping silver charms, had just emerged from the hospital doors and was now gliding towards them with hands outstretched. Her eyes were startlingly luminous, lined with kohl on a thin, dead-white face. Madame Davidova. Of course. She was Avery's favourite spirit medium, and, apparently, Lady Alice's as well. Eric had met her only once before, and once was enough.

Lady Alice herself was again the dignified but otherwise ordinary widow of Colonel Hadrian Russell's eldest son, George: the basalt Madonna was gone, and the last five minutes might never have happened. Eric had to marvel at her ability to put her best face forward as the situation demanded. She met Madame Davidova in a continental fashion, with a fleeting kiss on both cheeks, and her voice dropped in a reverence she showed no one else. "Madame. How did you know?"

"I have my ways," the medium purred in an accent ruthlessly appropriated from Eastern Europe—though Eric suspected that in unguarded moments, it would prove more St. Pancras than St. Petersburg. "You are here for Mr. Ferrett, yes? Come, we go together."

Madame Davidova had evidently just come down from visiting Avery, and while it was good to know that Avery was well enough now for that, Eric didn't much fancy having the likes of *her* fluttering around them with her pretentious nonsense. Judging by the look Penny gave him as they fell into step behind Lady Alice and the medium, he was not alone.

Avery's ward was a long, plain room with wide windows reaching up to the ceiling between the beds on either side. The result was sunny and airy, while a central heating system minimised any draughts. Avery, desperately pale and drawn, lay in the third bed. He looked up blearily as Madame Davidova swept in; his voice was weak and gasping as he said, "Back already? Oh, reinforcements!"

"Did I not tell you Mr. Peterkin would be here before day is out?"

"Well . . ." Avery began, momentarily taken aback. Eric guessed that Madame Davidova had, in fact, said no such thing—but Avery was in no condition to argue, and Madame Davidova had no intention of stopping long enough for doubt.

"Mr. Ferrett told me everything. But of course, I will direct all my powers to bring this fiend to justice. You are entwined in this, Lady Alice; as are you, Mr. Peterkin."

"What?" Eric turned to Avery, who, despite his pallor, smiled back with every indication of having pulled off a coup. "Avery, what did you do?"

"Duplessis said that Werner thinks he's Ward, didn't he? So, to find him, the question we should be asking is, *What would Gregory Ward do?* Isn't that right?"

Eric nodded. He could see where this was going, and he didn't like it.

Avery's grin widened as Lady Alice stifled a gasp of realisation. "Who knows better what Gregory Ward would do than *Gregory Ward himself?*"

# PART FOUR

# THE HARROWING OF MISS CASTLE

IT WAS RAINING when Eric and Penny got off the train at Harrow-on-the-Hill: a dark, miserable downpour uninterrupted by any catharsis of thunder or lightning—the sort of slow rain that lasted forever. Rather than wait in the station for goodness knows how long, the two hurried through the wet and finally arrived, thoroughly drenched, at a dark house with a skin-deep pretence of Tudor half-timbering and a white-trimmed bow window bulging out onto an unkempt square of lawn. A conjoined neighbour doubled the house's apparent size and, theoretically, its grandeur; the similarly semi-detached houses to the left and right were the same, as was every house on either side of the street, mirrored pairs repeating into the distant night.

This was Metro-land, and Harrow was regarded by some—others favouring Wembley—as its crown jewel. This middle-class suburbia spreading along the Metropolitan Railway line northwest of London had exploded since the War, to welcome the men coming home from it with a myth-made-real of cosy cottages set among hollyhocks and country lanes.

Eric got as far as fitting the provided key into the lock when a stone-faced policeman wrenched the door open and dragged both him and Penny inside. This was Sergeant Archer, and he had nothing to say to anyone who lacked a policeman's badge. Instead, he peered out into the rain in a manner certain to raise the suspicions of nosey neighbours, then shut the door tight and set about briskly locking everything.

"Why's it so dark?" asked Penny, taking off her hat to shake out her hair. "Is the electricity out?"

"Yes," Sergeant Archer responded shortly. But the lights were on in the neighbouring houses, so perhaps it was only that Scotland Yard hadn't seen fit to pay the utility bills for a place they used only now and again, and the electricity board was dragging its heels in getting things started again for what would almost certainly be no more than a week or two of operation. Sergeant Archer provided no explanations. He simply turned and lumbered off towards the kitchen, where Eric saw the soft glow of a kerosene lamp somewhere beyond the doorway.

With the house's faux-Tudor detailing draped in darkness, what might have been drab and impersonal in the light of day felt almost sinister. *I've grown too used to the modern electric light,* Eric thought. How had the previous generations survived?

"Oh my goodness! You're both soaked!" Lucy stood at the sitting room entrance with a candle, its yellow light floating around her like a ghost. "You'd better get out of those clothes before you catch your deaths of cold. We've got hot water in the taps, at least; so, Penny, if you like, I'll draw a hot bath for you. And Mr. Archer was kind enough to build a nice, cheery fire, so you can warm yourselves up there, too."

Penny would indeed like a hot bath, so Lucy ran upstairs to prepare it. Meanwhile, Eric could do little but strip off the worst of his wet clothing and hang it before the sitting room fire to dry. An extra dressing gown saved him the indecency of wandering a strange house in his underclothes, and he was warming himself at the fire when Lucy came down again. Eric had to remark at her transformation—or rather, her un-transformation. When he last saw her that morning, she was a shattered, listless wreck.

"I got better."

Eric remained incredulous. "Are you sure? I mean—"

"I don't want to talk about it." For a moment, the mask slipped—and then Lucy was smiling placidly again. She indicated a chessboard on the low table beside a trio of candles. "Do you play? None of the policemen do, so it's been dreadfully dull. Do sit down: I've already asked Mr. Archer to prepare us a pot of tea."

This was the stiff upper lip at work, of course: a fine and honourable approach—until the unrelieved pressure shattered you beyond repair; but if this was how Lucy wanted to deal with her distress, Eric could do nothing but play along.

Across the chessboard, the familiar black and white pieces cast long, wavering shadows from the combined light of the fireplace and the candles. White had been offered to Eric as a matter of courtesy due to the invited player, but he turned the board around to offer it back to Lucy. She accepted by moving a knight out towards the centre of the board.

"I don't know if I'm much good," she said, glancing up with mild concern. "You don't mind, I hope."

"So you say, but I'm sure you'll have me in mate within ten moves."

Archer emerged from the shadows five minutes later with the promised pot of tea and a pair of mismatched cups. He deposited the lot wordlessly beside them, then withdrew again to the kitchen to continue watching for the anticipated German attack. Penny came down another five minutes after that, but only to say good night, having elected to retire early to bed.

Eric settled into the game and into the sofa. The house was cheaply and indifferently furnished—hardly the lap of luxury—but that was masked by the darkness now, and there was comfort in the little patch of warmth and light between the candles and the fireplace. The soft patter of rain against the windows was both a soothing caress and a whispered warning against leaving the light.

It was clear to Eric that what Lucy wanted was a distraction, so, as they played, he told her what he'd told the others—about the meeting with Dr. Keller in Switzerland, Duplessis's assessment, and Avery's injury during the confrontation at the Britannia. Since, according to Lady Alice, Lucy already knew about Monique Garnier's letters, Eric told her about his inquiries in Paris as well, then added the day's attempts to track Werner down through the German community, visiting Avery at Saint Thomas' with Lady Alice, and the planned séance.

"Avery's in no condition yet to leave the hospital ward, and of course there's no question of disturbing the other patients with something like this. So Lady Alice has volunteered her drawing room tomorrow night for the event, while I'm to attend and report everything back to Avery the next day."

"You don't sound particularly enthused," Lucy remarked.

"I'm quite certain Madame Davidova's a thorough fraud. Avery believes in her, but he's a bit of an eccentric. What surprises me is that Lady Alice believes in her, too. She seems like such a sensible woman—Lady Alice, I mean."

Lucy toyed with a rook thoughtfully. "You know, I was still in school when the War broke out. One of our younger mistresses, Miss Castle, was very much like Alice in being sensible and ladylike. Her twin brother, meanwhile, was something of a black sheep; but black sheep have the best adventures, and when he went off to fight, he wrote about them to his sister in monthly letters. Miss Castle, in turn, would read those letters aloud for us. Then, on a night very much like this one, with rain like watered-down misery, something happened. Miss Castle woke up screaming for—well, for a 'medic,' which we assumed to mean the school nurse, not that *she* could do anything. Miss Castle refused to calm down until the rain stopped, sometime in the wee hours, and when morning came, she was like a different person. She forgot things she should have known, like our names and the things she was supposed to be teaching us, but she also seemed to know things she never knew before, like how to fix a motorcar. The third night afterwards, she sneaked out of the school to drink at the local pub, got into a brawl—and won! Such behaviour should have meant immediate dismissal, but it was also so shockingly uncharacteristic of the normally sensible and ladylike Miss Castle that the headmistress sent for a doctor instead."

"And what did the doctor say?"

"We never got that far. The postman arrived first, with Miss Castle's monthly letter from her brother; the doctor arrived a minute after, just in time to see her tear open the envelope. And the moment she laid eyes on the letter—oh! She let out such a shriek that the whole school heard and dropped senseless to the floor. They took her up to her room to lay her down in her own bed, and that's when they found it. The telegram. It had arrived the morning after the same rainy night when Miss Castle first went mad, to inform her of her brother's death by a sniper."

Somewhere in the house, a floorboard creaked, startling Lucy so she sat up, her pale face turned towards the shadows in fearful anticipation. Nothing followed but the continuing patter of rain on glass, and Eric found himself shifting closer to the fire for warmth. He said, "Dr. Duplessis would theorise that the telegram announcing her brother's death, arriving on top of her night terrors, shocked her into a delusion similar to what he thinks happened with Karl Werner; and then the letter, addressed to her as Miss Castle, snapped her out of it."

*Für meinen Bruder*. Just as Werner had been shaken by the sight of an old Christmas present from his own long-dead brother.

"Perhaps." Lucy put the knight she'd been toying with back down on the board and continued as though she'd forgotten the chess game altogether. "In any case, when Miss Castle woke up again that afternoon, she had no memory of the past three days—no memory of sneaking out to the pub, no memory of the brawl—but she remembered our names again, and she remembered our lessons. The headmistress saw her way to hushing things up, and Miss Castle went back to teaching us as though nothing had ever happened—though she refused to believe that her brother was truly dead. I left school that year, so I never found out if anything further occurred. Perhaps she's waiting for her brother still. Or perhaps, on nights like this, when the rain is slow and interminable, Private Castle walks again in his sister's shoes."

"*Private* Castle, is it?" Eric lined up a castle-shaped rook with Lucy's king. "Check. You know, only officers get their deaths reported by telegram. For other ranks, like privates, the records officer fills out a form and posts it to their families."

"Oh, you're no fun." Lucy placidly moved her king out of check and sat back. "All I'm saying is, there are too many ghost stories for us to not wonder if there might be a grain of truth in them somewhere."

"You'd go further without the fiction."

"The fiction is what makes it real. We were talking about Alice, so let me explain. As soon as the War ended, Alice threw herself into all sorts of charitable work to take her mind off George's death, and it was at one of these charity fundraisers that she met Madame Davidova. Madame Davidova knew things about George that she couldn't possibly have known—"

"The way your 'Miss Castle' knew things only her brother could know? You'd be surprised at the things you can find out if you put your mind to it."

"Well, it piqued Alice's curiosity. She went to one séance, and then another. I remember her coming back from one of them, red-eyed from weeping, but smiling. She'd talked to George again, she told me. He was happy where he was, and he wanted her to be happy, too, as long as she 'remained faithful to his memory,' which Alice took to mean perpetual mourning. She's worn nothing but black since, and while it might seem a bit morbid, she's finally happy."

Lady Alice was desperate for any sort of connection to her dead husband, of course. Eric wondered how many women, widowed by the War, had resorted to the likes of Madame Davidova for this forlorn scrap of false comfort. "She's being made a fool of by an unscrupulous fraud. You know that, don't you?"

"My point is that it doesn't matter. Checkmate, by the way."

What?

Eric jerked his attention down to the board, studying it backwards and forwards, side to side. Lucy was right. Checkmate. All those apparently reckless plays . . . had they been, in fact, part of a carefully calculated strategy of ruthless sacrifice?

"Not much good, you said! Good God. Where'd you learn to play like that?"

"Hadrian taught me." Lucy began setting the board back in order. "He always said that you must be prepared to sacrifice a few men if you really want to win. But you're like Alice: all you want to do is save everyone."

"I'm impressed. I had no idea."

"There wasn't much else to do, once dinner was done, though Hadrian cheated terribly. I don't suppose you noticed that as I was telling you about Miss Castle, I'd pick pieces up and put them down again, but in the wrong place? And then, you were so pleased with yourself at spotting the hole in the story that I could have made you walk into any trap I liked."

"You were cheating!"

Lucy grinned and tapped him on the nose. "Another thing Hadrian always said: if you cannot deal with cheats, then do not play at all. And now . . . Good night! Good night! And in the morning, wake bright!"

Picking up a candle, she twirled away, and Eric could only stare after her as the candle glow disappeared up the stairs into shadow.

# THE SÉANCE

PENNY CONSIDERED THE SÉANCE a break from the investigation, and had no interest in attending. Eric was secretly relieved: Flora would be there, and there was a certain delight in simply being in the same room as the lovely Flora Grace, which would be quite spoiled by the presence of an inquisitive younger sister. Until then, he had some reading to catch up on.

> Marlena Gudenoff was dangerous, that much was certain. At the moment, however, Harry Thompson only cared that her shapely hips were swaying like a hypnotist's pendulum as she drew closer, reddened lips pouting for a kiss. His gun wavered in his hand, then finally dropped to the floor as soft hands slid over his shoulders, and her warm, perfumed body pressed against his. The flash of a stiletto blade broke the spell only a split second before she could skewer him, but his reflexes were quicker—

An indiscretion was one thing, Eric mused, if one were sitting alone on duty with little to do, as in Harvey's case; but when the stakes were life and death, surely such lustful distraction was impossible? Then again, everyone had his or her own weakness. Avery and Lady Alice believed in spirit mediums, which Eric didn't fully understand, so who was he to judge a fictional detective for his peculiar inability to remember the danger of his situation when a beautiful temptress wandered into view?

Seven o'clock, and a fog was rising. Eric tossed the manuscript into his desk drawer, checked himself in a mirror, thought again of Flora, and set out for Lady Alice's Marylebone residence.

"Mr. Peterkin!" Lady Alice met Eric with bright eyes, flushed cheeks, and a nervous energy he'd never seen in her before. "Is your sister not joining us? That's a shame, but no matter: Dr. Duplessis is here, and he will round out our numbers quite nicely."

"Will your sons be joining us?"

"Oh no. This is hardly the sort of thing I'd like to expose their impressionable young minds to. Besides, with a dangerous fugitive on the loose, I thought it best they stay with my sister Charlotte's family in Brighton for the next little while."

Heavy curtains shielded the tall windows in the now-darkened, cavernous drawing room, while the Axminster carpet had been rolled away so a round table could be set on the bare parquetry. The only light came from a lamp set in the middle of the table; gathered beside it was a collection of unlit candles, all fat enough to stand on their own.

Madame Davidova reclined in the same chaise longue Flora had occupied yesterday, her face whiter and more corpse-like than ever. Kohl-rimmed eyes snapped to attention only briefly to receive Eric's greeting before wandering off again to some invisible thing in the middle distance.

Dr. Duplessis, peering at Lady Alice's framed photographs, nodded stiffly to Eric and whispered, "She is an interesting case, this Madame Davidova; though perhaps not so interesting as the sort of person who believes in her."

"I've no doubt," Eric whispered back. It sounded as though the alienist had, intellectually at least, forgiven Eric for daring to bring up the subject of his son's affliction.

The doorbell chimed, and a moment later, Lady Alice's efficient but taciturn maid stood silhouetted in the bright rectangle of light from the hallway to usher in the next guest. It took Eric a moment longer to recognise the slim, boyishly trousered figure as Miss Flora Grace.

The faintest hint of vanilla, leather, and smoke tickled his senses, so subtle it might have passed unnoticed at any other time, but now his imagination filled the cavernous void of the drawing room with thoughts of what he'd missed and what might have been.

"Flora."

"Mr. Peterkin." Her smile seemed genuine. Was he missing something in the shadows? "I'm surprised to see you here. I was under the impression that you had better things to do than chase after ghosts."

"Mr. Ferrett insisted I attend in his stead. And I do want to apologise."

"For telling Crane about Monique Garnier? I realise now that it couldn't be helped."

"Oh. Yes, I suppose. But—" *I want to apologise for not seeing you as soon as I got back from the continent. For not sparing you more attention yesterday when Penny and I visited.*

"Don't be a bore, darling."

Was she secretly angry at him? Or did she simply have no time to waste on the past? Elsewhere, Madame Davidova still seemed to be watching for fairies, and Duplessis's attention was back on the wall of photographs. Lady Alice was just now greeting Madam Eliot at the hall door.

"Alice," Madam Eliot was saying, "do you remember what you told me earlier, that this séance might fail because we haven't got anything of Captain Ward's to help with contacting his spirit? It got me thinking that since he was supposed to be friends with Andrew, there might be something of Andrew's that would count. But of course, I haven't kept any of Andrew's old things, and that's when I realised: you *do* have something to do with Captain Ward—I mean, *you* do. I gave it to you, remember? After Andrew died. It's right there on the wall."

What was this? Intrigued, both Eric and Flora followed as Madam Eliot all but dragged Lady Alice down the length of the wall to the glass-fronted toy cabinet with the framed family portrait above. Her goal, however, was one of the lesser photographs nearby, in which a row of bright-eyed, eager young soldiers proudly showed off their second lieutenant pips.

Flora gasped. "Of course! Ward trained with Andrew and David. He'd be with them in that photograph they all took together when they were commissioned. Alice, may I?" Reaching up, she lifted the framed photograph off its hook and turned it to catch the light from the hall.

The faces of men long dead smiled back at them, oblivious to their fates.

"That's David," Flora told Eric, pointing out one handsome, fair-haired fellow with a dashing moustache. The man next to him was taller, darker, not so handsome but heavier across the shoulders: Andrew Russell. And there, at the end of the row, was a man who might have been Werner's younger, unscarred brother.

"I won't say I'd guess them to be the same person," Madam Eliot remarked, "but if you told me they were, I'd have believed you."

"Well, I don't know if it's good enough," Lady Alice said doubtfully, then turned and brought the photograph to Madame Davidova for her opinion.

The medium received the photograph without a word and held it in both hands. She closed her eyes, exhaled slowly, and brushed one hand over the glass face of the picture. Another breath, and then a third . . . Finally, she intoned, "The psychic energies are weak—very weak—but I think they will do. Perhaps if Mr. Peterkin will take the seat directly opposite me? I sense a deep well of power within you, Mr. Peterkin, and crossing the table thus will allow me to tap into it—if I have your permission."

"Er. Of course." Eric gave the medium an utterly unnecessary hand to the table and took the indicated seat. Lady Alice was impressed, at least: she seemed to have cast aside both her reserve and a decade of her age at the prospect of this séance.

"My felicitations on your well of power," Duplessis whispered as he took the seat to Eric's right. "May it pay dividends."

"Shut up. I didn't know you went in for this sort of thing."

"Human behaviour is always of interest."

Perhaps.

Flora, Eric was gratified to see, had taken the seat to his other side. She smiled when she caught his eye, and the question of possibilities burned in his mind. A gentleman would have called on her earlier. A gentleman would have told her when he left the country. He'd been so focussed on the quest that he'd spared no thought for home, and Sir Kay, seneschal of Camelot, would be singularly unimpressed. But they'd barely begun anything, hadn't they? So perhaps the lapse of attention was not merely forgivable, but warranted. Eric wanted more than anything to clarify the situation with Flora, but there was nothing he could do right now, with everyone else sitting within earshot.

Lady Alice, at Madame Davidova's instruction, lit six fat candles and set one in front of each person—slapping Eric's hand away when he reached out for a closer examination. She'd claimed the seat to Madame Davidova's right, which left Madam Eliot seated between the medium and Duplessis. Once all the candles were in place, Lady Alice extinguished the lamp and replaced it with the photograph of Gregory Ward and his newly commissioned fellows. The door to the hall was closed. All around the table, faces glowed in the flickering light of the candles before them, like ghosts floating in the darkness. Madame Davidova's own face was a white mask with startling black-rimmed eyes, every line a grotesque exaggeration.

"Breathe."

Six sets of lungs synchronised in the silence.

"Join our hands. Complete the circle. Breathe."

The silence, rising and falling on waves of breath, stretched out into the night.

"There is a flame before you. Gaze into it. Deep, deep into the blackness at its core, that is neither fire nor water nor earth nor air . . . Neither life nor death. This is the threshold. Through that blackness is the way to worlds unknown, the one before and the one after, where spirits roam. Captain Gregory Algernon Ward. Picture in your mind the man as he was, and project that image into the gateway before you. Focus. Breathe."

The monotonous, hypnotic drone washed over Eric as he gazed into the nimbus of black around the candle wick. For some reason, he saw Waterloo Station: a schoolgirl seeing him off amid the scaffolding, and a woman welcoming him home under the completed Victory Arch . . . What was he missing? He was turning his back on a beautiful woman in trousers . . .

Eric blinked the vision away. How was everyone else taking this charade? Lady Alice was staring intently into her candle flame, of course; Madam Eliot was endeavouring to do the same but, thanks to a combination of curiosity and nerves, not succeeding quite as well. He could see Flora and Duplessis in profile to either side, but he'd have to turn his head for a better look. And Madame Davidova was staring over her candle straight at him.

Something crunched in the silence: a soft, grinding sound.

Lady Alice, sitting up straight in fevered anticipation, whispered, "The portal! It opens! I . . . I can *smell* it."

Eric sniffed. Roses? Yes, a strong odour of roses, sweet and cloying . . .

Madame Davidova let out a low moan. She whimpered. Her whisper carried across the table: "Yes . . . Come to us . . . Wait. No. Please. I mean, yes, but not like this . . . Oh . . ." She moaned again, this time in a deeper, more guttural timbre, and Eric felt the hairs on the back of his neck rise on end.

"The shame . . ."

Madame Davidova's voice had dropped an octave, and her posture contorted into one of straining tension. Her neighbours on either side could only stare—Madam Eliot in horrified fascination, Lady Alice with an eager excitement quite at odds with her usually respectable facade—as their hands were gripped in hers, too tight for them to pull away.

"This man who wears my face . . . who wears my name . . . I trusted him, once. He was kind to me. Once. The shame . . ."

"Are you Gregory Ward?" Eric couldn't help asking.

The voice emanating from Madame Davidova was a sepulchral creak: "I . . . am."

Impossible.

"Karl Werner," Lady Alice said. "Where is he now?"

The spirit medium's head rolled. She—or the spirit she was channelling—appeared not to hear. In the same low voice, she continued, "It was a mistake. He was open to possession. He was kind. I was new. I left . . . I left a piece of myself in him. The shame. Oh! The shame!"

"What must we do?"

"My gun. It was my father's . . . his legacy . . . my family's legacy. He used it. The shame, to have my name, my face, my family, my very self . . . embroiled in such a crime . . . Colonel Russell . . . he was like a father to me, in the War . . . I cannot rest while . . . oh!" Madame Davidova froze. Then her head snapped up to look directly at Eric, blue eyes burning with urgency. "You must clear my name. Restore my honour. Find my gun and send it to be buried where I am buried. It is of the utmost urgency—"

And then her head dropped to her chest, and her body went limp.

Madam Eliot wasted no time in extricating herself from her neighbours, only to have the medium jerk back into consciousness and seize her hand with a violence that made her cry out. "No!" Madame Davidova gasped. "Do not break the circle! Not yet, not while—ah!"

She stiffened again, both her neighbours wincing as her grip tightened on their hands. Eric felt Flora's hand slip back into his. He hadn't noticed losing her—was this an omen? She was staring at

Madame Davidova, her mouth half-open in fascination. On Eric's other side, Duplessis frowned across the table, utterly perplexed.

"Alice."

It was almost a growl, a guttural intonation emanating from deep within the medium as she rolled her head forwards, eyes glassy and unseeing. Lady Alice gave a start and turned, almost hesitantly, to face her.

"George?"

"Alice . . . I've missed you . . . I've been so lonely . . . Father . . . I can't find Father. He's lost. Alice . . . you must . . . you must . . . no!"

With a strangled gasp, Madame Davidova released her neighbours' hands and pitched forwards onto the table, unconscious.

# AFTERMATH

UNDER THE UNFORGIVING electric light, Lady Alice's drawing room lost all of the mystery fostered by Madame Davidova's stage management. The medium herself had been conveyed back to the chaise longue, on which she reclined with the melodramatic languor of a consumptive Victorian heroine. Eric, having recently encountered a sanatorium's worth of actual consumptives, was less impressed—but Lady Alice fussed in attendance over the woman as, admittedly, she probably would with any guest who'd collapsed in the middle of a visit.

Eric and Duplessis were left to move the furniture back in place, gather up the candles, and roll out the Axminster carpet again.

"What do you think?" Duplessis asked, keeping his voice low. "Are you convinced?"

"Don't tell me *you* are! Look." Eric rubbed at a barely perceptible stain on the floor where Madame Davidova's chair had been. "Rose scent. Break an ampoule of it under your heel, and when everyone wonders at the sudden inexplicable smell, you tell them it's the portal to the spirit world. Easy, and no wonder the carpet had to be rolled away: you want a hard surface underfoot to grind the ampoule into powder. And over here, look at the candles. There's a length of black thread tied to one, ready to be pulled over at the right dramatic moment. That's all this woman is: cheap tricks and theatricality."

Duplessis's frown deepened. "But it was Lady Alice who identified the so-called opening of portals, and Lady Alice who arranged the candles. Was she an accomplice?"

"Lady Alice has taken part in Madame Davidova's séances before, and I'm sure this is not the first time the trick with the rose scent was played. She's probably been told often enough what it's supposed to mean, and so now she's parroting the explanation back at us. As for the candle and the thread, it doesn't matter where the candle was placed, as long as the thread ended where Madame Davidova could get hold of it—"

"How, with both hands holding on to her neighbours? Anyone else might be forgiven for letting go, but not her."

"Perhaps she had the loose end tied to one shoe?" But when, after the placement of the candles, could she have done that? Eric shrugged. "Or perhaps that's why the trick went un-played."

Duplessis frowned, harder than when he was told about the death of the real Gregory Ward. "All the same, I wonder if Lady Alice believes less than we thought."

Eric recalled Lucy's peculiar brand of chess, and her apparent high spirits just half a day after being told that her lover never existed. "It never pays to take someone at their face value, does it? The Russell widows, especially."

"That is true. Otherwise, Lady Alice is very much like you in character."

Eric looked up sharply. It was the second time in as many nights that someone had compared him to Lady Alice, and he demanded to know what Duplessis meant.

Duplessis frowned at the collected candles, then at the chaise longue where Madame Davidova was accepting a cup of tea from Lady Alice with visibly trembling fingers. "She goes to great lengths for her causes," he said, though his mind seemed far away. "The same way you travelled to Switzerland for the Colonel's murder. Do you know, the day Monsieur Werner brought the Russell boys home from the train station, I saw her pay a large sum of money to him—to keep him away from Mademoiselle Lucy, I thought—"

"You saw what?"

Rather than elaborate, Duplessis said, "I asked you once before, why you saw the need to investigate these things yourself. Do you remember what you told me?"

"One does what one can before calling in the big guns. Why? Has something happened?"

"Perhaps." Duplessis lapsed into silence as they returned the séance table to its position under a window and rolled the rose-patterned Axminster back across the floor. Then he said, "I think I see the wisdom in what you say. If a thing can be resolved without the police, so much the better; and if not, you will have more evidence with which to convince them of the need to intervene. They would not listen to mere suspicion, is that not so? Please excuse me."

Duplessis would explain his concerns once he had them properly sorted, Eric supposed. As the alienist went to say his goodbyes to Lady Alice and Madame Davidova, Eric sought out the other participants of the séance: Flora and Madam Eliot, conversing by the glass-fronted toy cabinet under Lady Alice's family portrait, Flora still holding the photograph from the now-empty space above.

"Well, it has been a decidedly interesting evening, hasn't it?" Madam Eliot turned to include Eric into the conversation. "I was just telling Flora how I normally try to avoid Alice when she gets it into her head to have one of these séances, but now that I've actually seen one, I have to say I'm impressed."

"She'll be wanting each of us to contact our husbands next—for a fee, of course. It's a good thing Lucy isn't here. She'd be an easy mark without Hadrian to look out for her."

"You underestimate your sister-in-law, I think," Eric murmured. Sitting on top of the cabinet was an old chess set with pieces carved to represent nursery rhyme figures. Eric remembered Lady Alice's sons playing with it the day before, and hoped that neither Lucy nor the Colonel had taught the newest generation of Russell men to cheat.

"Poor Lucy," said Madam Eliot. "Whether this spiritualist business is real or not, it's probably for the best that no one encourages her to go looking for Patrick again. She's young, and one needs to live in this world rather than the next. Don't you agree? That's what I said to myself when I got the news about Andrew. One must carry on."

Flora smiled. "And you do it so well."

"Madam Eliot, I meant to ask," Eric said, idly picking up the white king. "Lucy mentioned you had reservations about Ward—back when we all thought he was Ward—and I was wondering why."

Madam Eliot's smile faltered. "I'm sure I don't know."

"Might it have been something your husband told you?"

"Andrew? No, certainly not. Well, perhaps. I never cared much for the few friends of his that I did meet, but as it's turned out that Mr. Werner was never one of them, that's hardly relevant, now, is it?"

Eric was about to press her for more details, when something rasped against the pad of his thumb. He looked down at the chess piece in his hands. Scratched into its base was a rectangle, divided by a cross into rectangular quarters—not quite the same mark as the one he now associated with the spies responsible for Andrew Russell's death, but remarkably similar.

Flora recognised it at once. "Oh, George used to mark everything he owned with that, when he was a boy. They were named for the patron saints of the British Isles: George, Andrew, David, and Patrick—England, Scotland, Wales, and Ireland. So George took the English flag, the cross of St. George, as his personal cipher. He grew out of it eventually, and neither David nor Patrick followed suit, the Welsh dragon and the Irish harp being a little more difficult to scratch into things with a penknife. But Andrew kept it up well into adulthood. Didn't he, Miranda?"

"Oh. It's been . . . I haven't thought about it in years."

Eric recognised the signs of Madam Eliot falling prey to her nerves. There was a sense of dread curdling the pit of his stomach as well.

Flora, however, seemed oblivious. She turned over the photograph of Andrew and David Russell's training mates, and began to open up the frame. "Didn't you say this used to be Andrew's? Here." Sliding the photograph out, she showed Eric the thing he guessed he'd see drawn onto its back: a rectangle quartered by diagonal lines into four triangles—the same symbol from the Webley in Ward's vault box, the same symbol carved into the sole of an assassin's shoe and printed in blood onto the scene of Andrew Russell's murder. A rectangular flag bearing the X-shaped cross of St. Andrew.

As if from a distance, he heard Flora continue, "It was his way of marking the things of particular importance to him, wasn't it, Miranda? Not his clothes or furniture, thank goodness—that would have been insufferable—but his favourite books, and of course his photographs—"

And then, Madam Eliot's high-pitched twittering: "Oh dear. Look at the time. I really must be off. Such a pleasure to see you again, Mr. Peterkin—we really must arrange another meeting to deal with that mess in the Britannia Club basement."

What was the same symbol doing on Ward's revolver, an assassin's shoe, and this photograph? Had Andrew Russell been one of the spies all along? To hell with the pipe room and the Roman mosaic! Who could think of such trivialities at a time like this?

Madam Eliot skittered away, pausing at the chaise longue to say a quick goodbye to Lady Alice and Madame Davidova before continuing out into the hall. Lady Alice's offer to have her maid show her out died before it was fully articulated. Duplessis, Eric noticed, was gone as well.

Eric wasn't sure how he found it in himself to offer Flora a ride home.

The fog outside had risen while they were at the séance, reducing the world to only about thirty yards in any direction. The house behind them was a dark, unwelcoming blank, punctuated by a dim light in an upstairs window. It was just as well they hadn't called Lady Alice's maid down for the trivial task of showing them the door, Eric thought as he noted the movement upstairs, if she was busy preparing her mistress's bed for her.

Once in their taxi, Flora said to Eric, "I'm not inviting you up for the night. I hope you understand that."

"That wasn't my intention." Whatever his intentions at the beginning of the evening, he wanted now to think about Andrew's mark and what it meant. Did the Webley that had killed Colonel Russell belong not to Ward, but to Andrew Russell? Whose footprint was it, then, that they'd found in his blood? But Flora was here now, and—"Look. I've treated you abominably."

"How so?"

"What happened between us usually implies all sorts of promises. Promises which I've failed to keep."

"Did something happen between us? As I recall, I gave you a kiss and let it be implied that I might welcome you into my bed. That was over a week ago. Do you imagine I've spent that time pining for you, or are you wondering how to ask if the offer is still open without appearing uncouth?"

Barely three feet away, the taxi driver drove on without a sign of having overheard anything. Eric shifted uncomfortably in his seat, sure that the hot flush creeping up his neck might have melted away the fog around them in an instant.

"Let me put your mind at ease," Flora said. "No, I expected nothing from you then, and I expect nothing from you now. We are not lovers."

"I can't help but think I've taken advantage of you," Eric mumbled.

"You never got far enough for that to be a concern. And if you did . . . Perhaps you'd find it was *I* who took advantage of *you*. Did you ever consider that?"

"I'm not—I wasn't the one in a state of grief."

Flora turned to stare at him, incredulous. Amusement tugged at her lips. "Grief! For Hadrian?"

"No, I meant—" Eric checked himself. It would be a bad idea to bring up David Russell now, or to suggest any sort of past analysis of Flora's psyche. Nobody liked having their own motivations explained to them.

But Flora saw exactly where he was going, and her amusement vanished. "You mean David."

"I know you still think of him."

"Mr. Peterkin." Flora looked dangerously close to spitting in anger. "If you dare suggest that I'm merely trying to replace David, I will scratch your eyes out. David was a precious and wonderful chapter of my life, and it ended with him setting me free. I told you, didn't I, what he said? 'Go. Leave me and move on. Live your life and be happy.' So if I take a lover, it is because I want to, nothing more and nothing less. And why shouldn't I, when men do what they want? If David's had any influence at all over my life now, it is in showing me that. It is not because I'm deluding myself into thinking I'd find him again in the likes of Thomas Harvey or even, God forbid, Eric Peterkin."

"But—" Eric stopped. But what? Flora was clearly unafraid of anything so trivial as people talking, and if there were societal difficulties beyond that, how could he bring them up without seeming to judge or castigate her?

"I've no patience for the old morality. That and the old men . . ." Flora took a deep breath, and declaimed:

*"But the old man would not so, but slew his son*
*And half the seed of Europe, one by one."*

The taxi came to a stop. Outside, Flora's block of flats was a monolithic wall, its height and boundaries obscured by the fog. Eric reached toward Flora as she slipped out onto the street. "I swear, Flora. There's no judgement meant."

Flora turned and leaned down to address him through the open door.

"This is what they call *liberation*, Mr. Peterkin. But let me tell you a secret: the point of it all isn't the right to lose myself in wanton dissolution with as many lovers as I can fit into my schedule. The point is that now, rather than simply wait to be chosen, I can myself choose—and I do not choose you."

Lust, not longing. But deeper than either of these, Eric realised, was *rage*.

Flora Grace might not be seeking to bring David Russell back in another lover, but she *was* punishing the world for having taken him away.

The door slammed. Fog swirled between the taxi and Flora's retreating form, leaving Eric to reflect that Harry Thompson's entanglement with the delectably dangerous Marlena Gudenoff was less complicated. There was a brief, diffuse glow as the building's door opened to let her in, and when the fog subsided enough to see again, there remained no indication she'd been there at all.

# CLYTEMNESTRA

THE OFFICES OF Carrington-Clarke & Associates were around the corner from the Willesden Green train station, one in a row of identical terraced houses in red brick and white stone trim, with a shallow forecourt before a wide bay window. Only a modest brass plaque gave any indication that this was not an ordinary residence—officially, anyway. Unofficially, there were the diazotype prints airing out on the balcony over the front door, spilling a faint ammoniac stench onto the heads of approaching visitors.

Eric paused in the shade of the balcony and turned back to Penny. Yesterday's clammy fog had given way to the sort of unusually hot day meant for lounging in the garden with a tall glass of lemonade, not for uncomfortable confrontations. "You don't have to do this if you don't want to, you know."

"But I *do* want to." Penny had been seized with an almost compulsive drive to involve herself in the ongoing inquiries since being forced to leave Barchester, which had only been exacerbated by the news that the séance had afforded a clue after all—specifically, the significance of St. Andrew's cross—and they'd spent the morning at St. Thomas' with Avery discussing it. "I shan't be left behind again. Besides, I really want to know what Madam Eliot has to say."

"Remember, we're here to get some answers. We don't actually know enough to make an accusation."

Andrew Russell's mark on that bloody footprint—a woman's shoe print—had shifted the weight of suspicion onto his wife. Why had she been so adamant that he'd killed himself? Had she been, in fact, deflecting suspicion from herself? If it was Madam Eliot, not Werner's spies, who'd actually shot Andrew Russell in his hotel room, why?

Avery had suggested a story of a conjugal visit gone wrong. Madam Eliot's arrival had been delayed, and Andrew Russell, giving in to impatience, had sought out a prostitute instead. "She caught him in the act, lost her head, seized his gun from the bedside table, and shot him."

Eric was more inclined to blame a temporary madness born from the horrors of war and too much time in the trenches. He imagined Madam Eliot entering the hotel room to find her husband drunk and violent, lost in some unwanted memory . . . "She picked up the gun to warn him off, and it went off by accident."

Penny, however, had a different idea: "She'd flourished in the absence of her husband, but she'd still be forced to give her job back to him when he came back from the War—even though he was never as good at it as she is. A man might start again elsewhere, but that's not really an option for a woman, is it? I'll bet she was pretty desperate about having to lose everything she'd built for herself."

That struck Eric as rather cold-blooded; but Penny had only ever met the woman twice, briefly.

"I doubt she'd tell us the *why* of it," Eric said as he opened the door for Penny. "But maybe she'll have an explanation that fully exonerates her, so none of this matters."

One could hope.

All he knew was that she'd lied to him, that it was indeed her footprint, and that she *had* been in Paris that night.

Inside, a secretary as polished as any of Madam Eliot's jewels directed them to wait in a cool, white-walled reception room. Framed images of housing projects surrounded them, with pride of place being one of Jocelyn Carrington-Clarke shaking hands with the powers that be at the Metropolitan Railway. Penny's attention, however, was drawn to a scale model of a housing estate in an idyllic country setting, clusters of little houses scattering outwards from the train station.

"So here is where Metro-land is born," she mused. "You'd think there were suddenly a lot more people in England now, but it's the reverse that's true, isn't it? Where did we house them all before the War?"

"Slums, perhaps?" Eric picked up one of the model houses for a closer look, thinking of the Working Lads Institute and its mission to lift up the lowly. Ten years from now, Thomas Harvey might be prospering in a suburban house just like this one with a wife, three children, and a dog, his years as a club attendant only a hazy memory. "Or the country? The servants' quarters of great houses? We used to have living quarters for the attendants at the club, but Cully's the only one still living on the premises now. The War changed things in a lot of complicated ways, moving a lot of people up and down the social ladder."

Eric went to put the model house back but realised he couldn't remember where exactly he'd got it from. He ended up placing it in the middle of a golf course, next to the fifth hole. That was bound to do unmentionable things to someone's handicap.

"Bitch!"

Heavy footsteps came stumbling down the stairs, and a red-faced, heavyset man came to a stop in the hall outside. He shouted, "We had a contract!"

Madam Eliot's voice rang down from above, crushing in its scorn. "Which you have failed to honour more than once. And don't think I don't know about the half-baked pottery you're trying to pass off as 'imported Venetian tile.'"

"You haven't seen the last of me!"

"Actually, I rather think I have. Goodbye, Mr. Stone."

Mr. Stone snarled and slammed out of the building. Madam Eliot, cool and triumphant, came down the stairs and into the reception room to address the secretary: "Moira, please arrange a meeting with the company solicitors. I don't think Mr. Stone is *that* stupid, but he's disappointed me before."

Eric thought of Madam Eliot perched on the edge of his desk, rolling over all opposition like a tiny armoured tank as she sorted out the matter of a burst pipe. He'd thought her *briskly businesslike* then, but might the right word be *ruthless*? What was it she'd said later, at the Colonel's funeral? *"I'm known for a spectacular lack of feeling."* Penny's theory as to motive might be closest to the truth, however cold-blooded it was.

"Mr. Peterkin! And Miss Peterkin! I do apologise for the scene. Some people see a woman in my position and imagine they can get away with anything. But what can I do for you? You wouldn't both be here if this is about the Britannia Club pipe room, so is it a house you're after? You'll never regret *that*, let me tell you. My own place in Chorleywood is the best financial decision I've ever made, and not just because property ownership gets me the vote—"

"We don't want a house," Eric hastened to inform her before he found himself suddenly saddled with Metro-land real estate. "At least, not a new one. I was hoping to have a few words with you. In private. Concerning a certain mutual friend."

Madam Eliot's smile didn't falter. "Oh! Yes, of course. Please, follow me."

It didn't escape Eric's notice that his sister snatched up one of the sales brochures as they followed Madam Eliot out into the hall and up the stairs. Perhaps it was just idle curiosity. "Let me do the talking," he whispered as she caught up to him.

"You're the one with the questions," Penny whispered back.

All he wanted were the answers.

Madam Eliot's office was at the top of the house, a cramped little attic room with a window looking onto the street from across the roof of the projecting bow windows below. The space was mostly swallowed up by a large desk and three mismatched cabinets; the warm weather that day made it stuffy as well. Stacks of paper were neatly arranged across the desk, from a telephone on one end to a Tiffany lamp on the other.

On the single chair available for visitors lay a man's hat—Mr. Stone's, presumably. Madam Eliot opened the window just long enough to fling the hat to the winds, then sat down behind her desk and gestured back to the now-vacated visitor chair. "When you say 'our mutual friend,' you mean Karl Werner, don't you? One must be clear about these things. But why have you come to me, and what do you think I'd be able to help you with?"

Eric chose to remain standing.

"Look. Ever since we found out who Werner really was, the assumption has been that he killed Colonel Russell. Werner was involved with the spies who supposedly killed your husband, and the last thing Colonel Russell did before he died was to send for information about the whole sordid affair. It seems reasonable to think that, somehow, Colonel Russell recognised Werner and was seeking confirmation."

"Or he simply knew him for an imposter, and any connection Mr. Werner may have had to Andrew's death is completely irrelevant."

"Yes. That is exactly what I'm saying."

Madam Eliot sat back in surprise. "It is?"

"What if your husband's death had nothing to do with Werner at all? What if he *wasn't* killed by German spies?"

"Mr. Peterkin, I told you already: Andrew shot himself, a suicide—"

"Here, look at this." Eric produced the photograph that Inspector Michaud had sent him and laid it on the desk before Madam Eliot. "This footprint was found in Andrew Russell's room after the murder. Someone else was there, in the minute between his death and the arrival of the concierge. A woman. And there's that symbol carved onto the sole . . . the same symbol your husband used to mark his things, isn't it? The cross of St. Andrew."

Madam Eliot paled. The imperious confidence with which she'd dispatched the dishonest Mr. Stone was gone.

Eric continued: "I didn't know what that symbol was until last night, but I'd seen it once before, on the Webley that Werner, as

Ward, claimed as his own. Now, that part is easily explained. I asked Inspector Crane this morning, and he confirmed that the gun is a Webley Mark V, which was produced only in the earlier half of the War. That would have been the gun your husband equipped himself with after his training. Gregory Ward, however, went to war with his late father's service revolver: it was one of the first things Colonel Russell told me about him, and Werner repeated the story to Lucy later. That would make Ward's gun a Mark IV or earlier. I think that means it was actually Andrew Russell's gun in Ward's box. Gregory Ward, the real Gregory Ward, removed it from the scene of Andrew Russell's death: he evidently feared it was a suicide and wanted to convince the police it was murder. But when the police found this bloody footprint, Ward must have realised his mistake. He wanted the murderer caught, but if he presented the gun to the French police, he risked casting doubt on everything else. So he carefully wrapped it in oilcloth to preserve the fingerprints, brought it back to England, and hid it in the club vault. And there it remained until Werner came and claimed it as his own."

"What we're having trouble with," Penny said, "is the footprint."

Eric nodded. "Can you explain it, Madam Eliot?"

Madam Eliot swallowed. "I know what you must think. That it's *my* footprint. Because if Andrew marked *his* things with that damned symbol, he must have marked mine as well. I . . . I don't know. I was never there. I was turned back at Le Havre."

"Flora did mention that you tried and failed to visit your husband in France. Was this the occasion she meant?"

"I was turned back at Le Havre," she repeated.

It was interesting, Eric thought, that she'd gone straight to that story of being turned back at Le Havre, rather than simply deny having gone at all. It sounded as though the story had been prepared a long time ago and was coming out now as a reflex.

"Madam Eliot, why did you suggest to me that Andrew Russell committed suicide? Ward might have had reason to assume that, given what he saw and heard—a single gunshot, and his friend's gun beside the body, still warm and smoking from having been fired. But you? You had the official police report explaining the circumstances, and no reason to suspect a suicide. The footprint proves that someone else was there. The policeman in charge of the inquiry told me there were no powder burns on the body, meaning he'd been shot from far enough away that he couldn't have done it himself. Were you simply trying to stop me from asking questions? Why?"

Penny said, "Did Colonel Russell ask for those newspaper clippings because he suspected Werner? Or because he suspected someone else?"

Madam Eliot remained silent for a full minute. Then she shook herself and stood up with her head held high. "I think you should leave. Now."

"As you wish. We'll show ourselves out."

Before the door fully closed behind them, Eric glanced back in time to see the brave facade crumble as Madam Eliot dropped back into her chair and snatched up the telephone. He thought she looked too fragile to have killed in cold blood over a matter of employment, but he could be wrong.

"I suppose," Penny said, once they were out on the street again, "there's no question that she killed her husband? I was hoping she'd have a convincing explanation for everything."

Eric shrugged. He'd been hoping for a convincing explanation, too, or he wouldn't have bothered with this interview at all. "There's nearly always room for unexpected alternatives to pop up."

They were no closer to knowing her motive, but did that really matter, in the end?

"Fingerprints," Penny said suddenly. "You said that Ward wrapped Andrew Russell's service revolver in oilcloth to preserve fingerprints."

"What of it?"

"That was six and a half years ago. Would fingerprints survive that long?"

"On something that's been carefully shut away in a vault? It's possible."

"Well, you've told me before about the mud and filth in the trenches, and how you had to clean your firearms regularly or risk them jamming at the worst possible moment. So any prints on that gun would have to be from within a week of his death, and certainly not from the last time he went home on leave. If Madam Eliot's fingerprints are on it—"

Eric sighed. He'd forgotten that it was spring and unseasonably hot—that the sky was a field of pale blue chased with puffy white clouds. He took a deep breath and smelt none of the diazotype ammonia that pervaded the offices of Carrington-Clarke & Associates.

"They're not," he told Penny. "They might have been, back when Werner showed the revolver to me in the club vault, but they've been hopelessly smeared since then. Crane told me that the only clear prints on it were Colonel Russell's. If Madam Eliot killed her husband—and, more importantly, if she killed Colonel Russell to hide it—the best we can hope for is that she confesses of her own free will."

# HER MASTER'S VOICE

ERIC AND PENNY returned to the Britannia Club in silence. Eric's thoughts revolved around Madam Eliot, and how well he knew her. Whatever her motive might be for killing her husband, she had a powerful one now for killing Colonel Russell: fear of exposure. Could she have done it? She had a key to the back door, for the benefit of the men working on the club basement. It would have been easy for her to slip into the building and confront the Colonel, but how would she have known he'd be there? If they'd arranged to meet, why meet at the club in secret?

But an overwhelming motive wasn't evidence of action, was it? Both Werner and Madam Eliot had motives now, and if one was guilty, the other must be innocent. Unless they were both innocent . . .

"Lieutenant Peterkin, sir!" Cully met them with his usual warm welcome. "Lady Alice came in just five minutes ago. She wants to see you—both of you. I thought it best that she wait in the downstairs meeting room, all things considered."

Lady Alice? If she knew to ask for Penny as well, it could only mean one thing . . .

"You were the one Madam Eliot rang," Eric said, two minutes later in the privacy of the meeting room. Penny was beside him, and Lady Alice was seated across the broad table from them. Around them, walnut-panelled walls glowed in the light from the tall windows overlooking King Street; but the black of Lady Alice's full mourning seemed to absorb all the warmth from her immediate vicinity, and her posture was that of a soldier anticipating battle.

"Can you blame her," she said. "It's a distressing situation. Of course she turned to me first. She wants moral support. You understand, don't you?"

Eric was about to reply when he realised that Lady Alice seemed to be addressing her words more to Penny than to him.

"I suppose that's true," Penny said, hazarding a glance at Eric.

"She hasn't told us anything," Eric added. "So if you could answer in her stead—"

"Of course she hasn't told you anything. The truth hurts her too much. Though you've certainly implied that you already know too much about it." Lady Alice looked from Penny to Eric and back, and Eric could almost see the mental calculations whirring in her head. "You think she killed her husband, don't you?"

"Did she?"

Rather tellingly, Lady Alice made no effort at denial. Instead, she said, "Have you ever shaken Miranda's hand?"

Penny shook her head, and Eric almost followed suit before remembering their meeting on New Year's Eve, when they were first formally introduced.

"If you listen hard," Lady Alice said, "you can hear the bones in her elbow click. Andrew did that. Miranda is a chatterbox, and it happened one day that she spoke over him—as one often does in an animated conversation. Heaven knows, George and I did as much to each other a million times over the course of our marriage. Andrew seemed to forget about it as soon as it happened, and so did I—until Miranda appeared the next morning with a broken arm. She'd had an accidental fall down the stairs, she said. She was always walking into doors or tripping on carpets. Funnily, her supposed clumsiness ended as soon as Andrew left for Flanders."

Was Lady Alice implying that Andrew Russell beat his wife? No, it appeared she was saying it outright. Andrew Russell, the gallant hero who'd been nothing but a gentleman to Flora over the matter of her letters—who'd moved heaven and earth, and paid with his life, to end the threat to the Empire's war effort.

"I suspected," Penny said. "At the funeral, remember? When she jumped at being touched? You told me it was because she was bombed in the War, and I thought . . . the stress of whatever my dear brother was saying to her . . ."

"If someone hurt her," Eric said gruffly, "I didn't think it would be *Andrew Russell*."

No, that wasn't strictly true. It had been Eric who'd suggested self-defence as a motive—but against war neurosis, not domestic violence. Eric had been deliberately shutting his eyes, he realised, to the idea of Andrew Russell being less than the hero his reputation described; and what was a hero, if not a gentleman? Were Andrew Russell's private inquiries not a mirror of Eric's own?

"Miss Peterkin," Lady Alice said, "I hope you never truly know what it is to have such a husband. My own George was always the perfect gentleman; David and Patrick, too, from what Flora and Lucy tell me. But Andrew? Andrew in his private life was a beast. Let me show you something."

Lady Alice snapped open her handbag and drew out a photograph—another one of the framed images from her wall of memories. The central figures this time were Flora and David Russell, newlyweds on the front steps of a church. The pair glowed with happiness, though Eric knew this was the eve of David Russell's departure for Flanders. Flora . . . Flora was Flora, lovely as always, but more so now in the joy of the man she loved; and flattering though her dress was, it occurred to Eric that he was far better used to seeing her in trousers. David Russell himself was handsome and proud in his dress uniform, as was his brother Andrew beside him, with the same bright, engaging grin.

"That's Andrew," Lady Alice said for Penny's benefit. "Look at the woman beside him."

The woman was more *behind* than *beside*, easy to miss: a drab little mouse with dull, dark hair pulled into a demure bun, in a dress so plain it might have sprouted savannah grass. Her half smile was hesitant, her eyes uncertain. Shorn of her crisp finger curls and bright jewellery, Madam Eliot was a different woman.

"Miranda before her marriage was only a little less gaudy than the Madam Eliot you know now. She married Andrew in 1912, two years before the War; and over those two years, I watched the glitter fade and all the brilliant stones she loved so much disappear one by one. God forbid she ever outshine her lord and master! Andrew made sure of that."

What would Andrew Russell have done to a woman who'd succeeded in the same business where he himself had failed?

Eric pushed the photograph away. "She practically bribed Bradshaw to get her husband's name up on the Roster of the Fallen. Why do that, if he beat her? Shouldn't she hate him?"

"Because," Lady Alice shot back, "if he's remembered as a hero, she can pretend that marrying him was never a mistake. She can sleep at night knowing she's not to be pitied. Think about it: Would Miranda really go to Paris with the intention of wrestling a revolver away from a man twice her size so she could kill him for having injured her four years earlier?"

Someone had rung the bell for the concierge. That must have been Madam Eliot. And if she was gone right after, it was because . . . because her husband, waiting in the hotel salon with a bottle of cognac, escorted her up to his room before the concierge arrived. He was expecting her, and she wasn't trying to hide her arrival.

"I've noticed," Eric said, "that she carries a pocket pistol in her purse."

"She got it *after* Andrew's death, and that's relevant only in showing that she feared being attacked again. And who could have given her cause for such fear, but Andrew Russell? Miranda was doing well, and I know that Andrew was already jealous. When she mentioned to him that Uncle Joss now had her signing contracts for Carrington-Clarke, Andrew took it as an insult, attempted to 'teach her a lesson,' and was shot in self-defence."

It was all too easy to picture little Madam Eliot cowering before the towering rage of her husband, scrambling away as he lashed out at her . . . In Eric's mind, he saw her fall against a bedside table, knocking Andrew Russell's Webley to the floor. That would only enrage him further. Her hands closed blindly over the revolver, she squeezed her eyes shut, pushing herself desperately into a corner and . . . *bang*! There was the thud of a body hitting the floor, a moment's silence amid the acrid odour of expended gunpowder, then running feet and someone pounding on the door—Ward demanding to know what had happened. Realising what she'd done, Madam Eliot would have dropped the revolver by the body of her now-late husband, and fled in a panic through the window to the balcony outside . . .

Far easier than to suppose that, having agreed to a pleasant conjugal visit, she'd decided on a whim to seize the opportunity for murder.

"Why meet him in Paris, though, if he'd hurt her so badly? Surely, she'd have wanted to see as little of him as possible. I don't doubt that he was the one who demanded they meet, but she could have come up with some excuse—gotten Mr. Carrington-Clarke to say she was too busy with work—"

"Oh, Eric." It was Penny who answered, though she was still examining the image of Madam Eliot in Flora's wedding photograph. "That's easy enough to say when you're only looking at the situation from the outside. But women seldom have the choices men think they do, and far less so when a forceful man frames himself as her lord and master."

"I know what you're thinking," Lady Alice said, turning to Eric. "You're thinking that men who beat their wives are as common as weeds and twice as awful. Why should Miranda be excused? But Andrew was a special kind of awful. Before he left for Flanders, he wanted Miranda to remember, always, that she belonged to him—that he owned her. You do know, don't you, what Andrew did with the things he owned?"

"He put his mark on the soles of her shoes. Yes, I know all about that."

"If only that were all! No. He took a knife and he carved that thing onto her back."

What?

That had to be nonsense, surely? No decent human being—no. No human being, decent or otherwise, would be so barbaric. Not in this day and age. As if through a fog, he heard Penny's gasp. "You're not serious!"

"The evidence is there," Lady Alice said, "if you can convince her to show you."

The claim would be so easily disproved that it had to be true.

Eric's throat was dry. He swallowed and said, "She wasn't actually in her house when it was bombed in the War, was she?"

"No. She was working late at the Carrington-Clarke offices."

Could these reactions have been born elsewhere? Could her scars have been inflicted by someone else? But who else would want to? Who else would care? There were stories passed around the Britannia in whispers, of once-good husbands who'd brought the violence of the War home with them—men who'd turned to drink, or who'd grown unable to tolerate the easy carelessness of peace. If such darkness already lurked behind Andrew Russell's bright grin and laughing eyes, what would it become after the ravages of war?

Eric glanced back at the photograph of Flora's wedding, and the woman hovering like a ghost in her husband's shadow. Was Madam Eliot's hesitant half smile hiding the pain of a fresh scar on her flesh, or would the atrocity be committed later that night, after the photograph was taken? Eric had to blink away an unbidden vision of that familiar symbol with dark blood beading up along its lines. It made him feel ill.

Then he heard Penny speaking to Lady Alice: "It won't be necessary. There's no real evidence of her crime, if you can call it that. The fingerprints on Andrew Russell's gun were quite useless—"

"Penny!"

"Lady Alice is right, and don't tell me that murder is a step too far. You men always assume everyone has the same options and escape routes you do. Honestly, I'd say justice has already been done, and if I were you, I'd see about taking Andrew Russell's name down from the club's Roster of the Fallen. He does *not* deserve to be there."

Eric pulled Penny to the other end of the meeting room and hissed, "What about Colonel Russell?"

That stopped Penny in her tracks.

"Don't forget," he continued, "why we went to Madam Eliot in the first place. Did she kill Colonel Russell to keep him from discovering the truth about Andrew Russell's death? Even if she was justified in the case of Andrew Russell, she wouldn't be in the case of the Colonel."

"Maybe we were right the first time, and Karl Werner killed him."

"We can't pretend she's out of it just because that possibility exists."

"Why don't we wait and see how it plays out with Werner first?"

"Should an innocent man have to die before we begin to consider alternatives?"

"Innocent? A German spymaster responsible for the death of how many Britons?"

"Innocent of *this*! You know what I mean!"

A knock on the meeting room door interrupted them, and Eric, with some relief, went to answer it.

It was Cully. "Inspector Crane wants you, sir. I told him you were with Lady Alice—"

Inspector Crane himself appeared behind Cully and pushed him aside. He did not look happy, which was only to be expected. "Lady Alice. Good. This will save us all a trip. I want a serious word with you and with Mr. Peterkin."

"Has something happened?" Eric glanced back at Lady Alice, who'd risen to her feet with trepidation colouring her cheeks.

"You were at a séance with Dr. Duplessis last night, were you not? I might as well tell you now. Dr. Duplessis was found dead in his flat about an hour ago—"

The Inspector stopped as, with a soft groan, Lady Alice sank to the floor in a dead faint.

# THE SURVIVOR'S BURDEN

INSPECTOR CRANE WAS needed at the scene of the crime, so it was a subordinate who, at Crane's instruction, questioned them about the previous night's séance. This took longer than expected, in no small part because the normally stalwart Lady Alice chose this moment to finally allow circumstances to overwhelm her. Of course, there was no question of abandoning her afterwards.

Eric emerged from his interview first and found Penny deep into a conversation on the club telephone. "Who was that?" he asked, as soon as she hung the receiver up.

"Scotland Yard."

As though Scotland Yard hadn't already invaded the Britannia. But Penny had an old flame at the Yard, and—"I'm assuming you haven't chosen this moment to rekindle a dead romance."

"Don't be stupid."

"So what have you found out?"

"Duplessis knew something. He visited Scotland Yard late last night, demanding to speak to Inspector Crane. Straight from Lady Alice's doorstep, apparently: they've already found the taxi driver who brought him there."

"Of course he did."

Eric had spent the past hour going over his last interaction with Duplessis. *"I think I see the wisdom in what you say. If a thing can be resolved without the police, so much the better; and if not, you will have more evidence with which to convince them of the need to intervene. They would not listen to mere suspicion, is that not so?"* That had been a direct result of Eric's own private inquiries. Eric might not have pushed Duplessis into doing the same, exactly, but he'd certainly encouraged it by example.

"He wouldn't speak to a constable," Penny continued. "He said he wanted to be sure. Then he asked about the telegraph office."

The Yard had its own telegraph, of course, but Eric doubted they'd have allowed Duplessis to use it. "Did you find out what that was about?"

"An old romance can only take one so far. What about you? That nice constable must have told you something about what happened, if only to scare you into telling him more."

The truth about Andrew Russell's homelife had left Eric sick enough already, and Duplessis's death made things infinitely worse. Still, he repeated what he'd gleaned from his interview: "Duplessis was supposed to meet with his colleagues at the Bethlem Hospital this morning. He failed to appear, so they thought to call on him at his flat later in the afternoon. When they got there, they found the door unlocked, and Duplessis lying dead beside the fireplace—he'd cracked the back of his head on a corner of the hearth."

Duplessis had fallen backwards, in other words. Did that mean he'd been struck down in a fight? Could this be an accident? Did he normally leave his door unlocked, or was that evidence of an intruder? Crane's man had been less than reciprocal when interviewing Eric; and to be fair, he likely knew very little at this point. If Eric wanted to know anything—

*If a thing can be resolved without the police—*

Eric forced back the bile rising in his throat. It was partly his fault that Duplessis was dead. The least he could do was ensure the man found justice.

Lady Alice had her own key, of course, but Eric elected not to trouble her for it when they arrived at her Marylebone house. The maid let them in and had nothing to say about her mistress's distress until Penny suggested they sit down in the kitchen instead. That request threw her for only the briefest of moments: *they* were free to do as they pleased; *she* would take this opportunity to clean out the drawing room grate, a task she normally reserved for after her mistress had retired for the night.

Efficient as she was, Lady Alice's maid possessed all the warmth of winter rain.

Five minutes later, Penny was watching for the kettle to boil on a cast-iron gas stove, while Eric studied the bank of bells meant to summon servants to different parts of the house. Lady Alice's kitchen was plain and spartan, with white-washed plaster walls and dark-stained cabinetry. The view through the window over the enamelled sink was of the bare retaining wall, now shrouded in shadow, of a narrow sunken court, and the only sound was the loud ticking of a kitchen clock. One of the new AB Arctic iceboxes—no ice necessary—from Sweden had been installed in a corner, and within it they'd found the dinner that Lady Alice had missed while speaking to the police.

Lady Alice, however, had no appetite. Her mood was as black as her dress. She'd cast off both hat and hatpin with careless exhaustion, and a lock of her long hair had come loose from her faux bob to ripple down over one shoulder.

"I've only made everything worse, haven't I?" she said at last. "If I hadn't organised that séance last night—"

Eric sat down and looked her fiercely in the eyes. "This was not your fault."

How often had he been told that by a superior officer, and how often had he repeated those words to another soldier? The sunken court outside was no more than a civilian trench, and they were the survivors.

*If only I'd been quicker—*

*If only I'd waited just five damned seconds—*

*If only I hadn't brought Duplessis into the investigation—*

*If only I hadn't chosen that moment to poke at Private Dent's shell shock—*

"You thought Madame Davidova could help," Penny said, setting a steaming cup of tea before her. "That's the important thing. You are not responsible for anyone taking advantage of your goodwill."

"Madame Davidova." Lady Alice scowled. "That old fraud. Taking advantage of one's goodwill, indeed! I don't know why I never realised it sooner. I shall have nothing more to do with her from this point on."

"A fraud?" Eric exchanged a puzzled glance with Penny. "I thought—I mean . . ."

"That I truly believed in her? I've been a fool, but I've had my eyes opened, thank goodness. And we shall speak no more of it."

Lady Alice was sitting up straight now, stirring sugar and milk into her tea with a ferocity reminiscent of the newly widowed Sister Russell: anger at the medium's duplicity seemed to have distracted her from her own distress, at least for the moment.

*Save your anger for the Germans, Peterkin. You're not at fault here: they are.*

"If *I* were Duplessis," Penny said, opting to move on from Madame Davidova, "I'd want my killer caught. Is there any way we could pay a visit to his flat? If the police missed anything, we can bring it to their attention."

Evidently, the shocking reality of Madam Eliot's plight hadn't dampened Penny's need to resolve the thing that had driven her from her home and from Mr. Stanhope's horses. Or was there something more to it?

*I shan't be left behind again.*

Lady Alice stared at Penny for a moment, then took a long sip of her tea. "I was the one who arranged his lodgings when he first came to consult about George's men. It's one of the flats let by Carrington-Clarke. I think . . . Yes, I think I would like to help. The police should be done with the flat by tomorrow, so if you come here at three, we can go together."

Duplessis's flat was on the north side of Bloomsbury, an easy walk to Euston station, University College London, and the British Museum. At first glance, the area was not much different from the street on which Lady Alice lived; but the modest terrace houses here had each been subdivided into even more modest flats, and Eric spotted a few "To Let" signs hung in the windows. Judging by snippets of their overheard conversations, most residents were scholars associated with UCL—Dr. Duplessis would have fit right in.

Lady Alice, back to her usual crisply competent self, led them to a house almost indistinguishable from its neighbours and fitted her key into the first flat door inside the entrance. "Miranda tells me that the police have given her leave to begin cleaning up after them, but she'll wait until we've seen whatever we need to see."

No mention had been made of Eric's visit to Madam Eliot the day before, and Eric had to marvel at Lady Alice's composure. She must have known, perhaps from the very beginning, the truth about Andrew Russell's murder, bearing that burden without turning a hair. Eric was just reflecting that the lady must be made of iron when Duplessis's flat door opened and Lady Alice suddenly faltered, looking quite green.

"No," she muttered. "This was a mistake. If you want to look around, please be my guest; but I'm not ready for this. I . . . I'll go speak to the neighbours instead. Ask if they've seen anything."

Her black skirts rustled up the stairs to the flats above, and Eric whispered to Penny, "I don't remember Lady Alice being quite this cut up over Colonel Russell's death. Then again, I didn't see her until the day after. She puts up quite a brave front, doesn't she?"

"I wonder if anyone's as brave as they pretend to be."

Though Lady Alice, it seemed, bore the weight of the entire family.

"She's got us in, at least. Better not let her efforts go to waste now."

Eric locked the door behind them as they ducked into the flat, using a handkerchief to protect himself from the inky fingerprint powder griming the brass doorknob. The main room of this ground-floor flat was large and graciously proportioned, with a fine bay window looking out into the street. By contrast, the bedroom was not much more than a cramped little alcove with space enough for only a bed and a wardrobe. Another tight alcove contained a gas ring, a sink, and a couple of pantry cabinets—a bachelor's kitchen, sufficient for a pot of tea and a package of store-bought biscuits but not much else. An equally small bathroom contained the usual amenities. The furniture had all come with the flat: stained dark and heavily varnished for the appearance of quality, but scuffed and scarred from a series of different and indifferent tenants. Duplessis had set his desk in the bay window, and Eric supposed that Crane would have claimed any incriminating material there; but the blotter remained, along with a scattering of blank notepaper. The same tricks he'd employed investigating Werner's possessions so long ago might serve well enough again to discover what the police now knew.

And then, of course, there was the fireplace.

The bloodstains were still there, a great blotch of red-brown covering one corner of the tiled hearth, dripping down the cracked ceramic to the parquet flooring, some of it trickling so far as to catch onto the edge of an enormous carpet.

Penny made her way to the far end of the carpet and nudged it with the toe of her shoe. "He can't have tripped on this, can he?"

"Backwards? What might he have been backing away from? And no, the distance is too great: I doubt he'd have reached the fireplace if he'd really tripped."

"Slipped, then?"

"The traction on the carpet's too good, I think."

Penny looked around the room, taking in the fingerprint powder dusted everywhere. "I hadn't really thought about it before, but how much of this might really have been evidence, and how much was just the police passing through? No wonder they get so upset at people meddling with crime scenes—it makes it so you can't be sure of anything."

"Not much we can do but try our best."

In a stand beside the fireplace were all the usual fireplace tools, including a heavy iron poker. Surely, if someone intended to do murder, they'd have availed themselves of such a convenient weapon? There was the pair of heavy candlesticks on the mantel, too, and the letter opener on the desk—quite a few options if one intended to kill a man and hadn't brought a weapon of one's own.

The desk blotter revealed nothing of note when held up against a mirror—only a bit of truncated French and a medical phrase or two. Shading the notepaper with a soft pencil revealed something far more interesting: very light traces of block letters, many too faint to discern, but enough to recognise names that Eric knew all too well.

Ypres. Artois. Neuve Chapelle.

These were battles and places across the Western Front. Curiously, there were clear places where Duplessis had borne down more heavily to score out and replace individual letters. *Artois* was consistently written as *ETRTOIS* before replacing the initial *ET* with an *A*.

Duplessis had been deciphering a coded message, with the clumsiness of an amateur.

"Penny, when Duplessis asked for the telegraph office last night, do you know if it was because he wanted to send a wire?"

"What?" Penny, who'd been sorting through the bin by the desk, looked up. "No, but why else would he want the telegraph office?"

"He might have wanted to borrow a telegraph operator's manual." Eric showed his sister the paper he'd shaded. "If I remember right, the Morse code for the letter A could easily be mistaken for the letters E and T set too close together."

"Espionage!"

"Ten-year-old espionage. To the best of my knowledge, we are not currently conducting any operations in Artois. Lady Alice might take some comfort, at least: this can't have had anything to do with her séance. What about you? What have you got there?"

"Only this."

Penny drew a large brown envelope from the bin, and Eric's eye was immediately caught by the name of Dr. Keller's sanatorium stamped into the upper left corner. Had Keller given this to Duplessis? Eric thought back to their interactions, and could only recall the envelope in which Keller had put his statement for Scotland Yard. Crane had that now—

*Werner dropped a fat envelope, self-addressed with the name of his old sanatorium, on top of the Webley in the vault box. "I'll keep this box a while longer. Put it back."*

If this was the same envelope, and it was connected to Duplessis's efforts at cryptography . . . why was Werner carrying around a parcel of encrypted documents referencing the War?

Well, Karl Josef von Werner of German military intelligence might have reason to possess such documents. Gregory Ward, on the other hand, even if he were only a delusion . . .

But Eric had never been completely convinced by Duplessis's theory, had he?

Did this mean that Werner killed Duplessis? There were ways of discovering where someone lived, ranging from simply asking them nicely to stalking them through the night. Once Werner knew . . . Eric imagined Werner appearing on Duplessis's doorstep, begging for help; and Duplessis letting him in, because he believed in giving help where he thought it was needed. Perhaps Werner was under no delusions, and this was a ploy to eliminate a perceived threat. Or perhaps he was exactly as Duplessis surmised, and the sight of his secret documents on the desk, half-decrypted, reawakened the beast within . . .

Eric was about to say more when a key rattled in the flat door. A moment later, Inspector Crane strode in. He scowled on seeing Eric and Penny standing in the middle of a crime scene.

"We were told," Eric said, "that you were finished with all this."

"And you wasted no time in sticking your nose in. Without my knowledge, I might add." Crane's scowl deepened. "They say you can count on any perpetrator to return to the scene of their crime—like a dog to its vomit, as the saying goes. Is there something you'd like to share with me, Mr. Peterkin?"

Eric looked down at the envelope and the shaded sheet of notepaper, and held them both out to the Inspector. "Just these. It looks like Duplessis found some old documents written in Morse code and was busy deciphering them. But I expect you already know all about that."

Inspector Crane sniffed disdainfully at Eric's offerings, then stepped aside and held the door open. "Out. Both of you."

"All right." But Eric stopped on the threshold and turned to face the Inspector. "Just one question. What was Duplessis wearing when he was found? His ordinary day clothes?"

"Out, Peterkin."

"Not a green overcoat?"

"No."

Eric gestured to the coatrack by the door. "I mention it because Duplessis only had the one overcoat—hence why he wore it to Colonel Russell's funeral despite the inappropriate colour. But unless you've taken it for some reason, that overcoat is now missing."

"So," said Penny as they walked back to the police house through the cool night air. "What have we learnt so far?"

"From the beginning?" They'd pressed on after Crane left, until Lady Alice had to take her leave, achieving no progress. It was easier to focus on the story as a whole than on *that*. "Colonel Russell, right before his death, developed a sudden interest in the death of his son Andrew Russell. Everyone thinks Andrew Russell was killed by the spies he was chasing, but Lady Alice has confirmed that, in fact, Madam Eliot killed him in an act of self-defence. There's also Karl Werner, who's been passing himself off as Gregory Ward. He was part of the spy ring that Andrew Russell uncovered, which means that both he and Madam Eliot are implicated in and potentially threatened by Colonel Russell's inquiries—"

"Don't forget Flora Grace. She's the one Werner was trying to get information from."

Eric nodded in acknowledgement. "Both Flora Grace and Karl Werner were in the club the night Colonel Russell was killed. Meanwhile, Madam Eliot has a key to the back door, for her workers. They all had opportunity."

"And Duplessis's death?"

*Am I responsible?*

Eric swallowed and pitted his focus on the facts. "None of his neighbours saw anything. All we know is that he seemed to be deciphering old military intelligence before he died, and there's that envelope you found. Werner put an envelope just like it in his vault when he first arrived, but emptied the box again right after the murder. If it's the same envelope, then . . . how did Duplessis get hold of it?"

They'd reached the house now, and Eric stopped outside the front door to look back at the street. The windows of the houses around them were glowing rectangles of light in the dark—a complacent middle class hopefully unaware of what was transpiring within this one member of their neighbourhood.

"I wonder," Penny said, "why Colonel Russell didn't denounce Werner on the spot. He knew the real Gregory Ward, didn't he? Could he have been trying to protect Miss Grace? I mean, if Werner really did get something damning out of her letters . . ."

"That would require Colonel Russell to know who Werner really was, not just that he wasn't the real Gregory Ward." Eric paused to consider. "It's possible, but I don't see how."

Turning, he unlocked the door, and the two slipped inside.

"Eric! Penny!" Lucy stood in the doorway of the sitting room. Her brightness, no doubt a comfort to anyone coming home from a hard day's work, grated on Eric's nerves instead.

"Have you been wandering all over Harrow?" Eric asked. With electricity restored and the hall light on, he could see fresh mud on the tyres of the bicycle by the stairs.

"Well, it's dreadfully dull here without you, and the policemen standing guard in the kitchen are no fun at all. Inspector Crane himself said it was quite all right if I went out for a bit, as long as one of his policemen went along—or if *you* were with me. Please say you'll join me tomorrow! Mr. Archer stayed so far behind me today, I spent half my time making sure I hadn't lost him, and I still had no one to talk to. It was solitude without the freedom, and company without the fun."

Inspector Crane had to know what he was doing, of course, but this was somewhat more freedom than Eric would have thought permissible under the circumstances.

"I can't," he said. "We're still looking for Werner."

"Oh, but aren't the police already doing that?"

"Yes. But . . ."

Werner had made himself wildly unpopular just being who he was, and if the police caught him first, it wouldn't matter if he was innocent.

"We're considering," Penny said, "the possibility that he was never under any delusions at all—that he might be looking to the German communities in London for help."

Without the delusion, Werner's courtship of Lucy Russell was a deliberate betrayal. Eric saw it in Lucy's expression, but only for a moment before the usual sunny smile smoothed it over. She turned to lead the way back into the sitting room, saying, "I'm surprised there are Germans in London, honestly, unless they only just came here in the last year or two. If I were an Englishwoman in Berlin in 1914, I'd have packed up and left the moment I heard of the War. They must really love—"

She stopped suddenly. Love? If Werner, in the midst of his deception, really had fallen in love with Lucy, did that make it less of a betrayal?

But Lucy's thoughts were on more prosaic matters. "If I were Karl Werner," she said slowly, "I would hide in the one place I knew no one would think to search."

"And where is that?"

"Hadrian's house, of course."

# BEHIND HADRIAN'S WALL

COLONEL RUSSELL LIVED in Knightsbridge, a well-heeled neighbourhood rubbing shoulders with Hyde Park to the north and the even more well-heeled Belgravia to the east. His house was number 189, four storeys of redbrick grandeur topped with an elaborately decorative gable. Its neighbours were similarly grand, and together, they formed a square around a leafy green park reserved for their exclusive enjoyment. Penny, gazing up at a portico only slightly less impressive than the Britannia's, remarked, "I'm surprised that no one has yet suggested money as a motive for murder. Lucy gave me the impression that the Russell household was rather more modest than a house like this would imply."

"Colonel Russell," Eric replied, "always gave the impression of caring more for his creature comforts than about flaunting; but he did have a reputation for openhanded generosity."

"Bought his popularity, did he?"

"Bite your tongue."

Before Penny could set foot on the front steps, however, Eric stopped her. "Wait. I'm going in first. Alone."

Penny turned, frowning. "I thought we'd already settled this."

Yes, they'd discussed it last night, after Eric reasoned that Lucy's suggestion was as good as any, and it wasn't as if they had any other options. And in the middle of that discussion, Lucy had retired to bed with a sleeping draught, forcing Eric to meet them at Harrow-on-the-Hill this morning for the house key. Lucy claimed then to have obtained Inspector Crane's permission to follow along—which had to be a lie, given the police protection she was under. Eric had put his foot down and sent her back to her police bodyguard, but Penny was more difficult. On the one hand, if he truly respected her as an equal, how could he object to her contributions? On the other, was an older brother not allowed his protective instincts? If the same thing were to happen to her as had happened to Avery and Duplessis—

"Think about it," Eric said. "What happens if we both get shot in there? Nobody would be the wiser, and Werner would be no closer to being found. Someone needs to stay out here, ready to sound the alarm in case of trouble."

Out here, where one could easily spot an approaching threat, where there were witnesses, and where safety was just a doorbell away.

"Afterwards," Eric assured her, "if Werner isn't here after all, we can conduct a more thorough investigation together."

"And why should you be the scout and I the lookout? Because you're a man?"

"Because I was a soldier and would stand a better chance against Werner if it came to a fight."

Penny considered and finally relented, albeit reluctantly. "All right. Fine. If you're not back in twenty minutes, I'll assume you've been brutally murdered and act accordingly."

"I'll keep that in mind."

Eric made his way up the front steps and fitted Lucy's key into the front door lock. He glanced back to see Penny at the park railing with her eye on her wristwatch, then turned the key, slipped inside, and locked the door behind him. Never mind that this might hinder the arrival of reinforcements, or his own exit if he had to run: it would help keep Werner in and, more importantly, keep Penny out.

Reaching into his jacket, he withdrew the gun he'd borrowed the night before, after leaving the police house. One advantage of old Army camaraderie was that there was always some contact somewhere on whom one could count for this sort of thing. In this case, he'd applied to old Forrester, a former sergeant with a collector's interest in firearms of all sorts.

*"If you haven't the proper certificate, you'd best not let the coppers catch you with this. It's three months' hard labour and a fifty-pound fine, last I checked."*

The gun was a Webley with a dramatically shortened barrel. Forrester had also provided a shoulder holster, which he declared was the only way to carry a gun around in the city. It wasn't quite what Eric knew from the War, but strapping it on had the same effect—like a bugle's call to a retired warhorse. The mission was vital. The smell of cordite and blood was in his nostrils and would not go away. Checking the gun was familiar, too, an almost comforting litany of motions drilled into him long ago.

What would a confrontation with Werner be like, with firearms between them? Eric recalled the shock on Werner's face when Avery was shot. Whoever he had been in the War—they'd all been someone else in the War—*this* Werner wasn't one to shoot an unarmed man. But Eric wasn't unarmed now, was he?

Shaking off his doubts, Eric looked around.

He was standing in a square, marble-clad entrance hall. Immediately before him was the dining room: oak panelling and green wallpaper stretching back to a distant set of French doors, and heavy dining chairs ranged along a heavier table with military precision. A wide staircase rose up on one side to the first-floor drawing room, and a corridor ran alongside the dining room to the back of the house. Right at his feet, the only untidy note to be seen, was a pile of mail that had accumulated under the letter box since Lucy's departure: condolences from those who'd heard of the Colonel's passing, and bills from those who hadn't.

When Lucy said that the house was empty, she'd meant it. No servants had been kept on to take care of the house, which increased the likelihood of Werner being here in hiding.

Eric shifted his grip on Forrester's Webley and glanced quickly around the dining room. No Werner. The corridor, as it turned out, led to a book-lined library. Again, no Werner. Back in the corridor, Eric found the door to the servants' stairs and descended to the basement.

Storage rooms, coal room, laundry room, pantry, wine cellar, furnace, servants' hall . . . The kitchen was a larger version of Lady Alice's, with similar windows looking out into a sunken courtyard. Eric tried but couldn't see the park—or, more to the point, Penny—from those windows. The tradesman's door, opening into that same courtyard, was locked: Werner wasn't coming and going that way.

Heading back up through the dead silence, Eric stopped on the ground floor to look out the window again, and was relieved to see Penny where he'd left her.

The first floor was almost entirely taken by a drawing room that stretched from front to back, with a grand marble fireplace and a succession of Impressionist landscapes brightening the walls. Still no Werner. Colonel Russell's private study was off one back corner, directly over the downstairs library. Here were framed prints of wildlife, a model ship, a tidy desk with a telephone, and a well-stocked liquor cabinet. No Werner, of course, but—

Eric looked around the study, then out into the drawing room. He couldn't put his finger on it, but something felt wrong.

Hackles raised, he ascended to the second floor, endeavouring to match the house's silence with his own. On the landing, he looked out the window to see Penny still waiting at the park railing.

Colonel Russell had the larger of the two second-floor bedrooms, comfortably furnished with luxurious fabrics. There were ashes still in the fireplace grate: no one had seen fit to clean it out since his death. The smaller bedroom, cheerfully wallpapered with a buttercup print, had to be Lucy's. A row of porcelain dolls ranged across the top of an open rolltop desk, under a framed photograph of a young man with a gap-toothed grin and ears that stuck comically out on either side. This was Patrick Russell, of course, and it suddenly dawned on Eric what he found disconcerting about the rooms downstairs.

Well-appointed as they were, only the Colonel's study felt lived-in. The others were impersonal museum pieces, dead things preserved under glass, for show rather than for use. And this photograph of Patrick Russell was the only thing he'd seen so far to suggest that anyone human lived here.

Perhaps Colonel Russell didn't like to be reminded of the family he'd lost. Or was Eric reading too much into things?

Eric continued silently to the next floor and looked out the window. Penny hadn't moved.

George Russell's old room was identified by the cross of St. George scratched into the doorpost. It had been rearranged as a nursery, and Eric recalled that Lady Alice's two sons had been sent here with their nanny during the War. Andrew's room, with a stained-glass mobile winking in the light of a window, was similarly identified by the cross of St. Andrew. If the room Lucy occupied downstairs had once been Patrick's, then the final bedroom here, notable for the now-empty bookcases flanking the bed, must be David's. All three were draped in sheets, with a layer of dust to assure Eric that no one had entered them since the end of the War.

Since the end of the War?

A sprawling country manor, Eric thought, might have a wing closed off for lack of use, just like this; but this Knightsbridge house wasn't on quite the same scale. Someone should have come in for some light cleaning from time to time, to keep the dust and cobwebs from spreading into the occupied parts of the house, or to keep at least one room ready for guests should the need arise. George Russell's room, in particular: Why was it still set up as a nursery, a supposedly temporary arrangement? It appeared as though the entire third floor had ceased to exist for Colonel Russell the moment the last of its occupants vacated it.

For all it looked like a four-storey mansion, Colonel Russell's house was really a two-bedroom cottage.

Up another floor, by the servants' stairs this time, to the attic and servants' quarters behind the decorative gable. Peering out the window, Eric was seized by a momentary panic when he failed to spot Penny at the park railing—but there she was, leaning in the gateway a few paces up and slightly obscured from view by the tall bushes flanking it.

The sooner this reconnaissance was done, the better.

Eric quickly satisfied himself that the storage rooms betrayed too much dust to have been recently disturbed. The servants' bedrooms, meanwhile, were empty. Too empty. They hadn't simply been vacated: they hadn't been used in years. Since the War, perhaps? Here was an abandoned work basket, and there was a discarded pulp novel; there must have been servants once, or no one would bother to wedge newspaper under the uneven legs of wardrobes and bedside tables. For the present, however, it appeared as though Colonel Russell employed no servants. No wonder the third-floor bedrooms were abandoned.

It wasn't until the last of the servants' bedrooms that Eric found signs of more recent occupation. The bed here had been made with military precision, and the wardrobe, though empty, was markedly free of dust. Under normal circumstances, Eric would have thought nothing of it; but empty as the other servants' bedrooms were, abandoned as the third-floor bedrooms were, he couldn't shake off a creeping suspicion that the last occupant of this room might not have been someone sanctioned by the Russells to stay here.

Karl Werner.

There was no guarantee that he might be waiting around during the day in the same place he slept at night, after all.

Or did the Russells, in fact, employ a single servant? Eric thought back to everything Lucy had ever said about the household. Had she mentioned any servants at all? Had she spoken only in generalities? Had he assumed?

There was an accounts ledger downstairs, in Lucy's room, which should contain a record of payments made to this hypothetical servant. Would Penny be upset if he looked without her, or did this count as part of his reconnaissance? Eric glanced out the window as he prepared to go downstairs and froze.

Penny was gone.

Could she have retreated farther behind the bushes? No, that would mean passing through the park gate, which was closed against trespassers. Had she wandered farther along the railing? No. Try as Eric might—and every second spent searching was another second wasted—he couldn't find Penny anywhere. In her place, a studiously nondescript man leaned against the railing with his hat pulled low and his nose in a newspaper. Was that Werner? This was a bad distance and angle to determine much of anything.

*Crash!*

Lieutenant Peterkin jumped, scanning his surroundings on high alert. The sound had come from downstairs, somewhere in the house. He wasn't alone in here.

Someone screamed. A woman. Penny?

Abandoning any further idea of stealth, Eric clattered down the stairs, practically sliding in his haste, leaping over the bottom four or five steps to hit the floor running.

*"Stop! Put that down!"*

Penny!

Eric skidded to a halt at the drawing room entrance, Webley up and at the ready. Penny was by the marble fireplace, locked in a desperate, flailing struggle with someone—he couldn't shoot one without also hitting the other—and it took him a moment to realise that her assailant was not Karl Werner, but . . . *Lucy Russell.*

# A FINE FACADE

"STOP! *STOP!*"

Eric dropped the Webley and dashed into the drawing room to prise the two women apart. Lucy, outnumbered and outmatched, struggled a moment in Eric's arms before finally sagging in defeat. Eric deposited her into an armchair and turned to Penny.

"What is going on here?"

He saw now that the landscape painting over the fireplace had been swung aside to reveal a small wall safe, also open but currently empty. A half-flattened matchbox lay on the floor, its contents scattered. Penny, picking some torn paper fragments out of the fireplace grate, said, "I saw her creep in by the tradesman's entrance, and . . . Lucy, what were you doing?"

Eric turned back to Lucy. "I thought we left you with your police bodyguard in Harrow."

Lucy scowled and looked away. "I wasn't lying about getting Inspector Crane's permission," she muttered.

She'd simply neglected to inform anyone that they'd turned her away, and followed regardless. These paper fragments had to be important, or Lucy wouldn't have gone to so much effort, and Eric quickly saw why.

*Chère Monique . . .*

An elegant cursive hand curled across each fragment with long, graceful loops. This was one of *Flora's* letters: her response to Monique Garnier's letters. For confirmation, there was Flora's signature at the end. And all up and down the margins was a dense pattern of dots and dashes, in the sickly yellow-brown of long-exposed invisible ink. Eric had no doubt that, once deciphered, the Morse code would resolve into something similar to what Dr. Duplessis must have discovered.

*Ypres. Artois. Neuve Chapelle.*

Werner's spies hadn't been probing Flora for information, after all: they were apparently receiving it outright and regularly in her letters. The sense of betrayal hit Eric in the gut, along with the realisation that Lucy had suggested the excursion to this house as a ploy to get hold of this letter. She'd never truly thought that Werner might be here. But if she was trying to destroy this evidence of espionage, did that mean she was somehow involved? Eric held up the letter fragments and glared at her. "Do you understand what this is?"

Lucy crossed her arms and continued to stare into the middle distance.

She looked like an admonished child, not a traitor caught red-handed. None of this made sense. Flora a spy? Lucy?

Eric took a deep breath. Calm. Anger would get him nowhere. He pulled an ottoman over and sat across from Lucy, leaning forwards to address her directly on her level. He said, as gently as he could, "Lucy. Look at me. You do understand how this looks, don't you?"

Lucy's expression remained sullen, but she did turn to meet his gaze.

"Can you tell us why you were trying to destroy what looks like evidence of espionage?"

Silence.

"Lucy. Werner was the spy who orchestrated all this. He's dangerous, and he's still on the loose. Colonel Russell, your father-in-law, is likely dead as a result of this espionage. I know you can't have anything to do with it, but—"

"Typical."

"What?"

"Typical!" Lucy's voice rose, shrill and trembling with pent-up emotion. "Of course I can't have anything to do with anything. I'm just Lucy, aren't I? 'Lucy's just a girl! She can't possibly have anything to say to the grown-ups! She doesn't matter!' You talk as though you're afraid I'll run crying to Nanny about someone being mean! Well, so what if I like games and toys and fairy tales? That doesn't mean I don't pay attention to the world. That doesn't mean I don't have my own opinions about . . . about communism, or Irish republicanism, or colonial rule. Hadrian would talk to me about politics and I'd tell him what I thought, and then he'd pat me on the head and forget I'd said anything at all—only I'd hear the same things I'd told him come out of his mouth again a week later at the club. And that's quite all right. I don't care. There's lots you can do when people don't take you seriously. If they catch you listening in on things you ought to know nothing about, they assume you don't understand. That's what happened with Hadrian and that letter. If I'd been Alice or Miranda or Flora, he would never have been so careless about reading it where I could see."

Penny laid a comforting hand on Lucy's shoulder. "You were like a daughter to him. Perhaps it wasn't so much that he thought nothing of you, and more that he trusted you."

Lucy shrugged off Penny's hand and replied instead with a withering look that said as plainly as words, *Don't be naive*.

"All right. Let's be adults, then." Eric sat back, adopting a more aloof, neutral tone. He indicated the letter fragments. "What's this all about?"

"It's not what it looks like."

"So tell me. Please."

"I saw Hadrian reading that before he died, and I recognised Flora's handwriting even if I couldn't see what she'd actually written. I didn't realise what it could mean until you told me about Gregory . . . about Karl Werner being a spy. And then, last night, I overheard you talking outside the house, and from what you said, I *knew.*" Her tone grew harsh as the storm gathered in her eyes. "But what was I supposed to do? I was stuck in bloody Harrow, with a damned policeman breathing down my neck every hour of the day. I couldn't even pick up the telephone without someone sticking his nose in!"

The facade was gone. The sailor dress, the butterfly buckle, the air of girlish innocence . . . Lucy Russell was not a child, and far more ingenious than ingenuous.

Eric said, "Flora told me she'd been duped by a German spy, but no one writes innocent messages in Morse code with invisible ink, especially not during a war. Was she in league with Werner all along?"

"No. Flora would never."

"How do you explain the coded message on the letter that *she* wrote, then?"

Lucy paused, considering her options, then said, "It was Hadrian, of course."

"Colonel Russell! You must be joking."

"Well, it wasn't Flora, so it had to be Hadrian." Lucy's tone picked up confidence. "Think about it. He was here in London through most of the War, working with the War Office. If anyone had information to sell, it would be Hadrian—not Flora, no matter what she might have overheard. And Flora never overhears anything: she's never had to worry about finding secret ways around other people, not once in her entire life, and that's left her blithely oblivious to half the world. She was living here in this house during the War, and she thought nothing of it when Hadrian offered to post her letters for her on his way to Whitehall every morning. Looking back at it now . . . Well, that gave him plenty of opportunity to go somewhere, steam those letters open, and add whatever he wanted to them, didn't it?"

It was plain to Eric that Lucy was forming her arguments on the spot, around a wild accusation. Colonel Hadrian Russell! It was as shocking as Lucy's nonchalant attitude towards the blackening of his name. Eric could see the man holding court in the Britannia

Club lounge, like King Arthur surrounded by his Knights. Wasn't it Colonel Russell who'd quelled any disagreement and unrest among the masses when Eric first took the helm as club secretary? With nothing more than a well-placed word—so great was his popularity—and for nothing in return. A man like that didn't hide behind his daughter-in-law, using her letters as a shield for his own wrongdoing.

Then again, it was no less believable than the idea of Flora Grace, who'd expressed such bitterness at the loss of Britain's young men, being party to the loss of thousands more.

Meanwhile, Lucy seemed to be descending from the initial elation of having hit on a plausible story, into the horror of what that story meant. She deflated and was once more the pale, staring girl Eric remembered from the Britannia Club dining room seven years ago—brought there by Colonel Russell in the hope that a change of scenery might stimulate her lost appetite.

"'*I never forget a face.*' That's what he said when he met Gregory—Werner, I mean. The way he said it was so odd. Quiet, as though he was reminding himself, or telling Werner that he knew who he really was. And he knew because he really did do it."

"But that's monstrous," Penny replied. "Colonel Russell had four sons in the War. Surely he wouldn't have endangered his family by giving the advantage to the enemy."

"And you think Flora would endanger hers?" Lucy shot back. "I overheard him on the telephone that night. I didn't understand what it meant, at the time, but I know now. He was talking to Werner. They were arranging to meet at the club."

Eric said, "Why didn't you tell the police about this?"

Lucy clapped a hand over her mouth, squeezed her eyes shut, and shook her head. She looked ill, and Eric guessed that she'd wanted to protect the man whom she believed at the time to be Gregory Ward. She didn't anymore. Her current objective was to protect Flora, and what she wanted now was for Eric to turn his ire on Werner instead—not that he blamed her. After everything

Werner had done to her and her family during the War, he was in every way the enemy.

Cully would know if such a telephone call had come through for Werner, even if he'd attached no importance to it before. But did that really mean anything, or even matter? Werner and Colonel Russell might have been communicating about the darkest treason, or they might have been discussing Lucy's marriage prospects.

Struggling to her feet, Lucy said, "Please. I can't stand to be here a minute longer. Hadrian . . . He's everywhere."

"Yes. Let's go." Eric stood and tucked the letter fragments into his jacket pocket. "This letter—"

"You're not showing it to Inspector Crane, are you? Talk to Flora first, at least. You told me what happened with the French police when they realised there was espionage mixed up in Andrew's death. They forgot all about him as they went after the spies, so no one knows if his murderer was actually caught or not. Flora didn't kill Hadrian. I know that for a fact. But Inspector Crane isn't going to care if he thinks he can get her for treason. And I told you, she didn't do *that* either."

Could Lucy be making a scapegoat of Colonel Russell simply because he was dead, while Flora Grace was alive? The letter implicated Flora, and there was nothing, really, to connect it to the Colonel. Then again . . .

"I wouldn't dream of giving this to the police," Eric assured Lucy. "Not yet. Not until I've investigated it myself first. To my fullest satisfaction."

Lucy kept her silence as Eric and Penny escorted her out of the house. The colour didn't quite return to her cheeks until they were out on the pavement, and then she turned to cast a critical eye at the four-storey-tall facade of artfully arranged red brick and the elaborate gable crowning it.

"Hadrian believed that a house makes all the difference," she said. "He always said that nothing changes for the common peasant whether he's ruled by the Romans or the Normans, but a man with a villa is someone for whom the Empire actually matters. I know he meant it as a metaphor for one's position in society, but I like to pretend he meant it literally."

"Perhaps he did," Penny replied. "Owning a house means you don't owe your living to anyone."

Recalling Penny's interest in Carrington-Clarke's Metro-land sales brochures, Eric wondered uncomfortably if this was something very much on her mind; she'd said nothing about it to him so far. To Lucy, he said, "You took care of this house all by yourself, didn't you? It didn't look as though Colonel Russell kept any servants."

"There was Mrs. Dunn, the cook. I can barely make sandwiches, and Hadrian wouldn't be caught dead anywhere near the kitchen. But I did most of the cleaning. I suppose, in the end, I was only a glorified housemaid."

That accounted for the one recently vacated attic bedroom.

"You've got a picture of Patrick Russell in your room. Should we get it for you, since we're here?" Eric thought he owed Lucy this one kindness, at least.

But Lucy only turned away from the house with a sigh. "I didn't pack it the first time, did I? It doesn't matter. Patrick never really loved me, anyway."

"Lucy!" Penny exclaimed.

"He thought he loved me, but what he really loved was the *idea* of me. I reminded him of the world before the War. I didn't care about the distinction then; I'm not even sure I understood it, not really. I was fond of him, though, and perhaps if he'd lived, we'd have grown to love each other the way Alice and George loved each other. That's what makes his death so awful."

"I'm sorry," said Eric, and he meant it.

"Werner was the same. I could tell from the way he looked at me when we first met, as though I were something on a pedestal. What did it matter? He was good for a bit of harmless fun, but I was never as mad about him as the others seem to think." Lucy glanced back again at the fine facade of Colonel Russell's Knightbridge house, and the lifeless finery hidden within. Then she turned and waved to the man loitering against the park fence across the street. “Constable? We’re ready to go now.”

# PART FIVE

# KRONOS DEVOURS

LUCY WAS HANDED over to Inspector Crane with little fanfare, then shuttled back to Harrow in a police motorcar with a constable to see she didn't slip away between here and there. Eric watched her go, his mind still churning over the letter fragments in his pocket. As promised, he wasn't about to hand them over, not yet—but he had a bone to pick with Inspector Benedict Crane.

Catching up to Crane outside his office, Eric said without preamble, "Lucy Russell isn't there for her safety, is she?"

"Don't waste my time, Peterkin." Crane looked tired and he sounded ill-tempered: the search for Karl Werner must be going badly. Inside the office, a grey-haired, black-clad woman half rose to her feet, but Crane closed the door on her before Eric could see more.

"You seem to think nothing of letting her wander all over Harrow with only a policeman watching from too far away to do much good should anyone actually pounce. You even expanded her boundaries to bloody Knightsbridge when you thought I'd be with her. You're actually using her as bait, aren't you? You think that if Werner is actively looking for her, you should make it easy for him to find her . . . and to follow her into a trap. Tell me the truth: If I were to go back to Barchester right now, would I find some clue there pointing to Harrow?"

The Inspector scowled. "Do you have any idea how many calls and reports I've had to sift through since this started, all about men with scars anywhere from Hampshire to the Hebrides? Do you think I have the manpower or resources to follow up on each and every one of them? Just last night, our most promising sighting turned out to be another Scotland Yard detective making inquiries on something quite unrelated, and didn't we look bloody intelligent then! So if there's a way to twist the odds in my favour, don't think I'm not going to take it."

"And Lucy's the Iphigenia to your Agamemnon, a sacrifice to get your ships moving! This sort of Machiavellian tactic might be quite all right in Hong Kong—"

Crane's fist was curled into Eric's shirtfront before he knew it, and the impact against the wall behind made him think, for a moment, of mortar shells and collapsing dugouts. But Crane was snarling inches from Eric's face, fiercely enough to pierce through any memory of long-ago battles, and Eric recognised the smell of a soldier who'd been living on his nerves all night.

"Don't you dare, Peterkin. Don't you bloody dare. I'll take it from the brass, and I'll even take it on occasion from some damned constable, but I'll not take it from the likes of you. Understand?"

Eric had touched a nerve, clearly: a nerve that had already been rubbed quite raw, and recently. He forced away the impulse to strike back and reached up only to push the offending hand away. Perhaps realising he'd overstepped himself, Crane let go of Eric and turned to enter his office.

"Go home, Peterkin. Just . . . go home. You don't belong here."

Eric did not go home. He fetched Penny from where she was having a nice gossip with a few policemen, and then . . . In truth, he was oblivious to the world and where he was going. He'd averted a scene with Crane, but his nerves still jangled from unwanted memories of violence. The earthy odour of churned mud was in his nostrils, with nothing to dispel it.

"Eric, slow down!"

Eric halted. They were by the Cenotaph, and he realised he'd been following the same route he'd taken with Flora almost two weeks ago. They'd stopped on this exact same spot then to look up with reverence at the monument's austere stateliness. Well, it was reverence on his part; was it the same for *her*? He remembered Flora's bitterness at the "old men" of the War Office, who'd survived the youths they'd sent off to fight. Had that bitterness led her to undermine their efforts?

Penny was saying something to him, but Eric heard none of it. He was imagining, instead, Flora Grace sitting up in what had been her husband's childhood bedroom, a bitter twist to her rosebud lips, carefully inscribing a message of dots and dashes along the margin of a chatty letter to a non-existent cousin . . . Sealing the letter with, perhaps, a spritz of perfume to mask the telltale lemon scent of invisible ink . . .

"What would she have to sell, though?" he wondered out loud.

"What?"

"Flora Grace," Eric clarified, turning away from the Cenotaph to continue up Whitehall. "This isn't a case of a German spy fishing for information. It's someone with a steady flow of intelligence. Lucy was right: Where would Flora get such intelligence? Just by talking to her father-in-law over breakfast?"

But the answer to that was obvious. Eric remembered the men wandering into the vicinity of the club lobby every Friday afternoon when she came to lunch with her sisters-in-law, and the spectacular lack of discretion exhibited by Thomas Harvey, her last known lover. Colonel Russell, popular as he was, would have given her ample opportunity to ply her considerable charms on men important to the war effort.

"So that's what's got you all of a bother," Penny said when he put it to her. "Well, I don't believe it. Wasn't she living with Colonel Russell at the time? Someone would have noticed."

"People have been finding ways to commit adultery without their families knowing since God created marriage."

"Would she have given you Monique Garnier's letters if she were guilty?"

Eric slowed once more to a stop, this time beside the War Office's baroque embellishments. Why draw attention to one's brush with espionage when the matter might never come up at all? Flora had more sense than that.

He turned to Penny. "What are you suggesting, then?"

"Someone at the post office? You needn't be a member of the Russell household to have had the opportunity to doctor their letters."

"A postal clerk wouldn't have access to Colonel Russell's War Office contacts. And with that advantage gone, why go through the effort of setting Flora Grace up as a stalking horse?"

"Then what about Colonel Russell himself, as Lucy suggested?"

"Impossible."

All the same, looking up at the War Office building, Eric couldn't help but picture the Colonel arriving here every morning during the War, alighting from a taxi because of course a man of his stature didn't deign to walk. The building would have been a hive of high anxiety, and there'd be Colonel Russell, cutting through the tension with his easy good humour . . . easier, perhaps, because he knew something his colleagues did not. Colonel Russell's specific role in the war machine was recruitment, which gave him little insight into the actual operation of the War; but his masculine popularity was at least as seductive as Flora's feminine charms. It wasn't hard to see him gossiping with a colleague over drinks about "what they'd planned for Jerry next." Failing that, he had only to wander across the corridor and see what everyone else was doing.

"Impossible," Eric repeated, and turned to continue up towards the shining beacon of Nelson's Column where Whitehall met Trafalgar Square. There, standing between the great bronze lions guarding its base, he gazed up to the dizzying heights of the column as though Admiral Nelson himself might come down and give him the answers he needed.

To be fair, was it really so impossible?

Across the square, the civilian population of London drifted in and out of the National Gallery; Edith Cavell, executed by the Germans on charges of treason, gazed directly at them from beyond the colonnaded porch of St. Martin-in-the-Fields. Eric thought he glimpsed that tramp Johnny, still watching for Werner to show up asking for his old berth in the church's vaults. The world seemed utterly heedless and innocent of his quandary.

*A memory of Colonel Russell gazing up at the Roster of the Fallen: "At least we name them, eh? The Cenotaph on Whitehall commemorates all the dead who never came home, grandly and simply, but we name them. We make it personal . . ."*

Were those the sentiments of a traitor?

"Why?" Eric asked. "Set aside for a moment the fact that Colonel Russell had four sons in the War. What on earth did he have to gain? Did he think Germany deserved to win—or that England deserved to lose? Might he have been blackmailed into it?" Eric thought of Colonel Russell holding court in the club lounge, silver whiskers flourishing over an indulgent smile. Might he—God forbid!—have done it simply for the sense of power it would give him over the fortunes of others? That wasn't the Colonel Russell he knew. Was it?

*Colonel Russell, once again before the Roster of the Fallen: "Perhaps, without the ideals of King Arthur . . ."*

"Filthy lucre," Penny replied, and that was enough. In a flash, Eric remembered the deserted servants' quarters of that grand house in Knightsbridge, and something Madam Eliot remarked to him once: *"The Russell men are hopeless when it comes to money. I know Hadrian lives*—lived—*closer to the bone than you'd expect."*

"Look," Penny continued, "if you want a reason why Colonel Russell must be innocent, it's really quite simple. Logistics. He'd have to steam those letters open, wouldn't he? Where and how would he have done that?"

"Are you serious? What household doesn't have a kettle and a hob?"

"If there's one thing the lord of the manor does not do, Eric, it's boil his own water. Don't you remember what Lucy said?"

*"Hadrian wouldn't be caught dead anywhere near the kitchen."* Yes, the sight of Colonel Russell waiting at the stove for his water to boil would be immediately suspicious. If he didn't want anyone walking in on him and asking questions, he'd have to get everyone out of the house first. Flora, Lucy, Madam Eliot, the cook . . . Lady Alice's two boys had been there, too, along with their nanny. Were there any other servants back then? Everyone's combined absence might be engineered a handful of times, but not consistently through the War.

"Unless," Penny added, "you know of a hotel nearby whose rooms come equipped with gas rings and tea kettles?"

Eric did not. But—

Something flashed at the top of the column: a pigeon's wing, perhaps, flapping across the sun. It was after Trafalgar that Fitzwilliam Peterkin and several like-minded friends—

Abruptly, Eric set off westwards, towards Pall Mall and St. James.

Penny scurried to catch up. "Eric! You've thought of something. What is it?"

"It's that you're right. There aren't many places where Colonel Russell could have sat down and done what Lucy's accusing him of. In fact, I can think of only one: a place situated conveniently between Knightsbridge and Whitehall; with private rooms, a few of which come equipped with gas rings and tea kettles; where Colonel Hadrian Russell was such a fixture that he could do anything and not be questioned."

Penny caught his arm, aghast. "You don't mean . . . ?"

Eric nodded grimly. "The Britannia Club."

"Lieutenant Peterkin, sir!" Cully, that stalwart of patriotic fervour, greeted Eric with a broad smile. "I was wondering when you'd stop in again. You know what day it is, don't you?"

Eric halted his steam-powered progress towards his office so suddenly that Penny almost walked into him. "The day? It's Monday, isn't it?"

"It's the thirtieth. Tomorrow's the thirty-first, and the end of the month. We need you to look over the bar receipts, the accounts, the stocktaking—"

Eric groaned. Who had time for such trivialities, now especially? "Honestly, Cully. Can't it wait? Or can't you handle it yourself?"

"No, sir. We've waited long enough, as it is. Next month's the annual general meeting, and you'll want all the club business in order for that. There's also that business with the pipe room in the basement. I've left everything that needs doing on your desk to go over, sir."

"Of course, of course. I'll get to it."

*Later.*

Eric hadn't set foot in his office since that disastrous confrontation with Werner. Werner's book, that Edgar Allan Poe anthology, still sat on one corner of the desk. Bradshaw's framed print of the tortoise on a bicycle was gone now, leaving a bare patch of unfaded wallpaper around an ugly bullet hole. A large section of wallpaper had been stripped away from the wall where Avery's blood had soaked into it, and the floor beneath had been so thoroughly scrubbed that a fresh coat of varnish would have to be put on. Even so, Eric thought he could still smell the coppery tang of blood. Every detail was still clear in his mind: Werner with his pocket pistol; Avery, heedless of his own safety, tackling the other man; the echoing gunshot and the horrified regret in Werner's expression . . .

Werner's intention had been to intimidate, not to injure. Eric felt sure of it. Dr. Keller was right, and it was not in that man's nature to do murder. Perhaps he'd chosen the more cerebral path of military intelligence to avoid direct bloodshed.

For now, Eric pulled out the guest room register covering the years of the War. He laid it on top of the bar receipts and bills that Cully had left on his desk. Looking up at Penny, he said, "There'll be nothing, of course."

"Of course."

They were only here to confirm that this was a mare's nest. Why, then, was anxiety gnawing at his bones? Why did it seem like a matter of urgency that they do this? Eric took a deep breath and opened the register.

Not a single room booked by the late Hadrian Russell through the months of 1912.

Just one instance in 1913.

Nothing in 1914, not even in the months of the War.

Eric began to relax as he turned the page and found nothing in January 1915, either. Then . . . once in February. Once in March. Once again in April. Like clockwork, once every month until August, when a room was noted as reserved for Colonel Russell's use indefinitely. It wasn't given up until October 1918, just days after the French police rounded up the members of Werner's spy ring.

"It's a coincidence," Penny said with false certainty. "He was in a demanding position and wanted time away from his family and their anxieties—"

"He was a widower by then and sleeping alone. What would he gain from sleeping here instead? And during the day, he had free use of the club facilities as well as his private study back at his house, so what difference would a guest room have made?"

"But . . . My God, Eric. If Colonel Russell really was selling military secrets to the Germans, he was doing it *from the Britannia*. He wouldn't have the gall to smile in the faces of men he'd secretly betrayed, every day, for over a decade. Would he? Even I know how much everyone loved him. I remember the turnout at his funeral."

"I don't have to be Madame Bloody Davidova to hear old Fitzwilliam Peterkin turning in his grave." Seizing a scrap of paper, Eric jotted down the room numbers from the register. "These rooms can't all be equipped with gas rings, not unless Colonel Russell insisted on them specifically. Come along: you'll be the first woman to have seen them since Great-Uncle Charlie's chorus girls."

"I'm not sure I appreciate the comparison," Penny began, but Eric was already hurrying out of the office and up to the comparatively shabby guest accommodations on the second floor.

The first room on Colonel Russell's list was the largest, directly over the front entrance and thus graced with a grander window than most. It was equipped, of course, with a gas ring and a teakettle, discreetly tucked away behind a Chinese screen. The second room was, in fact, the one that Werner had occupied until his unmasking, and Eric remembered quite well the gas ring he'd noted when he searched it two weeks ago. So it was with the next, and the one after that. Only a few of the club's guest rooms had gas rings equipped, but Colonel Russell appeared to have unerringly picked only those.

The last was a queer, crooked little cubby carved out of an inconvenient corner just beyond the bathroom, to help accommodate a new influx of members following the Crimean War. For a moment, Eric's heart lifted when he saw no gas ring immediately in evidence, only to plummet again when he realised the thing was hidden away in an alcove. This was the room Colonel Russell had reserved for himself from August 1915 to October 1918—an unattractive, uncomfortable space separated from the others by the intervening bathroom, with only its seclusion to recommend it.

Eric sat down heavily on the bed. "It's a coincidence," he said, echoing Penny's earlier words. "This isn't conclusive proof of anything. Is it? It doesn't mean anything that he took a room here during the War, and it means even less that he took this one in particular."

Penny picked up the kettle and peered into it. "Wet. Someone's been here recently, at any rate."

"Cully lets tramps in here from time to time, if they can say they fought in the War. Same as how St. Martin-in-the-Fields lets them bunk down in the church vaults. Bradshaw encouraged it; and so do I."

Penny replaced the kettle, and the bed creaked as she sat beside him. "Perhaps it was misinformation."

"What?"

"Misinformation." Penny sat up straighter, brightening at the idea. "Perhaps he was selling *mis*information to the Germans. He'd go through the motions of turning traitor, of course, in case the Germans were watching, and that would include the whole business of steaming Miss Grace's letters open in secret. But perhaps the War

Office knew exactly what he was doing, and was using him to pull the Kaiser's strings. That's something to think about, isn't it?"

"Surely the Germans would have smelled a rat within a month or two," Eric said doubtfully. "I wish Dad were here. He'd know."

"So would his friends."

"I've lost touch—no, wait, there's Major Kettering. I just saw him last Christmas, and I know he's usually at the Army and Navy this time of day." Eric pulled out the letter fragments from his pocket and considered the Morse code printed across them. "Better decipher this and show it to him. Should have started there, in fact. If the message says something different from what we know happened, we'll have cleared Colonel Russell's name."

Penny followed Eric wordlessly down to the book-lined reading room. Cloaked in discretion, the club lounge was quiet enough, but the reading room was even more so. Except for one white-whiskered admiral snoring in a corner over a battered copy of *The Picture of Dorian Gray*, they were alone. Penny sat down at a table to piece the letter fragments together while Eric went to fetch a signaller's handbook from the shelves. As he sat down again beside her, however, she looked up with troubled eyes and said:

"I'm not sure I want to know."

Eric paused with his hand spreading the handbook open and looked around at his sister curiously.

"If he really is guilty," Penny clarified, "then the Britannia Club will be party to treason."

Eric understood. They both felt that the institution stood for something more than comfortable armchairs and discreet attendants bearing gin and tonic. "Colonel Russell doesn't represent the club," he replied. "And we might discover something different."

"Eric, we started by saying that if . . . if . . ." She glanced over at the snoring admiral and lowered her voice further. "If Colonel Russell really were guilty of treason, then he'd have taken a guest room here. Lo and behold, we find that he did. If he were guilty, those rooms would all have the means to steam open a letter. Lo and behold, they all do. Now we're saying that if he were guilty, the information here would be good. The way things have been going, Eric, I'm almost certain that we'll find the information is good. I'd rather just trust that he was selling the Germans misinformation and leave it at that."

"You know we can't do that. For better or for worse, we've got to follow this thread to the end if we're to get to the bottom of his murder. Though I wonder if it would really be worth anything to find his killer, if he was playing Judas. He had four sons in the War, as you said. What kind of father does that to his own flesh and blood? That goes beyond Judas: that's . . ."

*Agamemnon sacrificing Iphigenia.*

No. Worse.

*Kronos devouring his young.*

The sleeping admiral gave a sudden snort as he jerked awake. Catching sight of Penny sitting where she was clearly not permitted to be, he muttered a baleful imprecation against the modern world and ambled out of the room with his book under his arm. Eric and Penny waited until he was gone, then set to work on Flora's letter. Ten minutes later, they had it: troop movements near Aveluy Wood, and a projected offensive set for the following month.

"Well?" asked Penny. "Does this clear the Colonel or does it further implicate him?"

"I don't know. I only know what happened in my corner of Flanders; even then, I couldn't swear to the exact dates."

"Respite, then."

"Until Major Kettering can weigh in."

A discreet cough behind them interrupted their reverie, and Eric instinctively threw an arm over their notes to cover up what they'd been doing. But it was only one of the attendants, with a message from Cully: "There's a lady to see you, sir. A Madame Duplessis."

*Who?*

Eric glanced down at the letter fragments and the accompanying decryption notes . . . For a moment, he felt ashamed. Did he care more about a seven-year-old case of treason than for a man who'd died by violence just two days ago? But Duplessis's death was linked directly to this very case of treason, and the treason itself might be the reason thousands of men never made it home from the trenches . . .

Eric wanted to flip the table over and smash something, anything, to pieces. Instead, he swept up the evidence of his investigations and, with Penny in tow, went to meet with Duplessis's widow.

# SINS OF THE FATHER

MADAME DUPLESSIS WAS withered and dry, with fine lines radiating from her lips as though they'd been pursed perhaps one time too many. This was the same lady, Eric realised, of whom he'd caught a brief glimpse earlier in Inspector Crane's office. It surprised him to find that Dr. Duplessis had a wife—at least, a wife still living. The alienist had given every impression of being as untethered as any bachelor. But he did have an amnesiac son in an asylum ward, whose dependence on him might mean a future in jeopardy now he was gone.

"Bonjour, Madame. Je suis très désolé que . . ."

Madame Duplessis winced—Eric had to admit that his French left much to be desired—and said, "I am happy to speak in English, thank you. You are Monsieur Eric Peterkin?"

"Oui. Yes." Catching the suspicious glance thrown in Penny's direction, Eric hastened to introduce his sister and, as Madame Duplessis expressed no objections to her presence, brought them all into his office to sit down together.

"Monsieur l'Inspecteur told me that you were with my husband on his last grand adventure." Madame Duplessis's mouth twisted at that, the creases around it deepening with disdain. "It is perhaps of no account, but I wish to know exactly what the old fool thought he was doing."

"Now, then. Dr. Duplessis's help has been indispensable. Quite above and beyond—"

Madame Duplessis snorted in derision.

Eric began again. "The Inspector must have told you about the murder that occurred here. We determined that German espionage was at the root of it, and Dr. Duplessis volunteered to come with me to seek out answers in Switzerland . . ."

Bit by bit, Eric told her about Duplessis's involvement in his investigation, getting as far as the confrontation with Werner when Avery was shot. At that, Madame Duplessis glanced at the bare patch of wall where the bloodstained wallpaper had been removed, and inched her chair away from it. "So Gérard was chasing Germans, though the War is this many years behind us! He has gotten your friend shot, and himself killed, for something that was no business of his. He is a doctor, not a policeman: his responsibilities are at home."

"He said it was for his son—*your* son." After the allegations against Colonel Russell, Dr. Duplessis's zeal on behalf of his institutionalised son was a balm for Eric's view of humanity in general and fatherhood in particular. "You have to understand how he felt, surely?"

But Madame Duplessis only looked contemptuous. "Oh, it was for Jean-Pierre, was it? As if that was any business of his."

"Any business of his? He's his father!"

"Some father!"

Madame Duplessis was more angry than anguished, that much was clear. Eric had seen grief take this form before: men resorting to fury at their friends for "daring" to die, as though the heat of their temper would cauterise the wound to their soul. Ordinarily, he would have left it at that—but the image of Kronos devouring his young was too fresh in his mind, which meant that Duplessis's devotion as a father had to be defended.

"Your husband said to me once that he'd 'lost' his son to the War, and I honestly believe that everything he's done since then has been for his sake. He turned his focus to psychology and began researching treatments for shell shock. He wanted to see that no one else suffered as his son did. Of course, he blamed the Germans for what happened, so—"

Madame Duplessis snapped. She leapt to her feet. "Blame! You dare to talk of blame! There is only one person to blame for what happened, and that is Dr. Gérard Duplessis himself!"

Both Eric and Penny were on their feet as well, the latter with a steadying hand on the older woman's arm, as Eric tried to soothe her with words: "I understand. Of course I understand. I know all about it."

Madame Duplessis swayed on her feet and allowed Penny to sit her back down. The fire left her. She looked up at Eric with haunted eyes and said, "You do?"

Eric nodded. Duplessis had encouraged his son to go to war, of course, as had half the fathers of Europe. Madame Duplessis's anger was a reiteration of Flora's bitterness at the "old men"—except that Flora wasn't faced with the daily care of a son she'd raised from infancy, now irretrievably damaged by the War. "Shell shock is a nasty business," Eric said, coming around the desk to hold Madame Duplessis's hand. It trembled in his grasp as she teetered on the edge of tears.

"Oui. It is terrible. Gérard should never have undertaken to treat Jean-Pierre himself."

"But he did," said Penny, and Eric nodded. If Madame Duplessis would only focus on *that,* surely she'd see how much, as a father, Dr. Duplessis cared for his son.

"I wish we had known more, back then. I wish no one ever thought of using electricity to stimulate the organs that appeared to be affected by the shell shock. And Gérard . . . I wish he'd never gotten it into his head that if he were to only increase the voltage, he might hasten our son's recovery. Now, Jean-Pierre will never recover at all."

*What?*

Eric looked up at Penny, who'd gone white with horror. Madame Duplessis, thankfully, did not notice that *this* was not what Eric meant when he said that he knew and understood.

"We separated." Madame Duplessis's voice cracked with a new and desperate tenderness. "How could I continue to live under the same roof, after what he'd done? What sort of a father does that to his own flesh and blood? I thought I would never forgive him. But now—"

*What sort of a father—*

Madame Duplessis crumpled into herself, like kindling collapsing into ashes, and her black-clad shoulders shook with her sobs. Penny wordlessly gathered her in, and the older woman clung to the younger with a desperation begun years ago, when laughter and light first faded from the eyes of a young French soldier deemed medically unfit for further combat.

For all her bitter invective, it seemed clear that Madame Duplessis deeply mourned the death of her husband, and was now determined to wring out every last tear from her grief by poking at it with a sharp stick wherever and whenever possible. Her next port of call, once she'd recovered herself, was a colleague of her husband's, who would tell her more than she needed to know—and less than she wanted—about his business in England. Penny, concerned for her well-being, offered to accompany her there, and the offer was accepted.

Eric suspected that Penny simply didn't care to continue questioning Colonel Russell's loyalties. He wasn't too keen on it either, but it had to be done—more so than the club's end-of-month paperwork. They'd meet later at St. Thomas' Hospital to look in on Avery; in the meantime, there was Major Bertie Kettering to call on.

Kettering's club was the Army and Navy, just around the corner where St. James's Square bled out onto Pall Mall. They'd recently acquired one or two of the neighbouring houses, expanding to meet an increased demand for bedrooms. The man who met Eric in the entrance hall at first supposed him to be connected with the construction work, and was taken aback when Eric assured him he was a gentleman asking after another member.

Eric had forgotten, over the past three months, what it was to be held at a polite arm's length when wandering these rarefied spaces—and why.

"Peterkin!" Bertie Kettering, a lean and sinewy gentleman of forty with an eye patch and prematurely white hair, met Eric with a heartiness designed to shame anyone questioning his presence. "Sorry to have kept you waiting. I was just concluding the purchase of a delightful Metro-land property practically on the fifth hole of the local golf course. Now, why don't you come with me into the morning room? Far more comfortable than hanging about here like a lost tradesman."

Eric was ushered into a grand reception hall with towering windows overlooking Pall Mall, and settled into a comfortable armchair. He declined the offer of a drink. "I'd prefer not to explain why I need to know this, and you don't have to tell me anything more than yes or no; but was Colonel Hadrian Russell involved with military intelligence in a misinformation campaign?"

Kettering chuckled, quite unfazed by Eric's reticence. "Probably no. Old General Cresswell didn't like Russell—thought him too short on brains for our line of work."

"What about this?" Eric produced a copy of the decrypted message. "At the given date, would this information have been considered reliable?"

"Hard to say. One troop movement's much like any other, and with this little context . . . Although I remember a spot of bother related to operations on this part of the front; plans changed at the last minute because of intercepted messages showing that the Germans somehow knew about them already." Kettering fixed Eric with a shrewd look. "You're suggesting that Colonel Russell passed this information to the Germans, aren't you? What happened to *de mortuis nil nisi bonum*?"

"I said nothing."

"You know damn well that your two questions put side by side are as good as an accusation. Here, I'll do some checks, see if this really is part and parcel of that leak I mentioned. That will make us even, yes?"

"Even? What do you mean?"

"You sorted out that strange affair last Christmas involving Sergeant Forrester—"

Oh. That. The trade in favours had been one of Bradshaw's best tools, but . . . "I'm not in the business of tallying favours," Eric assured him. "Certainly not for something that any decent human being should have done. You've never owed me anything."

Eric arrived at St. Thomas' Hospital to find Avery in significantly better health and spirits than before. He was performing a Tarot reading for Penny, and the late afternoon sun flooded the ward around them with a peculiar hushed brilliance. If Eric didn't know better, he'd wonder if his friend was malingering.

The look they gave him as he approached told him that Penny had already updated Avery with all the news.

"I'm sorry about Dr. Duplessis," Avery said as he put his cards away. "We didn't get on, but I really do think he was a decent fellow, when all was said and done. What happened to his son is simply tragic. This story about Colonel Russell, though . . . Surely there must be some mistake? Penny told me about a letter that Miss Grace supposedly wrote and which Lucy Russell was trying to destroy?"

Eric obligingly laid out the letter fragments on Avery's bedspread and repeated what he'd learnt from Major Kettering. "The idea seems too preposterous to be credited. Colonel Hadrian Russell! I liked him—everybody did. Well, everybody except General Cresswell. Point is, Colonel Russell was the heart and soul of the Britannia, and you know what the Britannia stands for. How does a man like that commit treason?" Eric sighed and rubbed his forehead. He felt more tired than anything else. "As Madame Duplessis said, 'What sort of a father does that to his own flesh and blood?'"

Avery, who'd been frowning at the fragment containing the salutation of *Chère Monique* as though it might burst into flame, glanced up in surprise. "You told her about Colonel Russell?"

"No, she was talking about her husband. The question seems to be the ongoing motif for the day, is what I meant."

"Well, you can't compare the two, can you? I mean, Duplessis meant well, surely? If there's one thing I've learned from having a doctor root around in my guts for a tiny lump of lead, it's that I'd much rather risk dying right now for a chance to live, than do nothing and die for certain in the next two hours. Duplessis thought he could cure his son. He was wrong, but that doesn't make him a monster."

"Yes," said Eric. "He meant well."

"Can you say the same of Colonel Russell?"

Eric considered. "Perhaps . . . Perhaps he wanted to leave a comfortable fortune to his sons. That's something every father wants and does, isn't it? A better future in exchange for some added risk now—a slightly higher voltage, if you will. I can understand that."

"Not I," Penny replied stoutly. "For shame! Treason is treason, and you know you can't buy your son's future with the lives of a hundred thousand strangers."

"I said I understood. I never said I agreed." But understanding Colonel Russell's treason only made it more believable, and believing it . . . Eric wasn't sure what to believe anymore. "According to Lady Alice, Colonel Russell once said that a son is a thing of his father's, which young Matthew supposedly misunderstood to mean that Colonel Russell didn't see his sons and grandsons as people in their own right. But now I wonder if perhaps the boy saw the truth more clearly than any of us adults."

Avery, still turning the letter fragments over in his hands, said, "That Colonel Russell's really got into your head, hasn't he?"

Eric remembered Colonel Russell holding court in the club lounge, the centre of attention without having said a word. How did one man amass such popularity? Looking back on it now, the scene seemed infused with a seductive faerie glamour, designed to befuddle the minds of mere mortals. He remembered the side glances and reserve he'd encountered at the Army and Navy earlier, none of which he'd had to endure since Colonel Russell took him under his wing. For the past three months, as far as the Britannia Club was concerned, he might as well have been as purebred a Briton as . . . as . . .

King Arthur.

*They had stopped on the landing of the grand staircase, and Colonel Russell was expounding on the historicity of Britain's once and future king . . .*

"He told me," Eric murmured, "that King Arthur was really a Roman centurion, and that Britain had inherited the glory of Rome. He said this inheritance was the only thing that mattered. I took it to mean that . . . that Arthur was English because he fought for England. It's allegiance that matters, not blood."

Who was Colonel Russell, really, if his allegiance did not lie with England and the things the Britannia Club stood for?

"'O what can ail thee, knight-at-arms,'" Penny quoted suddenly with a playful jab at Eric's ribs, "'Alone and palely loitering?'"

"Oh, shut it. Colonel Russell is hardly La Belle Dame Sans Merci." And quoting poetry only reminded Eric uncomfortably of Flora's penchant for the same. Though if Colonel Russell were La Belle Dame, perhaps Flora was the knight-at-arms—an innocent dupe.

"Isn't he, though? It sounds to me as though he knew exactly the sort of thing to draw you in and hath thee in thrall." When Eric remained unamused, Penny said with more seriousness, "Look, Eric. I'm every bit as shocked as you are, but you seem to be having more trouble accepting it and moving on. That's because Colonel Russell's put this picture in your head of who he is, isn't it? But it's like that grand house of his in Knightsbridge: empty rooms and empty words, purely there for show."

Across the river, Big Ben rang out the hour, and the low hum of conversation across the ward dropped into a momentary lull until the familiar chimes had faded. Eric blinked and looked away from the bright sun-filled windows. He felt as though he'd just been awakened from a hypnotic trance.

"Chin up, Eric," said Avery, finally putting down the letter fragments to reach for a familiar confectionery box on his bedside table. "We've all got to play the dupe from time to time. Stop worrying about it and have a marron glacé—I saved the last two for you and Penny."

"Oh, all right. Maybe it's best we all put Colonel Russell aside for the time being."

But as Eric swept up the letter fragments and began to shove them into his pocket, Avery suddenly let out a yelp. "That's it!"

"What? What's it?"

Avery winced and hugged a pillow to his stomach. "Monique! I've been wondering why that name seemed to ring a bell; and that letter, too. I've seen it before. Or, at least, something very much like it."

Penny, sitting across from Eric, froze with her hand in the confectionery box. Eric supposed his expression must be a mirror of hers as they both stared incredulously at Avery. "You have? When?"

"The day Colonel Russell got back from his fishing holiday. You were busy with Madam Eliot, but I was with him when he got his mail from the front desk. Nothing there he cared about, but then he came to this one, and I'll never forget the look on his face when he tore open the envelope and saw what was in it. Queer as a silver goldfish! And then he bundled it into his coat pocket, the same way you just did, before anyone could see. But I saw. Chère Monique. I remember thinking that Colonel Russell didn't look much like a 'Monique.' Miss Grace's penmanship is quite pretty, isn't it? I remembered that, too."

"And you didn't say anything?"

"Why should I? Colonel Russell didn't pull the letter all the way out of the envelope—just enough to see the salutation and some of the writing—so I never saw any of this invisible ink Morse code business, and it never occurred to me that this might be anything more important than a misdirected letter. Anyway, if you remember, I had a few other things on my mind."

Eric took the fragments out again and found the one bearing the salutation of *Chère Monique*. The yellow-brown Morse code crawling up the letter's margins didn't reach this far, leaving this fragment seemingly innocent and innocuous. "Werner sent this to Colonel Russell," Eric said, slowly connecting the dots in his mind. "It was a warning to keep his mouth shut. No wonder Colonel Russell didn't denounce Werner on sight. He knew exactly what this letter was and what it represented, without having to see the Morse code message on it. And he considered it sensitive enough that he hid it away in a safe when he got home, perhaps forgetting that Lucy knew the combination, too."

Avery shook the confectionery box at him, and Eric mechanically helped himself to the last of the amber-glazed chestnuts; but his mind had gone back to the day Avery meant. He remembered being buttonholed by Madam Eliot, and he remembered what happened next: Werner, in his guise as Ward, arrived with Lucy on his arm, and then there was that strange tension between him and the Colonel. At the time, Eric assumed it to be the usual paternal jealousy of a father encountering his daughter's suitor. He knew better now. Colonel Russell's reaction had nothing to do with Lucy and everything to do with connecting the man before him to the letter he'd just received.

"We talk of Werner being an imposter, but I'm beginning to think Colonel Russell was the real imposter." Eric turned his marron glacé over between his fingers. It was golden all around, a nugget of calcified sunlight. The last shreds of Colonel Russell's spell seemed to burn away, and Eric said with sudden passion, "All that fine talk about King Arthur and the legacy of Rome! You're right, Penny. Empty words. None of it matters."

"The worst lies," Avery said, "are fabricated from truth. Of course it matters, just not in the way he put it. I mean, for all their roads and aqueducts and governance, the ancient Romans were horrible people who fed anyone they didn't like to the lions for sport.

We're better than that because we learned from them. And a thousand years from now, when someone else is clamouring to be heir to the British Empire, they'll be better than we ever were. Sons are not 'things of their fathers'; rather, they learn from the sins of their fathers. These things cycle towards the light, don't you know. Now eat your marron glacé."

# LA BELLE DAME

"MR. PETERKIN." FLORA GRACE did not look at all pleased to find Eric on her doorstep. "I was just about to step out for a nice, jazz-filled evening."

"I have something that I think belongs to you. May I come in?"

Penny had gone back to Harrow, so Eric was alone. Flora showed him into her sleekly modern sitting room with evident reluctance, and turned on a single floor lamp. The modernist paintings on the white walls were indistinct shapes in the dim lighting, but the Chicago windows offered a fine, starlit view of Bloomsbury from above. Flora's perfume made Eric want to draw closer, like a moth about to immolate itself in a candle flame.

*Marlena Gudenoff*, Eric thought. That was the name of the vamp in his latest manuscript evaluation. The femme fatale. La Belle Dame Sans Merci. She was a familiar character archetype, whose role was always to distract the hero from his goals, and perhaps subvert them to her ends. If anyone fit the image, it was Miss Flora Grace. He'd agreed with Penny that Flora wouldn't have been so foolish as to hand him her letters from "Monique" if she'd really been guilty, but was that a certainty? Flora projected an image of sophisticated intelligence, but images could lie. He knew that all too well now.

"Well, Mr. Peterkin?"

Eric held up the torn fragments of her letter to "Monique," and Flora's annoyance turned instantly into consternation. She took them to the lamplight for a closer inspection, and when she finally looked up, her expression was more wary than shocked.

"Where did you get this?"

"Colonel Russell's house." Eric quickly outlined the morning's adventure, including Lucy's attempt to destroy the letter.

"I see. I always knew Lucy had more cunning than we gave her credit for."

"You don't want to know what the coded message says?"

"I can guess the nature of it." Would she point the finger at Colonel Russell, as Lucy had done? Instead, she turned to her liquor cabinet. "You might as well sit down, since you're here. I suppose you want a gin and tonic? I want a gin and more gin."

Sitting would make him too comfortable. Eric went to wait by the wide Chicago windows overlooking the asphalt roads of Bloomsbury four floors down. His eyes, however, remained on Flora, the white silk of her outfit shimmering like a mirage in the half-light from the room's solitary lamp. She mixed his drink first, poured her own, then took a large gulp directly from the bottle. The dim lighting, rather than softening the mood, only served to render the organically curved furniture more alien, and Flora's position more uncertain.

Flora returned with his drink, and he said, "Well? What's your answer?"

"I don't like to speak ill of the dead."

A disingenuous and therefore inherently dishonest way of accusing Colonel Russell. There was a tension there, too, signalling danger—but La Belle Dame was always a dangerous creature. Aloud, and perhaps more harshly than intended, Eric replied, "Don't you? You said something to me once: 'But the old man would not but slew his son, and half the seed of Europe, one by one—'"

"Wilfred Owen."

"You've always blamed Colonel Russell for what happened in the War. Why not now?"

Flora shuddered and took a large gulp of her drink. "That's different. Men like Hadrian start wars without question, but they generally imagine they're striving for something good. You can accept that they're still decent men—just stupid. But to start a war and deliberately hobble the efforts of your own men—your own sons—*David*—" Another gulp of gin, and then she set her glass down deliberately on a low table. Eric got the impression she would much rather hurl it at a wall. "It's true. I'm the reason David is dead. And George, and Patrick, and Andrew. I'm the reason they're all dead."

"Flora—"

"No, that's not right." Her fingers flexed, manicured nails curving into talons. "I'm not the reason: Hadrian is. I was just his fool. That's all. His stupid, stupid fool. For seven years, I worried that I might have inadvertently mentioned something in my letters, and all the time—*all the time*—it wasn't what I'd written that mattered, but what Hadrian put there. Of course it was Hadrian. It can't have been anyone else. That evil, *evil* bastard! If he weren't dead already, I'd murder him right now!"

She snatched up the glass she'd just put down, and this time she *did* hurl it against the wall. Glass shards exploded across the floor, and she would have followed it up with a heavy glass ashtray if Eric hadn't seized hold of her.

"Flora! Stop this! You're not solving anything."

Flora, with hot, angry tears streaming, let out an inarticulate howl of fury and struggled with a ferocity that had Eric worrying that she might do them both an injury. The ashtray fell from her hands and thumped on the carpet but did not break. Eric held on until the tears overwhelmed her, then half guided, half dragged her to a sofa and sat her down. He kept his arms protectively around her, and she curled up against him, trembling. They sat like that in silence for what seemed like hours.

A single lamp was hardly adequate to light the whole room, and the shadows seemed to throng with ghosts—"pale kings and princes, too," as Keats's poem went. Was David Russell among them? He'd supposedly released his soon-to-be widow from any notion of faithfulness to his memory, but . . . had he really? They only had Flora's word for it. A sudden thought: Eric had come here intending a confrontation with La Belle Dame, and now he was soothing her in his arms with all the fervour of a devoted lover . . . or a thrall. If David Russell's shade were hovering in the gloam, might that be a warning on his starved lips?

Flora hiccoughed as her sobs subsided, and her trembling eased into the steady in and out of long, heaving breaths. In a voice so small that Eric almost missed it, she murmured:

*"Then henceforth may earth grow trees!*
*No more roses!—hard straight lines*
*To score lies out! none of these*
*Fluctuant curves, but firs and pines,*
*Poplars, cedars, cypresses!"*

Across the room, Flora's modernist paintings offered no quotations of their own. They were honest in their formlessness. Eric said, "He knew how to charm people onto his side. I know that better than anyone."

"I hate him. I hate him for his betrayal, and I hate him for his hypocrisy. As if my taking a lover compares to what he did, if we're talking about bringing shame on the family! But almost as bad as all that—or maybe worse, I don't know—I hate him for making me, against my will and without my knowledge, complicit in the War."

"There's no complicity to speak of. War is inevitable."

*And people die in wars . . . If a man must number among the doomed, there is nothing you or I could do to make a difference.*

Colonel Russell had said that to him the night before he died. Eric recalled the darkened club lobby, the Roster of the Fallen, the ghosts of martyrs haunting the shadows as they seemed to haunt him now. He'd thought, at the time, that the Colonel was lamenting the loss of his sons. But as he repeated those words now for Flora's sake, he saw them for what they really meant to Colonel Russell: self-righteous justification. *Whether they live or die, it is Fate and nothing to do with me.*

"Inevitable?" Flora struggled out of Eric's arms and glared at him, her eyes and nose both reddened by her recent outburst. "Hadrian would have liked to think so, wouldn't he? I daresay *some* wars are unavoidable, but not all, and certainly not the last one. *That* was all vanity and ego—old men sending the masses off to die just so they can pretend they still matter."

Her native hardness was reasserting itself. She drew an arm roughly across her eyes, then glared at the smear of makeup on her wrist. "I must look a fright," she muttered, and hurried away. Eric followed her, stopping outside the bathroom door as she splashed water over her face and scrubbed it dry on a rough towel. With the polish stripped away, so was the mystique: this was Flora Grace laid bare . . . not La Belle Dame Sans Merci.

"Flora."

She ignored him.

"Flora, listen. You know this isn't over yet. You've got to think about what the police are going to say about this letter."

Flora stopped and fixed him with a frosty glare. "You're going to show it to them after all, are you?"

"How can I not? It's evidence. And the police will see this in one of two ways. One, that Colonel Russell was threatening to expose you, and you killed him to keep him quiet. Or two, that you learned somehow of his treason, and you killed him as revenge—not only for your husband's death, but for using you as his dupe. Five minutes ago, you said you'd murder him now if he weren't dead already."

Flora stared at him, then turned back to the bathroom mirror. "I thought we'd already settled on Karl Werner as the guilty party in Hadrian's murder."

"Help me out. Point me in the right direction. What really happened that night when Colonel Russell was murdered?"

"Don't you already know everything?"

"I know you've got your head screwed on a lot straighter than people give you credit for. I don't believe for a minute that you just happened one night to develop such an all-consuming passion for someone that you simply had to run all the way to King Street to interrupt him at his work. You've got more sense and self-control than that. So tell me, why were you really at the Britannia Club that night?"

Flora didn't answer. She turned her head left and right, still inspecting her face. "I think I shan't go out tonight after all. I'm utterly exhausted."

"Flora—"

She silenced him with a finger to his lips. Then she leaned in and brushed his cheek with a kiss, tantalisingly close to the corner of his mouth. When she stepped back, her eyes behind their redness were cool and aloof: she'd slipped once more into the role of the femme fatale. Even so, the image that came to Eric's mind was of her leaning against one of the Britannia's neoclassical columns with a cigarette holder in hand, declaring, *There's no such thing.* The femme fatale of popular fiction was no more than fiction herself.

"Thank you, Mr. Peterkin. Thank you for being here for me tonight, when I most needed a strong shoulder to cry on. But I am afraid I have nothing more to tell you."

"Consider it a lady's favour to her knight errant." Flora leaned in to kiss him, and her lips were as soft and delightful as he'd expected—and hot. So hot that they left a burning trail of blisters in their wake as she kissed her way down over his bare chest. Behind her, David Russell looked on in . . . approval? Judgement? His face was unreadable, and the blisters were spreading: the vile, yellow blisters of exposure to mustard gas . . .

*Pale kings and princes . . . starved lips in the gloam with horrid warning gapèd wide . . .*

He needed a medic. He struggled out of Flora's grasp, past David Russell, who'd gone from handsome to horrifyingly scarred in the blink of an eye. Out of the collapsed dugout where he'd been trapped with Private Dent—most of Private Dent—since the shelling began. Dr. Leonhard Keller, crowned with the horns of a mountain goat, stood on the stern of an Army transport vessel as it slid out of Southampton harbour, and Eric felt as though he was wading through molasses as he ran to catch it. What was the doctor saying? Something important. Eric strained to hear—

"Sir? Sir!"

Eric snorted and woke with a start. The blisters were gone, but he felt as though he'd just run all the way from Bloomsbury to . . . to his desk at the Britannia Club, and the paperwork demanding his attention. The electric light overhead was too bright and too harsh, and his awareness of every minute detail around him made it impossible to focus on any individual one.

Cully, framed in the dark rectangle of the office window, said, "Sir, it's past midnight, and I was locking up. Should I book you into a guest room?"

Eric gave his head a shake to clear it. What could Dr. Keller be trying to tell him? Perhaps it had been a mistake to force himself back to the club after visiting Flora, but he couldn't put off the paperwork forever. "No need," he decided. "I'm supposed to be club secretary, aren't I? I've got the room register right here, and I can do it myself."

Cully glanced down at the cluttered desk and grimaced. "Sorry to have stacked up all this bother for you, sir. Why don't you let it go for now and come back tomorrow? I'm sure no one will mind if things are late by a day."

Oh, but now it was a matter of pride. "Nonsense. This is what I get for questing all over Europe and leaving things to rot at home. Richard the Lionheart has nothing on me! Don't worry, this is a trifle compared to being imprisoned on the way home from the Crusades."

"As you say, sir. Couple of things, by the way: first, here's a telegram for you."

It was from Kettering and contained just one word: *Idem*. Latin, "the same thing"—confirmation that the "spot of bother" that Kettering had alluded to was, indeed, "the same thing" as the operation described in the coded message. Eric had accepted the idea of Colonel Russell's guilt by now, but the reminder still sparked an impotent fury. Damn Colonel Russell. Damn the traitorous bastard to hell. The bile rose in his throat as he recalled the blood and the maimed limbs, the men broken in more ways than the merely physical—

*Private Dent sat, shell-shocked, in the back of the dugout, fifteen minutes before the shelling began.*

How many had died because of secrets passed to Germany by hands free of mud?

"Second," Cully continued, "Lady Alice called. She said that you are to not do anything foolish; she has important information which she'll come and tell you in person tomorrow morning."

"I'm sure she does." No, that was unfair. He was allowing his anger at Colonel Russell to colour his treatment of Lady Alice. Calming his tone, if not his temper, he said, "I'll see her in the morning, then."

The office door closed on Cully's retreating back, and Eric looked down at the papers spread across his desk. Four weeks' worth of stocktaking. He'd managed precious little work on it since getting back from Flora's. The fact was, he was frustrated. He had gone to Flora seeking answers—or more to the point, the certainty that came with answers—and she had given him nothing of the sort. In fact, he was sure she was withholding something from him, which felt irrationally like a betrayal.

Why did it matter, Eric thought fiercely. If Colonel Russell was guilty of treason, did he deserve the effort Eric was putting into discovering the truth? Did Werner, as the foreign operative working with Colonel Russell? But another figure came to mind: a man of perhaps sixty, tall and narrow, with a pince-nez on a scarlet ribbon . . .

*If nothing else, I owe it to* him.

Eric pushed the memory away. He didn't want to think of Duplessis pondering the principles behind involving oneself in the pursuit of justice.

And he didn't want to speak to Lady Alice, either. Didn't the Russell widows all turn immediately to Lady Alice when trouble darkened their horizons? Perhaps the murder of Colonel Russell had been the work of all four women together—a righteous revenge for four dead husbands. Doubtless, Flora had got on the telephone to her sister-in-law the moment Eric left her flat.

*Flora. David Russell. "Do you know what mustard gas does to a man?"*

Eric blinked away an unbidden image of clean flesh blistering and melting like candle wax into twisted scars. He stood up. He needed a damned drink, and he needed to get it his own damn self. Anything but sit where he was and stew.

The halls of the Britannia were dark and silent as Eric crept out of his office. Cully had finished locking up and retired for the night: the only sign of life was the intermittent rattle of typewriter keys beyond the staff room door. Harvey was presumably occupied with seeking out new employment while awaiting surprise callers, unexpected emergencies, German raids, and murder. The last time Eric walked this way was just before Colonel Russell's death, when—

Eric pressed his lips together and banished the thought.

Through the lobby, and under the Roster of the Fallen. The names of the Russell brothers looked down in judgement where their father had walked every day since the War with seemingly no care for what he'd done to them. How many other names had been inscribed through Colonel Russell's treason?

*At least we name them, eh?*

Eric hoped the regret he'd heard was true. He hoped the Colonel woke up every day eaten up by guilt.

Up the stairs, past the painting of Arthur and his faithful knights—Sir Kay, smirking from the shadows: *Let the others quest as they will; I am the reason Camelot stands at all.* Eric averted his gaze and continued to the lounge. No one there but the ghosts of members past. He flicked on the switch for the light over the bar, then found his tab and pencilled in the drink he wanted. A gin and tonic? He was in no mood for anything more complicated than a straight pour. A gin and more gin it was, then.

Something was wrong.

Eric stopped, his hand hovering before the club's selection of gin. Something was missing, something he'd grown so used to seeing that he'd ceased to register its presence—only its absence. What was it? Why were alarm bells going off in his head?

The last time he'd had a good look at the bar was while overseeing the cleaning up after the murder. The only things missing then had been the gin and tonic water which Colonel Russell had had by his chair that night, but they'd been replaced since with identical bottles. Experimentally, Eric removed those from the shelf and looked again.

Something was still wrong. Missing. And it was neither the gin nor the tonic water.

Was this how Avery felt when he recognised the reference to "Monique" without remembering precisely where from?

Eric hurried back to his office for the stocktaking reports. The last one was compiled just this morning: he'd been going over it when he nodded off earlier. Setting it beside the one from the previous Monday, he checked off the entries until he identified the errant bottle.

Schnapps.

*Thomas Harvey. "No one's touched it since the War and especially since the British Empire Union came around telling everyone to say no to all things German . . ."*

Had someone suddenly and recently developed a taste for schnapps? No, not according to the bar receipts. Had it been accidentally knocked off the shelf and broken? No, there'd be some note of it if so. Had someone nicked it? There had never been a history of theft among the Britannia Club attendants, but there was a first time for everything; and, as Thomas Harvey had amply demonstrated, lapses of judgement did happen. But why take the club's only bottle of schnapps, a loss easily spotted, when one of the more popular liquors might be shrugged off as having fallen victim to a heavy-handed barman, assuming it was even missed at all?

Unless . . . unless one *didn't* know that the schnapps here saw no traffic . . .

*Dr. Keller. "He was fond of his schnapps . . . I suppose he was greatly affected by the loss, as I myself suffered the loss of a bottle of schnapps soon after the funeral . . ."*

Sitting back, Eric stared up at the ceiling, ears straining into the midnight silence. He had to be jumping at shadows, surely. There was no way. But . . . could Karl Werner have been hiding *here*, at the Britannia Club, all this time?

# RATS IN THE WALLS

THE PIPE ROOM had its own electric light now, and a new entrance from just outside the kitchens. The entrance from the vault anteroom had been sealed up, though more plaster work would have to be done to hide that it had ever been there at all. Only the hole in the floor remained—that, and the Roman mosaic at the bottom. Eric, accompanied by Harvey and Cully, crouched and peered under the crumbling lip of the hole. The light of his torch found that the cavity extended into a space under the floor just wide enough for a man to squeeze into and wait for the excitement of a shooting to die down.

Eric scowled in disgust. "You could still get in from the vault last week, couldn't you? The day Avery—Mr. Ferrett—was shot and everything went to hell. We were so used to this place being a dead end that we thought simply locking the door would trap anyone foolish enough to hide here. We didn't think Werner could escape out to the kitchens later."

After that, it would just be a matter of finding a safer and more comfortable hiding place to wait things out. Inspector Crane couldn't watch the train stations and roads out of London forever, and the public would eventually cease to care about scarred strangers in the street. Until it was safe to venture forth, enough food was made and consumed between the kitchens and the dining room that no one would notice a little bit trimmed off the daily leftovers. And where might this hiding place be, exactly? Not the basement, ground floor, or first floor: those rooms saw too much traffic throughout the day. Not the second-floor guest rooms, which might be taken by members at any inconvenient time. That left the unoccupied rooms in the attic from when the club attendants still lived on-site. One could sleep through the day there, safe and undisturbed; and during the night . . . Eric remembered Penny's observation that the kettle in one of the least attractive guest rooms showed signs of recent usage. During the night, when the building was quiet and the only man awake was the night attendant in the staff room, one might even avail oneself of a hot cup of tea.

Harvey, still the de facto night attendant until he found employment elsewhere, peered into the shadows outside the pipe room—the kitchens in one direction, the back stairs in the other. "Never thought I'd say this, but should we call the coppers?"

"And tell them what? That we think he's here, though we haven't seen him? There's a dozen false leads all over the city with more behind them than that."

"The missing liquor won't be proof enough, will it?"

"Not for the police, no."

"Perhaps we should wait for morning," Cully said. "You can speak with Inspector Crane then. He'll listen to you."

Eric was about to voice his doubts when a soft creak made all three men stop and stare off into the darkness. A joist expanding with the onset of spring? Or someone creeping through the shadows, close enough to know that his hours of hiding here were numbered?

"He'll be gone before morning, if that was him," Eric whispered. "I don't think we can wait. Harvey, lock the back door and make sure you remove the key, then meet me on the second-floor landing of the back stairs. Cully, see to the front door, then lock yourself in your office and keep your ears peeled. If you hear anything that sounds like a gunshot, call the police at once. Werner's still got his pocket pistol, so we'll want to be careful."

Eric wished he hadn't been quite so diligent in returning Forrester's gun. He couldn't help but remember Avery slumped against his office wall, the dark red of blood pouring over clutching fingers, the smell of expended gunpowder . . . and Werner, of course, with a smoking gun and a horrified expression . . .

Duplessis had theorised that Werner really believed himself to be Gregory Ward. Eric remembered the motorcar racing along the alpine roads, and the old alienist earnestly laying out his reasoning. Was he right, and did it make a difference? Eric only knew what he'd seen in that one unguarded moment, which was that Werner, whoever he thought he was, did not turn instinctively to violence. He wouldn't shoot unless he felt sufficiently threatened. Perhaps, in fact, they were safer without firearms of their own—though no amount of telling himself that could make him *feel* safer, and it would be the height of hubris to walk into this completely unarmed.

Harvey scurried off on his instructions, while Eric followed Cully as far as the lobby before continuing alone to his office. Harvey would probably double back to the kitchens for a knife, and Cully had already armed himself with a fireplace poker. Eric considered taking a master key to the vault and seeing if anyone had taken a German pistol for a trophy in the War and left it there; but that would take too much time, with no guarantee of suitable ammunition.

His eye fell on Great-Uncle Charlie's cavalry sabre.

And why not? Great-Uncle Charlie would be just as stout as any Peterkin from old Fitzwilliam up to Eric himself in his defence of the Britannia. His old sabre had lost most of its edge, but an experimental cut and thrust betrayed a nice balance, its point was still as wicked as ever, and it fit in Eric's hand as though it had been crafted specially for him.

Thus equipped, Eric stole up the back stairs to meet Harvey, who had indeed armed himself with a large kitchen knife. "Fat lot of good this will do," Harvey grumbled, "against a man with a gun. He'll kill us both."

"He can't shoot both of us at once," Eric responded lightly, the stiff upper lip of his officer training manifesting itself. "The other will have time to jump on him and wrestle the gun away. Besides, after Flanders, is this really something to fear?"

Harvey made a queer, choking sound. "Sorry. It's just . . . I think I read that exact same thing somewhere."

"Don't get distracted, now. Here, I'll take the lead."

With Harvey trailing a little farther behind than Eric liked, they continued up to the cluttered lumber rooms and abandoned staff bedrooms of the attics. It was a dim echo of Eric's search of Colonel Russell's house less than twenty-four hours earlier; but where that search had been lighted by the sun filtering in through high windows to soften the shadows, now they were carefully threading their way through the darkness: hard, black outlines against a backdrop of deeper black. There was just enough light, thank goodness, that they weren't groping blindly around. The last thing Eric wanted was for Werner—assuming he was there—to be alerted to their presence by the flash of an electric torch or the sound of their movement.

The lumber rooms afforded little but darkness and silence. Eric listened for anything to betray another human being's presence—a breath disturbing the still air, the creak of shifting weight on worn floorboards—but heard nothing. That did not mean that no one was hiding among the relics of ages past, but it would take far too much time and effort to properly poke through everything; and the resulting noise would ensure they found no one at all. Eric settled for closing the doors and locking them behind him. If Werner was indeed hiding in one of the lumber rooms, he would not be leaving easily or without drawing attention.

Next, the old staff bedrooms.

Empty. Empty. Empty. These rooms were wider than the guest bedrooms downstairs, but shallower, with empty bed frames at either end. A five-foot deep dormer alcove contained a chest of drawers and, up at the ceiling, a square window looking out to the sky over the buildings across the way. King Street itself was hidden from view by a wide ledge under the window, formed by the top of the club building's elaborate cornice.

Nothing could be done about the view, of course, but a bit of effort and paint might have turned these rooms into pleasant guest bedrooms for the use of the membership. Why hadn't that been done? The attendants who occupied these rooms at the time of the last expansion were gone now, after all. Then again, so was the demand. Somehow, even the Great War had failed to induce another expansion with a surge of new blood. Eric thought of the renovations currently underway at the Army and Navy to satisfy an increased demand for bedrooms, remembered that the Britannia had but one occupant the night of Colonel Russell's murder, and realised with a shock that the Britannia was stagnating. They'd grown so comfortable with where they were and what they'd been that they'd failed to notice the world leaving them behind—

What was that?

Movement in the next room?

Eric flattened himself against the wall on one side of the door and signalled Harvey to do the same on the other side. He put his hand on the doorknob and braced himself—

Something screeched, like heavy furniture dragged across the floor . . . or a long-disused sash window being forced open.

Eric tightened his grip on Great-Uncle Charlie's cavalry sabre and threw the door open, ducking as he did to get inside. The expected shots did not come. Instead, he found a room nearly identical to the others, except that a wafer-thin mattress had been pulled onto one bed, with a threadbare blanket sliding off onto the floor.

Perched with one foot on the chest of drawers and the other out the window, Karl Werner, the man formerly known as Captain Gregory Ward, looked back at Eric with the face of a haggard tramp, a man pushed to the end of his rope.

"Ward," Eric called out, hoping that Duplessis's assessment was correct after all; or, if it was not, that some persuasive argument might be derived from that opening.

Werner spat out something in German that Eric only understood as being terribly rude, and swung out the window.

Eric dashed into the room and leapt on top of the chest. Forgetting for a moment that he might get shot at, he stuck his head out and turned to see where Werner might have gone. He could hear the banging of shoes scrabbling over metal. Werner must have gone over the parapet and onto the roof. Eric turned to shout back to Harvey: “Call the police—”

But Harvey had already gone.

Eric slid the sabre blade behind the left side of his braces, where it teetered precariously without the weight of a scabbard to counter the weight of its hilt. Pulling his waistcoat tight around the thankfully blunted blade should hopefully provide enough of a hold to keep the thing from tipping forward and sliding free. Then he clambered out onto the cornice ledge in pursuit of Karl Werner.

# SOLVET SAECLUM IN FAVILLA

KING STREET, four storeys down, was a black void despite the streetlamps glowing along its edges. The cornice ledge seemed narrower than from the safety of the rooms within, and those four storeys a greater height than anticipated. The parapet stretched off on either side to the next dormer. Dark as it was, Eric hadn't noticed the rain clouds gathering earlier, but they were a roiling mass overhead, and a cold chill hung in the air.

Eric remembered humble cottages and towering steeples crumbling under mortar fire, and tried not to imagine the cornice giving way under his feet.

Finding a foothold on the neoclassical detailing around the dormer, Eric levered himself up over the parapet. He tumbled from there into a narrow trench, nearly losing the sabre in the process. The Britannia Club gave the impression, when seen from the street, of being no taller than its parapet; but if that were so, then the room that Eric just left would have had a ceiling no more than five feet high. In fact, the upper half of the attic rooms were contained within the corrugated green copper of a mansard roof that rose steeply up behind the parapet, and the sound of shoes on metal earlier must mean that Werner was attempting to escape over it.

Eric turned his back on the parapet and laid his hand on the green copper. *The world's gone backwards*, he thought. *The enemy is behind the parapet, and no-man's-land is homewards*.

He clambered up as best he could, somehow finding footholds in the copper, until he reached the ridge at the top of the slope, then cautiously peeked over it. Beyond this ridge, the copper roofing was almost flat, rising gently towards another ridge. Eric couldn't see beyond that second ridge, but he guessed that the roof must fall away after it towards the skylight over the club lobby. *That* would be no-man's-land, and to step into it could mean death by a four-storey drop to an unforgiving marble floor through a rain of broken glass.

A shot rang out, and Eric ducked instinctively. But he knew, somehow, that this was more warning than threat. Werner was aiming into the air. Looking up again, Eric saw his ragged silhouette step out from behind a towering chimney stack some forty or fifty feet away. The distant glow of the streetlamps below touched his scar with an infernal gleam, like a crack in the unforgiving material from which he'd been formed. His Bayard 1908 was held out to one side, as though he wanted nothing to do with it.

*He doesn't care whether I might have a gun, too,* Eric realised. *He knows this is the end, one way or another.*

Cautiously, Eric pulled himself onto the upper rooftop and stood up. "Werner?"

"I will kill you if you come any closer."

Eric checked the sabre tucked through his braces, surreptitiously to avoid drawing more attention to it, then began making his way along the roof slope towards Werner. He did not hold out his hands in any gesture of supplication or appeasement. He walked instead as though this were the most natural thing in the world, pretending he was not, in fact, keeping a careful eye out for the slightest threatening movement.

*No cause for alarm here. Everything is perfectly normal.*

Werner did not turn the pistol in his direction.

Eric could see the lobby skylight now: a dark expanse of smooth glass, like a treacherous ice field. It was designed for loads of snow heavier than London had seen in a hundred years; surely it would hold up to the impact of a man—or even two men—slamming into it? But that was a concern for later. For now, he had to keep Werner occupied until reinforcements arrived.

He had closed half the distance between them when Werner raised his pistol and turned it against his temple.

"Werner! Don't!"

"What is left for me, Mr. Peterkin? If they do not hang me or shoot me, I shall find myself lynched in the streets. This way, at least, it will be by my own choice." The German was coming out in his speech now, too strong to have been merely the influence of a few years among the Swiss. This was Werner, not Ward; though he wore the same face.

Eric said, "I know you didn't kill Colonel Russell."

Werner hesitated. The pistol began to lower, but only a few inches. "You know that, do you? And what of it? You think your English courts would give me justice?"

The situation had changed. The danger was no longer that Werner might escape, but that he might put a bullet through his head. The one saving grace was that he didn't really want to die. If he did, he'd have shot himself by now, with none of these rooftop dramatics. But if he should think he had no other choice—if, for instance, a fleet of black motorcars pulled up right now to disgorge an army of heavy-booted policemen . . .

Eric resumed his approach, praying he'd somehow get close enough to wrestle the gun away before the worst happened. He kept talking: if Werner was occupied with conversation, he wouldn't have time to shoot himself. Right? Eric hoped so.

"I know you didn't kill Colonel Russell because you still needed him. That's so, isn't it? You didn't want his money: you wanted him to vouch for you. That's why you came to the Britannia Club. If anyone should ever doubt you, there'd be Colonel Russell to say that you really are Captain Gregory Ward. And who would doubt the word of Colonel Hadrian Russell? His popularity was his greatest weapon. He told everyone that I'd be a good man for club secretary, and all my opposition disappeared. You see? I know better than anyone what his popularity could do."

"You know nothing about it."

"You're right." Eric had arrived at the corner of Werner's bit of roof. "You're absolutely right. I know nothing about it. Why don't you tell me?"

"Go away."

"Tell me about Gregory Ward. You met him in Switzerland."

"Why would you care?"

"You had everyone fooled. Dr. Duplessis thought you truly believed yourself to be Captain Ward. You must have known the real Captain Ward extraordinarily well."

Werner didn't respond.

"Were you friends?"

"We . . . we understood each other. We could talk about the War." The pistol shook in Werner's hand as the weight of his words sank in. His voice softened, as though at the wonder of realisation, and the German accent deepened. "You know the value of that, don't you? Your Britannia Club is not about the polish on your silverware or the expertise of your head chef. It is not even about prestige and exclusivity. A hundred other clubs offer that. It is . . . it is about being among others who understand."

And Eric understood. They were all the same, in the end: pawns pitted against one another by masters whose grudges they did not share.

"What was it like?" Eric asked. "In Germany, after the War?"

"What do you think?" Werner spat. The question had raised his ire—which, Eric told himself, was a good thing. "We'd exhausted ourselves on the war effort, and the Spanish flu was tearing us apart. We had to sign our pride away and honour such terms as dictated by a vindictive enemy. I came home to find that my brother had died in the trenches—not from a shell or a bullet, but from disease. The fatherland fell apart, and my family with it. My father—"

Oh no no no. Lucy had suggested that one of Werner's parents might have died by suicide, and if that was true . . .

"You must have hated Ward when you met him," Eric said before Werner could follow that thread back to the idea of shooting himself.

"At first." Werner's scar seemed to deepen. The pistol began to waver. "He had everything. He lost nothing to the War, and he was the enemy. I thought, perhaps, I might smother him with a pillow. But there is no honour in killing a man who is already sick and dying, ja? A pointless vengeance: it would bring back none of the friends and family I'd lost. And what was the use in crying for my old life again? One can never go back."

*One might as well protest the moon.*

"He came to see you as a brother."

"And I him."

"He wished to leave you his property."

"He wished to leave me his life."

The pistol drifted to point into the air as Werner seemed to forget, at least for the moment, that he had it at all. Eric shifted his trajectory. He had to approach from the side. Behind Werner, the mansard roof dropped down into a narrow trench between it and the parapet, but a full-frontal tackle might send them over both trench and parapet to the street four storeys down. Better if he could slam Werner up against the nearby chimney stack and hold him there.

"You weren't stealing his life," Eric said. "You were honouring it."

"Why else would I stay here? Why else would I want Colonel Russell to confirm my claims? Gregory, his last words to me . . . He did not wish for what he had to go to waste. He said that I should—" Werner stopped. The grip on his pistol tightened. "It was madness. I see it now. The ravings of a man facing his own mortality. And I embraced those ravings because, in truth, I envied him his life and wanted it for my own. I shall have to ask the good Dr. Duplessis about it, ja?" Suddenly realising just how close Eric had come, Werner turned his pistol on him and snarled, "Stay back! I will shoot!"

Tiny as the Bayard was, it might as well have been a howitzer, its muzzle an endless well of blackness drawing Eric in. Were the clouds gathering, and had the temperature dropped? Was there traffic in the streets of London? All of that had faded from Eric's consciousness. He could smell mud and blood and cordite.

"Tell me about Colonel Russell," Eric said, trying to ignore the threat. "You knew him from the War. How did that happen?"

"Do you know anything about how this works, Peterkin? We saw a weakness, and we exploited it. That is all."

Eric recalled his earlier conversation with Penny. "Money."

Werner's lip curled into a sneer. "I have no respect for traitors or for the murderers of their own children. Colonel Russell was both."

"And later, you threatened to expose his treason."

"He was too clever for that. When I confronted him with the intelligence he sold to us, he only laughed and said that it implicated his daughter-in-law, not him—and he did not care what happened to *her*. In the end, it was the other thing that convinced him to speak for me."

"The other thing?"

"Andrew Russell. You know that Colonel Russell killed him, don't you? His own son."

Eric hid his surprise. So, when Werner described the Colonel as a "murderer of his own children," he'd meant it literally. But surely—

"I dined with his widow," Werner went on, "my first evening here as Gregory Ward. I found her to be a devoted wife. Beyond rubies, as they say. Colonel Russell hated her for some reason—"

"He admitted to the murder?"

"Nein, he denied it. But I know it was not one of my own people, so who else was there? Only Colonel Hadrian Russell. Finding the weapon in Gregory's vault box was a gift—not that I knew at the time. But Colonel Russell knew—I don't know how—and the evening after he'd turned me away, he rang me here and said he would do whatever I wanted in exchange for that weapon. He was going to see Madam Eliot hanged, he said." Werner laughed bitterly. "Another scapegoat! When we met at midnight, I remarked on his habit of hiding behind his daughters-in-law, which he threw back in my face: I was happy enough doing the same in the War, so why turn chivalrous now? I was even free to sell Miss Grace's letters to the police if I liked! We parted then, and I resolved to warn Madam Eliot of the threat—though that proved unnecessary. Barely five minutes after I left him, Colonel Russell was dead. And now you know everything! Does it make you happy?"

"Werner—"

Lightning flickered through the heavy cloud cover; the accompanying thunder was a low rumble, and the chill in the air seemed to cut ever closer to the bone.

"Go home, Mr. Peterkin. Go back to your sister and your house in the pleasant countryside and the petty concerns of your club. This is not the world for me. It has only taken me this long to recognise that."

Werner began to raise his pistol back up to his temple, and Eric was still too far away—

"Hey!"

Both Eric and Werner turned, startled, as a shadow leapt out from behind the nearby chimney stack and seized Werner by the arm. Harvey! The young attendant was trying to wrestle the pistol away, and Werner, cursing and howling, lashed out at him with the fury of a wild beast.

Eric covered the distance between them at a run. All he could see was Avery bleeding out against his office wall, clutching at the growing crimson stain at his waist. The pistol went off like the crack of Armageddon, and Eric was running through muddy no-man's-land, seemingly an eternity from the pair struggling on the lip of a distant trench. They parted just as Eric laid a hand on Jerry: the English private stumbled back with a crow of triumph and a small handgun clutched in his hands. Meanwhile, Eric's momentum took both him and Jerry over the edge, sliding into the narrow trench beyond.

The mud felt as sharp as gravel when Eric fell into it, and he hit the parapet hard enough to knock the wind from his lungs. He clung to Jerry with all the desperation the mission required, even as

Jerry fought to free himself. They were wedged into a tight place; Eric had the advantage.

Werner. This Jerry had a name, and it was Karl Werner. The mission was to take him alive. And this wasn't mud: it really was gravel.

Eric blinked as the night sky above whirled back into reality with roiling clouds tinged an infernal orange by the city lights below. The parapet at his back was not made up of hard, compacted sandbags, but of even harder brickwork—on this side, at least: it was limestone blocks on the other. Eric knew this because he was in London, St. James, King Street, and the respectable edifices that made up this part of the world—

Something clipped him in the side of the head. Not hard enough to do any real damage—this was the awkward blow of someone struggling in blind desperation—but enough that the world flashed as bright as brass, his grip loosened, and Werner finally tore free. Eric shook his head and tried to struggle out of the awkwardly narrow space in which he lay. There was simultaneously too much light and too little, and there was Werner staggering against the parapet with a sword in his hand—the cavalry sabre formerly wielded by Charles Peterkin in the Crimea.

Eric could hear the roar of approaching motorcars in the street below. The police! Was there a proper roof access, or would they have to climb up from an attic window, as he'd done?

Werner swung one leg over the parapet. He was going to jump.

"Werner!" Eric threw himself again at the other man.

Whatever Werner shouted back at him, Eric neither heard nor understood. Metal flashed in his eyes, too bright for half a century in storage. Something stung on the side of his jaw, the world went red—

And he was squeezed on top of Private Dent, the walls of a collapsed dugout crushing in around him. He could hear the echo of distant gunfire and the shouts of his regimental mates, and he tasted blood. Mud and blood and cordite. Rain was coming down on him, somehow: a slow, dull drizzle as soft as floating ash, unheralded by any thunder or lightning.

This was how the world ended. This was how the world *had* ended—he'd forgotten—seven years ago. The shells and the rifles of war had been but a distraction while the world was washed away, far away, in frustration, desolation, and a gentle, inexorable rain.

# RETROSPECT

Reginald Butler's face twisted into a fierce scowl. "All I wanted was twenty thousand pounds to bring in a shipment of cocaine. Sold on the streets, that's a tenfold return on investment, and I've got gambling debts to pay. But the old man was going to cut me out of his will, just because I happened to kick one of his precious Spaniel puppies once. Of course I killed him. I killed five others to cover my tracks, and if you think I'd stop now—"

Harry Thompson's fist met Butler's jaw and laid him out flat before he could draw his revolver. "Why don't you tell it all to the jury and see what they think?"

The manuscript ended three pages later with order restored and the scales of justice perfectly rebalanced. Eric sat back and tapped a pencil against his teeth. What could he say about this? He thought about Madam Eliot, and what they'd learnt about Andrew Russell's appalling treatment of his wife. Murderers rarely turn out to be such grinning villains as this Reginald Butler character. Were the scales of justice already rebalanced, and who was he to make such a judgement? Would the denouement unbalance them again? If only real life were so comfortably black-and-white as in a book!

"Peterkin!"

Eric looked up to see Inspector Crane standing in the office door. Any annoyance at having been turned out of bed at two in the morning was gone, and the Inspector was all smiles.

"Just five hours and ten stitches later, and you're back at work. Conscientious old sod! Lucky, too: I'm told the sabre was an inch away from going through your throat. As it is, you might want to consider growing out your beard."

"A genuine duelling scar." Eric touched the dressing on his jaw. There was a tightness there that made it seem unwise to open his mouth too wide. "I'll be popular in Germany."

"You were supposed to have come back and signed this after the surgeon was done with that war wound of yours." Crane held out a typewritten version of Eric's police statement. "I'd be angry if not for what I owe you in this matter."

"Right. You've got Karl Werner and you've proven yourself to the rest of the Yard. Your career is safe, and coming home from Hong Kong has not been a complete waste, after all. That's what you've always wanted, isn't it? But do you know that Werner has no idea about Duplessis's death?"

Crane frowned. "He did seem quite taken aback when I mentioned the charge."

Eric shrugged and turned to read over the statement, everything he'd told the police since they'd come for him and for Werner. In the light of morning, the story felt about as real as the adventures of Harry Thompson. He took his time signing the document, wondering what guilt and innocence really meant, before handing it back.

"I've still got something of Werner's," Eric said. "A book of Poe, somewhere under this mess. Tell me, is it the gaoler who inspects the things given to prisoners, or is it you?"

"The gaoler, generally, but—"

"But you could do it instead? Good to know."

Eric walked the Inspector back out to the lobby, where the early morning light, no more than a warming glow in his office, seemed to explode through the skylight above like the divinity of a new Jerusalem. He watched as Crane departed into the light of a new day and a London blissfully unaware of what had passed here in the night. From the landing of the grand staircase, King Arthur and his Knights gazed knowingly down on him, as if to say, *Your case, Peterkin; you know what you have to do*.

Colonel Russell had spoken a great deal on the value of myths, and Eric could almost hear the old man whispering in his ear: *If the truth sows discord while the lie brings order, is it not better to choose the lie?* And Eric could almost believe it, if Colonel Russell hadn't amply demonstrated that his philosophy was suspect. The truth would damn the Colonel; and perhaps a handful of club members, his most ardent hangers-on, would end their memberships in a bid to distance themselves from what they'd see as a personal betrayal. That would be the extent of the resulting discord, in Eric's opinion—the stones of the Britannia's foundation were still too ancient and sturdy to be rocked by one man's lies. Besides, was the truth not worth the risk? Honour sustained by dishonour was no honour at all.

"Mr. Peterkin!"

"Eric!"

Lady Alice was expected, after her message last night; Penny was less expected, but more welcome. Eric went to meet them, saying, "You're up early."

"The police house was all in an uproar when I woke up," Penny replied. "Is it true? They've caught Karl Werner?"

"It's a relief," Lady Alice agreed, then pulled Eric aside, away from Penny, and hissed: "I saw Inspector Crane leaving. You didn't tell him anything about Flora, did you?"

"Why? What do you know about it?"

"I know that Flora is innocent. I know that Hadrian was the traitor, not her. I know that none of that really matters now. They can hang Mr. Werner without having to go into the sordid details of how Hadrian passed information on to him."

"And you'd like to see him hanged, would you?"

Lady Alice opened her mouth to answer but thought better of it.

Eric turned to draw Penny back into the conversation. "Early as it is, I'm going to guess that you rushed here without even stopping for a cup of tea. I know I'm starved. Come on. Things will make more sense once we've all had some breakfast."

Eric sat back and savoured his second cup of tea. This was the builder's brew generally reserved for staff consumption rather than one of the more genteel varieties on the menu, but Eric was club secretary and knew what he could or could not demand of his men. Across from him, Penny and Lady Alice picked at their continental breakfast rolls. Neither seemed hungry, though Eric had polished off a full English fry-up with a side of cheese. Elsewhere in the dining room, silverware clinked on fine china, while newspapers rustled in the hands of the few elderly bachelors who favoured the company of silent comrades over the silence of solitude. The sun streaming in through the tall windows outlined the entire scene in shimmering gold.

Lady Alice, reassured that Flora was in no immediate danger from the police, said, "All that matters now is sending word to my sister Charlotte that it's safe to send the boys home; but I think I shall join them instead and spend the Easter break in Brighton—"

"Easter break." Eric finished his tea and frowned into the bottom of his cup. "It must have been a shock when Werner brought your sons home from King's Cross. Lucy said you were quite upset with her for that."

"Considering what we know now, was I wrong?"

Penny said, "I thought you'd be over the moon, Eric, now that everything is over."

"This isn't over."

Silence descended on the table as Penny and Lady Alice stared back at him in surprise. Penny, recovering first, said, "I don't understand."

"There is a final decision yet to be made, and it's not my place to make it. All I can do is explain the situation." Eric poured himself another cup of tea and, when neither woman objected, began:

"Everything always seems to start with the War, so let's start there with Colonel Hadrian Russell: charming, expansive, popular. If you suggested two weeks ago that he flaunted his wealth, I'd have laughed in your face; but the truth is, his tastes are expensive, and half his charm lies in his apparent generosity. I don't know the exact history of his finances, but I think it's safe to say that, as the War begins, he finds his extravagance catching up to him. Enter Karl Josef von Werner of German military intelligence, offering a solution in the sale of military secrets. They devise a cunning plan to traffic this information. Colonel Russell, at this point, has three daughters-in-law: Lady Alice, who has left her sons and gone to France as a nurse—"

"A parent must be a hero," Lady Alice murmured. "No child deserves to be ashamed of his or her roots."

"Indeed. Lady Alice, who has gone to France as a nurse; Miranda, who is up to her ears in the stress of office work; and Flora—whose father lectures at Oxford, who enjoys the intellectual discourse of Hyde Park speakers, who habitually quotes poetry to make her point. Flora Russell would love nothing more than to exchange thoughts and ideas with someone in circumstances similar enough for sympathy but different enough for a new perspective. Von Werner invents just such a person—a distant cousin—and Colonel Russell endorses the idea. Flora begins corresponding with 'Monique Garnier,' and all Colonel Russell has to do is steam her letters open and insert what he knows in the form of Morse code printed in the margins with invisible ink. Morse code, invisible ink, and a stalking horse: three levels of subterfuge, and if they'd found a way to add a fourth, they would have."

"If Lucy had been married into the family at the time," Lady Alice said, "she'd be implicated, too. Bad enough to think of Flora framed for treason, but a child like Lucy? It's monstrous."

"Things simmer along for the duration of the War. One by one, Colonel Russell's sons are killed, until only Andrew Russell remains. Andrew cannot believe that his brother George's meticulously planned assault on the German lines could have failed so disastrously—surely, espionage must be involved. This suspicion is confirmed when he learns that 'Monique Garnier' does not exist. He communicates the news to Flora and obtains from her the address to which she has been sending her letters. His suspicions have been unceremoniously dismissed before, so he resolves to spend his next leave investigating on his own, though he has no intention of sacrificing his husbandly benefits. He demands that his wife, Miranda, meets him in Paris. She arrives unobserved, but the meeting goes bad: Andrew loses his temper with her, and she shoots him fatally with his own gun in self-defence. She flees the scene, leaving only a footprint bearing Andrew's personal cipher—the cipher of a possessive and jealous man, put on his wife's belongings not so they can be returned if lost, but so she knows that she is *his* property. At least, that's the story I pieced together, including what you told me yourself, Lady Alice. The interesting thing is that Karl Werner believes it was *Colonel Hadrian Russell* who shot Andrew Russell that night in Paris."

"What!" Lady Alice raised one black-gloved hand over her mouth in shock. "But why would he think that?"

"Werner assumed, as did everyone else, that Andrew Russell's death was directly related to his inquiries. He knew Andrew wasn't killed by a German spy. That left Colonel Russell, presumably willing to sacrifice his sole surviving son to hide his treachery."

"Could it be?" Penny wondered.

"No. But keep it in mind, as it'll become important later." Eric took a sip of his tea. "For now, we're in Paris with Gregory Ward, the real Gregory Ward, discovering Andrew Russell dead in his hotel room. Ward has heard one shot; here is one body with one gunshot wound; and here beside it is a smoking gun with Andrew's cipher on its grip. Clearly, Andrew must have shot himself. But his work mustn't go undone, so Ward takes and hides the gun, then tells the French police what he knows of Andrew's quest. The police find Miranda's footprint on the scene, confirming the presence of a suspected assassin—much to Ward's surprise. Ward realises now that Andrew's gun might be important evidence, but fears that his interference if known could upset the case against the spies. So he brings the gun back to London, stores it in the club vault, and watches the French news for any sign that this evidence might be needed. The War ends a month later. Less than a year after that, Ward is diagnosed with tuberculosis and sent to Switzerland for treatment."

Lady Alice leaned forward, hope and anxiety in her eyes. "Are you certain there's no possibility that Hadrian did it, after all? I can speak to Miranda. She might not have told me everything." *Or I could convince her to remember something different.*

"Whatever else Colonel Russell did, I don't believe he had it in him to actually level a gun at his own son, especially not the last surviving one. There is a reason the tale of Kronos devouring his young horrifies us, and Colonel Russell could never admit, even to himself, that he'd sacrificed his sons on the altar of his own ego. The last thing he ever said to me was that death in war was inevitable, and there was nothing he could have done to change their fates."

Penny's nose wrinkled in disgust, as did Lady Alice's.

"The War's over," Eric continued, "and now we come back to Karl Josef von Werner, who has lost everything in the aftermath. He dispenses with the 'von' prefix to reflect his fallen circumstances, and, as plain old Karl Werner, gets a job sweeping the floors of a Swiss sanatorium. Lady Alice, you said once that you understood his despair. Is that still true?"

Lady Alice nodded, albeit with some hesitation.

"Gregory Ward, by some sad coincidence, chooses the same sanatorium for his rest cure. Werner recognises him from the destruction of his espionage operation—this man represents the beginning of Werner's downfall. But rather than make an attempt on Ward's life, Werner turns the attempt against himself. And, irony of ironies, Ward is the man who saves him. What results is an odd but intense friendship between two men from opposite sides of a recent war. Ward even considers leaving all his worldly possessions to Werner, but dies before he can write his will. Werner, filled with grief for his dead friend and spurred by the knowledge of what Ward intended for him, resolves to *become* Ward and live his life for him. He begins identifying himself as Ward the moment he leaves the sanatorium. By the time he runs into Duplessis on the ferry from Calais, the role is enough of a second skin to convince Duplessis of his sincerity. Once in London, he spends a week living off the charity of St. Martin-in-the-Fields, scouting out the places that ought to be intimately familiar to the real Gregory Ward, before finally presenting himself at the Britannia Club. His objective here is Colonel Russell. He still has all the letters he received from Flora, with Colonel Russell's coded messages exposed on them. He believes this gives him a hold over the Colonel, whose endorsement will render his claims unimpeachable."

Penny said, "But Colonel Russell had just left for Scotland. Was that a case of bad timing, do you think, or was it intentional? An extra week of getting to know Ward's world and digging his heels in."

"I'm not sure how Werner could have known about this one habit of Colonel Russell's, unless it was known to Ward as well and Ward mentioned it to Werner. But I'm inclined to think the timing was intentional. Werner has shown himself so far to be nothing if not longheaded and careful. The one thing he never counted on was falling for Lucy Russell, and even that wouldn't be enough to stop him. And now, we arrive at the critical point of our story: the last thirty-six hours leading up to Colonel Russell's death."

All three leaned in, and Eric lowered his voice.

"Werner left an envelope for Colonel Russell at the club desk, containing one of Flora's letters. It's meant as a warning, to prepare the Colonel for their meeting. The Colonel recognises the letter immediately, and when Werner presents himself as 'Ward,' Colonel Russell accordingly addresses him as such. The Colonel is still unsure as to what Werner might have on him, and Werner himself is a stab at his conscience. That night, the Colonel drinks to excess and speaks to me of fate and inevitability. He also notices something I've doodled on my blotter: the symbol I saw on the revolver in Werner's vault box, which I attribute to Ward. Colonel Russell knows, of course, that the symbol identifies that revolver as Andrew's, but it means nothing to him for now. The next day, Saturday, he comes to the club and takes out all his fears and frustrations on Thomas Harvey, one of the club attendants. He doesn't get his interview with Werner until that evening, when Werner brings Lucy home from an afternoon's outing. In the privacy of the Colonel's study, Werner lays out what he has—Flora's letters—and Colonel Russell laughs in relief. Those three levels of subterfuge have paid off: the letters implicate Flora rather than him, and he, to Werner's surprise, cares nothing about her. Werner has no hold over Colonel Russell. Werner then accuses Colonel Russell of murdering Andrew Russell, which Colonel Russell also laughs off." Eric turned to Penny. "You remember what Lucy said? Colonel Russell emerged from that meeting in the best of spirits; Werner emerged looking 'quite glum.'"

"But they still met later, at midnight?"

"Yes. With time to think about it, Colonel Russell realises the implications of Werner's accusation. If Werner is being genuine, it means that Andrew wasn't killed by one of Werner's spies. But who else was there? He remembers that Miranda—Madam Eliot, now—attempted a journey to Paris that night, but claimed to have been turned back at Le Havre. Could that be a lie? He immediately makes a trunk call to Andrew's godfather, who he knows has collected all the newspaper articles surrounding Andrew's death, and asks that they be sent to him. Perhaps there is something in them to suggest the truth. He thinks some more. Madam Eliot carries a pocket pistol now, but she didn't own a firearm of any sort back then. How could she have shot Andrew? Andrew's service revolver was never recovered—but wait, I've all but told him that I've seen it in Ward's vault box. Why would Ward have had it unless he'd taken it from the scene, and why would he have done that unless it was significant somehow? It must be the murder weapon. Perhaps there are still fingerprints on it even after all these years. He rings the club, asks for Werner, and arranges a meeting at midnight. If Werner hands over the revolver, he will endorse Werner as 'Ward' to all the world. He tells Werner he means to see Madam Eliot hanged."

"That damned hypocrite," Penny exclaimed. "Excuse my language, Lady Alice, but you must agree: After what he did, who was he to judge anyone?"

*There will always be a certain percentage of slain, and if a man must number among the doomed, there is nothing you or I could do to make a difference. Not when David was drowned in mustard gas, not when George's attack on the German line went wrong, not when Patrick got picked off by a sniper . . .*

"It was a salve for his conscience," Eric replied. "If he could point to someone else as the direct agent of one son's death, and if that son's death could be attributed to a domestic squabble rather than any sort of enemy action, then *his* hands were clean. He could tell himself that he, Colonel Russell, was not responsible. Awful as he was, he could never put off his conscience forever."

"And what a way to satisfy it, the monster." Penny sat back and crossed her arms. "I suppose that was the telephone conversation that Lucy overheard."

Lady Alice cleared her throat. "If Lucy can confirm that when Hadrian came here that night, it was to meet Mr. Werner—"

"But I don't understand." Penny's frown deepened in consternation. "Did things go terribly wrong at that meeting? Werner needed Colonel Russell alive, didn't he?"

"And if he didn't, he would have used his own pocket pistol instead of the ill-maintained specimen that was Andrew Russell's old service revolver. No. I saw it when I questioned 'Ward' the night before the funeral, and I saw it again last night when I faced the real Werner on the roof. Whatever else he may have done, Werner didn't kill Colonel Russell." Eric turned to Lady Alice. "But you'd know that better than anyone, wouldn't you?"

# THE LADY OR THE TIGER?

THE BREAKFAST RUSH had died away while Eric was talking, and they were now alone amid the gleaming silverware and white linens of the dining room. The waiters were keeping their distance. The glow of early morning had dulled with the shifting sun into a shadowless stillness, in which the pulse of one's heart became a roar in one's ears.

Lady Alice, sitting stiff and motionless, said, "I beg your pardon?"

"A shadow in the street, the force of habit, a fallen idol, a length of black thread, and two instances of a maidservant's duties."

Both ladies stared at him.

"Let's carry on, shall we?" Eric cleared his throat. "Thomas Harvey is on duty that night. According to him, Colonel Russell arrives back here at half past eleven and settles into the lounge. Harvey retreats to the staff room but is summoned to the back door a few minutes later by the arrival of Miss Flora Grace. Harvey is the latest in a line of lovers Flora has taken since her husband's death, and she claims to be in the grips of a passion one only ever encounters in books. Harvey lets her in—he believes he's locked the door, but remember, Flora is there to unlock it, and he's somewhat distracted. They retire to a nearby storeroom, where Cully finds them. Harvey points Flora at the back door so she can let herself out.

Cully begins giving Harvey a dressing-down, when they hear two gunshots and the sound of breaking glass. They investigate and find Colonel Russell dead. They also encounter Werner, who has hurriedly changed into his pyjamas to hide the fact that he's actually just come up from a meeting with the dead man. Cully leaves the two to guard the scene while he calls the police and comes to get me; Harvey takes the opportunity to nip back inside and lock the back door, so there's no evidence of Flora having passed that way. Or so he thinks. One of the patrons of the Golden Lion claims to have seen a woman's silhouette leaving the service court. A shadow in the street."

"So she was seen, after all," Penny said.

"No, she wasn't. Flora Grace has her hair cut into a short bob, and Harvey mentions she was wearing trousers that night. Trousers for women might be the fashion of tomorrow, but it's certainly not the fashion of today. If you were to see a silhouette with short hair and trousers, would your first thought be that you saw a woman? Or a man of slender build? What that witness saw was the more traditionally feminine shape of a person in skirts. So, who was this other woman, if not Flora Grace? Madam Eliot was the one most directly threatened by Colonel Russell, and Lucy was the one with knowledge of the threat. What do you think, Lady Alice?"

"Neither of them. I'm not admitting to any sort of knowledge of that night: I'm only saying what should be obvious."

"It seemed quite plain to me, when I spoke to her last, that Flora was withholding information in a bid to protect someone—someone she knew was there that night. And the more I know her, the less I believe she was ever driven mad by some chance passion. I'm sure she didn't think this would end in murder, but I do think her seduction of Thomas Harvey was done with the express purpose of letting someone else into the club behind her. After all, that's the main difficulty for a non-member wanting entrance in the middle of the night, isn't it? No one's going to let you in; it might be too late if you wait for morning; and Colonel Russell certainly isn't going to pay any attention to a message admonishing him to 'not do anything foolish.'"

Lady Alice half rose from her seat, no doubt on the brink of declaring herself "insulted by such baseless accusations," but sat down again. She said, "Flora has nothing to do with this, either. None of them do. Not Miranda, not Flora, and certainly not Lucy."

"Madam Eliot has a key to the back door, for the benefit of her workers. She wouldn't have needed Flora's help to get in. And like Werner, she has a pocket pistol which she would certainly prefer over a weapon from a time she'd rather forget. She didn't do it. I'm wary of writing Lucy off, but here's the thing: What did Madam Eliot do when I confronted her about her husband's death? What did Flora do when I went to her about the coded message on her letter to 'Monique'? What did both of them do when they learned about Werner's true identity? They turned to you. What are the odds that Lucy didn't do the same when she overheard Colonel Russell declare on the telephone that he'd 'see Madam Eliot hanged'? The only reason she took matters into her own hands later, when she realised the importance of the letter in Colonel Russell's safe, was that she couldn't pick up the telephone without a policeman listening in. Otherwise I'm sure she would have sought the same help from you. The force of habit."

"Is it a crime to be dependable? Really, Mr. Peterkin—"

"Sit down. Please. This may come as a surprise, but I do sympathise. I understand. You want to save everyone. That's why I'm asking you to hear me out before you make a decision. Two men are dead, and three more lives are at stake."

Lady Alice's eyes blazed.

Eric took her hand and added, earnestly, "I'm telling all this to you now instead of to Inspector Crane, aren't I?"

Lady Alice pulled her hand out of his grasp but did not try again to rise. "Go on," she said, her voice hoarse. "Say your piece."

"Why did you—" Penny began, then stopped as Lady Alice fixed her with a withering glare. Turning to Eric, she began again,

"Why ask for Miss Grace's help getting into the club, if Madam Eliot had a key?"

"Madam Eliot lives in Chorleywood, and for all anyone knows, she might keep the key in her office in Willesden Green. Flora Grace, however, is just fifteen minutes away; and Harvey's speculation as to how the Colonel found out about his affair with her rather implies that it was an open secret among the Russell ladies."

Penny nodded, sat back, and gestured for Eric to continue.

Eric cleared his throat and turned back to Lady Alice. "I visit you on the Monday after the murder to pay my respects. That same day, your sons come home from their boarding school; not just for the funeral, but for the rest of the term as well. Werner meets them at King's Cross and shepherds them home at Lucy's behest. That upsets you, but I think you wanted a word with him regardless. Lucy did say he was going to call on you anyway—not 'call on us' in general, but 'call on Alice' specifically. I didn't think much of that until Duplessis told me he saw money change hands. He thought you were paying Werner to keep his distance from Lucy. But I think you were buying something from him: Flora's letters."

"That's preposterous. How would I even know he had them?"

"Consider the timing. We have Flora arriving, getting up to no good with Harvey, being discovered, and being shown the door; followed by Cully giving Harvey a good talking-to before they heard the gunshot. I find it highly unlikely that all of that took place in the five minutes after Werner parted ways with Colonel Russell. If someone slipped into the building behind Flora, they'd have arrived while Werner was still speaking with Colonel Russell, and they'd have overheard everything. They would know that Werner was an imposter, that he had Flora's letters, and what those letters could do in the wrong hands."

"Well, that may be, but I wasn't—"

"Let's change tacks and go backwards from Duplessis's death. Penny and I find evidence in his flat that he's been deciphering a message from Morse code about troop movements in the War. So he's got his hands on Flora's letters. How, and where? His death was early in the morning after the séance at your home, and I remember something else I noticed as I left your house that night: a light in an upstairs window, and a shadow of movement within. That's your maid preparing your bed, I thought; but it couldn't have been her, could it? You had guests, and might ring for her at any moment to show those guests out. Her place right then was in the kitchen, watching the bank of bells there for a summons. The first instance of a maidservant's duties. The shadow I saw was Duplessis, searching your rooms. Why was he doing that? Because he saw something at the séance to make him think you had something to hide. He saw the moment your faith in Madame Davidova died. A fallen idol."

A spot of colour rose on Lady Alice's pale cheeks. "That woman was a fraud."

"So you told us the next day, after the news of Duplessis's death. But you really did believe in her before then, didn't you? You couldn't refuse to let the séance be held without arousing suspicion, but you were afraid of Colonel Russell's spirit making an accusation from the other side. So you volunteered your home, where you had greater control over the proceedings; and . . . a length of black thread. That would enable you to disrupt the séance if necessary by pulling a candle off the table. I doubt we can trust Madame Davidova's word as to whether toppling candles is part of her repertoire of tricks, but Avery Ferrett can tell us what is or isn't likely to happen at one of her séances. What that bit of thread tells us is this: someone at that séance both believed in its authenticity and feared what it might reveal. And what was revealed? Madame Davidova, pretending to channel the spirit of Gregory Ward, kicks up a great fuss over how 'his' gun was used in the murder."

"Oh," said Penny. "We did think it was Ward's gun back then, didn't we? We know now that it wasn't. Which means—"

"Anyone who knew the truth then would know that Madame Davidova was a fraud." Eric nodded to Lady Alice. "Duplessis, sitting directly across from you, has a talent for reading faces, which has served him well against experienced poker players. He sees your reaction and realises that you must know something more about the murder than you're telling. At the first opportunity, he slips upstairs to search your room; and what does he find but a parcel of letters written by Flora Grace, dated during the War, with a yellow-brown pattern of dots and dashes printed down their margins. Morse code! Invisible ink! Espionage! He takes his find immediately to Scotland Yard, but Crane has left for the night. That is just well. He decides he has to be sure. He obtains a telegraph operator's handbook, deciphers the message, and finds that it indeed contains military secrets."

Lady Alice cleared her throat. "Have you considered the possibility that he got those letters directly from Mr. Werner instead?"

"Oh? And who killed him, then?"

"Mr. Werner. That should be obvious."

"Why would Werner give him those letters, then kill him to get them back? Suppose then that Duplessis obtained those letters by some other means. In that case, how would Werner know, and why would he care, given everything else already stacked against him? I should point out as well that when I spoke to Werner on the roof last night, he seemed quite unaware that Duplessis was dead. All right, so someone else killed Duplessis. When could he have obtained those letters? Not before the séance, or he'd have gone to the police first; and the police have established that he went straight from the séance to Scotland Yard. Very well, then. He got the letters from your house. You discover the loss the next morning and have to guess which of your guests took them. Flora and Madam Eliot pose no threat; Madame Davidova was never once out of your sight; and I had Flora as my alibi. That leaves Duplessis. You visit him immediately to plead for Flora, just as you came to me today. But Duplessis's patriotism borders on jingoism; he'd sacrificed his son to the War, and his rage is still raw. He refuses to turn a blind eye. Somehow, in the course of the altercation—perhaps you are trying to tear the letters from his hands—he falls and cracks his skull on the fireplace hearth. You escape with the letters. Duplessis's green overcoat was missing when we searched his flat, so I'm guessing you took it to hide your own distinctive black dress. Werner, with all of

London looking for him, would have sought out a disguise *before* rather than *after*."

Penny said, "Where's the overcoat now? And the letters?"

"I imagine the overcoat was discarded somewhere near Euston station and is now some tramp's prized possession. As for the letters . . . Penny, remember when we sat down in Lady Alice's kitchen later that afternoon? The maid said she'd leave us be and use the time to clean out the fireplace grate. But that day was unusually warm, so I wonder why the grate needed cleaning. The second instance of a maidservant's duties."

"Those letters were bought with money and silence," Lady Alice said. "But what if he'd held one or two back as some kind of a safeguard? I was studying them, looking for a break in the correspondence . . . I should have taken him at his word and burned them all immediately."

It was the closest she'd come to an admission of guilt.

In a gentler tone, Eric said, "What happened that night when Colonel Russell died? I know you didn't go there intending to kill him, or you'd have brought a weapon. But you must have arrived in time to hear some of his conversation with Werner. Werner told me how that conversation went. Enough was said about Flora's letters to implicate Colonel Russell as a traitor. After Werner left, you confronted your father-in-law—"

"George." The name came out in a hiss, and Lady Alice's eyes were hard. "Andrew was right: George would have lived if Hadrian hadn't alerted the Germans to the upcoming assault. My sons would have had a father."

The brightly lit dining room was a far cry from the shadowy lounge as it must have been that night two weeks ago, but Eric could picture the scene easily: Lady Alice, the Nemesis of that long-ago casualty clearing station, draped in a black that seemed to coalesce from the shadows around her, turning her wrath on a smiling villain. Colonel Russell was aiming to destroy Madam Eliot, he would happily destroy Flora, and he was effectively selling Lucy to a false lover . . . just as he'd sold all their husbands to the enemy.

Had he laughed? Had he dismissed her concerns as "feminine sentimentality"? The others might have moved on with their lives, but not Lady Alice. Lady Alice was still in full mourning. The death of George Russell was as fresh in his widow's mind today as it was seven years ago.

*Lady Alice strides over to scoop up the revolver from the table beside the Colonel; two steps more, and she's at the window, running her black-gloved hands over the revolver to wipe away Madam Eliot's fingerprints. The Colonel rises from his seat in anger and alarm. Lady Alice turns the revolver against him. Perhaps she realises that if the revolver had been kept as potential evidence against Andrew's killer, no one can have unloaded it since then; perhaps, in her fury, she simply hasn't considered it; or perhaps she pulls the trigger only instinctively, not expecting the revolver to be loaded. Regardless, she fires at the man now threatening her, and misses. He charges. He's stronger than she is, but she has momentum on her side. She swings around, letting off a fatal second shot as she does, and Colonel Russell is thrown, not simply* at, *but* through *the window.*

It was finely imagined, but Eric had to admit he couldn't know all the precise details.

Lady Alice stirred as though suddenly realising where she was, and straightened up. She said, crisply, "So the person spotted by the witness from the Golden Lion wasn't Flora; that doesn't mean it was me. Lucy might have rung me the moment Hadrian left his house that night; that doesn't mean I did anything. Madame Davidova is a fraud, but I might have realised that months ago. She had a multitude of tricks, and who's to say she didn't think of a new one for this last séance, even if it didn't work? Dr. Duplessis might have taken it into his head to search my room—terribly rude of him, if you ask me—but that doesn't mean he found anything, or that he acted in response to something he saw during the séance. And while Jane, my maid, might have occupied herself with cleaning out the fireplace grate the day Duplessis died, that doesn't mean the chore needed doing. You have nothing against me."

"That's true. Nothing that will hold up in court."

"And even if you did, can you say Hadrian didn't deserve his fate? After what he did?"

Eric sighed. "I'm not the police. Nor am I a judge, or a jury. It's not my place to say if the scales of justice are balanced over Colonel Hadrian Russell—nor is it yours. But then, there's Duplessis. Would he be alive but for Colonel Russell's death, and am *I* at least partly responsible, having encouraged his involvement? He certainly deserves justice, even if his death was only an unfortunate accident. And Werner . . . Lady Alice, are you going to send an innocent man to die for you?"

"Innocent! He stole another man's life. He lied to us. Say what you like about his friendship with Gregory Ward, how dreadfully romantic it was: that doesn't change the fact that what he did was fraud."

"Fraud is not a hanging offence. Lady Alice, everything that's happened so far may be justifiable, but not this. This is cold-blooded murder."

"I have nothing more to say to you."

Rising from her seat with a majestic sweep of her skirts, Lady Alice stood straight and tall, her head held high. She glared coldly at both Eric and Penny and turned to leave before a thought arrested her. "You said there were three more lives at stake. Mr. Werner is one. Who are the other two?"

"Matthew Russell. Mark Russell."

Lady Alice stared at Eric over her shoulder, brows raised in question.

"They're intelligent lads," Eric said. "And if there's one thing I've learnt from Lucy, it's that those we dismiss as 'children' frequently see, hear, and understand a great deal more than we give them credit for. I wouldn't be surprised if Matthew, at least, already knew the true shape of the crisis affecting his family."

*Matthew silenced his brother with a whisper, then picked up the chessboard to leave the room. The look he fixed on Eric—*

"I don't know them as you do, Lady Alice, so I can't say how the stakes lie—whether it would be better to see their mother keep silent while another man hangs for what might have been only an accident on her part, or to see her in the dock for the murder of a grandfather who'd turned traitor—"

"A grandfather who would burn the world for his own convenience," Lady Alice murmured, as if in a trance. "God forbid they learn *that* . . ."

The silence between them grew uncomfortable. Even Penny seemed to be holding her breath, until Eric finally cleared his throat. "As I said, I'm neither police, nor judge, nor jury. It's one thing to work out the story behind a murder; it's quite another to say what the story means, or how it ought to end. That part must be your decision and yours alone."

Lady Alice gazed back, saying nothing. She was silent and immobile, once more the basalt Madonna Eric had envisioned that day on the front steps of St. Thomas'. Just so might Boadicea, warrior queen of the Britons, have gazed upon the Roman governor Suetonius Paulinus after her final battle against the forces of Rome—knowing that her cause was just, but that this defeat meant death . . .

She thrust out a hand, palm up. "Flora's letter," she said, the iron of Nemesis in her voice. "If this is truly to be my decision alone, there must be no fear of interference."

Eric deposited the torn fragments into her hand without a word. Black lace closed over crinkled white paper. Lady Alice Russell, third daughter of the Earl of Colford, turned and processed out of the dining room with all the dignity of a condemned queen.

# LILACS OUT OF THE DEAD LAND

"PETERKIN!" INSPECTOR CRANE swaggered into Eric's office, shut the door behind him, and settled into a chair with all the smug satisfaction of a cat breaking into a creamery. "Still hard at work, I see? I thought you'd want to know: we're moving Werner to a more secure lockup tonight, and that will be the end of things until he goes to trial—not that there's any question how *that* will go. Man's guilty as sin, and all the world knows it."

Eric hid his concern. "Is that so?"

"All's well that ends well, as they say." Crane stretched luxuriously, picked up a book from the near corner of the desk—the Edgar Allan Poe anthology that had been Werner's Christmas present from his brother in happier times—and began leafing through it. "You'll never guess what happened yesterday evening. Lady Alice Russell came in and tried to confess to the murders of Colonel Russell and Dr. Duplessis. Can you believe it?"

"I take it you don't?"

"We get attention-seeking crackpots making false confessions all the time. Never thought Lady Alice would be one of them, but there you go."

"What exactly did she say?"

Crane tossed a crumpled sheet of paper onto the desk, then snapped the Poe anthology shut and stood up. "There's the confession she tried to sell us. We've got no use for it, so you might as well see it for yourself. Colonel Russell a traitor! What rubbish! Almost as implausible as *two* of his four daughters-in-law—we haven't forgotten about Miss Grace—coincidentally and quite by chance choosing the same night to invade a respectable gentlemen's club, don't you agree? No. Colonel Russell was killed by Karl Werner, whom he recognised as an imposter. That's all there is to it."

"I actually think," Eric said, his throat suddenly dry, "that Werner might be innocent."

"Hah! I'm not in the habit of hanging innocent men, Peterkin. So, this book belongs to him, does it? I might as well pass it on. He'll want the distraction, where he's going." At the door, Crane looked back and added, "You've had your go at glory. Now step aside: it's my turn."

*I, Lady Alice Russell, confess to having caused the deaths of Colonel Hadrian Russell and Dr. Gérard Duplessis.*

*On the night of Saturday, the fourteenth of March, I received a telephone call from my sister-in-law Lucy. She was frantic, having overheard our father-in-law, Colonel Hadrian Russell, arrange to meet with a German spy at the Britannia Club. Believing him to be in need of help, I went to the Britannia as well. Colonel Russell let me in, but bade me leave when I told him why I was there. I hid instead when his appointment arrived. It was Karl Werner, whom I'd known until then as Captain Gregory Ward. I heard enough of their conversation to know that Colonel Russell had been selling military secrets to the Germans during the War. Werner was blackmailing Colonel Russell with the letters containing their correspondence.*

*I confronted Colonel Russell after Werner left. There was a revolver on the table. I didn't know why it was there, but I picked it up to threaten him with it. I was in shock and did not know what he would do, now that I knew his secret. The gun went off unexpectedly, and he charged at me. I managed to throw him off, through the club window, shooting him in the process. People began coming out of the Golden Lion, so I ran while I could, escaping by the club's back door.*

*I later bought Werner's letters from him and kept them for further study. Dr. Duplessis discovered them after a séance at my home, accused me of espionage, and left with them. The next morning, I went to his flat to plead with him again. Our words grew heated, and I tried to snatch the letters out of his hands, pushing him away. He fell backwards and struck his head on the fireplace hearth. When I realised he was dead, I took the letters home and burned them, as I should have done when I first obtained them.*

Lady Alice had been careful about keeping Flora and Madam Eliot out of it. If Werner were to confess the whole substance of his conversation with the Colonel that night . . . Well, Lady Alice had explicitly claimed to not know why Andrew Russell's revolver was there, and she could easily claim that she didn't think Flora's involvement was relevant. Flora would be exonerated as an innocent victim, and they'd only have Werner's word as an untrustworthy foreign spy that Madam Eliot was involved in any way. Lady Alice's confession had been carefully crafted, Eric thought with grim respect, to incriminate no one but Lady Alice herself.

## SPYMASTER ESCAPES POLICE CUSTODY!

Karl Josef von Werner, the deranged German spymaster whose dramatic capture concluded a week of high anxiety not only in London but throughout the nation, is once again on the loose. Preliminary reports indicate he was being transported between prisons late last night when he managed to pick his handcuffs open and escape out the back of the police vehicle . . .

Avery dropped the newspaper to his lap with a loud rustle and leaned back into his pillows. "And the world will never know that the villain of the piece was really Lady Alice. I'm glad of it. She was never actually villainous, I think. Honestly, I'm amazed that she turned herself in—amazed and impressed."

Eric said, "She knew that an innocent man would hang, otherwise."

"I think the vast majority of people would have stayed silent."

"Coming forward was the only decent thing to do."

"Your standard for 'mere' decency, Eric, crosses into the heroic." Avery nodded sagely, then grinned. "Please, never change."

"Decent or not," Penny said, "it would have meant telling the world about Colonel Russell's treason. If the Britannia really is struggling as you say, this might have killed it."

"I think," Eric said, "that having two different murders in the space of six months is a little more damaging to our prospects. Colonel Russell was popular, yes, but at the end of the day, he was just a member. He wasn't the club. Whatever his treachery, there is still the honour and heroism of every man on the Roster. I hardly think one man's disgrace would outweigh the sacrifice of hundreds."

Penny turned back to the newspaper and said, "Inspector Crane must be tearing his hair out, at any rate. After all the accolades he got from catching Werner! The story's made a huge splash. Spies, shell shock, imposters, rooftop confrontations . . ."

"He's actually come out pretty well," Avery replied. "Have you seen this interview? Chin out, rugged determination, 'we did it once and we can do it again'—all that rot. On the balance, I'd say this has done wonders for his reputation."

Yes. It had, hadn't it? Eric recalled Crane's last words to him: *"You've had your go at glory . . ."* There was certainly more glory in capturing a deranged German spy than in receiving a respectable widow's confession.

"And what about Werner?" Penny asked. "Seems he picked his cuffs and the police wagon door. I did not know he could do that. Did you?"

Avery shook his head, but Eric had to admit he had some suspicion. "He had to get Andrew Russell's revolver from his vault box after Colonel Russell rang him that night, remember? And yet, Cully made no mention of being asked to open the vault for him. I think he must have broken in himself and got out with no one the wiser."

"But the police transport burglars and picklocks all the time. And surely he couldn't pick a lock without some sort of tool."

"I couldn't tell you the answer to that one, I'm afraid."

"Well." Penny put the papers down with an air of finality. "I'm glad this is over, anyway. I just hope Mr. Stanhope still has a job for me when I get home."

Eric blinked. "His horses, you mean? I thought that was a favour between neighbours."

"Much as I love horses, Eric, I'm not training them for free."

It occurred to Eric that he'd taken Penny for granted, the sister in the house he owned but seldom saw. This modern world afforded her opportunities that their mother never had, and if what she wanted was an escape from dependence on him—if her interest in Carrington-Clarke's real estate brochures was more than idle curiosity—could he be anything but happy for her?

Outside, gaily-coloured kites danced in the blue skies over St. James's Park, beyond the neo-Gothic hulk of Parliament, and Eric found himself sincerely wishing Werner well in his own escape. In spite of everything, Karl Werner was still Gregory Ward in Eric's mind—the man who'd wanted nothing more than a fresh start and a new life after the War, who'd whistled as he'd gone up the stairs with a spring in his step after an evening out with the girl he loved. Whether he loved Lucy or the idea of Lucy, that whistle was no imposter.

And Lady Alice was the loving mother and devoted sister whose only goal was to protect her family. Who could have guessed at how that would end? The important thing was that she'd tried to take responsibility for her actions, and perhaps halt the cycle of violence before it claimed another victim. Her sons would know she'd done the right thing now, as she'd done during the War when she went to France as a nurse. Still, there was a certain relief in seeing these particular consequences swept aside by powers beyond her control.

"Victorian, I'm afraid."

Dr. Linwood of the British Museum was younger than Eric expected, and the spitting image of King Arthur in the Knights painting on the club landing. Madam Eliot, consummate professional that she was, had arranged for his examination of the Roman mosaic unearthed in the pipe room—or, as it was turning out now, the Victorian faux-Roman mosaic—but she herself had no desire now to set foot within the Britannia. Needless to say, the Russell widows' Friday luncheons were a thing of the past.

"I knew," Dr. Linwood explained, "as soon as I saw the cement in which the tiles were embedded. The Romans had their own particular recipe for cement, lost to us for centuries. You can thank that recipe for the bits of Roman wall surviving into the modern day: as I've heard it said, Roman cement defies mere pickaxes, and will be defeated by nothing less than gunpowder. *This*, however, is Portland cement, dating it no earlier than 1824. As it happens, the recipe for Portland cement underwent significant scientific experimentation after its initial development, so we actually have records of different chemical compositions across those decades. I was thus able to narrow down the date of your mosaic to the mid-1850s."

The midst of the Crimean War, in other words, following which the club underwent its first expansion. Eric glanced over at his cabinet of ledgers and noted that the vault records went back no further than 1858. Presumably, that was when the vault was installed and the pipe room isolated. Presumably, too, the faux-Roman mosaic was meant to replace the existing mosaic flooring, but the project was cancelled for the sake of economy.

But did that really matter? Hadn't Colonel Russell once asserted that the myth was what mattered, being a distillation of meaning? Lucy, too: *"The fiction is what makes it real."*

"It's a fine piece of work, all the same," Dr. Linwood added as he got to his feet. "There's not much interest right now in the things of a mere seventy years ago, but give it another hundred years. The world will develop a fascination for the 1850s and they'll thank you for preserving this piece of history."

"So yesterday's rubbish becomes tomorrow's treasure, all for the romance it can weave about a forgotten time." As they left the office, Eric thought of Lucy's assertion that Werner's interest in her lay entirely in a nostalgia for the world as it was before the War. "We may not have to wait that long."

They were in the lobby now, and the afternoon light from the skylight above caught on Dr. Linwood's golden curls, making him look more than ever like the image of King Arthur up on the staircase landing. He said, "I don't know if I'd call it 'romance,' but people do hunger to know where they come from, don't they? Failing the guidance of scholarship, they make things up; but as far as I'm concerned, a history invented from whole cloth is as good as no history at all."

"You've got no use for myths, you mean."

Andrew Russell's plaque on the Roster of the Fallen shone just as bright as its fellows. The world would remember him as a hero, not as a wife-beating cad; but if that particular myth was what his long-suffering widow wanted, what was Eric to do? He had to remind himself that the Roster recognised service, and Andrew Russell had served better than most. Had this been a monument to his virtues, that would be a different matter.

Dr. Linwood, catching sight of the painting on the landing above, said, "Oh, I wouldn't discount the value of mythology, as long as it's kept distinct from actual history. There's King Arthur and his Knights: you wouldn't put them on the wall if they didn't represent the things you admire and wish to emulate, would you?"

Eric returned to his office lost in thought. He seemed to remember Colonel Russell saying something very similar—

A discreet knock on the door brought Eric back down to earth. It was Harvey.

"I came to hand in my notice, sir. It's been grand, but you did say me coming back wasn't to be forever."

"Ah, you've found another position, then?"

"Not exactly." Harvey grinned as though he was hiding a secret. "The important thing is I've found new digs. My new landlady's quite impressed by that story about nabbing old Werner on the roof. None of what happened before matters, now she can brag about that."

Eric stood and extended his hand. Harvey came to shake it and gave a start as his eye fell on the document lying among the papers on the desk. "How . . . What's this, sir?"

"I evaluate manuscripts for Looming Press. Did you not know? This one is *Harry Thompson and the Black Widow Curse*, by Gareth Bowman—"

"Pen name?"

"Possibly. His first book's just been accepted for publication."

"I know. I mean . . . Here, this came in the post, and Cully said to bring it to you since I was coming in." Oddly flustered, Harvey dropped a brown paper package on the desk and scuttled out of the office.

What on earth was that about?

But Thomas Harvey's discomfiture was immediately forgotten in the wake of this mysterious package. No return address. Eric had to inspect the stamps and the postmark to identify the package's origin as Casablanca, Morocco. Cutting away the brown paper revealed a battered Edgar Allan Poe anthology, with an attached note that said: *My thanks for this, but one can never go back.*

Werner. There was the telltale backwards flick on the tail of the lowercase *F*.

Crane had delivered the book to Werner, after all.

*I'm not in the habit of hanging innocent men . . . You've had your go . . . Now it's my turn.*

One could hardly pick a lock without some sort of tool, and who would think to search a Scotland Yard inspector's gift for such a thing tucked between its pages? And just in case the trick were discovered, Crane had kindly left Werner with the impression that the book had come from Eric—which wasn't entirely untrue.

Eric had to smile: a grim smile, tugging on the scar that would forever be a souvenir of his journey to the present—but a smile nonetheless.

At 4:43 p.m. on Thursday, the ninth of April, 1925, Eric Peterkin delivered the latest manuscript he'd evaluated, with his recommendations, to the Looming Press publishing house near Aldgate, and stepped out into the balmy spring afternoon. April was the cruellest month, or so T. S. Eliot claimed; but the blue sky above, deepening towards a daily more distant evening, and the sense of quickening life all around him—"lilacs out of the dead land"—made Eric think it a delightful cruelty.

The name of the poet reminded Eric of Madam Eliot, and poetry itself reminded him of Flora Grace . . . Perhaps the cruelty of April was in the illusion of having moved on.

Rather than get back on the Underground, he turned his steps towards St. George's Lutheran Church. Nothing had changed since his last visit: brown brick grimed with East End soot, but underneath it, the universal search for community. Eric considered going in, but stopped when he heard voices just beyond the threshold.

Crane's men were questioning John Miller—the former Hans Mueller—on the possible whereabouts of Karl Werner. For the second or third time, presumably: it had been a week since the escape. The policemen had their backs to the door, but Mr. Miller, looking over their shoulders, caught sight of Eric. His gaze was brave but cold as he strove to assure his visitors that the community as a whole was English enough, whatever their roots; he hadn't the time, energy, or desire to entertain Eric.

Eric turned away and continued towards the Tower of London and the Thames. This was the same route he'd walked on New Year's Eve, when he first shook hands with Colonel Russell and his daughters-in-law. Before then, he'd known them only by their masks: the magnanimous patriarch, the gracious widow, the glittering professional, the glamorous vamp, the girlish ingénue . . . Masks were less than skin-deep: the people themselves were so much more.

Nearing the Tower of London, however, he slowed to a stop as he spotted a familiar figure on Trinity Square, strolling towards the newly built Port of London Authority Building: Flora Grace, the only woman he knew who walked about London in trousers, looking like an exotic flower among these drab streets . . .

*Lilacs out of the dead land . . .*

She ducked into an anonymous-seeming alley, and Eric, following curiously, found her staring up at a blank wall.

"Flora?"

Alarm flickered, then faded when she saw it was only him. Perhaps it was only the contrast with their dingy surroundings, but she seemed lovelier than ever—eyes as green as alpine forests, golden hair shining in the light of the setting sun . . . "Mr. Peterkin," she said, rosebud lips twisting with amused mockery. "April really is the cruellest month."

"Somehow I knew you'd say that." He joined her in looking up at the wall. It formed the back of the buildings on Trinity Square: grey stone or brick, with a yellowish tint, layered between three bands of what appeared to be dust-covered red tile . . . "We missed you at the Britannia last Friday."

"Did you really expect us to continue our Friday luncheons, after everything?" Flora paused, searching his expression, then turned back to the wall. "I'm getting on well enough, if you must know. There's a gentleman at the Port of London Authority—"

"That's why you're here."

Flora smiled and nodded. "Meanwhile, Miranda's carrying on as if nothing's happened. She's happy that way, and I can't blame her. Alice wants to go to Paris, to help care for Dr. Duplessis's amnesiac son—I think you can guess why—but Madame Duplessis wants nothing to do with her."

"And Lucy?"

"She plans to spend some time living abroad—Casablanca, of all places. The change could be good for her, but I wonder if the shock will be too much."

Eric blinked, remembering the stamps on Werner's parcel. Casablanca? He stared at Flora, wondering how much she knew, or whether this was only a marvellous coincidence. Finally, he turned back to the wall and changed the subject. "What are we looking at?"

"Londinium."

Of course. This was a piece of the old Roman wall that, for centuries, had defined and defended the city of London. Eric knew it was somewhere in this area, but he'd never thought to seek it out.

"Hadrian was obsessed with Roman history," Flora said, with an undercurrent of scorn. "All our neoclassical architecture, why we still study Latin and read classical mythology—he used to say that we harken back to the legends of Rome because of what they reveal about us."

*We put this myth on the wall because it reveals who we are.*

And what of the literal wall before them? Now that he knew, Eric could almost imagine that the warm honey tint of these bricks was, in fact, the lingering kiss of imperial Rome. He said, "I was told the same thing just earlier today, about that painting at the Britannia of King Arthur and his Knights. 'You wouldn't put them on the wall if they didn't represent the things you admire and wish to emulate, would you?'"

"That's not the same thing at all. Hadrian thought that a myth defines who you are; you're saying that a myth defines who you should strive to be. It's the difference between identity and ideals." Flora paused, then leaned in to whisper, "I think I like your version better."

Subtle hints of smoke and vanilla—Flora's perfume—set Eric's mind reeling, but she was right. The distinction made all the difference. He thought of Madam Eliot's insistence on honouring her cad of a husband on the club's Roster of the Fallen, a lie that continued even now to set Eric's teeth on edge. The truth was generally superior—but even an ass like Andrew Russell, dressed up in a lion's skin, might still teach future lions to roar.

Stepping away from the intoxicating scent of *her*, Eric laid a hand on the old Roman wall and took a deep breath. He half expected to be assailed with visions of golden eagles rising from the swirling dust of antiquity . . . but that was a romantic fantasy. His hand encountered cold masonry and nothing more. The streets and alleys around him were drab and ordinary, their focus more on the nearby Port of London Authority Building—an icon of a new empire, Britannia ruling the waves.

Eric brushed the dust of empires from his hands, and remembered what Dr. Linwood had told him about Roman cement: that it was a recipe lost to antiquity, for a thing of such strength that, even now, London continued to derive its structure from Rome.

Much as Eric derived strength from the experience of war, terrible as it was.

These remnants of Londinium were relegated now to the obscurity of a house's back wall, and it was the buildings surrounding them that defined modern London. He'd been thinking earlier about the facades presented by the Russells, and it occurred to him that much the same could be said here. From the faux-Tudor cottages of Metro-land to the baroque extravagance of the Port of London Authority Building, London was all of those things; but—scratch the surface, strip off the mask—so much more.

Eric turned to say as much to Flora; but the sun had fully set while he'd stepped away, and she was gone.

# HISTORICAL NOTES

ONE THING I'VE found, as a writer of historical fiction, is that history is far messier than anyone would like. One must filter fact from fiction, and while some things are easily discerned as true or false, there are always narratives embraced long ago that are not strictly lies, but have more to do with romance than truth. The present diverges from the past, leaving it far behind, and these myths evolve to bridge that gap. But myths are seductive in their romance, the true Belle Dame Sans Merci, and there is a real danger in buying too heavily into them.

Case in point: as someone with a particular fondness for all things British, I am disposed to focus on the mythic positives of the British Empire; meanwhile, Eric, as a product of his time and upbringing, naturally believes the Empire to be by and large a good thing. But the negatives do exist, perhaps even outweighing the positives. Colonialism has historically served as a system of exploitation, and the life I love was built on top of that. The present, too, is far messier than anyone would like.

It is my belief that to truly love something, one must acknowledge its flaws and love it still. To pretend that any earthly thing is perfect and incapable of wrong—that is not love, but idolatry. I cannot change the past, and I cannot pretend it is perfect: all I can do is hope we do better—make the myths of nobility real; filter out the oppressive lies; and take the accompanying truths, both good and bad, as the lessons they are.

Rome was, of course, a model for European civilisation in the centuries after its fall. In a similar vein, the wall they built for their outpost at Londinium continued to shape that city through most of its history. However, with the Industrial Revolution came an explosion in urban growth, and a great deal of the wall was destroyed over the 1800s to make way for urban development. The section that Eric examines on Tower Hill was preserved by virtue of having been previously incorporated into newer buildings. In 1938, that piece of wall was given over to public guardianship, and the attached buildings were demolished. Today, the wall stands alone as a monument to London's heritage. Only the lower half is actually Roman in origin, however: the upper half was added in mediaeval times to raise the wall's height.

The discussion that Eric overhears when he first approaches Colonel Russell concerns the Imperial Airways de Havilland crash on Christmas Eve, 1924. The flight was scheduled to leave Croydon for Le Bourget, Paris, but crashed and exploded less than two miles out with no survivors. An inquest and public inquiry conducted over the following months exonerated both pilot and airline, and resulted in large-scale improvements to Croydon airport.

While it had already been suggested for a while that the name "Arthur" might be derived from the Latin "Artorius," it seems that the actual identification of King Arthur with Lucius Artorius Castus was first made by American philologist Kemp Malone in a May 1925 issue of *Modern Philology*. Unless Mr. Malone was already discussing the theory before the publication of that article, Colonel Russell's knowledge on the subject must therefore be an anachronism—albeit one of only a few months.

Growing up in Singapore, I often saw "Madam" used by divorcees and by married women going by their maiden names. I'd always assumed that we'd adopted this practice from the British, but now I find myself unable to unearth any evidence of this usage in early twentieth-century England. "Madam Eliot," therefore, should not be taken as representative of common practice, but as an ad hoc solution to new issues arising from married women entering the workplace.

The British Empire Union was founded in 1916 from the Anti-German Union, which had itself been founded just the previous year. One would like to think that the shift was due to a renunciation of xenophobia in favour of patriotism; but the infamous "Once a German" post-war poster rather suggests that this xenophobia remained a driving force for a while longer. In the years following, they turned their focus to promoting nationalistic protectionism over both labour-centric socialism and laissez-faire capitalism. They became the British Commonwealth Union in 1960, and eventually ceased political activities in the 1970s.

I first learned about Roman curse tablets while visiting the Roman baths in Bath. As Avery says, the ancient Romans would inscribe curses (some of them hilariously petty) on small, paper-thin lead tablets; in the case of Bath, these tablets were then folded up and thrown into the sacred hot water springs. The Bath tablets would not be unearthed until the late 1970s, but similar tablets had been discovered long before then across Europe and North Africa.

The teashop where Eric finds Crane at his breakfast is fictional, but this is not to say that Chinese eateries didn't exist in 1925 London. The Chinese Restaurant (yes, that was its name) was established in 1909 on Glasshouse Street, off Piccadilly Circus, by a Mr. Chang Choy, and would continue operation until well after the Second World War. This was "fine dining," however, and perhaps a bit much if all you want is congee for breakfast.

*Honi soit qui mal y pense* is, of course, the motto of the Order of the Knights of the Garter, supposedly founded when King Edward III retrieved the fallen garter of the Countess of Salisbury at a ball.

This is probably only a fairy tale, and there are two or three different women at the time of the Order's founding who might have been the countess in question. There are reports of Edward III having sexually assaulted one of these women, leading me to think that the tale of the fallen garter might be a euphemism—though, to be fair, the events may, in fact, be wholly unrelated. Today, the Order of the Garter is the highest British order of knighthood, honouring distinguished service to crown and country: as Eric notes, even an ass dressed up in a lion's skin might teach future lions to roar.

The Working Lads Institute was founded in 1876, though it would be another eight or nine years before the building on Whitechapel Road was completed. Following a financial crisis in 1891, control was passed on to Reverend Thomas Jackson, a Methodist clergyman who continued in the Institute's original mission of outreach to the troubled and impoverished boys of Whitechapel, regardless of race or creed. This included many taken from the courts with Reverend Jackson serving as a probation officer—our Thomas Harvey might already be familiar with the wrong side of the law. By 1925, the mission had expanded to other buildings, with the original Institute building serving primarily as a hostel. The Institute building was sold in 1971 and converted into residential flats in 1997; the organisation itself, meanwhile, continues to this day as the Whitechapel Mission, serving the homeless and marginalised of London.

The train times for Eric's journey to Switzerland and back are cobbled together from what timetables I could find on timetableworld.com, as well as the 1923 ABC guide in my possession. The journey thus assumes it is 1923 from London to Calais, 1928 from Calais to Paris, 1920 from Paris to Basel, and 1910 in Switzerland. One hopes that the scheduling differences across that time period will be minor.

I don't know exactly when Citroën's plan for the Eiffel Tower was conceived, so the rumour heard by Inspector Michaud may or may not be a minor anachronism. Nevertheless, the Eiffel Tower was lit up with thousands of electric lights spelling the name of Citroën in July 1925, and remained so until 1934 when electric bills bankrupted the company. The mastermind behind this project was a lighting engineer named Fernand Jacopozzi, who had previously been contracted to help light up a false Paris to draw German night bombers away from the real city. The War ended before that project could truly take off, and Jacopozzi's new project with Citroën would instead help draw aviators like Charles Lindbergh *to* Paris.

The iron harvest continues across northern France to this day, more than a century after the end of the First World War, with farmers still unearthing unexploded ordnance and other relics of the trenches while working in their fields. Other parts of this region remain off-limits due to the amount of dangerous material, both chemical and mechanical, still in the ground. This is the *zone rouge*, or "red zone," and while the iron harvest is slowly reducing it over time, it may be another three hundred years at least before it is completely cleared.

Dr. Keller's sanatorium is fictional. Its attached village is based on the town of Brigels (Breil in the local Romansh), which I chose on the grounds of having visited once for a cousin's wedding. It is not far from Davos, where the first closed Alpine sanatorium for tuberculosis treatment was established in 1889 and which became, over the next few decades, the central hub to at least forty different such facilities. The progress of modern medicine seems to have cut back on the need for such treatment, but the rise of skiing as a sport has seen the region's focus transition over to athleticism—a different sort of healthcare for a more conspicuous sort of consumption.

Madame Anna Tchaikovsky is better known today as Anna Anderson. DNA analysis has since disproven her claims of being the Grand Duchess Anastasia, but the idea of Anastasia's survival remains a fascinating myth.

The neoclassical bell tower of St. George's Lutheran Church was removed at some point prior to 1934. The church itself ceased regular services in 1997 after its adoption by the Historic Chapels Trust, though it is still available for special events.

The advent of the railways enabled workers to commute over greater distances between home and work, and the late 1800s thus saw the rise of suburban development for the middle classes outside and around London. The Metropolitan Railway line, reaching out to the villages northwest of London, provided an excellent breeding ground for these suburban housing estates, and the term *Metro-land* was coined just before the War to describe the phenomenon. At the same time, the Metropolitan Railway was looking for a way to turn a profit on the surplus land it had acquired in the process of expansion—land which they, unlike other British railways, were permitted to keep and use as they saw fit. A pair of housing estates were developed around Pinner at the turn of the century, but further forays into suburban housing were halted by the War. In 1919, recognising the increased demand for housing after the War, the Metropolitan Railway Country Estates Company was formed to join other building companies in making Britain, as then-Prime Minister David Lloyd George put it, "a fit country for heroes to live in," and the development of Metro-land took off in earnest.

All characters here are fictional, though mention is made of various real-life figures: Lucius Artorius Castus, Edith Cavell, Guy de Maupassant, Julius Caesar, Emperor Hadrian, Robert Baden-Powell, Jack the Ripper, King Edward III, the Countess of Salisbury (though historians are unsure as to which specific one), Mary Ann Nichols, Annie Chapman, Queen Boudica (here spelled Boadicea), Siegfried Sassoon, King Edward VII, Eric Liddell, Gaston Leroux, Louis Armstrong, Eugene Bullard, Wolfgang Amadeus Mozart, Edgar Allan Poe, Anna Anderson (identified here as Anna Tchaikovsky), Pyotr Ilyich Tchaikovsky, Antonina Tchaikovskaia (here spelled Tchaikovsky—folks in the 1920s seemed generally oblivious to the Russian practise of feminising surnames for women), the Grand Duchesses Tatiana and Anastasia, Tsar Nicholas II, King George III, Horatio Nelson, Wilfred Owen, John Keats, King Richard I, Gaius Suetonius Paulinus, and T. S. Eliot.

The pastor of St. George's is meant to be Georg Mätzold, who indeed was repatriated to Germany in 1917 but returned in 1920; Eric barely misses him and speaks with a fictional warden instead because I am uncomfortable with putting words in the mouth of someone I only know from a *Survey of London* article. Likewise, the vicar of St. Martin's, referenced by Inspector Crane in his war council, is Reverend Dick Sheppard, who did indeed open the church's vaults to the homeless after the War.

# ACKNOWLEDGEMENTS

MANY THANKS TO the usual suspects at Inkshares: Adam especially for the long months of editing and for pulling things together, but also Noah, Sorcha, Marjorie, Ryan, and Pam for their insights and for helping to pummel the text into shape; and to Kevin and Tim for their excellent design work on the finished product. It has been quite a journey since *A Gentleman's Murder*, and the people who have extended the hand of friendship along the way are too numerous to name without inadvertently leaving someone out; nevertheless, I am grateful for their kindness and hope for all the best as we continue together on the next leg of this ongoing journey.

# INKSHARES

INKSHARES is a community, publisher, and producer for debut writers. Our books are selected not just by a group of editors, but also by readers worldwide. Our aim is to find and develop the most captivating and intelligent new voices in fiction. We have no genre—our genre is debut.

Previously unknown Inkshares authors have received starred reviews in every trade publication. They have been featured in every major review, including on the front page of the *New York Times*. Their books are on the front tables of booksellers worldwide, topping bestseller lists. They have been translated in major markets by the world's biggest publishers. And they are being adapted at the biggest studios and networks.

Interested in making your own story a reality? Visit Inkshares.com to start your own project, connect with other writers, and find other great books.